PORKY BAYCANN

Tank Gunner

Tank Gunner is the pen name of a retired combat cavalry trooper, Senior Parachutist, and Jumpmaster awarded a Combat Infantry Badge and decorated with a Silver Star, three Bronze Stars, one for Valor, and a Purple Heart. He served his nation with pride and honor for more than a quarter century as an enlisted soldier and officer. An award-winning author, Tank wrote and published *Prompts a collection of stories* at age 76, *Prompts Too another collection of stories* at 77, *Cookie Johnson*, his Vietnam historical fiction novel at 78, *Palomino*, his immensely popular WWII historical fiction novel at 79, and *Porky Baycann* at age 80. He and his wife live with Toby, 100 miles southwest of Palomino.

OTHER WORKS

PROMPTS
a collection of stories
(fiction)

PROMPTS TOO
another collection of stories
(fiction)

COOKIE JOHNSON
(Vietnam Historical Fiction Novel)

PALOMINO
(WWII Historical Fiction Novel)

War Stories of an Armed Savage
(nonfiction)

Any Name But Smith!
(play)

Direct Hit
(newspaper column)

For Sylviane, Rob, Rich,

and

for Terry, Chloe, Zak, & Toby

ACKNOWLEDGMENT

A special thanks to Capn Lee Sneath and writers who supported this creative success; and, heaps of gratitude to managers of the Dallas-Fort Worth area Half Price Books stores who have hosted more than two hundred of my book signings to permit enthusiastic readers and pleased fans to find and enjoy my work.

Boy Scouts of America granted permission to use the Scout Oath, Law, Motto, and Slogan.

PLAYERS

Portland "Porky" Alvin Baycann, Junior
Son & Boy Scout wannabe

Agnes Baycann
Mother & Nurse

Sally Edmonds
Friend

June Edmonds
Mother

Thomas James "T J" Workman
Friend

Irene Adams
T J's Granmomma

Gene Autry
US Army Air Corps Sergeant

Sandy
Driver

Winston Tanner
Scoutmaster

Clifford Douglass
Assistant Scoutmaster

Woodrow Collins
Friend, Boy Scout

Grover Lindsey
Friend, Boy Scout

i

PLAYERS

Bessie Books
Friend

Rochelle Tucker
Friend

Warrene Culp
Palomino Palace

Yvonne Leonard
Palomino Palace

Bobbie Jo Evans
Manager, Jeeps Cafe

Maybelle Winters
Owner, Editor, Publisher of the *Palomino Press*

Ruby Bostick
Owner, Palomino Palace & the Porter House

Ethel Watson
Miss Ruby's Housekeeper

Julius Watson
Miss Ruby's Chauffer

Carsey Belew
Palomino Switchboard Operator

Bastion Albert
Vegetable Framer

Martin Church
Cotton Field Supervisor

PLAYERS

Dallas Church
Daughter, Senior Palomino High School

Odessa Church
Daughter

Preacher Adams
Cotton Field Hand, Minister

Major Clay Monroe
WWI Hero & Cotton Farmer

Casey Shipp
Palomino Mayor

Porter Skaggs
Principal, Palomino School

Nate Dulfeine
Co-Owner, Dulfeine's Grocery

Margie Dulfeine
Co-Owner, Dulfeine's Grocery

Wolf Hunter
Gas Station Owner

Pearson Keenan
City Meter Reader

Caleb Joiner
Gas Station Helper

Francoise "Tub" Tubane, Junior
Boy Scout

PLAYERS

Bobbett Moon
Teenager

Blackie Beck
Barber & Babe's Daddy

Barber Beck
Ne'er Do Well

Wyatt Posey
Ne'er Do Well

Babe Beck
Boy Scout

Eliot Thurgood
Palomino Tormenter

Doc Garland Burns
Doctor, Palomino Hospital

Doctor Greffen "Pearly" Gates
Doctor, Palomino Hospital

Linda Salter
Nurse, Palomino Hospital

Geraldine Skinner
Nurse, Palomino Hospital

Sheriff Jim Dudley
Lamar County Sheriff

Deputy Gary Gully
Lamar County Deputy Sheriff

PLAYERS

Sergeant Willow "Twig" Chestnutt
MP Guard & Palomino Constable

Teresa Chestnutt
Wife & Cafe Waitress

Tina Chestnutt
Daughter & Grade School Student

Kraus "Duke" Hopplendagger
German POW

Edwin "Eddy" Becker
German POW

Wilhelm "Will" Weiss
German POW

Kingston Kline
Co-Owner, Kline's Drugs

Dora Kline
Co-Owner, Kline's Drugs

Major General Everett Evans
Commanding General, Camp Maxey

Brigadier General Charles Pace, Junior
Deputy Commanding General, Camp Maxey

Colonel Benicio Sardanna-Sanchez
Provost Marshal, Camp Maxey

Colonel R. J. Jones
Administrator, Camp Maxey

PLAYERS

Waldo Sutherland
Boy Scout

Patricia Ann "Patsy" Parker
Friend

Rayfield Paramore "Pinky" Pinkston, Junior
Friend & Paperboy

Vito Scarpinello
Mafioso Don

Sofia
Housekeeper

Captain Harry Hayworth
7th Army Staff Officer

Sergeant Vick Sorvino
7th Army Staff NCO

Corporal Dennis Raymond
Acting Squad Leader, 1st Infantry Division

Private Ross Connors
Rifleman, 1st Infantry Division

Private Grant Sweeney
Rifleman, 1st Infantry Division

PORKY BAYCANN

1

It was the summer of 1943. America had been at war with Japan, Italy, and Germany for twenty-one months. Operation Husky, the invasion of Sicily with George Patton and Bernard Montgomery's combat forces, was underway. Up to this point life had not varied much for Porky Baycann in the small town of Palomino, Texas, but that was about to change.

Martin Church counted out three Mercury dimes, a Buffalo nickel, and three steel, zinc-coated pennies of wages into Porky's open palm.

"Whachu gonna do with all that money, Master Porky?" Preacher Adams asked.   Porky looked up. The large black man stood in freshly picked cotton piled hip-deep in the wire-caged trailer.

"I'm going to Mister Dulfeine's for a loaf of bread and pork and beans for Momma. She's gonna fix weenies and beans for supper tonight."

"Well, you tell Mister Nate and Miss Margie, Preacher say hi."

Portland Alvin Baycann, Junior was a normal-sized young boy for his age, his nickname notwithstanding.

"Okay, I will."

"You watch out for cars and trucks, you hear? How come you didn't ride your bicycle?"

"Flat tire, Mister Church. I left it at Mister Hunter's station. He said Mister Joiner could get to it this afternoon. It's not much of a walk."

"Well, you be real careful, you hear?" Preacher cautioned.

"Are you going to hep out tomorrow?" Martin asked.

"Yessir."

"Okay, be here about seven. The earlier we start, the more we can get done before the August sun gets too hot in the field."

"I'll be here on time. Momma let me use her alarm clock."

"What have you heard from your Papa?"

"Momma said he's probably in Sillalee, sorry, Sissalee, that's in Italy. I remember Miss Pruitt talkin bout it and pointin at it on the big map in our classroom."

Preacher removed his hat and wiped sweat from his brow. "I pray your Papa is gonna be alright over there, the good Lord will look after him." He replaced his hat and nodded. "And all our boys over there fightin them Nazis."

Porky looked up again, this time shielding his eyes from the sun with the hand clutching the coins. "Thank you, Preacher Adams. Momma prays everday, too. I'm going now, see yall in the morning."

From Major Monroe's field to Dulfeine's grocery was a half-mile walk up Highway 271 and a half-mile walk down Main Street. Porky struck out from the cotton trailer, a man on a mission to shop for his Momma.

In the half-mile along 271, Porky managed to count

sixteen trucks and nine cars roaring past on their way to Camp Maxey and twelve trucks and six cars headed toward Bogata.

He had only taken forty paces down Main Street when he heard an approaching car. He stopped, turned, and watched.

The big, long automobile slowed and pulled up beside him. The shiny paint and chrome on the grill sparkled and gleamed from the late afternoon sun.

Porky recognized the Army chevrons. Sergeant stripes were prominent on the khaki-sleeved arm propped on the open passenger-side window frame of the black Cadillac.

"Hello, Son," the familiar voice said. "Can you give me directions to the nearest cafe in town?"

He lifted his eyes and raised his hand to shield the blaze from blinding him. He recognized the smiling face, but was surprised as he peered into the bright brown eyes.

Porky knew the voice well – and the face. He had heard the songs and sat in the *Palomino Palace* on Saturday afternoons watching the Singing Cowboy take care of villains, scoundrels, crooked ranchers, and bad hombres, and ride off into the sunset with the girl sitting behind him on his beautiful horse.

"You're Gene Autry," Porky heard his voice squeak.

Gene laughed and leaned farther out of the car window. "That I am, Son. What's your name?"

"Porky . . . Portland . . . Baycann . . . Junior."

"Porky. Porky *Bacon*. Well, Porky, where you headed?"

"To town. To Mister Dulfeine's grocery store. I have to get a loaf of bread and a can of beans for my Momma."

"Can I give you a ride into town?"

Porky grinned. "In your car?"

Gene laughed again. "Why, sure, Pardner. Champion rode the train to Paris and made me ride in this car with Sandy, my driver."

"Champion's in Paris?"

"Sure is." Gene leaned over and held open the back door. "Come on, get in, let's go. Tell me how to get to the best cafe in town."

Porky climbed into car. He settled on the back seat and slid the palm of his hand across the fabric. It felt as smooth as his mother's silk scarf.

"Go straight ahead, straight down Main Street. Jeeps is on the left hand side."

"Jeeps?"

"That's the cafe. The only cafe. Jeeps Cafe."

Sandy eased the clutch out and the Cadillac's engine hummed softly as the big car rolled forward.

"What's the name of your town, Porky?"

"Palomino."

"Like the horse?"

"Yessir. Palomino was named after a horse."

"Palomino. A Texas town named after a horse. Palomino." Gene and Sandy gave a hearty laugh.

"That would make Champion awful jealous," Sandy said.

"I sure would like to see Champion."

"Well, Son, maybe we can make that happen. Okay, Sandy. Take us into Palomino and to Jeeps."

"You're in the Army? You're a Sergeant."

"Sure am. Been in over a year. On my way to Camp Maxey to entertain our boys there. Sometimes, I go to the Army hospital in San Antonio. After Camp Maxey, I'll go to Dallas, to Love Field. I'm going to be a

4

pilot."

"You're going to fly airplanes?"

"Sure am."

"You're not going to be in the *pitchursho* anymore?"

"I'm going to do my part for the war, Son. Everbody has a role to play and my role is to fly airplanes. I'll be back in the saddle again. After the war."

Porky grinned. "I've heard you sing that song a hundred times, Mister Autry."

"What song is that, Son?"

"*Back in the Saddle Again.*"

Gene looked at Sandy and sang the first lines – "*I'm back in the saddle again, Out where a friend is a friend . . .*" He turned to look at Porky, continuing with the lyrics, singing the song for his passenger.

Porky was amazed, thrilled, moved. He was sitting in Gene Autry's car, watching Gene Autry's chin move, listening to the Singing Cowboy sing his signature song. Porky's mouth was so wide open a buzzard could have swooped in and landed on his tongue.

"Goll-lee," Porky whispered. He applauded when Gene grinned.

"I see the sign, Gene. Jeeps Cafe. Looks like we can park right in front. The grocery store is right there, too."

Sandy steered the long sedan into the slot and shut the engine.

Gene turned on the seat and leaned toward Porky.

"Would you like to come in with Sandy and me and have a hamburger, Porky?"

First, Porky didn't quite know how to handle the invitation. Secondly, he wasn't sure if Gene and Sandy would expect him to pay for the hamburgers. His thirty-eight cents was earmarked for bread and beans. There was no way he could pay for three hamburgers and three drinks – and buy a loaf of bread and a can of pork and beans.

Gene picked up on Porky's hesitation.

"Sandy, do you have enough money to buy all of us hamburgers, French fries, and Cokes? And maybe an ice cream soda, afterwards?"

Sandy nodded. "I think so, Gene." He looked into his rearview mirror. "But I need to know how many hamburgers you think you can eat, Porky, so I know if I have enough money?"

His hesitation was enough for Gene to look. "Don't you worry, Porky. If Sandy doesn't have enough money, I'll sing for our supper. Okay?"

Relieved, Porky nodded and grinned. "I'll eat just one hamburger and drink one Co-Cola, Mister Autry."

"Porky, we're friends. You call me, Gene, okay?"

Out of the car and up the steps onto the sidewalk, Porky led the way.

Passersby nodded greetings toward Porky and Sandy; they gawked at Gene, who smiled and touched the brim of his Army cap.

Porky opened the screen door and led his new friends into the cafe.

"Hey, Porky." A brief glance up from stacking two plates across her arm supplemented Teresa's welcome. She paused and did a double take. "Bobbie Jo? Come out here. *Bobbie Jo. Come out here, now.*"

"Let's sit at the counter, Porky."

Porky's grin would have impressed any opossum living near Palomino.

"Okay, Gene."

Patrons, Bobbie Jo, and Teresa were immobilized. They gaped, mouths wide. Some lips formed an "O" in

6

wonderment that Gene Autry came into the cafe with Porky Baycann and sat next to him at the counter.

Bobbie Jo broke the trance.

"Hello, Mister Autry.   Welcome to Jeeps Cafe, welcome to Palomino. My name is Bobbie Jo, I'm the manager. This is Teresa Chestnutt."

"Howdy, Bobbie Jo. Howdy, Teresa." Gene turned on the stool and touched the brim of his cap. "Howdy, folks. Please don't mind us. Sandy and me are going to have hamburgers with our new friend, Porky."

Somehow, time marched on. Teresa served their fresh cooked burgers, and the trio quickly consumed them, rarely speaking.   Bobbie Jo opened ice-cold bottles of Coca-Cola she pulled from the double-lid red box and set them beside glasses. Teresa refilled the glasses with ice.

"Tell me, Porky, how did your nickname come about?" Sandy asked.

"My Daddy gave it to me when I was two. He told me with a first name of Portland and last name of Baycann kids at school would nickname me anyway. He called me Porky all the time and people never made fun of me. I've been called Porky all my life."

"Does anybody call you by your real name . . . Portland?"

"Momma does, sometimes, when I'm in trouble. But she uses both names, Portland Alvin. Teachers call me Portland most of the time. I guess they're supposed to do that. I kinda like Porky, anyway. It's unusual."

Sandy smiled. "That it is, Porky. I think your Daddy did the right thing, that way you didn't have to fight bullies in school because of your nickname."

"How old are you?" Gene asked.

"Fourteen.   I'll be fifteen after school starts in

September."

"Are you a Boy Scout?"

Porky was puzzled by Sandy's question.

"No, I never thought about being in the Scouts."

"Do they have a Troop in Palomino?" Gene asked.

"We do, Mister Autry."

Gene and Sandy turned, seeking the source of the voice at a table behind them.

"My name is Winston Tanner, Mister Autry. I teach Texas History to Juniors and Seniors at Palomino High School. I'm also the Scoutmaster of our Troop."

"Thank you, Mister Tanner."

Gene and Sandy turned back to pin Porky.

"How bout it, Porky? Why don't you talk with Mister Tanner about becoming a Boy Scout? You know Scouts and Cowboys come close to sharing the same code."

"You mean like keep your word and always tell the truth?"

"That's right," Gene said.

"And be a good worker and help people in distress," Sandy said.

"And respect women, your parents, and our laws," Bobbie Jo added.

"Do your best, do your duty to God and country, obey the Scout Law, help other people at all times, and stay physically strong, mentally awake, and morally straight," the Scout Leader said.

"And be a patriot," Teresa said. "Just like Mister . . . Sergeant Autry and Sergeant Chestnutt."

Porky didn't know where to look. He felt like a criminal under interrogation. The only word he could think to say was, "Okay."

Gene nodded and cleared his throat.

The adults realized what they had done and felt

guilty.

"If you want to talk Scouting, Porky, come see me at my home or at the school," Winston Tanner said in a soft voice. "Any time, okay?"

Porky faced him. "Okay, Mister Tanner."

Quietness prevailed before Gene spoke.

"Well, Sandy, Porky has some shopping to do for his Momma. Maybe we should be on the road."

"How much do we owe you, Miss Bobbie Jo?" Sandy asked.

Bobbie Jo shook her head. "It is on the house, it is my pleasure to serve you. Friends of Porky are friends of ours. But I need to ask why you're over here in Palomino in a Army uniform?"

Gene canted his head and smiled. "At the Pentagon's request, I joined the Army at the end of July, last year. I took the oath on my live radio show, *Melody Ranch.*"

Gene put his arm around Porky and matched his grin.

"After my swearing-in, I was promoted to Technical Sergeant."

Chair legs scraped the cafe's floor as customers scooted back, stood, and inched closer to hear Gene's explanation.

As he continued, Gene looked into all the faces gathering close.

"A week later, early August, *Melody Ranch* became the *Sergeant Gene Autry Show* and that was part of my Army duties."

"Why you here, in Palomino, Mister Autry?"

"On my way to Paris and Camp Maxey from Shreveport. I'll do a show for our boys there, stay overnight, and then Sandy and me will drive down to

Dallas."

"Germans from Camp Maxey are coming to Palomino," a voice said.

Sandy and Gene turned toward the voice.

"Germans?" Sandy asked.

"POWs.   Three are coming to live and work in Palomino," Bobbie Jo said.   "Our Mayor made the announcement a week or so ago."

"They're going to live here?" Gene asked.

"They'll do labor work, pick cotton, dig ditches, whatever the town needs. They'll be under guard," Teresa said. "My husband is military police sergeant Twig Chestnutt, out there at Camp Maxey. He's assigned as their guard and supervisor. Maybe you'll see him there, at Camp Maxey."

There was a pause. Everyone waited. They wanted to hear more about Gene's life. The crowd in Jeeps Cafe was mesmerized to be the presence of a famous movie star.

"Gene is going to fly airplanes," Porky ventured.

"I have a pilot's license. That's why I'm going to Dallas. I'll go through the Army Air Corps flight training and become a Flight Officer. I'll fly transport aircraft to bring supplies and equipment to our boys who are doing the hard work in this war."

Sandy looked at his watch. "We might better be on our way, Gene."

"Okay, Sandy.   Before we go maybe these fine people of Palomino would like a song or two."

Sandy moved off his stool right away and rushed to the car.

No one spoke.   In the stillness, their awe and admiration to be near greatness filled the cafe.

In a few moments, Sandy returned and weaved

10

through the onlookers with Gene's guitar.

"What would you like to hear, Porky?"

"*Back in the Saddle Again* and *Deep in the Heart of Texas.*"

As Gene sang the songs, he tilted his head inviting the customers to join in on the choruses.

The loud voices brought onlookers to the screen door, and eventually many slipped into the cafe to join in.

At the appropriate time during *Deep in the Heart of Texas*, they clapped hands, banged tabletops, and stomped boots.

It was a great, memorable time in Jeeps for Porky. Dozens stood with him on the sidewalk outside the cafe and waved goodbye as the sedan pulled away.

Only when Sandy and Gene drove down Main Street toward Highway 271 did Porky think about an autograph. He shrugged off the oversight when the rear end of the long, black Cadillac disappeared.

Life in Palomino returned to normal in the silence that followed.

Porky thought about the boys he'd seen in their Scout khakis. He reflected on what it might be like being a Boy Scout, but now he needed to buy a small loaf of Wonder Bread and a can of Campbell's Pork and Beans for his Momma.

Portland Alvin Baycann, Junior looked up Main Street once more after Gene, turned, and strolled down the sidewalk, headed to Dulfeine's grocery store humming the refrain of *Back in the Saddle Again*.

2

Bastion Albert owned and farmed the largest vegetable fields around Palomino. In the twenty-one months America had been at war, he had fed many residents in Lamar and Red River Counties. Every week, Bastion's farm hands loaded their pick-ups and drove his produce to markets in Paris, Powderly, Clarksville, Bogata, Sumner, Blossom, and Detroit. Under a lucrative, long-term Army contract, thousands of civilians, soldiers, and POWs enjoyed Bastion's plants every day at Camp Maxey.

Bastion was a short, heavy, wealthy man by any measure – whether by ancestry, money, reputation, adoration, height, weight, or girth.

At least one day every month, he was also the town drunk. He was on that timetable as Porky approached Dulfeine's grocery.

Nate Dulfeine came out of his store holding Bastion. Porky stopped and stared.

Bastion's left arm was across the back of Dulfeine's neck and the grocer held Bastion's left wrist. Dulfeine's flowery red tie accented his starched white shirt with sleeves neatly folded across ample biceps, his right arm wrapped around Bastion's back.

To Porky, when Mister Dulfeine stood erect, he seemed taller than five-seven, which was average for men who remained in Palomino. At that height, though, he was a head and a half above Mister Albert. So together, there on the sidewalk joined in an awkward position, the two of them reminded Porky of *Mutt and Jeff* in the comics.

Dulfeine was a striking, rugged man and his bright blue eyes pinned the boy. The storeowner's affable smile drew Porky in.

"Help me, Porky," the grocer implored. "Take Bastion's arm."

Porky stepped up and grasped Bastion's right wrist and elbow.

Bastion looked at him, their noses almost touching. "Hello, Porky."

Porky frowned at the whisky-breath odor. "Hello, Mister Albert."

"You're a good boy, Porky."

"Thank you, Mister Albert."

"Okay, Porky. Put his right arm across your shoulders and help me get him down the sidewalk steps to my car."

The movement of Porky raising Bastion's arm and placing it across his shoulder caused Bastion's ample waist to stretch and flatten. His trousers slid down hairy legs and settled into a clump around his ankles.

It was immediately obvious Bastion wore no underwear.

Where only Porky had remained on the sidewalk after Gene and Sandy drove away, now pedestrians filled the scene and gawked at Bastion Albert's privates.

Captivated by the large spectacle, so to speak, no one moved to help Porky and Dulfeine bring Bastion down the steps to Dulfeine's car, or to step forward and raise Bastion's clothing.

With pants on top of his Brogans, Bastion could only shuffle. It became apparent they could not safely maneuver down the three concrete steps, so Dulfeine placed his right hip into Bastion, leaned left, and lifted the farmer off his feet. Porky held Bastion's right arm across his shoulders, clasping his right wrist. He stumbled down the steps, too, in stride with Dulfeine.

At the car door, Dulfeine gave instructions.

"Pull his pants up, Porky."

Embarrassed, for himself and the farmer, Porky turned his face to the rear as he stooped to clutch a handful of khaki waistband. He pulled the trousers up and placed Bastion's right hand on the wide belt buckle.

Once Bastion was in the passenger seat, Dulfeine did not slam but firmly closed the car door.

"Okay, folks," Dulfeine said, "it's all over, I'll take Bastion home."

Later, the operative description was, *it was a sight to behold, for a short, fat man*.

Porky mounted the steps and paused.

"Thank you, Porky," Dulfeine said.   "Tell Miss Dulfeine I said you could have a Fudgsicle."

"He didn't have any underwear on," Porky said.

"Well, you never mind about that, okay?"

Porky smiled. "Okay, Mister Dulfeine. I'd never seen a naked man before."

Not only in Palomino but also in both counties, Dulfeine was well known as a man's man. He met Porky's smile. "We're all just like you, Porky. God made us all the same way."

14

Porky's smile spread into a wide grin. He shook his head. "Not quite, Mister Dulfeine."

Dulfeine chuckled, got into the car, and started the engine.

Porky turned and walked into the store.

Margie Dulfeine stood behind the counter and cash register. "You did a good job, Porky, helping Mister Albert and Mister Dulfeine. Shame Mister Albert's pants fell down. He'll hear about that for a long time to come."

"Momma sent me for a small loaf of Wonder Bread and a can of Campbell's Pork and Beans. And, Mister Dulfeine said I could have a Fudgsicle for helping him."

"Okay, Porky, you go right ahead and get your Fudgsicle. When you've finished it, bring your bread and can of beans up here to the counter."

Porky went to the icebox and withdrew the ice cream. He split the wrapper and nibbled small bits from the top to make the delight last longer. Licking, mouthing, and nipping his Fudgsicle, he wandered aimlessly to the tall comic book stand, stood there, and gazed at the covers. He slowly turned the rack with his free hand as he scanned artwork – *Archie, Gene Autry, Action, The Fighting Yank, United States Marines, Superman, Captain Marvel, Captain America, Marvel Mystery, Wonder Woman, Batman, Mutt and Jeff,* and a dozen others. In one form or another, even *Wonder Woman,* characters depicted in military uniforms of bright, bold colors fought, shot, bayoneted, savagely beat, and kicked butts of German, Italian, and Japanese soldiers. It was the war years and comics stories were a creative, artistic form of propaganda.

Porky finished the chocolate bar, lapped the wood clean of sugary remnants, and stuck the stick in his

Pillsbury flour-sack shirt pocket.

Palomino boys saved Popsicle and Fudgsicle sticks because . . . well, just because.

He pulled the latest edition of *The Fighting Yank* out of its foxhole slot and fanned the pages.

Miss Dulfeine's voice found his ears. "Tomorrow?"

"That's what Twig told Casey."

His ears tuned in to the familiar voice. Porky side-eyed from the book and confirmed the other female voice came from Carsey Belew, the primary Palomino telephone switchboard operator. With her in the store, Porky surmised, Maxine Gleason was on the switchboard.

"Twig is bringing his Germans to town by late afternoon," Miss Belew revealed.

"Well, the Mayor met with the Army and made all the arrangements, so he would need to know when Twig and the prisoners are coming."

"Twig asked Casey's opinion about which street to use to come into town."

"Why would he ask that?"

"To avoid a *welcoming committee*, if you know what I mean."

"Oh."

"I mean, they're Germans, Margie. They're the enemy. They're folks here who have husbands, sons, brothers, uncles, cousins, whatever, fightin over there in Sicily, and gettin ready to go after Hitler, Himmler, and all the Nazi henchmen."

"They're prisoners, Carsey. Captives. The Mayor told us they passed the test to come here to live and work. I trust the Mayor. He wouldn't put us in danger."

"Well, Twig was concerned about their safety."

"What street is he going to use?"

"Clark. Casey said everbody would be standin on the sidewalks, expecting him to drive down Main."

Porky turned to look at the two women.

"Well, Carsey, who all have you told about the Mayor and Sergeant Chestnutt's private conversation?"

He grinned when Miss Dulfeine made her accusation.

"Who all have you told about Twig and the prisoners coming into Palomino driving down Clark Street?"

"Just you, Margie. And Ruby. And Teresa. And Bobbie Jo."

"And?"

"Maybelle. And Casey told me to find Major Monroe and Wolf and Martha – the town council – and tell them. He knew I was listening. He never said it was a private conversation. He knows the rule."

Porky replaced the comic book. He picked up a small loaf of Wonder Bread and grabbed a can of beans on the way to the checkout counter. He waited until Miss Belew sidestepped to give him space. He laid his items down.

"Hello, Porky," Carsey Belew greeted.

"Hello, Miss Belew."

She smiled at Miss Dulfeine. "You know, Margie, Porky is now a famous resident of Palomino and Lamar and Red River Counties."

"Oh, my, Carsey, you didn't, did you?"

"Just a few good folks know that Porky is a pal of Gene Autry. Did you get an autographed picture of your new friend, Porky?"

Porky shrugged and frowned. "No, Mam, I forgot to ask."

To Margie. "Well, Porky ate a hamburger and drank an ice-cold Co-Cola in Jeeps with a real movie star. And

17

Gene Autry sang two of his songs."

Miss Dulfeine looked at Porky. "I heard the racket, banging and stomping. Was that what was going on?"

"Yes, Mam. Mister Autry asked me what songs I wanted him to sing, and I said *Back in the Saddle Again* and *Deep in the Heart of Texas.*"

"I remember Gene singing that song at the *pitchursho* in *Back in the Saddle*, a couple of years ago," Miss Dulfeine said.

"I guess you're gonna be a big shot in town, now, Porky. People will be askin for your autograph because you ate a hamburger with Gene Autry."

Miss Dulfeine sighed at Porky's blush. "Miss Belew is just playin around."

Carsey Belew reached out, grabbed Porky by his shoulders and pulled him in for a hug. "You're a good boy, Porky, I was just kidding."

"Is this all you want?" Miss Dulfeine asked.

"Yes, Mam."

She called the item, price, and pressed the number keys on the cash register. "Small Wonder Bread, ten cents. Campbell Pork and Beans, five cents. Is that all?"

"Yes, Mam."

A pull on the lever raised a white metal tag in the register window. Imprinted on the tag was a black numeral fifteen and a cent symbol. "Fifteen cents." The cash drawer slid open.

Porky plucked a Mercury dime and a Buffalo nickel from his cotton-picking wages and dropped the coins into Miss Dulfeine's open palm.

Three steps out through the grocery store door, he could still hear Miss Belew and Miss Dulfeine's voices.

"His pants dropped down to his ankles and exposed

18

everything . . . to the world, mind you."

"Did you look?"

"Had to, Margie. Couldn't help it. I mean it was right there. It was a sight to behold."

"Really?"

"It really was nothing special, if you know what I mean."

Their laughter faded away as he strolled down the sidewalk with sack in hand, on his way to Mister Wolf Hunter's Gulf Station at the end of Main Street. He could see Caleb Joiner holding the nozzle, pumping gas into a Model-A Ford, waving his free arm and hand in expansive gestures as he jawed with the driver.

Tank filled, payment made, goodbyes said, the driver pulled away.

Porky wasn't within hailing distance as Mister Joiner went into the gas station office, so he hurried his pace.

Caleb Joiner looked up while putting a one-dollar silver certificate and three gasoline-rationing coupons in a King Edward cigar box. "Hey, Porky. Come for your bicycle?"

"Yessir, is it ready?"

"All patched up and ready to roll. The tube had a pinhole. I scraped the rubber with my rough file, put a dab of glue, and pressed on a sticky pad. Did the job."

"How much do I owe, Mister Joiner?"

"Twenty. Ten cents for the glue and pad, ten cents for labor."

Porky pulled the coins from his pocket and handed over the remaining two Mercury dimes. "Thank, you for repairing my flat tire, Mister Joiner."

"You're a good boy, Porky. I hear you brought a new friend to the cafe and had him sing songs for Bobbie Jo's customers."

Porky didn't know how to correct Mister Joiner's misunderstanding, so he let it be. "Yessir, and I rode in Mister Autry's car, too."

Caleb Joiner chuckled. "My, my, you're gonna be a big shot in Palomino. Everbody'll be wantin your autograph cause you know Gene Autry. Did he give you one of his autographed pictures?"

"No, Sir. I forgot to ask."

"Whachu got in that sack?"

"Wonder Bread and beans for Momma. At the store, I heard Miss Belew tellin Miss Dulfeine Sergeant Twig's bringin his Germans to town tomorrow. They gonna come down Clark street to avoid the committee."

"Yep, they gonna live with me at Miss Ruby's. You know she got a lot of money from the Army for them to stay and eat at her place."

"Are you afraid?"

"Of what?"

"The Germans."

"No, I guess not. We was told they are okay to come live and work in Palomino. Anyway, Twig is their guard. He's got a gun and they don't. No, I guess I'm not afraid of them Germans comin to town. Are you?"

Porky thought on it a moment, shrugged, and shook his head. "No, I guess not."

"Are you gonna stand on the street and watch them come into town?"

"I hadn't thought about it. Maybe."

"Well, your bicycle is over there in the second bay, ready to go. Can you manage with a sack full of groceries?"

"It's just a small loaf of Wonder Bread and a small can of Campbell's Pork and Beans."

"Okay. Thank you for your business, Porky. I'll talk

to you later."

Porky's mind swirled and swam and flooded with thoughts on his ride home. He needed to tell his mother about Gene, Mister Tanner's offer, Mister Albert's pants, Twig's arrival with his Germans, about Clark Street and the committee, Miss Ruby's Army money, his flat tire, and, of course, the hamburger and Coca-Cola and all the singing and clapping and stomping in Jeeps Cafe. He knew his mother would ask if he got an autographed picture of Gene.

It was then the idea flashed in his mind that somebody should have made their picture together. Somebody with a Kodak, somebody should have thought to take their picture, there, in front of Jeeps. Dang it, he could of had his picture made with Gene Autry, maybe even standing next to Gene by his big car.

That image faded away as Porky imagined being dressed in a Scout uniform, almost like his Daddy in the Army. Woodrow and Grover were Scouts, but his two friends had never pressured him to come into the Scout Troop with them. Now, maybe he would join up after he talked with his mother.

He knew he had to tell his friends about Twig and his Germans coming to town tomorrow. Woodrow would want to stand on Clark Street for their arrival. And Grover would tag along with Woodrow. He would be there too. He'd never seen a German.

He let his bicycle fall over in the yard and took his front steps two at a time. He brought the groceries into the kitchen. His mother sat at the kitchen table, a letter clasped in her hand.

She looked at him and smiled but did not speak.

Porky saw she had been crying.

He removed the bread and beans from the sack and

left them on the kitchen counter.

Porky quietly folded the paper sack; then he sat across from his mother.

"What's wrong, Momma?"

3

On bicycles, Woodrow Collins and Grover Lindsey made their way up quiet, carless Borden Lane to Porky's house.

They dropped their bikes in the yard, next to Porky's, and mounted the six plank steps. Woodrow nodded, and Grover firmly planted his knuckles four times on the faded, weather-stained doorframe.

Grover called out on the fourth knock. "Porky? It's Grover and Woodrow. Anybody home?"

Agnes stood, wiped her eyes with a corner of the white apron with red polka dots and nodded.

Porky rose from their kitchen table, wiped his eyes on a shirtsleeve and moved into his mother's arms.

"It'll be alright, Porky. We'll be alright," she whispered. She hugged Porky, grasped his shoulders, and kissed her son's forehead. "Go see your friends."

Porky stood behind the screen door. He did not speak to Grover and Woodrow. He did not push it open and invite his friends in nor did he step out on the porch to join them.

Woodrow spoke first. "Can you come outside?"

Agnes Baycann came up behind Porky. She placed both hands on his shoulders, only her forehead, nose, and eyes were visible to the two boys on the porch.

Both visitors spoke at the same time. "Hello, Miss Baycann."

"Hello, Grover. Hello, Woodrow."

"Can Porky come outside?" Grover asked.

"Of course. Porky might prefer to sit on the steps with you rather than go off somewhere." She patted his arms. "Maybe for an hour, then it'll be suppertime."

On the porch, feet on the top step, Grover sat on Porky's left, Woodrow on the right.

"Is something wrong?" Woodrow's voice was soft.

Porky sniffled and lowered his head. He swiped liquid hurt sliding down his cheeks.

Grover and Woodrow looked away, embarrassed, avoiding watching their friend weep.

Porky dabbed at his eyes with his shirtsleeve.

"The Army can't find my Daddy."

Neither of his friends spoke, waiting for him to continue.

"Momma got a letter from a General at Fort Sam Houston in San Antonio. The General said a month ago Daddy was in a boat that sunk when it was hit by enemy shelling. Two hundred men was dumped in the water, some drowned. Some got pulled out, but they're tryin to find all of the others. The General said it is perzoomed my Daddy may have been lost in the ocean. Momma got the General's letter and my Daddy's letter today. Daddy said his company was playin in boats, learnin how to go to Italy to fight the Germans."

The three sat in silence. At a loss for what to say, Grover squirmed. Woodrow bent forward resting his chin on his arm that lay across his knees. He picked at his shoelaces. Porky stared at the three bicycles laying in his front yard.

Finally, Grover put an arm around Porky and ventured solace. "Maybe he swimmed out, maybe they'll find him eatin biskettie somewhere."

Porky smiled. "You never could say spaghetti."

Before removing his arm, Grover gently shook Porky. "I may not know how to say it right, but I sure like to eat it."

Woodrow chimed in. "I like that white stuff my Momma shakes on it."

"Pamenjohn cheese."

"Yeah, that tastes good."

"Pinky said you ate hamburgers in Jeeps with Gene Autry," Woodrow said.

Their conversation was a respite from the grief he felt over news of his father. Porky grinned and nodded. "He's in the Army."

"Gene Autry is in the Army?"

"He's a Sergeant. He's going to Camp Maxey to sing for the soldiers. He goes to the hospital in San Antonio, too, where Momma worked. He's gonna go to Dallas and fly airplanes."

"He's not gonna be in the *pitchursho* no more?" Grover questioned.

"He's doin his part for the war, then he'll be *back in the saddle again*." Porky sang the last words.

They fell silent once more. Grover yawned . . . Woodrow spat into the grass alongside the steps . . . Porky remembered Miss Belew telling Miss Dulfeine about the Germans coming to town.

"Sergeant Chestnutt is bringing the Germans from Camp Maxey tomorrow," Porky said.

"Yeah, I'm gonna go watch. Momma said they'll be

comin down Clark Street late afternoon," Woodrow said.

Porky looked at Woodrow. "Miss Belew told that to Miss Dulfeine at the store.   She musta told your momma, too. She musta told a lot of people."

"She listens to everbody's phone calls," Woodrow said.

"Unless you teller not to," Grover amended. "One time I heard my momma say it's a private call, Carsey."

"Do you hate the Germans?" Woodrow asked.

"I don't know any Germans.   I've never seen a German," Porky answered.

"I mean, because of what happened to your Papa? The Germans blew up your daddy's boat," Woodrow calrified.

Porky shrugged. "I dunno." He nodded. "I guess I do.   If they didn't start the war, my daddy would be home."

"The Japs started the war."

"Well, the Germans started it over there," Grover said. "I'm bringin my Red Ryder tomorrow. If they try to run away, I'll shoot em down," Grover said.

"Your B-B gun ain't gonna scare no Nazis, Grover. You better leave your gun at home. They may jump on you and take it away," Woodrow said.

"My Grandpa calls them Jerry's," Grover said. "He said they eat krap and drink a lot of beer."

"They don't eat crap, Grover. It's krout, like our sourkrout with pork chops," Woodrow countered. "They drink snaps, too."

"How do you know all that?" Porky asked.

"Mister Tanner told us."

Porky leaned forward and rested his chin on his arm across his knees as Woodrow had done.

"He told me to come see him if I wanted to be a

Scout, if I had any questions."

"That'd be great if you'd be a Scout with Woodrow and me."

"Tomorrow night we're going camping," Woodrow said.

"Where?"

"In the woods on the other side of the highway and the Katy station," Grover said. "We camped there before. We earn merit badges for doing chores, readin stuff, makin stuff, learnin stuff."

"I think Mister Tanner owns the place. There's a shack and two old wagons there. Some sleep on the ground and some sleep in the wagons," Woodrow said.

"I've never slept in the woods."

"Why don't you come with us. We ride our bicycles to the station and leave em there. We cross the train tracks, and hike up the trail. It ain't a far walk," Grover said.

"It's about a mile," Woodrow added.

"Next month we're going to a Scout Jamboree in Paris," Grover said. "We do all kinds of stuff, like lifesaving, tellin stories, buildin fires, listenin to Scout leaders, just all kinds of stuff."

"We get badges for doin that stuff, too," Woodrow said. "I've got eight badges so far."

"I got six," Grover said. "I'll get another tomorrow night for tellin a story about a good deed I done for Miss Chambers."

"Wad you do?"

"I found her dog, Raleigh. He run off, and I found him snoopin round the Ice House."

"I guess I'll ask momma if I can talk to Mister Tanner about it. I'm thinkin about it."

Woodrow sneezed. "Well, talk to Mister Tanner

about it, don't talk to Mister Douglass." Woodrow sneezed again and wiped his nose on his arm. He spat again on the grass next to the front steps.

"Our math teacher, Mister Douglass, at school?"

"Yeah, he's the Assistant Scoutmaster," Woodrow said. "You know how creepy he is. Remember that time Hale Perkins said Mister Douglass wanted to kiss him?"

Grover snorted. "I didn't believe that story. A man don't want to kiss boys. Anyway, who'd want to kiss a cripple."

"My daddy kissed me," Porky said. "Not on the lips, though. He's kissed me on my head or my cheek."

"Well, that was your daddy. Daddies can kiss their sons, sometimes, like birthdays and Christmas," Grover retorted. "Math teachers don't kiss boys. Anywhere. Lips, head, or cheek."

"I've kissed Sally," Porky said. "I think she's cute. I'm going to ask her to go to the *pitchursho* with me. Maybe she'll be my girlfriend."

"I like Bessie. She sat beside me at the *pitchursho*," Grover said. "I held her hand, and she leaned over and kissed me."

"Where?" Woodrow asked.

"In the *pitchursho*."

"I mean where? On the lips, on your cheek, on . . ."

"The lips. And I kissed her back. She giggled, too."

The boys thought about girls for several seconds before returning to Grover's disparaging remarks about Hale Perkins.

"I believed Hale," Woodrow said.

"Hale ain't no cripple, Grover," Porky said.

"Why would he say somethin crazy like that if it wasn't true?" Woodrow shook his head. "Mister

Douglass is scary." Woodrow paused before his voice was softer, quieter, almost a whisper. "He wanted to kiss me one time, but I pushed away. When I did, he laughed."

Grover and Porky looked at Woodrow.

Woodrow shrugged. "I never told nobody." He looked at his companions and shrugged again. "Who'd believe me? He's a teacher."

Miss Baycann's voice penetrated their subsequent silence.

"It's about time for supper, Porky."

Startled, they stood and turned.

She was immobile, one hand rested on the screen door spring, the other on the frame. She pushed open the door. "Would you boys like to come in and eat supper with us? We're having beans and franks."

Porky wondered how long his mother had been standing at the door while they talked. Had she heard Woodrow tell about Hale and himself and Mister Douglass?

"No, Mam, I better get on home," Woodrow said.

"Me, too," Grover said.

They bounded down the steps, picked up their bicycles, and pedaled away not looking back.

Porky poured a glass of cold milk and a glass of tea for his mother.

She served their supper, sat across from Porky.

"Did you tell them about your father?"

"Grover asked if I hate Germans. Because of what happened. Do you think Daddy is dead?"

Agnes canted her head and smiled at her son. "No, I think your daddy is safe somewhere in a hospital. The General said it was difficult to know where all the men were."

Porky smiled too. "I think he's alright. We'll get a letter from him, Momma, and he'll tell us he's okay."

Agnes turned her head away so Porky could not see tears shimmering. She brought her plate to the sink to gain composure. She peered through the kitchen window.

"What did you tell Grover?"

"I dunno. I don't know any Germans. Do we hate Germans, Momma?" He watched his mother, aware she felt sad.

Agnes wiped her eyes and sat at the table. "We hate Hitler and all the Nazis. He's a bad man who hurt a lot of people."

"Sergeant Chestnutt is bringing his Germans to Palomino tomorrow."

"Where did you hear that?"

"When I went to the store for the bread and beans, Miss Belew was tellin Miss Dulfeine. They're gonna come down Clark Street because of the committee."

"What committee?"

Porky didn't remember. "Miss Belew said the committee would be waiting if they came down Main Street."

He finished his franks and beans and wiped his plate with the remaining half slice of Wonder Bread.

"Can I join the Boy Scouts, Momma?"

"The Boy Scouts? Where did that idea come from?"

"Sandy asked me if I was a Boy Scout."

"Who is Sandy?"

"He's Gene Autry's driver. They were in a big black car. Gene asked me if I wanted a ride into town. I sat on the back seat. It was soft."

Agnes leaned forward and placed her elbows on the table. She grinned.

"Sandy. Gene Autry. And you rode into town with Gene Autry in his big black car?"

Porky matched her grin.

"And I ate a hamburger and drank a Co-Cola with Gene Autry in Jeeps."

His mother shook her head. "Reeeely."

Porky's grin grew larger. His eyes sparkled with joy to see his mother's happy face. He nodded emphatically. "Really, Momma. Cross my heart and hope to die."

"Well, I've never known you to be a fibber, so I guess it's true."

"You wanna know what else?"

"There's more?"

"Mister Albert's pants fell down and he waden wearin no underwear . . ."

His mother's bellowing, boisterous laughter interrupted the report.

"Everbody stopped and looked."

"Goodness gracious. I guess that was a sight to behold."

"I helped Mister Dulfeine help Mister Albert down the steps in front of the store."

They fell silent for a few moments. She detected there was more. She waited.

"Mister Tanner said I could come see him at school or his house if I had questions about being a scout. He's the head of the scouts."

"He's the Scoutmaster of a Troop of Boy Scouts."

"And Mister Douglass is his assistant."

"Yes. Who told you that?"

"Woodrow."

"Well, I guess it's alright for you to talk to Mister Tanner. I don't want you talking to Mister Douglass about Boy Scout stuff."

Porky decided not to tell his mother about Mister Douglass wanting to kiss Hale . . . and Woodrow.

"Is Hale a cripple, Momma?"

"No, Porky. Hale's brain was not right when he was born. His mother was sick with an infection, and they think that affected Hale."

"He walks and talks funny, that's why Grover said he's a cripple."

"He has Cerebral Palsy. He's not a cripple."

He also decided not to reveal his plan to go with Grover and Woodrow tomorrow to watch the Germans come into Palomino.

"Go listen to your programs while I do the dishes. Then I want you to read the next chapter of *Robinson Crusoe*."

Agnes Baycann planned asking Sergeant Chestnutt for help to find Private First Class Portland Alvin Baycann, Senior who she was sure was safe in a hospital somewhere over there.

4

Porky enjoyed the radio programs his mother listened to as much as she did. He tried to pay attention for clues as Ellery Queen solved baffling murders. He laughed with her at mishaps and predicaments *Lum and Abner* managed to find in Pine Ridge.

It never occurred to him that almost half of radio programming in 1943 was comedies. Laughter soothed the psyche from the strain of anxiety about loved ones fighting in Sicily, as well as those involved in the island-hopping war in the Pacific and preparing to take the war onto the European mainland.

During an advertising break, he posed his question. "Since Mister Madison left, are we gonna get a new Constable?"

"Why do you ask that?"

"If we have a murder, who's gonna solve it?"

Agnes thought for several seconds while the announcer proclaimed Alka-Seltzer would relieve an uncomfortable feeling. The distinctive plop-plop, fizz-fizz as tablets dropped into a glass of water preceded the pitchman's testimony of instant relief.

"Well, Jimmy Madison sure wouldn't if he was still here, that's for sure."

"Ellery Queen always solves the murder." Porky watched his mother's face and waited.

"I guess Sheriff Blake or Sheriff Dudley would, depending on which side of Pecan Creek it happened."

"Why don't you be the Constable, Momma? You're good at solving murders on the radio."

She smiled. "Radio is not the real thing. Clues are for listeners to play along, to see if they can figure out whodunit before the end of the program. On the radio, there is misdirection, wrong solutions, and red herrings before the crime is solved."

"Like a fish?"

"Well, no, it's a technique to try to fool the listener. Or the reader. People who write books do it all the time. Solving real murders is hard, sometimes they don't get solved. Anyway, I like my job at the hospital."

"This hospital is little, not like where you worked in San Antonio, at the Station Hospital."

"Last year it was renamed Brooke General Hospital."

"Do you miss being there?"

She thought for a couple of seconds. "In a way, I do."

"I know we came here because Daddy was at Camp Maxey, but I like San Antonio. Do you think we'll go back there?"

The reason they moved to Palomino was no longer present. Portland shipped out from Camp Maxey as a replacement and ended up in Sicily. Agnes had mulled over the possibility of returning to San Antonio and her job at the hospital there. Then the letter, and now . . .

"You like it here. You have friends here, Grover and

Woodrow. They're your best friends. And Pinky and Patsy."

On the radio, Carleton Young, as Ellery, and Santos Ortega, as Inspector Queen, reading their lines was an undertone to a mother talking with her son.

"It's okay, I guess. They're my friends. Daddy is . . ."

The radio characters continued in the silence.

Porky got up off the floor. "I'm goin to bed. Mister Church wants me at the field at seven."

"Let's go to the *pitchursho* tomorrow night to see *Heaven Can Wait.*"

Porky didn't mind walking with his mother three nights a week to the *Palomino Palace* because he knew his mother loved to see films. But this time he had other plans.

"I'm supposed to go camping. Anyway, *Heaven Can Wait* is next week, Momma."

"Camping? With who?"

"Woodrow and Grover. They asked me to go with them."

"You've never been camping."

"It's a Boy Scout camping. They do stuff. They earn badges for doin stuff. They sleep in the woods."

"Where?"

"Across from the Katy. Mister Tanner has a special place over there, a house and wagons. Some sleep in the house and some in the wagons."

Agnes was hesitant, but she knew her son needed experience, adventure. "I don't know, Porky. You've never slept anywhere except in your bed."

Porky smiled. "I'm growing up, Momma. You can't baby me forever."

She matched his smile and nodded. "Yes, I can,

young man. I'm your Mother. You'll always be my baby, forever and ever."

"Can I go camping with Woodrow and Grover, Momma?"

Her smile broadened, and she shrugged. "I suppose so. When you come from the field, I'll have a thermos of water and a snack ready for you. You'll need a blanket and jacket. What time are you supposed to be there?"

Porky hadn't thought about time. He didn't have a watch. "I dunno."

"How are you going to get there?"

"I'm gonna ride my bicycle to the Katy and meet them there. We'll walk to the camping place. Woodrow said it's about a mile."

"You don't know what time?"

"I didn't think about the time. I'll ask them when we're over on Clark."

Her antennae shot up. "What's going on over on Clark?"

"You know, Momma, the Germans. We're gonna watch for Sergeant Twig and the Germans."

"What time are they coming?"

"I dunno."

She smiled again. "So, Sergeant Chestnutt is bringing Germans to Palomino, and you want to go watch their arrival, but you don't know when they're coming?"

"Miss Belew said late afternoon."

"Miss Belew told you . . ."

"She told Miss Dulfeine late afternoon when I was in the store. I heard them talking. Grover and Woodrow are gonna go, Momma. I want to go with them."

His mother sighed. "Okay. I guess it'll be okay for

you to go watch. But you be careful. There's a lot of people upset and uneasy about German prisoners coming to live and work here."

In the darkness, he grasped the hand and gripped it tightly. It was a struggle; the weight was more than he expected. He planted his feet for support and strained against the resistance. Yelling reached his ears, and rumbling *gunfire* – was there *gunfire*? A huge object came out of the blackness, boring down on him. He clasped the extended hand with both of his . . . and grunted . . . and pulled harder . . . and pushed with both feet. Now there was movement, shaking, the yelling grew louder.

"*Porky. Porky*?"

The ceiling light was on. He blinked at the brightness. He opened his eyes wide and peered at his mother standing over him.

His bed sheet was tangled around his feet, and his hands clutched the balled edge of the sheet at the top.

"You were having a nightmare, Sweetheart."

Tears formed in his eyes.

His mother sat on the edge of his bed.

"Oh, Son, what's wrong?"

"Daddy. I was pulling Daddy out of the water. There was gunfire and yelling."

She shook her head and brushed wet hair from his brow. "You were yelling, Darling. It was you."

"Daddy wanted my help. He held his hand up to me. I had his hand. I was helping him out of the water. A big ship was going to run over us. I pulled as hard as I could but . . ." He caught his breath, his bottom lip quivered.

She leaned forward and kissed his forehead. "Your

Daddy is alright. He's safe."

Porky wiped his nose and eyes with the sheet. "How do you know that?"

Her lips made a slight movement but did not form into a smile. "I've got connections. I had a conversation before bed. I've been told not to worry, it'll be alright. Now, go back to sleep. It'll soon be time for you and me to go to work."

Porky's nightmare was ending as another was beginning in Pecan Park.

They sat in the '37 Willys sedan, seventeen-year-old Barber Beck behind the wheel, sixteen-year-old Bobbette Moon next to him.

Sixteen-year-old Wyatt Posey lounged on the back seat. Between asides, he swigged moonshine from a Mason jar. They had pulled the whiskey out of a tree stump, stolen from the hiding place near Barber's daddy's still. The rotgut, mostly clear liquid had passed between the three of them most of the night. Their lubrication oiled rising anger.

"Did you hear what she said, Posey?"

"Yeah, I heard. I told you she was bad news, but naw, you wouldn't listen to me. You shoulda cut her loose sooner. Now you're in a fix."

"I ain't in no fix. Miss Bobbette, here, is the one who's in a fix. And I might just fix the whole mess."

In the darkness, Barber grabbed fingers full of dark hair and jerked her head back. "If you think I'm gonna marry you, you got another think comin."

"You got to. It's your baby, Barber."

"That's a lie, and you know it."

"You shut your mouth, Wyatt," Bobbette snapped. "This ain't none of your business."

"I seen you with Tub, all snugglin up at the *pitchursho*. Cuddlin up comes after snugglin up. And then . . ."

"Did you go with Tub?" Barber demanded.

"No . . . I mean, not really."

"What does 'not really' mean?" Barber jerked harder.

"You're hurtin me."

"You ain't hurt yet. Answer me. What does 'not really' mean?"

"We just talked."

Wyatt fueled the fire flaming Barber's temper. "Yeah, he talked you right into the back seat of his car."

"Did he?" Barber demanded.

"What if he did? Since you and me ain't together no more, I do what I want to do with the people I want to do it with. You ain't my boss."

Barber shoved her head toward the door. "Get outta the car." He got out, went to the passenger door and opened it. "Get out, I'm gonna see if you carryin a baby."

"You're crazy. What're you gonna do? You're crazy drunk, leave me alone, Barber. Take me home."

As he reached for her, Bobbette pushed Barber back, leaned away, and raised her feet to kick him.

He grabbed an ankle and reached under her dress.

Bobbette felt his fingers dig into her abdomen, scratching her skin, and grip the waistband of her panties. She resisted, struggled, fought as he pulled the cotton garment down and off.

His balled fist to her jaw and then to her cheek cut short her first scream.

Wyatt reached over the front seat and grabbed her.

He yelped when she sank strong fingernails into the back of his hand and bit his wrist.

Bobbette felt the knife slice her belly. "Oh, Barber, no. Oh, no. Oh, no, please."

Her second and third screams were haunting and painfully murderous.

"Porky? *Porky?*"

He smelled Spam frying as the alarm rang. He rushed out of bed.   "Yes, Momma."

Morning toiletry complete, he splashed cold water on his face and dressed.

He chomped the small slab of pork laid over a slice of dry toast and washed breakfast down with a glass of milk.

Twelve minutes flat and he was out the door on his way to work. He stood on his pedals, pumping his two-wheeler to the cotton field.

Agnes saw her son off, tidied up, and began her walk to the hospital. She decided to leave their car in the driveway and walk the half mile. Gas rationing was a way to save fuel for the war effort, but it also encouraged people to be mindful of being thrifty.

Anyway, the August heat had not yet waked, so her journey was a pleasant stroll. Agnes spoke to friends who were up early, toiling in their flowerbeds.

As Agnes came through the doorway, Greffen Gates stood behind the reception counter. He held a tray filled with bottles, cups, and syringes. His greeting was somber.

"Something's happened. What's wrong, Pearly?"

"Bobbette Moon was brought in before daybreak. Doctor Burns and Nurse Salter have been in the operating room for a couple of hours, trying to save her."

"Should I go in there?"

"Linda said you better make the rounds for her and Doc. Check vitals and pass out everbody's medications. I was just getting everything ready for you."

"Where's Geraldine?"

"Kline's drugstore, for Doc Burns."

"Has Lucile and Delbart brought everbody their breakfast?"

"Breakfast rounds will be a little late, I think."

"What happened to Bobbette?"

"Somebody cut her open. Barber Beck and Wyatt Posey brought her to the hospital about four this morning. They found her up there in the park. They had come from workin a job at Camp Maxey and stopped to relieve themselves. She was layin on the ground with her underwear off. Linda called me to come in right away, she's been helping Doc Burns."

"What do you mean Bobbette was cut open?"

"Her belly was sliced from one side to the other."

"My goodness. Who could've done such a thing? Why?"

"We don't know. She wasn't conscious when they brought her in. Linda said it don't look good. Doc told me to call the Sheriff."

Voices down the hall drew their attention.

Doctor Burns and Nurse Salter came to them.

The Doctor shook his head. His weary eyes and grim face broadcast bad news.

"Oh, my goodness. Oh, dear Lord," Agnes Baycann whispered.

"We couldn't save her. Her jaw was broke and her eye swollen," Nurse Salter said. "Somebody beat on this poor girl before they killed her."

"And her baby," Doc Burns growled.

41

5

An hour after Porky pedaled past the hospital, Lamar County Sheriff Jim Dudley and Deputy Gary Gully parked in front.

Inside, the medical staff gathered with the officers in a small meeting room. They sat around a table with a checkered gray and white Formica top.

The investigators sat stoic and held their tongues as reports played out.

Dudley let the pause linger before he leaned forward and placed his forearms on the table. He clasped his fingers together.

"I know it's gonna sound like we didn't listen to all of you, but I want to ask for your patience and understanding in answering our questions."

They nodded.

Dudley looked at Doctor Burns. "She was alive but unconscious?"

"Yes. Barely, though. The wound was deep and long, she had lost a lot of blood. I knew right away her chances of surviving were slim."

"You said her breathing was shallow and heartbeat

was weak?"

"Yes. Her blood pressure was on the bottom rung, pulse extremely faint."

"Didn't open her eyes or move in any way?"

"No. Well . . ."

Dudley waited, then, "Go on, Sir."

"Her lips moved, like she was trying to close her mouth."

"But she said nothing?"

"No, nothing. It could have been a contraction or reflex of sorts."

"In your experience, Doctor, are you able to determine the type of blade used?"

"I don't understand, Sheriff? You mean like a . . ."

"Like a scalpel, pocketknife, serrated hunting knife, stiletto, bayonet, sword, saber?"

"Oh, yes, I see. I can rule out a serrated edge, and certainly no sword or saber, but any of the others you mentioned is possible. A very sharp and large blade made the incision, from side to side. No small pocketknife, for sure."

Dudley looked at Greffen. "You came on at midnight, Mister Gates?"

Greffen nodded. "I go by Pearly, Sheriff. Yes, midnight to nine. It's my regular shift. They came in about four."

Dudley and Gully smiled.

"Pearly Gates?" Gully asked.

"Picked it up in school, years ago."

"Wyatt Posey and Barber Beck brought Miss Moon in?"

"Yes, Deputy, I know both those boys. We've had them in here over the years, patching them up from one scrape or another."

A knock drew attention.

Nurse Salter rose and opened the door. "Hello, Mayor. Hello, Jonathan." She made introductions. "Deputy Gully, the Sheriff knows Mayor Casey Shipp and Jonathan Bell, our undertaker, but you don't."

Handshakes and how-dos finished, Casey got down to business. "We've notified Frank and Francine about Bobbette and they asked Jonathan to come for her, Doc."

"Yes, of course. May we release the body, Sheriff?"

"That's fine, Doc, you've listed the cause of death and we'll investigate it as a homicide. You can take Miss Moon, Mister Bell."

The interruption was over quickly. Doctor Burns escorted Jonathan to retrieve Bobbette Moon's body. Everyone remained standing.

"Mayor, with thousands of soldiers and workers out at Maxey and thousands of strangers comin into the county, our hands are full. I'm gonna need some help with this investigation, to find the person who killed Miss Bobbette Moon. Have you found a replacement for Jimmy Madison?"

"I have, Sheriff, but he hasn't been officially appointed. Army Sergeant Twig Chestnutt will be our Constable."

"An Army Sergeant is gonna be your Constable?"

"He's a Military Police Sergeant and former Constable in Vivian, Louisiana. He's got law enforcement training and experience. He'll fit right in."

"Why's he comin here?"

"We made arrangements with General Pace at Camp Maxey for three German prisoners to come to Palomino to live and work. Sergeant Chestnutt's wife and daughter live here. The General agreed Sergeant

Chestnutt could do double duty as our Constable, and guard and supervise the German prisoners."

"They're gonna live here?"

"Yes. They're arriving late this afternoon. After they settle in at Miss Ruby's place, I'll go over and tell him to come to my office tomorrow morning for his swearing in."

"Okay, after your Sergeant is Constable, have him contact me so he can help in the investigation. Maybe he can develop some leads."

"Yes, I'll do that, Sheriff."

"Now, we need some directions, Mayor. Deputy Gully and I will go up to Pecan Park first. After we have a look around there, we'll stop by to talk to Mister Beck and Mister Posey. Maybe they have information that can assist in finding who killed Miss Moon."

"Master Porky, this here is T J. He's my sister Irene's boy, my nephew. It's his first day in the field. Could he work alongside you on the next row over?"

Porky looked at T J. His skin was not quite as dark as Hazelnut but not as light as the color of bronze, certainly not black like Preacher Adams. Deep dimples formed in T J's smooth cheeks and his dark eyes shined with delightful anticipation.

Porky matched T J's wide friendly grin. "Sure, Preacher Adams."

"Okay, you boys go on up yonder, ten rows up," Martin Church directed. "Walk all the way up to the top and start pickin your way back down this side."

"Okay, come on, T J."

They walked past three rows, shoulder to shoulder, before Porky spoke.

"Where you live?"

"Over yonder, in Minter."

"Where you go to school?"

"We don't have no school. My Momma teaches me readin and writin. I've read a thousand books."

"That's a lot of readin. How old are you?"

"Fourteen years old. How old are you?"

"Fourteen, almost fifteen."

"Why my uncle call you Porky?"

"It's my nickname. My daddy give it to me when I was a baby. My real name is Portland. Portland Albert Baycann, Junior."

"My real name is Thomas James Workman. I don't have a white friend."

Porky stopped. Thomas took two more steps before he stopped and turned to face Porky.

"I don't have a colored friend."

"I ain't colored. My momma says I'm a black child and to be proud of it."

"You don't look black to me. Your uncle is black, but you're . . . you're . . . you're like the middle of a Reese's Peanut Butter Cup."

T J shrugged and raised his hands, palms up. His beautiful grin flashed again. "Then we can be friends with each other. You be my white friend, and I be your butter cup friend."

Porky grinned and stepped forward. He put his arm across T J's shoulders. "Okay, Butter Cup, let's go pick Major Monroe's cotton."

T J put his arm around Porky. They turned as one and marched between matured green stalks of fully bloomed rows of white fluff, headed to the top.

This new pair of friends would begin working together at more than picking cotton in Major Clay Monroe's field.

Gray, stringy hair framed a haggard face. Her pale blue eyes peered through the frayed screen; arthritic fingers clutched a worn and faded apron.

Jim Dudley touched the brim of his white felt Stetson. "Howdy, Mam. We come from Paris. I'm Lamar County Sheriff Jim Dudley, and this is Deputy Gary Gully. I'm looking for Wyatt Posey. We were told Wyatt lives here."

"What'd he do now?" Her voice was anxious, nervous.

"Are you Wyatt's momma, Mam?"

"Yes." It was a quick, blunt response.

"We'd like to speak with Wyatt, Mam. Is your son home?"

She held her gaze on them. "WYATT? WYATT? The law is here for you. Come to the door." She turned away and disappeared.

A scrawny, unkempt teenager appeared. Red pimples filled cheeks scarred by acne. His brown eyes were flat, unpredictable. He remained behind the screen door, a barrier for safety.

Dudley went through the introductions again. "We'd like to talk to you about last night. About Miss Bobbette Moon, the girl you found in Pecan Park and brought to the hospital."

"Uh huh."

"Do you mind comin out on the porch with us, Wyatt?" Deputy Gully asked.

Dudley and Gully both detected Posey's hesitancy, reluctance.

"You're not in trouble, Posey," Gully said. "Come on out for just a couple of minutes, to clear up some questions."

He pushed open the flimsy, wooden frame and took two steps sideways. The spring snapped the door shut.

Posey seemed embarrassed when he shook Dudley's extended hand and then Gully's.

Sheriff let his Deputy conduct the interview.

"At the hospital, they said you and Barber Beck found Miss Bobbette when you stopped in the park to pee. Where was she, like by one of the trash barrels, a picnic table, alongside the road, by Clark Street?"

"I . . . I don't remember. It was dark."

"Oh, that's right. It was early morning, like two or three?"

"Yeah, that's about right. About three, I think."

"And you and Beck were comin home from workin at Camp Maxey. At three in the mornin?"

"Yeah."

"What do you do at Camp Maxey? What kind of work?"

"Construction, roofing, framing, that kind of thing. Whatever strawboss say, we do."

"And the job you worked on last night? The one where you worked so late, that you'd be gettin home at three in the morning?"

"We was finishin up interior walls of a new mess hall. Puttin on some paint."

"Who's your boss out there, at Maxey?"

"John Young."

Deputy Gully looked at Sheriff Dudley.

"The old man, John, Senior? or Junior?" Jim Dudley asked.

"Junior."

Dudley nodded.

Gully continued. "So you and Beck found Miss Moon in the park in the dark, picked her up, put her in the car, and brought her to the hospital?"

"Yeah. Well . . . Well, it wadn in the dark. We saw her with the headlights."

"Oh, so there was some light. You could see where she was layin. By the road, the street, or . . ."

"Yeah, by the road. She was layin on her side, by the road."

"Did you talk to her? Did she tell you what happened? Who cut her?"

"No. I mean we ask, but she didn't say nothin."

"She must have been awful bloody with a knife wound across her abdomen?" Gully prodded.

"Where?"

"Her stomach," the Sheriff added. "She was cut open, Wyatt. There musta been a lot of blood on her and in your car?"

Posey's face drained. He grew pale. He smacked his lips together. "We was in Barber's car."

"I see."

Gully continued. "In the light, the lights from the car, did you see anything layin on the ground?"

"Like what?"

"I dunno. Trash, beer bottles, whiskey bottles, rubbers, clothing?"

"Clothing?"

"Yeah, like a shirt, or pants, or underwear?"

Wyatt closed his mouth and swallowed hard. His bobbing Adam's apple accented a skinny neck. "No. No we didn't see none of that stuff . . . I mean I didn't see nothing."

The Deputy nodded. "Well, we did. We went by the park just a little while ago." He watched Wyatt's face. "I'm surprised you didn't see them, just layin beside the road there, in the park, with the car's headlights shinin

49

on em."

"See what?"

"A pair of woman's white cotton underwear."

Wyatt blinked, his eyelids flashed, danger lay ahead.

"Damn," Dudley exclaimed. "This splinter is killin me." He raised his hand and squeezed his right thumb with his left fingers.

"Maybe Wyatt's got a pocketknife, Sheriff, to pick it out? Could the Sheriff use your knife, Wyatt?"

"No. No, I ain't got no pocketknife." He reached for the screen door. "Maybe Momma's got a pair of tweezers."

Dudley released his thumb and held out his left hand toward the door. "No, that's alright, don't bother your momma."

"Just a couple of more questions," Gary Gully continued. "Who picked up Miss Moon?"

"Barber did."

"What did you do?"

"I held the door open."

"What kind of car does Barber have?"

"Willys. A Thirty-Seven Willys."

"Coupe or sedan?"

"Sedan. Four-door sedan."

"So, which door did you hold open?

"The front. The front passenger door."

"So, you held open the front passenger door and Barber put Miss Moon on the front seat?"

"Yeah. And I got in the back. Barber drove as fast as he could down Clark Street and we went to the hospital."

"So, you didn't touch Miss Moon?"

"I didn't lay a hand on her, I mean, I didn't pick her up. I mean, I helped Barber pick her up and brought her to the car. Then I opened the door."

"I see. Were you wearin these clothes last night?"

Wyatt looked at his shirt and pants before shaking his head. "No, I was wearin overalls."

"So, did any of Miss Moon's blood get on your overalls?"

"No. When Barber picked her up I held her ankles, he held under her arms. We brung her to the car and then to the hospital."

"Where's your overalls?"

"Momma's washin em now. I used turpentine to get paint off and momma put em in the washtub to soak."

The investigators let the silence extend for dramatic effect. Tension hung in the August morning warmth.

Posey shifted his weight to his left foot and canted his head. "Is that all?"

"I'm kinda puzzled about something, Wyatt?" The Sheriff cupped fingers over his mouth for a couple of seconds before letting them slide down his chin. "Aren't you interested in how Miss Moon is doing?"

Wyatt Posey clasped his lips together and physically swallowed with difficulty. "Is she . . . is Bobbette alright, Sheriff?"

"No, Mister Posey. Miss Bobbette Moon is not alright. That poor child succumbed to her wound," Gary Gully said. "A shame."

"Subcomed?"

"She died, Wyatt," Sheriff Dudley said. His voice was solemn. "She bled to death." His tone was stern, threatening. "We're now searching for her killer."

"Or, killers," the Lamar County Deputy added.

Posey blinked, his mouth open and slack.

"Well, we'll be on our way. We gonna go have a talk with Barber, to see if he remembers anything you might have missed." Sheriff Dudley smiled. "Oh, there's one other thing before we go, Wyatt. The Mister John Young that we know in Paris has three grown daughters. There is no John Young, Junior. Maybe you made a mistake."

They turned to leave but stopped.

"We may have other questions, Mister Posey. I'd like for you to stay close at hand," the Sheriff cautioned, "so you tell your momma where you're gonna be. Don't you make us have to come lookin for you."

A young boy, twelve or thirteen, responded to the knocks.

"How do, son. I'm Sheriff Dudley. We're here to see Barber Beck. Is he home?"

An older man with a walking cane shuffled up behind the boy.

"I heard you, Sheriff. I'm Beck, Barber's pa. This here is Billy. Barber ain't here. Can I help you?"

"How do, Mister Beck. This is Deputy Gully. We wanted to thank Barber for what he did last night and ask a few follow-up questions."

"What'd my boy do?"

"He helped a young girl who had been bad cut and brought her to the hospital. Maybe you know her? Miss Bobbette Moon?"

"Billy, you go help your momma shell them peas?"

The three men waited until the youngster disappeared.

"Yeah, I know her. Her and Barber was goin together for a while, before he quit her. She's a wild one. Seems she'd go with any boy who give her a look. They'd fight, split up, and fore you know it she was back here wantin him. Wouldn't leave my boy alone, stuck two of his tires with a ice pick. I told Barber he better cut bait for good fore it turned sour."

"We think it might have, Mister Beck."

"How so?"

"Miss Bobbette Moon is dead," Sheriff Dudley said. "Somebody cut her open in the park and left her there. Your boy and Wyatt Posey found her this morning there, in the park, when they stopped to pee, comin in from workin at Maxey."

"Barber don't work over there at Maxey."

"Does your boy own a pocketknife?"

"He does. It was his grandpa's."

"Can you describe it, Sir?" Deputy Gully asked.

"It's a Case XX, with a Stag handle. It's a pretty big, heavy knife to be called a pocketknife. Four full inches when it's folded up, fills a man's hand. His grandpa used it to skin rabbits, coons, squirrels, and possums. Kept all the blades sharp as a razor. I give it to Barber after his grandpa was buried."

"Do you know where your boy is now, Mister Beck?" Gully asked.

"You thinkin my boy had somethin to do with this Moon girl's killin. With his knife. His grandpa's knife."

"If you know where Barber is, you need to tell us," Gully said. "This is serious business, Sir."

"I'm sorry, Sir. We really need to talk with your boy, Mister Beck," Sheriff Dudley said softly.

6

In Major Clay Monroe's central cotton field, the largest of his sixteen, there were more than four dozen adult pickers. Two dozen kids, along with T J and Porky, were out for a few dimes of spending money and adventure, well before Labor Day and the start of their new year of school.

This acreage was nearest to town. The Major's other spreads stretched east toward Bogata, west toward Pattonville, north toward Detroit, and south toward Cunningham and Minter. A rich man, in wealth, property, and influence, the Major was the perennial councilman representing the First Section of Palomino.

He was a favorite of Ma Ferguson since the day her husband, the Texas Chief Executive, visited the Major in Station Hospital and decorated him, on behalf of President Wilson and General Pershing, for bravery during the first war. Following medical discharge from the Army, he became a supporter, fundraiser, and contributor for Governor Pa Ferguson.

Throughout the years, he was a letter, telegram, or phone call away from all of the Texas Democratic bigwigs and wheelers and dealers, including Governors Bill Hobby, Ma Ferguson, Pappy O'Daniel, and current incumbent, Coke Stevenson. He had broken bread with and served as confidant to President Franklin Roosevelt.

Every four years since the crash in '29, the Major had been in the background, but instrumental, in the continuing elections of Lamar County Sheriff Jim Dudley and Red River County Sheriff Billy Blake.

They paid homage to the Major, knew he was their benefactor, and gave important consideration to his thoughts and wishes, which were fulfilled often.

The Major was astute at using power to wield sway over the goings-on in Palomino. People judged him as a double-edged sword, he could be benevolent or malevolent – he benefitted either way.

The boys had been at it for an hour. They stopped mid row on the third turn and shielded their eyes from the sun. Odessa Church was coming their way with a pail of water.

Odessa was Martin's oldest daughter and earned a little spending money by serving as water bearer for hands in Major Monroe's cotton field. She was twenty and a second-year student at Paris Junior College. She had been a member of the famed bevy of beautiful, full-bodied young women who performed at rodeos, parades, and social events, but was serving a suspension for inappropriate Christian behavior.

The Assistant Dean of the English Department had observed Odessa and a star football player in a comprising position in the back seat of a Packard parked under the stadium bleachers and reported the incident. Because the Junior College staff matrons probably behaved in a similar fashion when younger, they support Odessa and asked the school's President to not dismiss her.

She set the bucket down and pulled the dipper full up to Porky. "I have water for you, Porky."

Porky took the handle and swallowed several gulps of the warm water. He reached the dipper over the top of the stalks to T J.

Odessa intervened. "No, Porky. What're you doin? You can't do that."

"T J is my friend, Miss Odessa, he's thirsty, too."

"But he can't drink from this water . . . this bucket of water . . . and dipper."

Porky knew the answer and reason. He prodded, anyway. "Why not?"

"Because. Because he's a . . . because."

"T J is my friend, Miss Odessa. He needs a drink of water like everbody else. Even if it's warm water like this is. You left the bucket in the sun."

"I did not. Anyhow, the water for your friend is at the cotton trailer. He can go there if he wants a drink."

All this time, Odessa did not look at T J.

"I ain't thirsty now. I'll go to the cotton trailer when I want a drink of water."

"No, here." Porky shoved the dipper towards T J. Water sloshed over the brim and covered Porky's hand. "Drink from this dipper."

T J took it, glanced at Odessa, looked at Porky, peered into the water, and glared at Odessa as he tilted the cup over and let the clear liquid spill out onto the black dirt between his bare feet.

"Okay, now both of you come with me to the trailer. I'm gonna tell what you did here." Odessa stuck her hand out, palm up, toward T J and wiggled her fingers. "Now, give me the dipper."

T J handed it over to Porky who took it and jabbed it

at Odessa.

"Both of you come with me.

She turned on her heels and marched down the row.

Porky grinned. "We might as well go. We can dump what we've picked, get a good drink of cool water, and sit in the shade a bit. It's almost dinner time anyway."

They pulled on the shoulder straps and hefted their quarter-filled bags across their shoulders. They trudged along in their row, trailing after Odessa.

At the trailer, she stood by while they handed over their loads. "Porky gave the dipper full of water to this boy here to drink," Odessa reported.

Martin looked at both boys. "He did, did he?" He grinned and deftly grasped Porky's strap and looped it around the end of the bag to form a sling. Then he lifted the bag and placed the sling/strap onto the scale hook. "Nine and three-quarter pounds," he announced.

Dallas Church, Martin's youngest daughter, recorded the weight on Porky's sheet in her notebook. "Ten pounds for six and a half cents."

Martin unhooked the bag and tossed it over the trailer's high railing to Preacher Adams.

Preacher was, indeed, a recognized and properly ordained minister by legitimate officials of the Northeast Texas Counties Baptist Convention. Besides weddings, baptisms, and funerals in and around Palomino, Preacher often was invited by the Palomino Baptist church elders to conduct a Sunday sermon for their congregation.

Preacher was a huge black man who had worked in Major Monroe's fields for decades. He never confirmed his age – he would only say he was born in the piney woods of East Texas on the day the Lord permitted his arrival. Many believed Preacher was near seventy.

Preacher shook Porky's bag violently, so all the cotton spilled into the trailer.

"Did you drink the water, T J?"

T J looked at Odessa. "No, Sir. She say I have to drink the water here at the trailer."

Martin repeated the process. He deftly looped T J's strap around the end of the bag to form a sling. Then he lifted the bag and placed the sling/strap onto the scale hook. "Ten pounds," he announced.

"Do I write your name in my book as T J or Thomas?"

"T J, Miss Dallas. My momma calls me Thomas, but I go by T J all the time. Everbody knows me be T J."

Dallas turned to a clear page in her book, wrote his name, and recorded the weight on T J's sheet. "Okay, I made a new sheet for you, T J. Ten pounds for four cents."

"He gets six and a half cents for ten pounds like me, Miss Dallas," Porky said. He looked at Martin. "Don't he, Mister Church?"

Martin looked up at Preacher.

Preacher leaned on the railing of the trailer and peered down at Porky and T J.

"Goin rate is sixty-five cents a hundredweight, Master Porky. But T J gets less than you."

"Why?"

"Why, indeed?"

They turned toward the voice and all, except Preacher, took a step back.

Preacher raised and stood erect. He spoke in the silence. "We was about to explain the why to the boy, Major."

Clay Monroe was a highly decorated, disabled World

War One hero, and retired Major, United States Army Reserve. He had no right hand. Upon new introductions, the Major found it amusing people felt awkward holding and shaking his left hand with their right.

Tall at six-two and broad-shouldered, he stood with a statesman's stature. His black eyes sat deep in a face dime novel writers described as chiseled, and his magnetic broad smile was contagious. Neatly trimmed white hair peeked from under the sides of a clean, gray Panama hat.

Old and new acquaintances described the Major as a rich owner of many large fields in Lamar and Red River Counties and the larger of the two cotton gins in Palomino. Widespread word of mouth in Texas said he ran the town, was a politically active patron with deep pockets, and could buy what he wanted, including people.

Porky stood his ground. "He picked the same cotton as me, Major. A little more. He's supposed to get six and a half cents, same as me."

The Major stepped between the youngsters and laid his stub on Porky's shoulder and his left hand on T J's. He peered down at Porky. "You have always had a lot of spunk, Porky. You take that from your momma. I like that. Is T J your friend?"

"Yes, Sir."

"That's what good friends are for. To fight for one another. Do you agree?"

"Yes, Sir."

"Well, then, what do you think, Mister Church?" The Major looked up at Preacher. "Preacher?"

"He picked a little more, Major, he deserves the same wage."

"Yes, you're right, Preacher. Mister Church, Miss Dallas, mark it so on T J's sheet from here on out. He's paid the same wage as his friend, Porky Baycann."

All the adults grinned, except Odessa. "Porky gave him the dipper to drink water from this pail."

The Major looked at Odessa, then at T J. "Did you get a drink?"

"No, Sir. I poured it out cause Miss Odessa say I have to drink the water at the trailer."

The Major nodded. "Dip me a cup of your water, Miss Odessa, please."

He took the dipper and handed it to T J. "Here, Son, have a drink of water."

After five hungry swallows, T J handed over the dipper.

They watched in astonished silence as the Major tilted the cup to his lips and swigged from it.

The rattling Ford pick-up drew their attention. When it stopped, a woman got out and marched to the group clustered around the trailer.

"Miss Irene," the Major said, "you're just in time. Ring the bell, Preacher, for all hands to come in for dinner."

Odessa took the tin from the Major as he patted Porky on the back with his stub. "Porky," he said, "I'm glad you're my friend. When I need help, I'm gonna come see you. You know how to get results."

The pay line shuffled toward Dallas and Martin who sat at a table next to the trailer. Preacher perched on a corner of railings watching the procession. Dallas called off the total and Martin paid wages for the day.

Porky put T J in front so he could see the amount announced by Miss Dallas and paid by Mister Church was as promised by the Major.

"You said you read a thousand books." Porky's voice did not hide his suspicions and disbelief. "What were they?"

T J shrugged. "I don't member all the titles."

"Well, tell me three."

T J turned to face Porky. "You don't believe me?"

Porky nodded. "Do you know how long it takes to read a thousand books?"

T J grinned. "For me, it would be a thousand days, cause I read a book a day."

Porky did not grin, doubt covered his face. "A thousand days is more than three years. You didn't read no thousand books."

T J's grin grew broader. He shrugged. "Maybe I meant a hundred. I meant to say a hundred. I've read a hundred books."

Porky thought on it for a minute and concluded it was possible, but he still had misgivings. He challenged the number. "You might of read ten instead of a hundred."

"I've read all of *Uncle Arthur's Bedtime Stories.*"

"I've read some of those," Porky admitted. "They're close to being religious stories, sort of."

"I read *Treasure Island* three times."

"Yeah, I've read that too."

"And *Lassie Come Home.*"

Porky waited. "Is that all?"

T J took three steps closer to Dallas and the paymaster.

He nodded at T J's back. "Okay, you read three books. Just like I guessed."

"I've read some of the *Hardy Boys* books."

Porky was impressed. "I liked them. They are good

detectives. You and me could be the Palomino Boys, T
J, findin out about all kinds of stuff."

T J ignored the possibility and continued. "I've read
Robinson Crusoe and *Moby Dick*."

"I'm reading *Robinson Crusoe* now. I read most of a
chapter every night before I go to bed. I just read
Chapter Four where he was on his way to buy slaves
and ends up on the island."

"My momma tells me her great grannies and great
aunts and great uncles was slaves a hundred years ago.
They all lived in Africa, and their Chief sold them to
somebody. That's how they got to Texas and why I'm a
black child."

"Well, your skin *is* a bit dark, darker than mine, but
it ain't black. Why you keep sayin that all the time?"

T J shrugged, then, "My blood is red though, just
like yours."

They fell silent. The line moved up two steps.

"My momma lets me read her *Holy Bible*, too," T J
said.

"I've never read a bible, but my momma sometimes
reads from it for me."

They were now third and fourth from the front.

"*Where there is no vision, the people perish*," T J
said. "That's one of my favorite sayings in the Bible.
Proverbs 29:18."

"What do you mean *one*?" Porky asked. "You have
more of em?"

"I remember some."

"Okay, say another one."

"*A soft answer turns away wrath, Proverbs 15:1.*"

"Like you said to Miss Odessa when you poured out
the water."

They both moved forward, and T J stood in front of

the pay table. Miss Dallas read the amount. Martin Church counted out the thirty-six cents as he dropped the coins onto T J's open palm.

T J wrapped his fingers around the money and grinned. He looked up at Preacher Adams.

"Whachu gonna do with all that money, Boy?"

"I'm gonna give all of it to momma, cept ten cents."

Preacher laughed. "Well, your momma can use twenty-six cents for sure. And whachu gonna do with the other ten cents?"

"I'm gonna buy a strawberry ice cream cone and a Baby Ruth."

"Well, don't tarry none," Preacher cautioned. "After your ice cream and candy, get on over to the gin where your momma will come to pick us up."

"I'm goin with Porky. I'll come to the gin after that."

Preacher's voice took on a tone of cautious alertness. "Whachu gonna do with Porky?"

"We gonna go over yonder to watch the Germans."

Preacher shook his head. "I don't think you better go wanderin around the streets of town, T J. You in Texas now. Palomino ain't like where you come from."

Porky looked from Preacher to T J then back to Preacher. "He'll be with me, Preacher." Porky nodded his reassurance. "Won't nobody bother T J when he's with me."

"They'll be a lot of people out there on Clark Street waitin for them Germans to come to town," Martin said.

Porky remembered the exchange in the store between Miss Belew and Miss Dulfeine. A smile tempted his lips. Miss Belew *is* the town crier, he thought, recalling *Chicken Little*, a character from one of his books, and she's done told Miss Dulfeine, and now all in Palomino knows the Germans are coming down

Clark Street instead of Main to avoid the committee.

"Thirty-six cents for Porky," Dallas said.

Martin counted out the wages and dropped the coins onto Porky's outstretched palm.

"You see, Porky," Martin said, "we did like the Major wanted. You and T J picked about the same amount of cotton and yall got paid the same."

Porky nodded. "Yessir, Mister Church. I was watchin."

Dallas smiled. Martin and Preacher laughed out loud.

"You boys done a good day's work. I'm gonna miss you when school starts." Porky looked at T J. "My school is gonna start on the Monday after the Labor Day."

"That's right, it'll be startin on Tuesday, September the seventh," Dallas said.

Martin and Dallas looked at T J.

"T J don't have no school. His momma is his teacher," Porky said. "He's read a hundred books."

Martin waved his hand to shoo them away. "Okay, yall better move along, there's people standin behind you waitin to get paid too."

Preacher watched the two friends walk toward Porky's bicycle. He called after them. "Yall be careful now, you hear? Don't be ridin off into no trouble and get locked up in the *Calaboose*."

7

Sally Edmonds matured early. She was proud of the noticeable developments her body had achieved since school year ended last May. She had celebrated her fourteenth birthday ten months ago and now in her mind she was a woman. Physical transformations had sped up in the one hundred days of summer vacation.

She stood a few feet away in front of her dresser mirror admiring her nude figure. She turned sideways to the left, paused, then to the right and paused, back to the left and again to the right. She faced her reflection and smiled, pleased how her breasts had evolved and filled out. Her dark nipples grew taut from the caressing touch of her fingertips. The rush of exciting, sensual pleasure flushed her cheeks. She thought of Porky and the possibilities with him, squeezed her lips into a pucker, and kissed at her likeness in the glass.

"SAL-LEE?"

Startled, she jerked around at the shrill call. "Yes, Momma?" Immediate embarrassment replaced her admiration.

"I'm ready to go," June Edmonds announced. "Where are you? Are you ready yet? Hurry up or we'll be late."

"Yes, Momma. I'm getting dressed." She slipped into her pink underwear, fastened and adjusted the new white bra, pulled on and buttoned the white blouse, and stepped into the faded blue overalls she loved. She flipped the denim straps over her shoulders hooking the wire loop onto the brass clasp. She smiled again. Her lips puckered for another imaginary kiss at the mirror.

"You don't wear a dress anymore?"

"I wear dresses, Momma."

June smiled, pressed her lips together, canted her head, and then said, "A young lady ought to wear a dress. You're growing up nice."

"Do you notice, Momma?"

"I sure do. But them overalls are hidin everything."

Sally blushed. "I just like these overalls, Momma."

"Well, I guess it'll be alright. They won't be nobody but Doctor Dunnfree at the office anyway, everbody'll be waitin to see the Germans."

"Can I go watch the Germans? After the dentist fills my tooth?"

June started the car. "Don't you want to go to the grocery store with me?"

"Bessie and Rochelle are gonna go watch."

June looked left and shook her head. There was no need to stick her arm out of the window to signal the turn. In Palomino, nobody ever signaled before turning or stopping – it wasn't anticipated or expected. "Those two are always into something."

"I told them I'd ask you to let me go."

Sally's mother parked in front of the office and shut the engine.

"Makes me nervous when I know you're out running around with those two. Sometimes I think they're a breath away from trouble, double trouble. Especially that Bessie. She's a bold one. I've heard say she smokes cigarettes and even drinks beer."

Sally avoided confronting the truth, but defended them. "They're my best friends, Momma. They're alright. We won't get into any trouble just standing on the street watching Germans. Porky might be there too."

"Porky." June smiled. "He's a nice boy. His momma is a good woman, helpin people at the hospital." She looked at her daughter. "You really like that boy, don't you?"

"I think he's cute. I just like talking with him, being with him. Sometimes we just sit side by side and don't say anything for a long time. He makes me laugh, makes me feel special. I think he might ask me to be his girlfriend."

June Edmonds nodded. "I understand. Your daddy made me feel special."

They got out of the car and moved up the walkway.

"How old were you when you kissed a boy?"

"Fourteen, like you. His name was Raymond."

"Did you love him?"

"I did." June thought on it, the pause seemed longer than four seconds. "Until your daddy came along."

"What happened to Raymond?"

"He went away. His daddy worked on an oil rig over there in Kilgore but got a job out west, and the family moved to Midland. After Raymond, there was another boy or two before your daddy."

"What did daddy do to change your mind about the

67

other boys?"

June opened the door to the dentist office for her daughter. "He did the right thing."

"Daddy says you got to do the right thing, Barber."

Barber remained seated on the floor. He did not look up. "You member when Buster and Butch built this tree house for us, Babe?"

Babe scanned the ramshackle boarding before sitting next to his older brother. "It was three years ago, on my eleventh birthday."

"It was our hideout, the Beck brother's getaway," Barber said. "Buster and Butch went off to fight in the war." His voice was a whisper. "Now they're dead. It's just you and me that's left."

"And Billy." With a side-eye glance at Barber, Babe spoke again. "I come to tell you the law was at the house looking for you."

Barber did not speak.

"It was Lamar County Sheriff Dudley and one of his deputies from Paris. Daddy said they wanted to talk to you about finding Bobbette Moon. He asked me if I knew where you was."

Barber Beck shook his head. "Did you tell Daddy where I'm at?"

"No. But I knew you'd be here." Babe leaned forward and turned. He looked at Barber's face. It was blank.

"Daddy said they asked if you owned a knife."

Babe wondered if his words had registered. His brother remained stoic; there was no emotion, no recognition that he heard Babe talking.

"He told em you did, it was Grandpa's. Daddy said the Sheriff talked liked he thought you cut her with your knife. Did you?"

Barber drew in a deep breath and exhaled slowly. He looked at the floor and spoke with a quiet voice. "I don't know what to do, Babe. Wyatt cut that girl. I tried to stop him. He was mean crazy. You know how Wyatt is, sometimes. I thought he might cut me too. I brought her to the hospital in my car. I thought they might just fix it, sew her up."

"Why is the law asking about *your* knife if Wyatt cut Bobbette?"

"I dunno why."

"Where's the knife, your knife, the one Grandpa had?"

"I dunno. I guess I lost it someplace."

"Daddy says you got to do the right thing, Barber. You got to go talk to the Sheriff, tell him what happened. Tell him about Wyatt cutting Bobbette."

"Wyatt lied about that."

Babe furrowed his brow, puzzled. "What do you mean?"

"He told the guy there at the hospital, Doctor Gates, that we was comin home from workin at Maxey and stopped to pee. We found her layin in the park, all cut and stuff."

"Jesus."

He turned to face Babe. "They gonna put me back behind bars. I can't do no more hard time."

Babe was shocked to see scratches on his brother's cheek and chin. He shook his head, his eyes remained fixed on the red lines. "No. No, they not. You didn't cut Bobbette. You tried to save her."

"Save her?"

"Yeah. Sheriff told Daddy she died."

Barber nodded. He looked down again, staring at

the worn, weather-beaten one-by-four planking of the tree house floor. "They gonna put me in the chair, then, if she's dead."

"Why you say that?" His heart raced, creeping doubt blossomed into anxiety. "You tried to save her by bringing her to the hospital."

"I'm in big trouble, Babe. I don't know what to do. I been sittin here all day thinkin bout drivin off, goin away somewhere. Maybe to San Antonio, maybe to Mexico."

"Where's your car?"

"Over there, on the other side of the Katy. At Winston Tanner's place."

"What's it doin there?"

"I was thinkin to go down to his pond to clean it up. It has a lot of blood on the front seat and door where we put Bobbette. I got scared and come here. I left it over there. I ain't had a chance to clean it up, to wash all the blood off."

"Well, Mister Tanner is gonna find it tonight."

"Why you say that?"

"We gonna go out there camping."

"We? Your Scout Troop?"

"Yeah, the Scouts are gonna camp at Mister Tanner's place tonight."

"Well, little brother, then you can help me."

"How?"

"By bringin my car back here. You could go early and be there when everbody comes in. You could tell Tanner and everbody that you drove my car, I let you have it for a joy ride, and you're gonna bring it back tomorrow mornin after camping."

"I can't do that, Barber."

Babe stood and peered down on Barber.

Barber looked up.

Babe saw no life in Barber's eyes.

"I can't help you anymore, Barber, and you know it. You've got to do the right thing and go to see Sheriff Dudley. Tell him the truth."

"The Sheriff is gonna try to pin everything on me, Babe. You know that. I did two years in county jail, it'll be Huntsville and the chair next."

"You gonna run, aren't chu?"

Barber fixed Babe with a menacing glare. "I ask you to help me, and you say no? You say no to your family? You really disappoint me, little brother. If you're not gonna help me, then I ain't got no choice."

Babe dropped to his knees. Tears welled in his eyes. "Oh, Lord. You killed her. That's why you got scratches on your face." His voice was soft, beseeching. "You killed Bobbette Moon, didn't you, Barber?"

From Dulfeine's, Porky could have gone up the back way to Clark Street. Instead, he chose to ride his bicycle straight down Main from the store and straight up the middle of Clark. People were lined up on both sides of the wide thoroughfare. He knew why everybody stared and pointed as they cruised up the street, but he enjoyed their bafflement.

Porky imagined the spectators' gossiping – it was an unusual sight for a colored boy to be eating an ice cream cone while sitting on the bicycle a white boy pedaled – *but we seen it, sure enough*, they would say.

Porky spied Grover and Woodrow and steered toward them. As he approached, Bessie, Rochelle, and Sally came into view. Adults stood on both sides of his friends but apart from them as if to separate themselves from the children.

Porky braked to a stop, put both feet down, and steadied the bicycle. He grinned at all five of them as they gaped at T J.

T J dismounted, licked the last tad of strawberry ice cream, and chomped the remaining morsel of vanilla cone. He eyed the white kids while he chewed.

Porky said nothing and pushed the bicycle through the gauntlet. He dropped the bike and stood by Sally.

"This is my friend. His name is T J," Porky said. "This here is my friend, her name is Sally."

T J's grin was as wide as the Grand Canyon. "Are you Porky's girlfriend?"

Everybody looked at Sally anticipating her affirmation.

"Hello, T J," Sally said. She looked at Porky. "We're just good friends, schoolmates."

Porky looked into Sally's soul. He did not move his eyes from hers. "And this is Bessie, Rochelle, Grover, and Woodrow."

"You're a neg . . ."

Porky glared at Bessie and cut off her reaction. "T J is my colored friend. We picked cotton together, bought ice cream cones, and ate candy bars."

"I ain't colored, Porky." T J met Bessie's stare. The grin remained plastered on his face. "I've told you before, my momma says I'm a black child."

"Where you from T J?" Woodrow asked.

T J's grin settled into a faint smile. As he spoke, T J met each one's gaze. "I'm from Tacoma."

"You said you lived in Minter," Porky challenged.

"I do. I live with my Granmomma."

"Miss Irene?"

"Yeah."

Grover wanted to know more.   "Where at's Tamoma?"

"Washington."

"Where the President lives?" Rochelle asked.

"No, no, it's a state. Like Texas is." T J pointed a slim finger in the vicinity of a direction toward the north-northwest. "The State of Washington."

"I know where that is," Rochelle said. "Did you go to school there?"

"I did. I finished eighth grade."

"But he don't go to school here," Porky said.

"My Momma teaches me. I've read a thousand books."

"Yeah, I'll bet that's a lie," Bessie said.

Grover persisted.   "What did your folks do in Tamoma?"

"It's Tacoma, Grover," Rochelle snapped. "Ta-com-ma. Tacoma, Washington. It's close to Seattle."

"My daddy worked at Todd Shipbuilders. He worked on ships, building ships for the war. He was a welder. My momma worked there too, as a cook."

"How come you're here when your momma and daddy are over there, in Ta-com-ma?" Grover asked.

"My daddy joined the Army and got killed. He was weldin on somethin and it blowed up. My momma jumped off the Tacoma Bridge." T J looked at Porky. "I come all the way here by myself on the train to live with my Granmomma in Minter and be with my Uncle Preacher Adams.   Uncle Preacher Adams is my Grandmomma's brother."

They grew solemn, pensive. T J and Porky turned and with the others faced empty Clark Street.

"My daddy might be killed, too," Porky said quietly.

Sally put her arm around Porky's shoulder and pulled

73

him close.

"Here they come," a voice said.

The children stepped up and leaned forward to be able to look around the line of adults blocking their view.

Porky had seen the effects in short films after Saturday matinees and it seemed to him now, as the Army jeep pulling a trailer approached, it was rolling down the street in slow motion.

He watched Sergeant Twig Chestnutt at first, then took in the three others – one German sat in the passenger seat, and two sat on the back seat.

The only Germans Portland Alvin Baycann, Junior had seen were in *Movietone News* newsreels narrated by Lowell Thomas at the *pitchursho*. Of course, there were town folk and school classmates whose grandparents or parents had come to America from Germany and were Germans, but Porky never thought about that depth of lineage or grasped the concept of ancestry.

Since attending the meeting in the school gym and hearing Mayor Casey Shipp's announcement, no topic held greater import than the arrival of the enemy.

Now, here they were, coming into Palomino aboard a United States Army jeep, chauffeured by an Army Sergeant.

Remarkably, the street was silent. There was no chatter, no conversations.

Then, "They killed my boy."

Porky turned toward the voice and saw it was Babe Beck's momma. Her gray hair was parted down the middle. It was straight and tight on the sides and gathered at the back. She wore rimless glasses. A faint line of mustache ran across the top of her colorless lip.

Her overworked hands clutched a checkered apron.

"These boys didn't kill our Buster, Mother," Mister Beck said. He hefted the shotgun in the bend of his arm. "He died in the Philippines."

"They don't look so tough." Grover's voice was subdued.

"You ain't so tough, yourself," Woodrow laughed.

Porky gawked, mouth ajar. The German prisoners of war sat erect and did not look at him as the Army jeep glided past. "They look just like Curtis Kline and Oscar Fant, and the high school football team," he heard his voice say.

"What?" Sally asked. "What'd you say?"

Porky faced her. "They look like us."

"They don't look like me," T J said.

Those words broke Porky's reverie.

He faced his friend. "I know. I didn't mean it that way, T J. The Germans don't look like devils. I didn't see no pointed tails or no horns stickin outta their heads."

T J shrugged. "I don't want to get close enough to find out. I need to be at the gin. My momma's gonna come for Uncle Preacher and me."

"You mean your Granmomma."

"She's my Granmomma, for sure, but now she's my momma."

Porky nodded. "Why don't you go camping with us tonight?"

"*Por-Ky* . . .?" Sally's caution was preempted.

Bessie and Rochelle interceded. "He caint do that, Porky."

"He caint do that," Woodrow said.

"Why not?"

"Cause. First, he ain't been invited by Mister Tanner

75

or Mister Douglass," Grover said. "And, second, you know . . . well, you know . . . he just caint be a Boy Scout."

Porky searched Woodrow and Grover's faces. He looked at T J. He looked back at Woodrow and Grover. "I didn't ask him if he wanted to be a Boy Scout. I asked if he wanted to go camping."

"It ain't your place to ask, Porky. It's a Scout camping, we asked you because Mister Tanner wanted us to."

Porky blinked.

"I'm different, Porky. In Tacoma it was better, not a whole lot better, but it wadn like it is here. Ride me down to the gin on your bicycle. I really don't feel like walkin down this street in front of all these people, these white folk who are mad at Germans and holdin guns."

"I'll talk to Mister Tanner, the Scoutmaster," Porky said.

"We better get goin. I gotta go home and get my stuff," Grover said. "I'll meet you at the Katy."

"*Bye yall*," Bessie and Rochelle sang. They weaved among adults and children who were walking away.

"Will you see me tomorrow, Porky?" Sally asked.

Porky grinned. "Yeah, I'd like that."

"You not even a Scout yourself, Porky," Woodrow said. "You gotta be a Scout fore you go askin favors."

8

They mounted the bicycle and Porky, standing on the pedals, propelled them down the center of Clark Street toward the gin. As they approached Ruby Bostick's Porter House, Porky braked and let the bicycle coast on a slow roll.

"Why you slowin down?" T J asked.

Porky steered the bicycle to the side of the street and stopped. He put both feet down and steadied the handlebars for balance. "Look there. That's where the Germans are gonna live."

T J put a foot down and slid off the saddle. He stood next to Porky.

The boys watched Sergeant Chestnutt and the three Germans standing in the yard, talking with Teresa, and Tina Chestnutt their young daughter, and Miss Ruby. Ethel and Julius Watson, Miss Ruby's housekeeper and chauffeur, stood on the porch.

"That's my Aunt Ethel and Uncle Julius," T J said.

Porky looked at his friend. "They your kin?"

"Naw, not really, but they come to visit a lot. Miss Ethel brings a pot of her leftover stew sometime. She makes some good stew, and I really like her cornbread."

"Have you ever been in Miss Ruby's house?"

"Not on your life. My Auntie says Miss Ruby would cut off my ears if I set foot in her house. Have you?"

"Naw. But I heard my momma and her friends talk about it though. It has three floors and nine bedrooms. I went on the front porch one time and sat in the swing when Miss Ruby was gone. I been on the back porch one time, too. There's a big barn in the back, you can see part of the tin top from here."

"That's a awful nice house. Them Germans are gonna live bettern we do."

Porky looked back at the house. "They gonna live bettern anybody in Palomino. Cept maybe the Major and Mister Albert."

The boys could not hear his words, but they realized Sergeant Chestnutt was giving orders with his pointing finger. They watched the prisoners move to the jeep's trailer, lift the tarpaulin, and pull out baggage and gear before replacing the cover. Then the Germans tagged along behind Miss Ruby up the steps and through the front door, trailed by the Chestnutt family, and Julius and Miss Ethel.

"The Army will pay a lot of money to Miss Ruby for them Germans to live in her house."

"Who told you that?"

"Mister Joiner, down at the Gulf station, and other people."

"They gonna eat bettern we do, too, cause Auntie said she'll have to buy a lot of good food from Mister Dulfeine's grocery for the Germans."

"What kind of food do they eat?"

T J shrugged. "I dunno. I guess they gonna eat

what we got since they here in Palomino and aint in Germany?"

"Beans and weenies?"

"I guess so."

"I ate hamburgers with Gene Autry."

Great doubt covered T J's face as he eyed Porky with serious suspicion.

"Aw, go on."

"I did. Cross my heart and hope to die. Right there in Jeeps. And a Co-Cola, too."

T J canted his head, impressed by Porky's oath of truthfulness. "The real Gene Autry? In the *pitchursho*?"

Porky nodded. He couldn't resist a triumphant grin.

"He's gonna fly airplanes, too."

"No lie?"

"He said we was friends and I could call him Gene."

"No lie?"

Porky's grin grew wider, larger, more animated, enjoying the attention of impressing his friend.

"No lie, T J. I sat on a stool right next to him."

"In the cafe?"

Porky nodded with great emphasis.

"And he asked me what song I wanted him to sing."

He waited for T J to ask the question.

"Wadchu tell im?"

"Whachu think?"

"*Back in the Saddle Again*?"

"That's what I asked, and that's what he sung. And he did another one too."

T J grinned too. "No lie, Eli?"

"Yep. *Deep in the Heart of Texas*."

They laughed and punched each other on the arm.

"You friends with Gene Autry? Did you get his autograph? Did you get a picture?"

79

Those oversights came back to haunt him and took the wind out of Porky's sail. "Naw, I forgot."

"Then you ain't got no proof."

"Yeah, I do. A lot of people was there. Miss Bobbie Jo, Miss Teresa, and Mister Tanner, the Scoutmaster. They saw it. They know about it. They sung with him too."

"But you didn't get no picture. You shoulda got your picture with him. If you got a picture, everbody would believe you was with Gene Autry."

The omission was defeating. Porky shrugged, surrendering. "I know. Okay, get on, we better go on to the gin."

"Well, I believe you anyway." T J held onto Porky's arm and mounted the bicycle. He pointed over Porky's shoulder. "Look up there, on the water tower."

Porky shoved off and gained speed. Both glanced at the house as they cruised past.

T J began. "I'm back in the saddle . . ."

Porky joined in.

Their harmony, loudly singing Gene's song, rolling down the middle of the street, attracted the attention of neighbors standing in their yard. Pedestrians walking home shook their heads and pointed at the duo. Thinking they had seen everything by watching an Army sergeant drive Germans into peaceful Palomino, residents now were amazed and amused at a white child pedaling a black child on a bicycle while murdering Gene Autry's signature song at the top of their voices.

A quarter mile farther down, Porky turned off Clark Street. With their weight and the incline, he strained to pump the bicycle up the winding, rising path leading to the gin. Noisy, roaring machinery grew louder. Rumbling and thrashing of clashing iron and steel shook the ground.

Men and boys scurried about, busy with the day's pickings. Idle wagons and trailers brimming with freshly harvested cotton stretched all the way down the driveway to the street. Teams of contented horses hitched to wagons rested on three legs while munching chopped vegetables and oats from muzzle feedbags. Drivers sat atop their tractors and smoked cigarettes or pipes, or spat tobacco juice over a rear steel wheel while waiting their turn to inch forward to the gin's vacuum pipe.

Porky stopped close to the office door, and T J got off.

The boys scanned their surroundings.

"I don't see my uncle nowhere."

Sensing uneasiness in T J's voice, Porky laid his bicycle down. "Okay, I'll stay with you. Come on, let's go look for him."

They trekked past the wagons and animals quickly but did not see Mister Church on his tractor or T J's uncle in the trailer filled with cotton.

"Maybe they're in the gin," T J suggested. He headed for the opened double doors. Porky followed.

Slices of sunlight slipped between spaces of the dried, worn boards of the west wall. A darkened wedge, sandwiched among slivers of yellow, cloaked them inside the tin-roofed structure. They paused, letting their eyes adjust. Porky stepped ahead of T J.

"Comere, Boy." The booming voice startled both youngsters.

T J's struggling gagging gurgling jolted Porky who jerked around.

In the dimness, Porky could see a big man holding T J by a shoulder with one hand, the fingers of the other

81

hand around T J's neck.

"What are you doin in my gin, Boy?"

T J thrashed and twisted and kicked in the tight grip.

Porky charged and flayed the arm and hand holding T J by the throat.

"Let him go," Porky shouted. "Let him go." His small fists landed on muscle and bone. He aimed higher, jabbing and punching a shoulder and back. He kicked twice, three times at a leg.

Released from the choking grip, T J fell forward and dropped to his knees. He coughed and gasped for air.

A big palm slammed onto Porky's forehead. Large fingers and a thumb squeezed his head and pressed his temples, but Porky kept fighting and yelling.

Behind the boys, an approaching man's voice demanded an explanation. "What's goin on here? Why these boys yellin so? Let that boy go, Eliot."

Porky stumbled back when the painful grip released him.

The two retreated and backed away when the huge man moved toward them from out of the darkened recess.

"Them boys was in here to steal, and I caught em," Eliot Thurgood bellowed.

"That's a lie," Porky shouted. He moved to T J and reached down, grasping an arm and bony shoulder.

T J rose and faltered, leaning against his friend.

Porky's anger was boiling. "We aint in here to steal nothin of yours, we was lookin for his uncle."

"Boys sneakin in here all the time, stealin all the time. Colored boys, mostly."

Porky found his normal voice. He pulled on T J's arm and stepped in front of him, standing between his friend and Thurgood. "You aint got nothin we want,

Mister Thurgood. We was lookin for Mister Church and Preacher Adams. You hurt my friend. He didn't do nothin to you."

Thurgood ignored the accusation. "Well, Church and Adams ain't in my gin." He pointed toward the door. "They probably over yonder, at Monroe's gin. Now git."

Porky nodded and stepped back, his anger still alive. "We be goin now. If I was big enough I'd fight you."

Thurgood laughed. "Aint *nobody* in this town big enough to fight me, Boy. Now, yall git. And don't come back in here, you hear? Boys always stealin stuff outta my gin."

The man who intervened led the boys out of the gin. In the sunlight, he looked closely for any injuries.

"Thank you, Mister Bennett. I thought he was gonna kill T J."

Bennett nodded. "Portland, you know better than being around Eliot. That boy's got bats in his belfry."

Porky and T J frowned.

Bennett smiled and patted T J's shoulder. "You're going to be alright, Son." He then fixed Porky with a grimace and shook his head. "He's crazy, Son. Now, you boys be on your way over to the Major's gin. And stay away from Eliot, you hear?"

Porky picked up his bike and wheeled it around. He put his leg over the frame and held it steady for T J to mount. "Thank you, Mister Bennett. Thank you for helping us."

T J put his hands on Porky's shoulders. "Ready."

Porky pushed forward and they were on their way — he steered down the winding path, dodged potholes as they crossed Dawson Road, and pumped the pedals to gain momentum up the sidewalk leading to the office door of Monroe's Lint and Seed Company. Even before they got off the bicycle, Preacher Adams called to them.

"Where yall been?"

Porky pointed. "Over there, I got mixed up."

"We found a bad man, Uncle Jim."

Preacher canted his head and peered at Porky.

Porky nodded. "Mister Thurgood."

"Goodness sakes. Whachall doin with Mister Eliot?"

"He said we was there to steal his stuff," Porky said. "He grabbed T J."

Preacher reached out for his nephew. "Did he hurtchu, Boy?"

T J moved in close and put his arms around his uncle in an embrace. "He grabbed me by the neck, but I'm alright. Porky beat him off me. Porky's a fighter."

Preacher released T J and shoved his hand out. "Thank you, Master Porky."

Porky grasped the calloused palm and felt strong, long fingers engulf and grip his hand. "Aint nobody gonna grab my friend again, like he did. But Mister Bennett helped us, too."

Martin Church came up. "Is everthing alright?"

"It is now, Mister Church," Preacher said. "Everthing be alright."

Porky looked at the men, from one face to the other. "If I was big enough, I'd fight him. Maybe a big stick can do the trick. T J and me gotta teach Mister Thurgood how to leave boys alone. Teach him how to be kind to others."

T J stepped back from his uncle and nodded agreement at Porky. "We can do it too."

Preacher shook his head and turned T J to face him. "Now you boys stay away from Eliot Thurgood. He aint right."

"He got bats in his bref-free," Porky said.

Martin chuckled at Porky's mispronunciation. "That's for sure."

Porky looked at T J and smiled. "Well, I got to go home and get my stuff for the camping. I'm supposed to meet Grover and Woodrow at the Katy station."

T J stuck his hands in his overall pockets and shrugged. "Well, thank you for the ridin and singin."

"I'll see you in the field in the mornin."

"I'll be there. We only work half a day on Saturday."

"I'm gonna ask Sally to go to the *pitchursho* tomorrow night. I'll probably ask her to be my girlfriend."

T J nodded and smiled. "I like Sally. I think she'll make you a good girlfriend."

"Will you be there?"

"I might be, I'll have to ask my momma. She'll have to come with me cause I caint be by myself in town at night."

Porky nodded understanding. "I know." After a brief pause. "Well, I gotta go. Bye."

Preacher Adams and Martin Church bade Porky farewell.

"Bye." T J grinned. "Thank you for bein my friend, Porky . . . Portland."

"You are my friend, Butter Cup . . . Thomas."

Porky dropped his bicycle in the front yard and bounded up the steps. He rushed past his mother.

"I have to go to the bathroom, Momma."

"I'll be in the kitchen."

Porky peed for twenty-seven seconds.

In the kitchen, he took a glass from a cabinet, filled it half full of water, and gulped it down.

"I gotta go, Momma."

"Who's going to be there?" Agnes asked.

"Woodrow and Grover, for sure. Mister Tanner and Mister Douglass, I guess. Maybe Tub, maybe Babe. Those are the only ones I can think of. Oh, and maybe Pinky, Waldo, and Hale."

"Well, you be careful." Agnes clasped her son's shoulders and pulled him close. She kissed his forehead. "If you think you might like to become a Boy Scout after tonight's camping, we'll talk about it, okay?"

"Okay, Momma." Porky looked at his mother. "Was Daddy a Boy Scout?"

"Yes. Yes, he was for a while. He had to quit because your Grandpa Ike needed him to work after the Depression. I'm surprised he never told you. I think he might like for you to be one, too."

"I asked T J if he wanted to come tonight. But Woodrow said I had no right to ask him because I'm not a Boy Scout."

"Well, Woodrow is right about that. Who's T J?"

"He's my new friend. He's Preacher Adams' nephew, Miss Irene's son, ah, granson, I guess."

Agnes nodded. "Oh, Thomas. I've seen the boy in town. He comes in with Preacher or with Miss Irene sometimes. He came to the hospital for a vaccination. Miss Irene's his Granmomma, not his Momma."

"That's what he said, later, when we was talkin. When we was waitin for Sergeant Chestnutt and the Germans, he said his daddy was killed, and his momma jumped off a bridge, but his Granmomma was now his Momma."

"He can't be a Boy Scout, Porky."

Porky shrugged. "I know, Momma. I know why. He does too. I'm gonna ask Mister Tanner if T J can be our mascot."

"Goodness gracious, Porky. NO."

The sharpness in his mother's tone surprised Porky. He could count on one hand the number of times he had heard his mother raise her voice.

"That boy is not a mascot and don't you ever think of him that way."

Porky hesitated. "Okay, Momma." He judged it was safe to continue. "I just wanted T J to be part of it if I am."

Agnes smiled. "Well, maybe you can ask Mister Tanner if T J can be an honorary member."

"What's a honorary . . . ?"

"It means Mister Tanner *might* let T J come to meetings or go camping, but that's all. Other families might not want T J to even do that with the other boys."

Even though Porky felt the need to get to the Katy station, he paused, thought on it, and decided to tell his mother about the run-in with Eliot Thurgood.

"After we watched the Germans I took T J to the wrong gin."

"Why?"

"His momma was gonna come get him and his uncle, Preacher Adams."

"No, I mean why did you take him to the wrong gin? Which gin did you go to?"

"Mister Thurgood's. And he grabbed T J by the throat."

"Oh, my."

"But I beat him off. And Mister Bennett helped."

"Oh, my."

"Mister Thurgood said we was there to steal his stuff. He was pretty mad, he hurt T J."

"Why in the world did you go into Eliot's gin, for goodness sake?"

"I got mixed up cause we was singing. I meant to go to Major Monroe's gin."

"You stay away from Eliot Thurgood, you hear?"

"He's got bats in his bref-free."

His mother grasped her stomach and laughed. "Where in the world did you hear that?"

"Mister Bennett. We didn't know what it meant when he said it."

"What did he tell you?"

"That Eliot Thurgood is crazy."

Porky's mother nodded. "You stay away from Eliot Thurgood, Son."

He knew that would not be possible, but knew it was not the time to reveal he and T J might teach Eliot Thurgood a lesson. "I will, Momma."

Porky collected the bag his mother had prepared. "I better go now. I know Grover and Woodrow are waiting for me at the Katy station."

Agnes put her arms around Porky and hugged him. "I want you to be careful. I put a blanket and thermos of water in the bag. I wrapped some cheese and crackers in wax paper for your bedtime snack."

Porky beamed at his mother and put his free arm around her. "I love you, Momma."

She matched Porky's smile and kissed his forehead. "I also put your daddy's flashlight in the bag with the other things."

9

They were waiting when he pedaled up. Their impatience evident to Porky from the way Grover and Woodrow jumped off the station platform. Both were confrontational, aggressive.

"Where you been?" Woodrow challenged.

"We been waitin on you for over an hour," Grover scolded. "We gonna be late now."

Porky felt humbled, his friends' edginess chastising. He tried to remember if either of them had told him there was a schedule, a timetable he needed to adhere to. In any case, it didn't matter, he didn't have a watch. He offered a weak shrug. "I had things to do. I took T J to the gin, had a fight with Eliot Thurgood, and went home for my stuff. Momma had things to tell me."

They knew if a momma had something to tell her boy, the boy was gonna stay in place and listen. But that was of lesser importance than fighting.

"What did Eliot Thurgood do to you?"

"He didn't do nothing to me, well he gripped my head and squeezed it. But he grabbed and choked T J."

89

They waited.

"How did you fight im?" Woodrow asked.

"With my fists. I hit him on his arm and back and kicked his leg. I beat him up pretty bad."

"He's crazy," Grover said.

"Mister Bennett said he had bats in his bref-free."

Grover nodded. "Sure enough."

"What does that mean?" Woodrow asked.

"It means he's crazy," Grover shot back.

"You said that already," Woodrow retorted. "What does bats and bref-free mean, Porky?"

"It means he's crazy, Woodrow." Grover's exasperation was pronounced. "I read about it someplace in a book."

They looked at Porky. "That man's crazy."

"You lucky he didn't kill you," Grover said. "They say he shot his daddy with a rat gun. Right there in the gin."

Porky blinked, the thought was chilling.

"Okay, put your bike over there with ours," Woodrow said. "We'll walk to Mister Tanner's place."

"Why can't we just ride our bicycles?"

"Cause, Porky, there ain't no direct road from here. If we rode our bicycles, we'd have to go all the way round the other way, the back way, the road to the pond. We can walk straight through the woods. Okay, come on, let's go," Grover said.

They walked abreast, a tree or a clump of bushes occasionally separating them. "There's three of us, we're just like the Musketeers in the *pitchursho*," Grover said.

Woodrow laughed. "Pinky told me Tina called them the 'Mustard Tears'."

Grover snorted. "Three mustard tears?"

"Pinky and Patsy and Tina?" Porky asked.

"Yeah." Woodrow continued. "Pinky said Patsy was with him on his paper route and Tina met them in the street. Tina wanted to be Pinky's girlfriend, but Pinky said Patsy was his girlfriend. Patsy told Tina she needed help with Pinky. Then Pinky said Patsy was his senior girlfriend and Tina could be his junior girlfriend."

"That don't make no sense," Grover said.

"Well, it did to Tina," Woodrow said. "Pinky said he never saw her grin as big as she did cause she always wanted to hide her missing front teeth."

They kept walking at a steady pace, ducking under low hanging tree limbs, skirting bramble, thickets, and undergrowth.

Grover made an assessment he thought completely logical. "That don't make no sense, neither. You caint hide somethin that's missin. How could she hide missing front teeth?"

Porky and Woodrow looked at each other and grinned. "By keepin your mouth shut, Grover," they said.

As the trio approached the clearing where the house sat, they saw two wagons, three cars, and a gaggle of kids facing Mister Tanner and Mister Douglass who stood on the porch.

"Here they come," Mister Douglass said, pointing.

"We were wondering where you were," Mister Tanner said.

"We had to wait for Porky," Woodrow explained.

"Well, welcome, Portland," Mister Tanner said. "I'm glad you decided to come see for yourself what scouting is all about."

"Woodrow and Grover wanted me to come," Porky submitted. "They told me you said it was okay, Mister

Tanner."

"You are welcome. Everyone's here except Walter. Walter had his tonsils removed and he's still in the hospital."

Andrew, Waldo, Grady, J W, Pinky, Tub, Babe, Hale, Emmett, and Leroy looked at Grover, Woodrow, and Porky and greeted then with a smile or nod. It was not their time to speak when the Scoutmaster was presiding.

Mister Tanner recounted plans for the evening. "Now, boys, we'll say our Pledge of Allegiance, our Scout Oath, and review our Scout Laws. Then we'll build a fire, burn hot dogs and marshmallows. Mister Douglass and me brought a tub of ice with Co-Colas. After we eat supper, we'll have a couple of games and a story activity. Then we'll bed down for the night."

Porky listened while surveying the surroundings. He spied a wooden, carved plaque on the right side of the front door proclaiming Troop 2255. On Mister Tanner's right, an American Flag hung from a staff attached to a porch column. A Scout Ensign hung from another staff attached to a column on Mister Douglass' left. On the right side of the house were two Fords, on the left side was a four-door Willys. He knew the two on the right belonged to Mister Tanner and Mister Douglass. Porky looked at the back of Babe's neck, wondering why Barber's car was parked beside Mister Tanner's house.

"Porky? *Porky*?"

Mister Tanner's voice penetrated the trance. Porky shook his head to clear it. "Yes, Sir?"

"I was just saying there's a water faucet on that side of the house, the bathroom is on left from the kitchen, so you know where they are," Mister Tanner said. "Pinky, will you lead us in the Pledge?"

Tanner and Douglass faced the flag and placed their right arm across their chests with their hands over their hearts. The Boy Scouts stood at attention and took up the position. Porky followed their lead.

Pinky and the Scout leaders began. Porky's mumbled murmur was subordinate to the Scouts' strong voices.

"*I pledge allegiance to the flag of the United States of America, and to the Republic for which it stands, one Nation indivisible, with liberty and justice for all.*"

Tanner and Douglass faced the boys.

"Babe, will you lead us in the Scout Oath?"

Tanner and Douglass faced the Ensign. They raised their right hands, forming the salute with their thumb and first three fingers.

Unsure what to do, Porky started to raise his hand before deciding to keep still. He watched the Scouts' performance.

Babe's voice was firm, steady, leading the others. "*On my honor, I will do my best, to do my duty to God and my country and to obey the Scout Law. To help other people at all times. To keep myself physically strong, mentally awake, and morally straight.*"

"*Be prepared,*" Mister Tanner concluded.

"*Be prepared,*" Mister Douglass and the Scouts responded.

"Okay, J W, you and Tub are working for your Merit Badges. So, collect some wood for the fire," Mister Tanner directed, "and remember, everbody, our outdoor code. What is it?"

"*Be clean in my outdoor manners,*" four voices said.

"*Be considerate in the outdoors,*" three boys said.

"And, *be conservation-minded,*" Mister Douglass added.

"And, *be careful with fire*, Mister Tanner," Grady said.

"That's a good boy," Mister Tanner said.

Porky realized he stood in the middle of swift-moving traffic and became uneasy about it. Activity was brisk. Everyone seemed to have a responsibility or helped another with a job they were doing. He decided to get out of the way, sat on the porch steps, and followed, as if observing fast-paced worker ants, his friends dashing around taking care of their tasks.

Firelight flared as twilight faded. Porky came off the steps and joined the others gathered in a circle in the glow J W and Tub created.

Mister Tanner congratulated them. "That's a great fire, boys. Perfectly built with safety in mind. You've earned your Merit Badge."

Leroy and Pinky handed out their whittled spikes. Emmett and Babe passed around the wieners. Waldo and Hale handled the buns. Andrew and Carl spooned a dab of mustard on the buns. Woodrow and Grover opened the bottles and passed around the cold drinks.

Porky gulped two hot dogs, swallowed four marshmallows, and was on his second Coca-Cola when Mister Tanner asked for the Scout Laws.

"We'll go around the circle and recite one Scout Law," Mister Tanner directed. "Pinky, you start, please."

"*Trustworthy,*" Pinky said.

"*Loyal,*" J W said.

"*Helpful,*" Hale answered. "I'm helpful."

"*Friendly,*" Andrew said.

"*Kind,*" Pinky said.

"You already said one, Pinky," Leroy admonished. "*Be courteous.*"

94

Everyone laughed, including Pinky and Porky.

"*Cheerful*," Woodrow said.

"*Obedient*," Tub said.

"*Thrifty*," Waldo said.

"You're more than thrifty, Waldo," J W said, "you're cheap."

"Now, boys," Mister Tanner chided. "What law comes in play that way, Grady?"

"Kind, Sir. Be kind, Mister Tanner."

"Good," the Scoutmaster nodded. "Now, there's three more."

"*Brave*," Babe said.

Porky watched the reflection of flames lick Babe's glassy eyes.

"A Scout must be brave," Babe said, "even if he is afraid. He must have courage to stand for what he thinks is the right thing . . ."

Crackling, popping wood filled the silence.

Porky saw that everyone was looking at Babe.

"*Clean*," Emmett said. "A Scout must be clean."

"Very good, Emmett," Mister Douglass said.

"*Reverent*," Grover said.

Porky searched faces, pausing, judging, wondering, moving from one friend's feature to another, unaware nighttime had cloaked the Troop. He had no idea they had sat around the campfire for two hours in the dark woods south of Palomino.

The Scoutmaster rose and walked to house. On the porch, he went from one Kerosene lamp to the other, raised the chimney's, touched a match to the wicks, and adjusted the flames. He went in the house and lighted two lamps there before coming back to the group.

"Okay, we've got time for one game and one story before we turn in. Mister Douglass selected the message game. Let's see they're twelve, no, thirteen, with Porky. So, here are the positions. One Scout at each corner of the house, one scout at each wagon wheel. So, let's see, that's . . ."

"That's twelve, Mister Tanner," Leroy said.

"Okay, then, Porky, you're number thirteen, you'll be the King. You sit on the porch steps. Criers pass the message through your Kingdom in relays. The objective of the game is clear communication. We do this to see if the message given to the first crier is the same message received by the King. Everbody understand?"

No one spoke.

"Okay, we'll start with you, Hale, count off."

"One," Hale said.

"Two," Emmett said.

"Three," Babe said.

The rest of the boys caught a number, and all took up positions assigned by Mister Tanner.

Once all the boys were in position, Mister Douglass came up to Hale. "Here is the ten-word message for the King, Hale. *Three mad miggies come round blow your castle's crown down.*"

Hale moved to the corner of the house and whispered the message to Emmett.

Douglass mounted the steps and spoke quietly to Tanner, but Porky thought he heard three of his words . . . *Barber . . . driedblood . . . Casey.*

Douglass jumped from the other end of the porch.

Mister Tanner sat beside Porky.

"What do you think about scouting, Portland? Do you have any questions? Think you'd like to join us?"

"Why is the salute with three fingers and not like the Army?"

"That's a good question, Son." Tanner formed the

scout salute, extending his index, middle, and ring fingers while clasping his little finger with his thumb. "These three fingers represent the Scout Promise – *Honor God and Country*, *Help Others*, and *Obey the Scout Law.*"

"I want to be a Boy Scout. Momma said my daddy was a Boy Scout but had to quit to work."

Tanner let the pause last five seconds before he spoke. "I heard about your daddy, Portland. But I think he's going to be alright, I think he'll come home to you. Before you know it, your momma will get a letter telling her the Army found him."

Porky wiped his eyes and under his nose. "I watched the Germans come to town. Woodrow and Grover asked me if I hated the Germans, hated them because my daddy is missing."

"Do you?"

"I dunno." Porky shrugged. "They didn't hurt my daddy." He looked at the Scoutmaster. "They looked like the football team, they looked like us."

"Those boys were in Africa, not where your daddy is, in Sicily, so they couldn't have hurt your daddy."

Douglass approached with Leroy in tow. The other boys closed in. Douglass and Leroy stood at the bottom step. "Here is the message for the King," Douglass said.

"*Three glad little piggies are gonna blow your castle down*," Leroy said.

Groans and moans swelled from the messengers.

Tanner and Douglass laughed. "What was the message, Hale?"

"*Three mad miggies come round blow your castle's crown down.*"

Jostling and arm punching ensued. Caught up in

the fun, Porky grinned and laughed with the Scouts. Porky's thoughts of his daddy being a Scout warmed his heart.   Porky wanted to be part of this group, by becoming a Boy Scout he knew he would make his daddy proud.

"What did we learn from that game?" the Scoutmaster asked.

"Be trustworthy," a voice said.

"Be helpful," another said.

"Tell the truth," someone said.

"Tell the whole truth," a voice said.

"*And nothing but the truth,*" all of the boys squeaked.

"Good. That's very good." Tanner stood. "Now, remember your number. Mister Douglass will assign where you will sleep by your number. Some will sleep in the house, some on the porch, and others in the wagons. Before Mister Douglass tells you a good story, we'll take a bathroom break. After that, gather round the fire. Who needs to go to the bathroom?"

Mister Tanner, Mister Douglass, and all the boys raised their hands. They all roared with laughter.

"Okay, Hale, you're number one, you go first. We'll go to the bathroom in number order. Emmett, you go after Hale. Now, I have to go into town. Mister Douglass will stay with you through the night."

10

Like sparrows on a telephone line, the teenagers perched on the wooden plank bench. They sat shoulder to shoulder with their feet flat on the grassy turf of Pecan Park.

Bessie and Rochelle's skirts were up over their knees. They were leaning forward, forearms atop their skinny legs.

With her crossed legs covered by overalls, Sally sat more erect.

The three of them faced the street, smoking pilfered Old Gold cigarettes.

"I like Pall Malls better," Bessie said. "They last longer." She flicked ashes out toward the ground.

"Chesterfields are milder and taste better," Rochelle said. "A B Cs."

"That's what the radio announcer says all the time, A B Cs," Sally said. "Always buy Chesterfield. They make me cough less than Camels or Lucky Strikes."

Bessie mockingly sang the familiar refrain from a placard advertising a cigarette brand. "*L S . . . M F T.*"

Rochelle cheerfully emphasized the words for the

letters. "*Lucky Strikes Means Fine Tobacco.*"

Neither of them spoke for several seconds. The orange glow of burning tobacco brightened with each inhaling gulp of strong, unfiltered nicotine.

Rochelle sniffed. "Anyway, Old Gold is what my mother had in her purse." Through her nose and mouth, she released two long strings of smoke into the August night's slight breeze. The wispy cloud of gray aroma sailed away from them toward the subdued lights of town. "So that's what we got. I don't think she'll miss these three."

"I wonder what was new that was added?"

"To what?"

"The cigarettes. Old Gold says 'something new has been added'."

They thought on it for a minute and found no answer. To these young girls, experimenting with adult ways was all that was significant. If facts were important in advertising, a test would have revealed that tobacco was tobacco, notwithstanding the company's claim of something new in Old Gold cigarettes.

"I like coming to the park and smoking," Bessie said.

"It'd be better if we had beer," Rochelle said,

"There's no light in the park, nobody ever comes up in the dark. That's why it's so peaceful."

"It's almost like a cemetery."

Bessie snickered. "Yeah. In both places, we can relax and talk."

"About school?"

"No, Sally, about *boys*," Rochelle said.

They giggled.

Bessie took a long drag and slowly exhaled the smoke, attempting to blow smoke circles with the last bit of her puffing breath. "When do you think Porky will ask you to be his girlfriend?"

"Probably tomorrow night. We're going to the *pitchursho.*"

"*Casablanca,*" Bessie said. "Humphrey Bogart and Ingrid Bergman. It's about Germans . . . Nazis."

"Has he kissed you yet?" Rochelle asked.

"Um . . . we've kissed."

"Did you like it?" Bessie asked.

"Uh huh. It was nice," Sally said.

"Did he try to French kiss you?" Rochelle asked.

"Ugh." Bessie shuddered. "A boy sticking his tongue down your throat? Ugh."

"That's not how it's done," Rochelle said. "His tongue is in your mouth, not down your throat. A girl don't want a tongue down her throat. His tongue touches *your* tongue, like this."

In the darkness, neither Sally nor Bessie could see how Rochelle darted her tongue out and slipped it back between her lips three times. "It don't go down your throat, Bessie. Who'd want a boy's tongue down their throat?"

"So, who did you do it with?" Bessie wanted to know.

"Tub and me tried it," Rochelle confessed. "It felt nice. It was soft and warm. It made me tingle when he did it. I liked it. And he liked it when I did it to him."

"He said that?" Sally asked.

"Uh huh. We did it three or four times."

"Where?"

"Here, in the park. Laying on the tabletop."

"No, I mean where did you tingle?"

"I dunno, just all over. My skin felt alive, hot, and

my heart beat fast. It was hard to breathe. I mean, I even felt pressure in my ears and nose. I felt like . . . well, I just felt good, happy. I didn't want to stop. I kinda wanted to go all the way."

The girls fell silent. In darkness, they were consumed in their own thoughts of exploration, kissing, imagining, fantasizing.

"They're over at Mister Tanner's place, camping," Bessie remarked.

"It's a Scout camping. They spend the night."

"We should go over to Mister Tanner's place and swim in his pond while it's still . . . while it's still summer," Bessie suggested.

Sally giggled. "Somebody might see us."

"I've seen the boys swimmin in the pond. They was all naked."

They thought about those images for a few seconds.

"I didn't think anybody ever went there, except the Boy Scouts once a month when they go camping," Rochelle surmised.

"Porky's there, with them . . . he went with Grover and Woodrow. I think he wants to be a Scout with them."

"Maybe we ought to be Scouts."

"We could have our own group, just like the boys."

"It's called a Troop, not a group. A Scout Troop."

"The three of us could be the first three in the *Troop*. We'd be the senior Scouts."

"I think Peggy and Lucile would join. And, Janice."

"Ruth and Liz."

"And Lena."

"And Lana."

Rochelle groaned. That sound made it clear enough that Lana's nomination lacked support.

"No, no, not Lana."

"Yeah, not Lana."

"She's such a snob, always bragging about going to Dallas and buying clothes and stuff at Neiman-Marcus."

"Well, her momma and daddy's got the money. They're probably as rich as Major Monroe. Maybe richer."

"They got two Cadillacs."

"I bet they have people who steal gas coupons for them. My momma says those big cars must drink gasoline like a baby drains a bottle of warm milk."

"Lana is such a big put-on. She wants everbody to know about her being on the mailing list for the store's Christmas catalog."

"I saw their catalog from last year. There was some really fancy stuff in there. And expensive, too. Some clothes cost more than fifty dollars."

"I've never been in Neiman-Marcus. I've never even been to Dallas," Sally said.

"I've been to Dallas, a year ago. Last summer, we went to a funeral in Irving," Rochelle said.

"I remember you telling us about your poor aunt."

"Yeah, my Aunt Ina, one of my mother's sisters. A cotton trailer at the gin mashed her flat, the two horses pulling the trailer got scared and ran. After Aunt Ina's funeral, we even went into the store."

"You went into Neiman-Marcus?"

"Uh huh."

"You never told that."

"Well, we did."

"What did you buy?"

"Nothing. Momma couldn't afford to buy anything in there, even the ordinary stuff. We just went in to look. We were in there for two hours, just walking around admiring everything. I touched all the fancy dresses and underwear and coats and hats and purses and shoes and stuff."

"I've seen pictures of their stuff," Sally said.

"I smelled all the expensive perfumes. A nice lady sprayed some on my wrist.

"They even had cowboy boots that cost two hundred dollars. I put a pretty, red silk scarf around my neck before a woman poked me on my arm and told me to take it off. 'Don't touch anything unless you're going to buy it', she said. She folded it up neat and put it back with the others."

They fell silent once more, daydreaming about fashionable clothes, fine scents, and unaffordable accessories.

"Why don't we go to Dallas to the fair."

"They don't have the fair no more."

"Oh, that's right. I forgot. The war."

"Before the war, they took kids on school buses . . . two school buses . . . to the fair. The buses left early Saturday morning before the sun was up. They spent the day at the fair and stayed overnight at a college dormitory someplace. They ate Sunday breakfast at the college and got home before dark."

"Somebody said the school might let buses go to the Daingerfield State Park."

"That would be fun."

"We could go together."

"The boys would go, too."

"Yes. Yes, we could be with our boyfriends at the fair, I mean, the park."

They thought about the possibilities.

"Scouts got in free at the fair."

"Would your mother be our Scout Leader, Sally?"

"I dunno. I can ask."

Headlights of a car turning toward them off Highway 271 brought the girls upright. Rochelle and Bessie lowered their skirts, and Sally uncrossed her legs. Instead of flipping away their cigarettes, they lowered their hands in front of their shins, so the smoking stem was not obvious. In unison, they turned to peer into the approaching light and followed the car as it sped down Clark Street toward town.

Douglass sat on a chair brought from the porch. The Scouts formed a circle round the dying embers, an amber glow and dark shadows highlighted anticipation on their curious faces.

"Has everyone heard about Mad Dog Callahan and Snapper, his fierce hound with fang-like teeth that always are showing?"

They nodded.

"Mister Bastion Albert hired Mad Dog and Snapper to find the boys who took watermelons from the patch north of town."

Douglass paused. His mention of *the boys* was intentional, although Douglass and Bastion knew *boys* lifted a watermelon or three from the patch every season. These boys, every one of these Boy Scouts, and Porky, had pinched a watermelon now and then.

"Well, my story is about what happened last year when Mad Dog and Snapper were put on the trail of two boys from Bogata."

Safe, so far, the boys around the campfire wiggled and squirmed to relieve pressure on boney butts sitting on hard dirt. They strained to not look at each other, knowing, or at least suspecting, Mister Douglass would realize glances would pinpoint the watermelon thieves in their cluster.

All eyes, with great struggle, remained fixed on their assistant Scoutmaster.

"Mad Dog and Snapper set up one night in the middle of the patch. Snapper was a well-trained attack dog. When the watermelon thieves came rolling up on their bicycles, Snapper knew not to bark. Instead, he raised up and sat on his haunches, alerting Mad Dog that their prey was present.

"Mad Dog reached out and patted Snapper's head and whispered, 'Good Boy'.

"Snapper looked at Mad Dog and licked his chops with his long pink tongue. Snapper knew he was about to enjoy a nip or two of a tender leg."

Some Scouts moved their legs, others rubbed where they imagined Snapper's bite might clamp on.

"Now, Mister Albert did not want these boys to be harmed. He preferred they be captured and stand trial for theft of property. He also expected the boys to be forced to pay a dollar for each melon and spend time in *The Calaboose*."

"A watermelon don't cost no dollar," a voice said.

Douglass smiled aware he had their attention. "Well, that's right. If you *buy* a watermelon at Mister Dulfeine's grocery store, you'll pay fifteen or twenty cents for it. But buying and stealing are different, aren't they?"

Every head nodded. Only then were surreptitious telltale glances at known watermelon thieves attempted. Culprits' heads were lowered hoping no finger pointing or name-calling would erupt. Accomplices knew if they identified ringleaders, they were just as likely to spend time in *The Calaboose*.

Douglass saw the quick peeks and understood he

faced a Troop of watermelon bandits. He could not stop a grin growing on his face.

"In the bright moonlight, Mad Dog and Snapper could see the thieves had found melons they wanted. Mad Dog and Snapper could hear them talking about whether to take the larger or smaller one.

"He waited until they decided on the smaller one and cut it open before he stood and announced he was there to bring them to justice."

Loud gulps of oxygen filled the tense night air.

"The boys started to run, but they were no match for the fast Snapper. The big dog dashed after them and brought the slowest boy to ground. The screams could be heard all the way to Dallas, but Mad Dog was too late. Snapper had the boy by the leg and was just gnawing away."

Douglass paused.

"What happened?" a weak voice asked.

"Well, Doctor Burns mended the leg, and the boy recovered. But he no longer could walk straight. His new nickname is Gimpy."

"What about the one who got away?"

"He did the right thing."

They waited. What was the right thing?

Douglass did not elaborate.

"Okay, it's time to turn in."

He made assignments of sleeping areas by numbers.

Porky, Woodrow, Grover, and Pinky were directed to sleep in the first wagon.

Andrew, Waldo, Grady, and J W – the other wagon.

Tub and Leroy had the porch all to themselves.

"Hale, Emmett, and Babe will sleep in the house with me," Mister Douglass said.

11

They used the large, sturdy rear wheel spokes as a ladder and climbed aboard the aged, dilapidated wagon. With its bed only three feet wide and ten feet deep, the boys staked out their sleeping spaces parallel to the sideboards and began to settle down in the four corners. Woodrow dropped his bag at the left rear; Pinky chose the right rear. Porky picked the right front side, up under the bench, and Grover took the left spot.

Porky pulled out the blanket and his daddy's bullet-style Ray-O-Vac, but did not turn on the flashlight. He shoved his hand back into the bag and brought out the snack and thermos. Before speaking, he gulped four swallows of cool water. His voice was low, slightly above a whisper. "Anybody want some cheese and crackers?"

Even though their stomachs were full of Coca-Cola, weenies, and buns, Woodrow and Pinky crawled on hands and knees and, with Grover sliding over, sidled up to Porky. They sat facing each other, knees almost touching. Dim light from the dying campfire aided in the handing out of the nibbles.

"I think Babe is sick," Pinky whispered.

"Yeah." Grover's nodded agreement went unnoticed by the others. "Spooky, too."

Woodrow held broken pieces of saltine between his lips; his voice was subdued, soft. "Why you say that?"

Pinky responded. "Didn't you see how he stared into the fire when he was talking about being brave and doin the right thing?"

"I did," Porky said. "He looked like he was thinkin deep. Like he was thinkin about doin the right thing about somethin."

"I'm thinkin deep about Hale havin to sleep in the house with pansy-wansy Douglass," Woodrow said. "I'm afraid Douglass will do somethin to Hale that aint the right thing to do."

"Was you tellin the truth about Mister Douglass kissin you?" Grover asked.

"I never said he *kissed* me, I said he *wanted to*," Woodrow offered, "I think he did, anyway. I think he wanted to."

They fell silent.

Doubt crept into Porky's thoughts. He wondered now if Woodrow, known to be truthful, was making up this story about the Assistant Scoutmaster.

"I believed Hale when he told about Douglass wanting to kiss *him*," Woodrow said.

"I kissed Sally," Porky said.

Nobody said anything for several seconds.

Porky continued. "We're goin to the *pitchursho* tomorrow night, and I'm gonna ask her to be my girlfriend."

"I thought she *was* your girlfriend," Grover said. "Like Patsy is Pinky's." Grover didn't take a breath. "Did Tina call you the three mustard tears?"

Pinky laughed. "Miss Chestnutt told me Tina said that."

"See, I told you," Woodrow said. "I'm a good Scout. I always tell the truth."

Porky persisted. "We are . . . she is . . . we are . . . well, we're always together, anyway. I'm just gonna make it official."

"Will she say yes?"

Hope was in Porky's voice. "I think so." He added reinforcement to the prospect. "We really like each other. T J said Sally would be a good girlfriend for me."

"T J said that?" Grover asked. "About you and Sally?"

"He's my friend," Porky said.

"Did you say anything to Mister Tanner about T J?" Woodrow asked.

Porky snapped his fingers. "No, I forgot. I told Mister Tanner I wanted to be a Scout, though."

"He may not let you join our Troop." Grover's voice was solemn.

"Why not?"

"Cause T J is a colored boy, cause you have a colored boy as a friend," Woodrow said.

"What's wrong with havin a colored boy as a friend?" Anger tainted Pinky's question. "I know T J. I like him. He's smart. Smartern some of the kids round here, Grover."

Porky joined forces with Pinky. "Nothin's wrong with havin him as a friend. T J's just like us, just like them Germans, only his skin is different, a different color. He's read a lot of books. He's read the same books I have, more than I have I think, maybe a thousand books."

"He aint read no thousand books," Woodrow said,

"and he aint like no Germans, that's for sure."

Four bullfrogs on different sides of the pond filled the silence, mimicking the exchange in the wagon bed.

Grover was placated. "This afternoon he had to fight for T J."

"Why did you fight T J?" Pinky asked.

"I didn't fight *him*, Pinky, I fought for him."

"Who? Who did you fight?" Pinky asked.

"Eliot Thurgood."

His gasp was pronounced. "Uh, oh." Pinky's tsks tsks were distinct. "That man's crazy, Porky. He mighta killed you."

"Mister Bennett said he had bats in his bref-free." Porky remembered his momma correcting the word. "Belfry. It means he's crazy."

"Told you," Pinky said. "Why did you fight Thurgood?"

"He grabbed T J and was chokin him."

"Okay, tell Pinky the whole story instead of a just a piece at a time," Woodrow said.

And, Porky did. He told Pinky about mistaking Eliot Thurgood's gin for the Major's, fighting Thurgood, and how Mister Bennett stepped in.

"You and T J better stay away from crazy Thurgood," Pinky said. "We all better stay away from him."

"He killed his daddy," Woodrow said.

They knew the story, heard it told and repeated in multiple versions by family and friends over the years. It was even in the *Palomino Press*. But there in the wagon with the fresh news of Porky's fight with a suspected, but not charged or convicted, killer, they rehashed the myth.

"His daddy beat him with a leather whip. I guess he

got tired of the floggin," Grover said. "He shot his daddy with a rat gun, right there in the gin."

"Doctor Gates tried to save him," Woodrow said.

"My momma said Doctor Gates killed two people in Houston and went to Huntsville. When he went to prison he wadna doctor no more," Pinky said. "He got out on a peel and came here to work in the hospital."

"My momma likes him," Porky said. "She calls him Doctor. I always call him Doctor, so I guess he's a doctor again."

"My Granmomma said Doctor Gates was the best one cause he helped her with her arthur-rightus. Even lookin at her fingers made my hands and fingers hurt, they all knotted up like she's got two knuckles on every finger," Woodrow said. "She likes to get the shots he gives her to relieve her pain. She calls him her candy man, her god of dreams. She said she now has the 'soldier's disease'."

"What's that? What's 'soldier disease'?"

"I dunno, but it has somethin to do with the shots Doctor Gates gives her."

"That's what he was doin, that's what Doctor Gates was doin when he killed those two old people," Grover said, "givin em morphine shots to stop their pain."

"Well, Doc Burns wouldn't have let him work in our hospital if he thought Doctor Gates was gonna hurt people."

"He goes by Pearly."

"Everbody knows that, Grover."

Grover couldn't stop himself, couldn't rein it in. "Pearly Gates."

"We know that, Grover."

"Momma says he has a magic touch," Porky said. "She told me how Doctor Gates made a really sick baby

112

get well after Doc Burns said the baby wouldn't live another day. Momma said a man had a heart attack and died in his hospital bed. She said Doctor Gates came in, checked him, sat on the side of the bed, held the dead man's hand and wiped his head, and the man sat up in the bed."

"What do you mean, wiped his head?" Pinky asked.

Porky caressed his brow. "Like this."

"He set up in the bed, dead?"

"No, he set up and was alive. Talkin to Doctor Gates."

"That's scary," Grover said.

"He was dead and Doctor Gates made him alive?" Woodrow asked.

"Yeah, that's what momma said."

"That's like bringin Snow White back," Grover said. His pause was not long lived. "Maybe Pearly's got voodoo medicine. You know, like a voodoo doctor can put his hand on you and make you well. He might even have a magic pill.

"I seen a Baptist preacher do that one time at a meetin on Pecan Creek. He put his hand on a woman's head and yelled 'HEAL', and she walked again." Grover put his palm on Woodrow's forehead. "HEAL," he whispered.

They snickered at the thought.

Woodrow brushed Grover's hand away.

"You're funny, Grover," Porky said.

"I wish I had a cigarette," Pinky said. "With all that food, a good smoke, a good Chesterfield, would suit me just fine right about now."

"I shoulda brought some Camels," Grover said.

"Pall Malls are better," Woodrow said. "They last longer and taste better."

Porky thought on it a few seconds. "Can Boy Scouts smoke?"

In the diminished light, Porky could see their heads turn to him but could not see their sheepish expressions. He felt embarrassed, realizing his question exposed a violation of one of the Scout Laws – he just didn't know which one.

"I saw Mister Albert's pants fall down and he was naked."

"No lie?"

"Right there on the sidewalk, in front of Mister Dulfeine's store. Mister Albert had been drinkin again. I helped Mister Dulfeine bring Mister Albert to his car."

"He didn't have no clothes on?"

"He didn't have no underwear on."

They thought on it for several seconds, each picturing an image of a man with no underwear.

"I got to go to the bathroom," Woodrow said.

"Me too," Grover said. "We can just stand in the wagon and do a number one over the sideboard. Let's see who can pee the longest."

"You can't do that," Pinky said.

"Why not? I pee in the woods all the time," Grover said.

"Well, you ain't in the woods. You're at Mister Tanner's house, in his yard."

Porky tried one of the Scout Laws. "Scouts have to be clean. Peein in Mister Tanner's yard aint bein clean . . . or, even bein considerate."

"I need to do a number two, anyway," Woodrow said. "Let me use your flashlight."

"I'll go with you, I need to do a number one, too."

"Okay, we'll all go," Grover said. "But hurry up, or I'll go in my pants."

"I don't need to do a number one or a number two. I'm goin to bed. Yall be quiet, don't wake nobody up," Pinky said.

The trio crawled over the side and used wheel spokes to climb down. Exhausted campfire embers guided their crossing of the yard. Turned low, the two porch lanterns gave a little light for the porch steps, so Porky did not turn on his flashlight.

They all had been to the bathroom before Assistant Scoutmaster passed out sleeping assignments, but now, inside the darkened room, they became disoriented. Porky aimed the Ray-O-Vac toward the wall, pushed the switch forward, and pressed the button for a quick flash of light on a door for two seconds – the door he thought was to the bathroom. When Grover and Woodrow stepped toward the door, Porky released the button to extinguish the light. The quick illumination wiped out their night vision. They eased forward in total blackness cautiously.

Woodrow reached out with a hand, searching in the empty darkness. He found the wall, slid his fingers down and along to the knob, turned it, and opened the door.

From the smell, they could sense it was not the bathroom.

"Turn on your light," Woodrow whispered.

The brightness against the starkness of three bright, white robes draped on wire hangers startled the boys. The ornamental red, black, and white patches sewn on the front of each dressing gown was unmistakable.

Porky moved the light across, down, and up on the clothing. On a closet shelf above the hanger rod laid four pointed, white hoods, their tops drooping down. Across each hood was a scarlet and black sash.

A rush of exhaled air forced Grover's whispered shock. "KKK."

Porky's heart pounded in his chest, his throat felt constricted.

Awe was inimitable in Woodrow's whisper. "That's KKK stuff."

Hale's voice from the floor behind them shook the boys. "What're yall lookin for?"

Porky released the button as Woodrow eased the door closed.

"The bathroom," Porky said. "We lookin for the bathroom, Hale."

"It's on the other side of the room, over there on the right."

"Quit shinin that light all over," Emmett protested.

Now, standing there deeply blinded and with absolutely no visibility, Porky and Grover placed a hand on Woodrow's shoulder as he moved to the right. They took baby steps, shuffling toward the other door.

"Turn on your light," Woodrow whispered.

Porky pressed the button as Woodrow opened the door.

The glow flared and filled the small enclosure exposing man and boy.

The three searchers froze, mesmerized by the gripping, heart-stopping image. Babe stood in front of and faced the Assistant Scoutmaster.

Douglass sat on the commode, his hands holding the Scout's hips.

Both turned and squinted, staring into the blinding beam.

"You son-of-a-bitch," Woodrow screamed and charged.

"I'm sorry to disturb your supper, Mayor."

"Come in, Winston, come in. My goodness, the look on your face tells me something's wrong. Has something happened to one of the boys?"

"No, no, Mayor. The boys are alright. They're at the house. Clifford is with them, I've come to tell you what he found."

"Hello, Winston, how are you doing?"

"Hello, Sue. Fine, just fine. I'm sorry to barge in on you at supper."

"We were just having coffee and a little of my lemon icebox pie for dessert. Come into the kitchen and have some with us."

"Okay, Sue, just coffee, though. I really love your icebox pie, but I ate too many hot dogs with the boys tonight."

Winston Tanner sat at one end of the kitchen table, Casey sat on his right.

Sue did not serve pie to her husband. After pouring coffee for them, she sat at the other end of the table. "Casey was just telling me that you and Clifford were camping out with your Scouts tonight. Has something happened to the boys?"

Tanner shook his head. "No, no, Sue. I was just telling Casey the boys are okay. We have thirteen boys."

He sipped the brew before he spoke again. "Mayor, I've come to tell you that Barber Beck's car is out there, parked beside the house, and Clifford saw blood in it."

Sue's gasp was audible. "Oh, my."

"Was Barber there?"

"No, Casey, no, he wasn't, just the car. It was there when I drove up late this afternoon, but I never looked in it. I thought he might be fishing in the pond or rabbit

117

hunting. When he arrived, Clifford went to look in it. He went down to the pond, too, to look for Barber. I thought it . . . I thought it important enough to come report it right away."

"It is, I'm glad you came, Winston." Mayor Casey Shipp sighed. He looked at his wife, then at the Scoutmaster. "Apparently you don't know what's happened."

"Something's happened to Barber?"

"No. No, not to Barber. It's Bobbette Moon. She died in the hospital. Barber and Wyatt Posey brought her in. Pearly said they found her lying in the park, bleeding. Somebody cut her open with a big knife. The blood in Barber's car must be from Bobbette's wounds."

"Poor girl," Sue whispered. "The baby died too."

"Baby?"

The Mayor nodded. "Yeah, I'm afraid so. Pearly called Sheriff Dudley. He drove over here right away to the hospital with one of his deputies, Gary Gully. They talked with Doc Burns, Doctor Gates, and Nurse Baycann. I came in later with Jonathan for Bobbette. Her momma and daddy wanted Jonathan to bring her to his funeral home. Sheriff said they were gonna go talk with Barber and Wyatt."

"Beck and Posey is a wild pair," Tanner said. "Babe is out at the house with the other Scouts." The Scoutmaster took a deep breath and exhaled as he continued. "He appeared distracted, really strange for Babe. Something was going on in that boy's head."

"You don't say?" Casey glanced at Sue. As he spoke, he turned back to Tanner. "I have to admit that my first thought was mean."

Tanner waited.

Sue filled in the silence. "Casey believes Barber and

Wyatt may have had something to do with Bobbette, rather than just finding that poor girl laying cut open in the park."

Tanner took another sip of coffee and set the cup gently on Sue Shipp's exquisite porcelain saucer. She treasured the tea and dinnerware she had bought from the Paragon China Company Limited before the war and was pleased her fine bone china matched the set used by King George VI and Queen Elizabeth. He canted his head, measuring his words.

"Maybe that's what's bothering Babe."

"I hope my thoughts turn out all wrong," the Mayor said. "Anyway, the Sheriff said that with all that's going on at Maxey and in Lamar County, he needed help to sort things out here. He asked if I'd found a replacement for Jimmy. I told him I had."

"You have?"

"After having some of Sue's delicious pie and coffee, I was going over to the Porter House. I want you to come with me, Winston."

"What're we gonna do at Ruby's?"

"I'm gonna get a replacement for Jimmy Madison, to get help for Sheriff Dudley in his investigation."

"Twig?"

"Yes, that's right. I'm gonna ask Sergeant Chestnutt to come to my office in the morning where I'll swear him in as Palomino Constable.

12

The white beam was blinding.

As the light approached, he narrowed his eyes. He looked to the right of the illumination, trying to see the figure behind the flashlight.

The light stopped six feet away, below.

"Barber? Barber, you up there?"

Barber sighed. "Yeah, Wyatt, I'm here. Come on up."

Wyatt held the flashlight with two fingers and a thumb, grasped the boards nailed to the tree, and climbed the makeshift ladder through the hole in the flooring of the rickety tree house. Once inside, with light filling the cramped space, he saw the red and brown ribbons where Bobbette's fingernails had ripped Barber's cheek. He sat on the planks and turned off the flashlight.

"How'd you know I was here?"

"I went to your house. Your daddy said he ain't seen you since yesterday. For some reason, he seemed to be mad at me."

"He didn't say why? Pa ain't one to hold back."

"Naw, he didn't say why but I guess cause the law come snoopin round askin about you and me. Your daddy said the Lamar County Sheriff and a deputy came and wanted to talk to you about Bobbette. Asked me if they come to my house."

"Did they?"

"Yeah. Your daddy said the Sheriff was interested in knowing about your knife."

"Wadchu tell the Sheriff?"

"I told im we found Bobbette in the park all cut up and brought her to the hospital. The Deputy, Gully, asked me if I had a knife."

"Wadchu tell im?"

"I don't have no knife. I told im I didn't have no knife. The Sheriff said he had a splinter in his thumb, and Gully asked if I had my knife so he could pick it out."

"Uh huh. Like that didn't register with you, Wyatt? Him wantin your knife?"

"What was there to redster?"

"You don't get it, do you?"

In the dark, they sat in silence for six seconds while Wyatt tried to register.

"The knife. I see. Where ats your knife, that big one you always carry?"

"I lost it."

"In the park? You left it in the park? It's still in the park?"

Barber's voice was filled with resignation. "Yeah, okay, so what?"

Momentarily, Wyatt was speechless. Then, "So what? They gonna find . . ."

"Did you bring anything to eat or to drink?"

"Naw. Well, I got a Baby Ruth."

"Give it to me. I ain't had nothin to drink or eat since we come from Madame Estelle's place."

Barber peeled back the candy wrapper and chomped a parcel of the peanut, caramel, and milk chocolate bar. His smacking and chewing was distinguishingly audible.

"I told em we'd been at Maxey and was comin home and found Bobbette in the park."

"Why'd you tell em that?"

"Well, you told Gates that. I was just keepin the story straight."

"Yeah, well. You ain't never been so good at keepin any story straight. Like that time at Miss Ruby's house, when the housekeeper found us in the barn."

"You won't let that go, will you?"

"The next minute after I said we was lookin for my dog, you said you was lookin for your goat. I know the housekeeper told on us. I'm surprised Miss Ruby didn't come lookin for us to pin our ears back. You know how mean Miss Ruby can get."

"Well, I was nervous."

"Uh huh. And that time Byrd caught us in the gym with a sack full of gloves and uniforms. The minute I said we volunteered to clean em, you said we found em outside and was bringin em back in."

"I knew Coach Byrd knew we didn't volunteer to clean no baseball gloves and uniforms." Wyatt listened to Barber chew. "You ain't seen your face have you?"

"No, but I know I got scratches on my left side. It hurts, burns, feels like it's all swolled up."

"Her fingernails cut you deep. They're three scratches that are red and brown from the dried blood and scabs."

"I can't show my face like this. The minute somebody sees me they gonna ask what happened, if I got in a fight with a cat. I got to get away, and you can help me. We'll use your light to go get my car."

"Where ats your car?"

"Over there at Tanner's place, side of the house. I took it over there to use the pond to wash the blood out, but I didn't get around to it. Somebody was comin up the road, and I left it."

"I dunno, Barber."

"Whachu mean you don't know?   What's that mean?"

"Bobbette is dead."

"I know."

"Bobbette is dead, Barber.   The Sheriff said Bobbette bled to death. You killed Bobbette."

"I said I know it, Wyatt. Babe told me. Babe told me she died in the hospital."

"You're in big trouble."

"We're in big trouble. It's all your fault, anyway, Wyatt. I shoulda cut you, too."

"You are crazy. Why is it my fault?"

"Cause you said Bobbette went and did it with Tub. You said her baby was probably Tub's."

"I said no such thing. I said I seen her snugglin up with Tub, that's all. That don't mean they did it. It was your baby like Bobbette said it was."

"Well, I got to get my car and get outta Palomino. I might go down to Dallas or San Antonio . . . or maybe even all the way down to Del Rio, or cross the border into Villa Acuna. So, you can help me. Ain't nobody in town this late, we'll walk through town and use your flashlight through the woods to Tanner's place."

"Naw, I ain't gonna do that."

"You know they'll convict us of murder and send us to Huntsville for the chair."

"I didn't kill nobody."

"Yes, you did."

"You had the knife. The one that's layin somewhere in the park. You the one who cut Bobbette, not me."

"You're in this neck deep just as I am, Wyatt. They might put you in the chair first."

"I think all this is gotta stop. You got to do the right thing."

Barber snorted. "That's what Babe said. My baby brother said he wadn gonna help me neither. Babe said I had to do the right thing. He said my Pa said I had to do the right thing. The right thing is gonna put me in old Sparky."

"I'll walk to town with you but I ain't goin out there to Tanner's place with you. I'll give you my flashlight and you go on by yourself to Tanner's and on to wherever else."

"Yeah, and after I'm gone whachu gonna do? Run to the High Sheriff and tell im I killed Bobbette and tell im where I'm at?"

"Naw, I won't say nothin like that."

"Uh huh. I know you, Wyatt Posey. Now, come on, let's go get my car."

After climbing down from the tree house, they zigzagged across backyards and around houses down to Clark Street. They were surprised to see all the lights, including the two on the front porch, and paused to see if there was movement in the Porter House.

Barber's stride was swift, and Wyatt intermittently trotted to keep up. They saw the car's headlights coming down Clark Street and slowed their pace. They paused behind a fence, waiting for the car to pass.

"That's Tanner's Ford," Wyatt said. "Wonder where he's goin in such a hurry?"

"Oh, I forgot," Barber said. "Tanner and Douglass is out there by the pond with Scout camping. Babe is out there, too."

"Well, if the Scouts are out there, there ain't no way you can get your car without them seein you."

"Yeah I can. I'll just sneak up, crank it up, and drive off."

"They'll hear you."

"I'll be long gone fore they figure it out. Come on, let's get goin."

Once in town, Barber and Wyatt slowed their pace and strolled down the sidewalk along Main Street. They kept moving as theatergoers came out of the Palomino Palace.

"Humphrey Bogart and Ingrid Bergman in *Casablanca*. Did you see it?" Wyatt asked. "I liked it. Twig is bringin his Germans tomorrow. But they ain't Nazis like in the *pitchursho*."

"How you know that? How you know they ain't Nazis?"

"Cause Casey said they wadn. That they went through a lot of processin to be able to live and work here."

When they reached the highway, even this late, heavy traffic barreling along 271 east and west, gave them pause. Judging a safe distance from approaching trucks from both directions, they jogged across the military and civilian supply artery.

Wyatt stopped at the Katy station. "Here, take my flashlight. I'm goin home."

Barber took the light and turned it on and off twice. "You got to come with me, Wyatt. A house apart is gonna fall. As long as we together we can look out for each other. If you go home, you know the Sheriff is gonna come pick you up sooner or later."

"If I come with you now, will you do the right thing?"

"What is all this business about doin the right thing? What do you think the right thing to do is, anyway?"

"Go see the Sheriff."

"If we do that, whachu think the Sheriff is gonna do? He gonna ask a lot of questions and figure out what happened to Bobbette."

"The right thing, Barber, is to tell the truth. You got to tell that you cut Bobbette. You didn't mean to kill her."

Barber sighed. "Oh, okay. Alright. You're right. I didn't mean to kill her. Now, I'll get my car. My pistol's in the glove box. You come with me. I'll do the right thing, you'll see."

Wyatt agreed. "Okay. Let's get your car and we'll go to Paris and see Sheriff Dudley."

They maneuvered through the woods, trailing the direction where Barber occasionally turned the light on.

They could see faint smoldering from a campfire and dim, yellow glows from two lanterns on the porch, thirty yards ahead.

Before they reached the tree line twenty yards from the house, hollering and screaming erupted. White lines from three different flashlights swayed and bobbed and sliced and flashed along the house, the ground, toward them, and skyward.

Barber and Wyatt stopped and peered through the brush. They watched figures shuffling off the porch carrying a heavy burden to a car. They heard the car's engine roar to life and saw its headlights come on. They stood dumbfounded, immobile, as it pulled away.

They crouched down as yelling and bawling Scouts

ran toward them, crashing through brush and low hanging limbs and branches of trees, rushing past, heading toward town.

"Something bad's happened," Wyatt said. "Looks like everbody sure is scared of something and running for home. Maybe they saw a ghost."

Barber rose from the ground. "Come on, now's our chance to get the car and get away without nobody seein us."

Fear and anxiety in Wyatt's voice were unmistakable. "Maybe there's a ghost up there. I'm scared of ghosts. I want to go home."

"You ain't never seen no ghost. And they ain't no ghost at Tanner's house. Now come on, let's get outta here."

Nurse Baycann anxiously pressed her teeth against her bottom lip. She slowly and gingerly lifted the tape and gauze away. Clifford Douglass did not flinch or grimace. With the covering removed, the sutured gash across the left eyebrow and swollen, black eye of the Assistant Scoutmaster lay ghastly exposed. For the moment, she did not strip the bandages from his fractured nose. Douglass breathed calmly and deeply through his gaping mouth.

She used a sterile patch soaked with alcohol dabbing and patting the wound and stitches to clean them. Her exhale mixed with a sorrowful sigh.

"Maybe it's a good thing Clifford's out. Can't feel the pain," Doc Burns said.

"Yes." Agnes did not look up. "He has no fever, so that's good."

"But it's going hurt bad when he wakes up." Doc Burns cleared his throat. "I told the boys to go home,

127

told Portland to go home, too."

Agnes paused in the swabbing, nodded, and returned to her cleaning chore. "Twig will have to sort things out."

Doc Burns chuckled. "That boy's been on duty as our Constable for just a few hours, and already he's been given the Sheriff's request to help with the Bobbette Moon matter, and now he'll have this thing with the Scouts and Clifford. Wonder he doesn't pack up his Germans and go back to Maxey."

"He's not that kind of man, he wouldn't skunk away like that," Nurse Baycann said. "Anyway, Teresa wouldn't let him."

Greffen Gates came into the room. "Vernetta wants to go home. She needs to go take care of Clifford's sick momma. I asked her to wait until I spoke with you, Garland."

"I think she probably should go home, Pearly. Clifford is unresponsive, there's not much any of us can do while he's in a coma. What do you think, Agnes?"

Nurse Baycann looked from one doctor to the other. "Going home and taking care of Miss Bertha will take Vernetta's mind off her husband. It'll keep her busy. I think you should tell her we'll call when Clifford wakes up."

Doc Burns shrugged and looked at Gates. "Do you think he's gonna come out of it?"

Pearly's small nod was reassuring. "He will. One way or the other." He looked at Burns. "You've never second guessed yourself, Garland.

Vernetta rose from the slatted, wooden bench when Greffen came into the waiting room.

"Is he awake?"

Doctor Gates smiled. "He's coming round, Vernetta,

128

but it'll be a while before he's fully awake. Why don't you go on home and take care of Miss Bertha? Agnes will call you when Clifford is alert. Okay?"

Tears shimmered in her eyes. "He's all we got, Miss Bertha and me, Doctor. Please make him well."

Greffen opened his arms, and Vernetta stepped into his embrace. He held her close, warmly, and spoke in a soft, consoling voice. "Your man is going to be alright, Vernetta. Clifford is strong hearted, he loves life, he's a fighter. The injury looks bad because you can see it, but the wound is only superficial. It'll heal in no time." He grasped her shoulders and held Vernetta at arm's length. "You know I'll do the best for Clifford, don't you?"

Vernetta flashed a wisp of a smile before tears slid down her cheeks. "I do, Doctor Gates. I know you will." She wiped her face with both hands. "Thank you."

"Now, Twig is going to get involved and talk to the Scouts. He's going to find out what happened."

"I'm here, Doctor Gates."

Vernetta leaned and peered around Gate's form as he turned.

Sergeant Chestnutt stood in the doorway, his three Germans behind him.   "Sorry to interrupt. The Mayor sent me over. Hello, Miss Vernetta."

"You brought *them*?" She pointed a finger, aimed like a pistol, at the three men trailing the Constable.

"Yes, Mam. They're prisoners of war, Miss Vernetta. I'm their guard. They must go with me everywhere I go, day and night."

"I'm just so used to seeing you in town by yourself or with Teresa and Tina."

"Yes, Mam, I know." Twig softened his voice. "How

is Mister Douglass?"

"He's . . . Doctor Gates said Clifford is coming round, not alert just yet."

"Good. That's good." Chestnutt paused. In front of Vernetta, he was unsure what to say or what to do.

"Vernetta was just leaving, Twig," Gates said. He put an arm around her and moved toward the door.

Twig stepped aside and spoke to his prisoners. "Against the wall."

Twig thought he saw Vernetta shrink in Gates' grasp as they passed the Germans.

At the door, she turned and addressed them. "I don't hate you boys. Welcome to America."

Gates closed the door and swept his hand toward the waiting room. "Let's go in there. We'll have a little privacy."

Twig pointed at the Germans. "Stay here, sit on the floor." He followed the doctor through the doorway of the waiting room and sat with Gates on the divan.

"Clifford is in a coma. He's banged up pretty bad. Nasty cut along his right eyebrow and a fractured nose. He's suffered a blunt force trauma. Tub drove Clifford's car, brought him in about two this morning. We stitched up the wound and repaired his nose. He's had ice packs on and off for the last few hours. A little later, maybe twenty-thirty minutes or so after Tub brought Clifford, Woodrow Collins, Grover Lindsey, Babe Beck, and Portland Baycann came in. After we put Clifford to bed, I asked the boys what happened. Woodrow seemed to speak for the group . . . he said Clifford must have tripped in the dark and fallen."

"But you don't believe that?"

Gates smiled. "No, I don't. Bumping your head, bumping your nose, in a fall is one thing. Clifford's gash is deep and three inches long. The bridge of his nose was broken. A fall didn't cause those injuries. He was hit in the face with a blunt object. Each of the boys said they didn't know what happened. It was obvious they didn't want to talk to me or Doctor Burns about it, so he sent them home. Doctor Burns asked me to call the Mayor and report it. And the Mayor dropped it in your lap."

Twig took a small notepad and short pencil out of his shirt pocket. "Those names again, Doctor Gates."

"Tub brought Clifford in."

"Tub?"

"Nickname.   Real name is Francoise Tubane. French. Francoise, with an e, is the feminine spelling instead of Francois, without the e."

Twig frowned and nodded. "I come from Louisiana, I know the difference."

Gates shrugged. "Anyway, Woodrow Collins, Grover Lindsey, Babe Beck and Portland Baycann, Agnes' boy, are the others."

"So, the boys are at home now?"

"Yes, probably."

"It sounds to me like Mister Douglass was attacked and beaten. One or two of those five boys know what happened. If there's a weak link, I'll find it. It's my job to find out the truth. Then we'll know what path to follow."

13

They had talked for twenty minutes – strategy, mostly, and priorities. Palomino school Principal Porter Skaggs, Mayor Casey Shipp, Constable Twig Chestnutt, and the three prisoners stood on the sidewalk in front of the screen door of the Constable's office. Passersby stared at the Germans, but they cordially dipped their heads and greeted the Americans. No one stopped to chitchat.

Because he knew the answer, the Mayor's question was more for a breather from the seriousness of topics rather than for information.

Twig nodded, took a deep breath in the pause. He checked his impatience before answering. "A year, Mayor. They've been in Palomino a year. Teresa and Tina moved into the Porter House July, a year ago. Teresa's worked for Bobbie Jo at Jeeps for that long, too, and through her and my weekend passes from Maxey, I've met and got to know most of the good people here. All that time, it was as peaceful as where we came from. I thought the job as Constable would be easy, a walk in the park, like Vivian."

"Well, it was, Twig. It was. But not anymore. Now we've got our hands full, a lot to do."

"Well, Mayor, to go back to your point, it's a matter of time and resources," Twig said. "Talking with Barber Beck, to get his story is certainly the priority, for us, as well as for the Sheriff and Miss Bobbette's family. But we don't know where he is. We don't even have an idea where to look. Believe me, if I knew where he was, I'd be on my way to get him for the Sheriff."

Twig shifted from one foot to the other. He hooked his left thumb under the Army web belt and grasped the leather holster in his right. "You told me you don't believe Beck and Posey. If the Sheriff didn't take Posey away, it's because he didn't have the evidence to do so." He pulled up with his thumb and hefted the heavy Army Colt pistol with his right hand to relieve the weight. "I'm a force of one man, that's why I suggested we talk to the boys first about Mister Douglass and get that out of the way. Then I'll hunt up Posey and talk with him, maybe he'll tell me where Beck is. Maybe his brother, Babe, knows where Barber is."

"Twig, his three Germans, and thirteen boys can't fit into the Constable's small office," Casey said to Porter. "It's not any larger than the bank's vault or the broom closet. So, I want you to call Floyd and ask him to open his school gym."

Principal Skaggs hesitated. "They'll scratch the gym floor, Mayor, and I'll never hear the end of it from Coach Byrd. You know how Floyd threw a fit when you used the gym to make the announcement these Germans were coming."

Casey, Twig, and the Principal looked at the prisoners whose blank faces did not reveal their deep interest in the goings-on in a small Texas town. They

133

were enthralled with all the drama the few hours they had been in Palomino.

Casey shrugged. "I know, Porter, I know. The Coach still bends my ear about having our Christmas cakewalks on his floor. But Twig wants all the boys together, wants them to watch when he's talking to the others."

Twig's attempt at reassurance was lame. "The only time they'll be on the gym floor, Mister Skaggs, is when I call them over. They won't be running and jumping around on your floor, Sir."

Porter Skaggs waved it off. "Why can't all yall just sit on one side or the other? Everbody sit in the bleachers on one side, then nobody would have to cross the floor."

"I'll sit on the bottom row and conduct interviews one-by-one," Twig said. "My Germans will sit on the very top row, out of the way. I'll put the boys on the bleachers on the other side and space them out on different rows so they can't talk to each other. I want them to feel the pressure as they watch me interview their friends. It's standard police work when conducting interviews with a lot of people. They don't know what the person is saying and get anxious. Helps get people to open up."

The Principal's surrender was weak. "Well . . . well, you're our lawman now, so I guess what you say is the way to do it. But tell the boys Coach Byrd will skin em alive if they scratch his floor." He took a deep breath and let it out with a defeated sigh. "I know Floyd is gonna scream bloody murder when I tell him to open the gym."

"Thank you, Porter," Mayor Shipp said. "We've talked to all the parents, or parent in a few cases, and they agreed to let their boys come. We'll meet you over there at one."

"You're gonna sit in with the Constable?"

"Yes. Yes, I will, Porter. Many of the parents asked me to. This is a really sensitive situation with Clifford. We need to know what happened . . . what happened out there. We need to find out if one of the boys attacked and hit or beat Clifford. This could turn out to be a serious criminal matter."

"Or several boys," Twig interjected. "Why would Boy Scouts attack or beat their Assistant Scoutmaster?"

"You don't know, do you?" the Principal asked.

Twig frowned. "Know what?"

"Clifford's ways."

"Okay, tell me what you want to tell me, don't beat around the bush."

The Principal did not elaborate. Instead, he pointed at the approaching owner of Dulfeine's Grocery, the only grocery in Palomino.

"Hello, Nate," the three greeted in unison.

"Hello Mayor, Porter, Twig. I heard your math teacher is in the hospital with a serious injury . . . what happened to Clifford?" Nate Dulfeine asked.

"The Mayor and Constable are about to go talk with the boys to try to find out," the Principal said.

"Mister Douglass' injuries could turn out to be life threatening, Nate," Twig said. "If he dies, it's really serious."

"Okay," the Principal said. "I'll go call Floyd and meet him at the school. We'll open the gym for you and stay there."

"Well, Principal Skaggs, I don't mind you and the Coach stayin, but neither one of you can come into the gym while I'm conducting the interviews."

135

Skaggs nodded. "Yes, of course. I understand. We'll stay out of your way, Constable. We'll stay in my office till it's over."

At one, after dinner, the Mayor and the Constable greeted the boys at the front door of the gymnasium as all thirteen arrived within a couple of minutes of each other.

As they entered the gym, the Mayor directed they walk outside the boundary line. Twig pointed to where he wanted his prisoners to go. He noted that each boy watched the Germans mount the left-side bleachers and sit on the top row.

The Constable told the youngsters to sit in a group. He selected seven to sit on the bottom row and six to sit on the second row of the right side bleachers.

"Mayor Shipp and me have talked with your folks, and that's why you're here. Mister Douglass is in pretty bad shape. Someone told Doctor Gates that Mister Douglass may have tripped and fell in the dark. We need to find out exactly what happened. Some of you may have seen him trip, may have seen him fall. So, I'm goin to ask a few questions here as a group, then I'm going to interview each of you over there in the other bleachers. Once we've talked, you'll be able to go home unless I want you to stay."

"Are we under arrest?"

Twig smiled. "No, Andrew, nobody is under arrest."

"We just need to find out what happened," Casey said. "That's all."

"Let's start with where everbody was at the house and what they were doin before Mister Douglass, ah, fell." Twig pointed to each boy in turn to maintain orderly responses.

One by one, they told where they were – wagon,

porch, or house. All said they were asleep, except Babe, Woodrow, Grover, and Porky.

As each boy spoke, Twig paid attention to facial expressions and body language. He quickly picked out the seven boys he needed to interrogate.

"That's good. Thank you for tellin the Mayor and me where you were and what you were doin," Twig said.

The Constable's long pause was for effect. He cleared his throat. "As you grow up, there'll be a point in your life where you'll have to decide what is right. Until that time comes, you'll have to depend on others who know, to show you, to teach you, what is right.

"Does anybody have any questions?"

Twig counted to ten. When there were no questions from the boys, he continued.

"Okay, Andrew, Grady, Waldo, and J W, since you boys were asleep in one of the wagons, I think it'll be alright if you go on home. And, you can go too, Pinky.

"Leroy, you and Tub were on the porch, and Tub, you drove Mister Douglass' car and brought him to the hospital, so I want to talk a little more with both of you. Hale and Emmett, since you were sleeping in the house, I want to talk a little bit more with yall. And, Babe, I want you to stay a little longer, too."

The Constable paused again. "And, Woodrow, Grover, and Porky, I need to talk with yall more since you three came into the house to use the bathroom."

The five that Twig dismissed did not say a word before leaving the gym.

"Is Mister Douglass gonna die?"

"Mister Douglass is in pretty bad shape, but Doctor Gates and Doctor Burns don't think so, Hale," the Mayor said.

"Did Mister Douglass say what happened to him?"

"No, Hale," Twig said. "Mister Douglass is in a coma right now, and he hasn't been able to talk. When he wakes up, we're gonna want him to tell us what happened. Any other questions?"

Twig scanned the faces, waiting. No one spoke but all looked at him and made eye contact. Twig pointed out who was to sit where until called and each boy took his place.

"Let's start with you, Tub," Twig said. He led the way across the floor to the other bleachers.

Casey sat on the second row, positioning himself between Tub and Twig who sat on the bottom row.

Tub looked up, toward the prisoners. "They don't look like devils."

Twig glanced up. "No, they're not devils, Tub. Are you afraid of them?"

"No, Sir. My daddy is at Barksdale hospital."

"Your daddy is in the Air Corps?" Twig asked.

"Tub's daddy, Frank, is recovering from burns he sustained in a belly landing. He was a nose-gunner in a B-Twenty-Four," Casey said.

"He's gonna be okay," Tub said. "Momma and me went to see him a couple of weeks ago. We took the train over there."

"You drove the car, Tub. You brought Mister Douglass to the hospital. Tell me what you know."

Tub was not fat, but at five-three and one-hundred-fifteen pounds, he was larger than the average size. His black eyes, dark hair, and olive skin presented the handsome and distinct appearance of a Middle Easterner, yet Tub was of French stock.

Teresa had told Twig about Tub. How girls and young women enjoyed Tub's attention; they were attracted to him because he knew how to speak softly and listen.

"His manner and confidence are like a magnet," Teresa had said. "Tub knows how to flirt. He's in the early stages of his development to becoming a lady's man.

"Tub, in a manner of speaking," she had said, "has a way with women, and *we* enjoy it."

Teresa had laughed at Twig's frown. "You wouldn't understand, Sweetheart."

Teresa had continued when Twig asked how in the world a boy who attracted girls ended up with the nickname of Tub. "Bobbie Jo told me," Teresa had said. "Instead of Francois Alois Tubane, Junior, the Clarksville hospital clerk spelled the names Francoise Aloise Tubane, Junior on the birth certificate, exactly as Tub's father, Frank, had printed on the back of a cafe check.

"Frank and Mary Tubane had been in The Spot Cafe, in Bogata, having a blue-plate special supper when she exclaimed, shrieked, that it was time for Junior's arrival. Instead of paying, which he was in the process of doing when Madeleine screamed, Frank stuffed the check in his pocket.

"After Mary delivered, Mister Tubane suspected a hick from Northeast Texas, who had never been out of Red River County, would be ignorant of the different meanings and would not know how to spell his son's name, so he printed F-r-a-n-c-o-i-s-e, the female equivalent of the male Francois, without the e, and A-l-o-i-s-e, the female equivalent of Alois, without the e. Trouble was, Bobbie Jo said, the clerk knew better, but she did not correct the Northeast Texas ignorant hick's, Mister Tubane's, misspelling."

"Doctor Gates told me the same story," Twig had

said. "All the spelling business is so confusing, it makes my head hurt." Twig had shook his head and shrugged. "It just don't make any sense. Anyway, I still don't know why he's called Tub."

Teresa had huffed when Twig told her he had already heard the spelling story from Gates. Even though Teresa had smacked her lips in disappointment that Twig hadn't appreciated her telling of the spelling story, she enjoyed sharing the gossip.

Grinning, Teresa had continued. "It was Miss Evelyn Pruitt. When he was in her second-grade class, Evelyn inadvertently nicknamed him Tub because she continually mispronounced his last name as Tub-bane. Of course, the kids picked it up right away. Fortunately, Frank, Junior preferred and tolerated Tub more than the *Junior.*"

Tub looked up at the Germans again before answering Twig's question.

"Do they talk?" Tub asked.

"They talk to me when it's necessary, Tub," Twig said. Casey and Twig looked up at the prisoners.

"It's best they stay quiet," the Mayor said.

"Tub?"

Tub looked at Twig. "Yes, Sir."

"You're fourteen, Tub?" Twig asked.

"I'm almost sixteen."

"Been drivin cars long?"

"I learned how to drive a car when I was ten, Mister Chestnutt." He looked at Casey then back to Twig. "My daddy taught me how to drive. He was a mechanic at Mister Casey's Chevrolet place."

"Tub knows how to ride a motorcycle, too," the Mayor said.

Tub smiled. "Actually, it's a forty-two Cushman

140

motor scooter, but since it has two wheels, a throttle, and a two-cylinder engine, everbody calls it a motorcycle."

"Tub's a bit of a showoff. It's nice, though, to see a kid have fun because, well, because it was somethin different for the war-weary folks here in town."

All the time Casey was talking about Tub, Twig watched the boy's face, saw there was sincerity in the dark eyes. Twig remembered Teresa's gossip and now could see that Tub was more mature for his age.

"I see. Tell me when you were aware Mister Douglass was hurt."

"First, the yelling started and then Woodrow and Grover and Porky and Babe brought Mister Douglass out of the bathroom hollering that Mister Douglass was hurt."

"What do you mean, the yelling started?"

"Woodrow."

"What did Woodrow yell?"

"Son-of-a-bitch."

Twig looked at Casey.

"Are you sure?" Casey asked. "You were out on the porch with Leroy."

"We was kinda awake anyway when Porky and nem came up on the porch. They weren't very quiet."

"Woodrow told us they were coming to use the bathroom?"

"Yes, Sir."

"So you heard Woodrow yell . . ."

"Yes, Sir. That's what he yelled. And Babe yelled, and then Porky, and then . . . Well, it seemed like everbody was hollering and screaming, and for me, hollering for me to drive him to the hospital. I jumped up and ran down the porch goin to Barber's car . . ."

"Barber's car?"

"Yes, Sir. But Babe yelled to take Mister Douglass' car, so I turned around and ran the other way, to the other side of the house."

"They brought him to the car? They brought Mister Douglass to his car?"

"Yes, Sir."

"What'd you think had happened?"

"When they put him on the front seat, I could see there was a lot of blood. In the light, I could see the cut above Mister Douglass' eye. He was cut bad."

"What light?"

"Flashlight. Porky had his flashlight. I thought maybe somebody had hit Mister Douglass with a stick . . . or . . . with . . . a flashlight. That's how bad the cut was."

14

It was late morning.   Their snoring, and the perceptible hissing of the two kerosene lanterns, filled the heavy air.   The battling frogs had long slipped into the pond or burrowed into their mud-huts to escape the rising temperature.

A sharp, biting, baritone woofing from a nearby hound waked them.   They lay on the porch, on their backs, without moving.   Both were weary from exhausting anxious arguing. In their words, it was clear they feared what lay in the future. Both smacked their lips and clacked tongues against palettes to moisten dry mouths.   They scratched and rubbed familiar places, lazily waiting for nothing.

Their hunger and thirst were on the verge of awakening too, with a ravenous vengeance.   Neither had eaten since the *incident*, as Barber called it.

"I'm hungry and thirsty.   I wonder if Tanner has anything in his Frigidaire to eat or drink?" Wyatt asked. "I sure could use a cold bottle of Lone Star right about now."

"Tanner ain't got no Frigidaire in there.   You see

them coal-oil lamps, Wyatt? He ain't got no electricity out here, that's why he ain't got no Frigidaire in there."

"Well, maybe he's got a icebox with a big block of ice in it. And it's full of cold beer. And it has somethin to eat in it."

"If he *has* a icebox, you can bet there ain't no food in it, with all em kids out here."

The jarring, ear-piercing cock-a-doodle-doo from the large male gallinaceous bird startled them.

The rooster stood elegantly at the opposite end of the porch. Between each set of crowing, he clucked and pranced in place as if the worn, warped plank was a hot plate.

Fully awake now and alert, Barber rolled onto his side. "What is a rooster doin crowin this late of a mornin? Shoo, bird. Shoo."

The brown and green and purple chicken craned his neck. He did not like sharing his roost with strangers. He canted his head and eyed the intruders, perhaps checking to see if they paid attention to his warning. He stretched his neck and chimed again.

Barber sat up. "SHOO, I said. Git."

The rooster ignored the command and clucked faster, louder. He faced Barber. The bird dipped and stuck his head forward before raising it in a challenging position. With hackles rising, the bird erected his crimson, flappy comb to an aggressive posture.

Wyatt sat up and yawned. "You in the boss' territory. You better be careful. That old boy might attack you. His hens are somewhere close and he's crowin to tell em where at he is. And what he's doin is tellin you to vacate his primanisses."

Barber snorted. "I'll wring his scrawny skinny neck for im, then he won't have no hens and no territory.

I've a good mind to catch and pluck him, and eat him right here for dinner."

Wyatt got to his feet and stretched. "I've got to go to the bathroom."

"Well, see if there's a ice box with food and beer while you're in there," Barber said. "And hurry up. I gotta pee, too."

Wyatt took two steps, bent at the waist, and charged the rooster. "Come here you little loudmouth banty, I like fried drumsticks."

The chicken squawked, pirouetted, and dug his claws in for grip on the rough timber to gain traction. He flapped his wings for lift and sailed off the porch. On the ground, he trotted away clucking indignation, tail feathers majestically flared.

Wyatt laughed. "You chickened out, chicken." He went into the house.

Barber pushed on over and did five pushups before scampering to his feet. Standing on the front of the porch, he watched the rooster herd the hens. He thought about making plans – what he should do with Wyatt? Bring him along? Leave him here?

He thought about money, which he had very little of. He'd have to rob a bank, a gas station, a couple of soldiers, to get money to buy food. And gas for the car. He couldn't remember how much gas was in the car. And the pistol. The pistol's in the car.

He looked to the left, toward the car. The images, thoughts, and internal conversations ran through Barber's mind. His brain could barely keep up.

The car. He'd have to clean the blood out. He'd drive the car down close to the pond, that way it'd be easier to wash and wipe the bloodstains away. He'd get Wyatt to help.

Help. Wyatt said he wasn't going to help.

But he came here, to Tanner's place. He came this far. Maybe?

Barber turned toward the door. If Wyatt don't come along with him, then he'll spill his guts to Dudley. Dudley. The High Sheriff. An ornery cuss, too. Dudley had pistol-whipped Buster, beat him down on their own front porch.

Barber had run-ins with Dudley. The ration coupons thing and the car tires. Even Papa with his whiskey still, which Dudley destroyed with a pick-ax.

He remembered his Papa fighting a deputy in the front yard. His Papa knocked the deputy down and stood over him. The deputy pleaded for help, he'd lost his wedding ring. The fighting stopped, and everybody was looking for the ring. Butch found it and handed it to the deputy. That ended the fight.

All of us, Barber thought, have had run-ins with Big Jim Dudley. All the Beck men, except Babe and Billy.

Yeah, Wyatt would spill his guts all over Dudley's shiny Luccheses. Wyatt couldn't be trusted, even if he came along to . . . Dallas . . . or, San Antone . . . or . . . or, across the border. Villa Acuna, that's where it would be safer. Then after the war maybe come back. The *incident* would be old news, probably forgotten by then.

And Tub. Yeah. Tub Tubane. He'd have to make Tub pay for this trouble. Tub and Wyatt, they were in this together, it was all their fault. Yeah. They'd have to pay. When he came back from . . . wherever . . . wherever he ended up. Mexico, maybe. He'd have to leave Palomino, for sure.

He thought about the pistol again, looked again to his left. He could see the rear bumper of the Willys.

He needed to go get the pistol.

He needed to pee first.

"Hurry up, Wyatt. I gotta go. Hurry up."

Fizzing in the nearest lantern attracted his attention. He moved closer, peered, and listened. He squinted at the short wick and small, linear, flickering yellow flame. He thumped the glass with his middle finger. He fiddled with the contraption. When he pinched and turned the burner knob, the lantern swung away.

Making his way through the front room, Wyatt announced his findings. "There ain't no food, there ain't no icebox, and there ain't no cold beer neither."

To steady the lantern, Barber reached up and wrapped his fingers around the chimney, absentmindedly. Reacting to the intense, blazing heat, he screamed and yelped and stomped his feet in an agonizing dance. Painfully shocked – unable to release the searing globe still in his grasp – he jerked his hand away and flung it aside.

Wyatt stood in the doorway buttoning his trousers. The lantern slammed into the doorframe. The seam between the burner and fuel reservoir split apart. Sloshing and spewing, flaming fuel splashed across Wyatt's face and drenched his neck, the front of his cotton shirt, and his hands holding the lead buttons. Fire swallowed the boy and engulfed the aged, Texas sun-dried wooden structure – both shrieked in excruciating agony.

Stunned, frozen in place, Barber gaped. He watched Wyatt twist, turn, slap at the blazes, and fall to the floor.

Barber closed his mouth with decided determination and jumped off the porch. He grimaced and cringed as Wyatt writhed in screeching, crying pain.

"Help me, Barber. Help me. Barber, help . . ."

Wyatt's voice trailed off.

In no hurry, Barber walked past the steps and climbed onto the porch at the other end. Casually, he took the other lantern off its hook and unscrewed the fuel cap. He aimed, did two quick practice tosses, and chucked the lantern through the doorway behind Wyatt. The spilling flammable liquid flared the pyre before exploding into a bonfire.

Barber jumped down from the porch and moved away from the heat. Transfixed, he moved his eyes to follow the strings of fire climbing the porch columns and gulping the desiccated shingles. Flicks of yellow, red, and black crept toward the top of the roof. Glass creaked and cracked. Now, he saw that the full structure was a roiling inferno.

Reflections of dancing calamity shone in his eyes.

The overhang collapsed, and the porch imploded.

In a dart for safety, three huge rats scurried from the house, ears pinned against small heads and their long hairless tails stuck straight out like pencils.

Barber waited until Wyatt's legs stopped kicking and his body stopped flopping before unbuttoning his pants and peeing in Tanner's yard. "You wouldn't be in this fix if you'd agreed to help me. You shoulda done the right thing. Now look at chu." He gave a mock salute toward the house. "Adios, Amighost."

As he buttoned up, the framing leaned toward the Willys.

The pistol.

Barber was afraid the house was going to fall on his car. He needed to get the pistol. He dashed to the Willys and flung open the passenger door.

The house made a crumbling rumble. Boards and ash crashed.

Barber looked up from fumbling with the glove box door button. Still focused on the house, he got the compartment opened and withdrew the .38 caliber, short barrel revolver. In reflex, he hastily opened and rolled the cylinder, eyeing the caps of six unfired cartridges. He closed and rolled the cylinder into its stop and held the gun in his hand.

The house sagged, tilted, and began a slow tumble toward him.

Barber staggered backwards from the car and turned away to run. His legs locked, he twisted an ankle, stumbled, and fell forward. He reached out with both hands to break his fall. When the heels of his palms hit the ground, his finger jerked the trigger. The gun fired. The slug punctured a hole into his temple. A volcano of blood spurted before spilling across his eye and streaming off the tip of his nose.

The burning building came plunging down onto the Willys. The fiery roof toppled off the crashing house and covered Barber. It took only a few seconds for the quarter-tank of Gulf gasoline from Wolf Hunter's gas station to ignite and erupt in a thunderous conflagration.

Safely away from roasting, the rooster and his hens gazed and clucked at the horrendous destruction. The boss flapped his massive wings and sang victory. Soon, they became disinterested in the goings-on of crazy humans, and the rooster's brood returned to pecking and scratching the black, dried dirt of Winston Tanner's place.

The month-old golden, fluffy clutch of curious chicks craned tiny necks to blink at the billowing funnel of black smoke veiling the high noon sun.

15

Tub explained how the boys put Mister Douglass on the front seat.

"At first everbody was quiet bringin Mister Douglass to the car. Porky was shinin his flashlight. Woodrow had Mister Douglass in his arms. Grover opened the door and I run around to the other side. There was a box of stuff on the seat. Woodrow said get the box outta the way and Babe, I think it was Babe, coulda been Grover, well it coulda been Porky. Anyway, somebody put it on the floor, behind the seat, or on the back seat. I think everbody was scared."

Twig placed a palm over his mouth and swiped fingers down his cheeks. He held the tip of his chin between a finger and thumb. He said nothing, waiting.

"What do you think they were scared of?"

Tub looked at the Mayor. "That Mister Douglass was dead." He looked at Twig. "I know I was." He looked at the Mayor. "Mister Douglass didn't move or talk after they put him in the car. Porky shined his flashlight on Mister Douglass and I asked if he was alright."

"You asked Porky?" Twig's voice was soft, inviting. "You asked Porky if he was alright?"

"No, Sir.   Well, yes, Sir, but I meant Mister Douglass. I meant was Mister Douglass alright."

"Did you ask what happened to Mister Douglass?" Twig asked.

"No, Sir. I mean, I sorta knew what happened."

Tub looked at the Mayor.

"Go on, Son," Casey said.

"Well, when Woodrow yelled . . . I mean it was a . . . it sounded like Woodrow was mad, that kind of yell. I've heard Woodrow yell before, when he was mad, I mean."

"What did he yell?"

"He yelled 'son-of-a-bitch'?"

Twig nodded. "Son-of-a-bitch?"

"Yes, Sir."

"Who was Woodrow mad at, you think?"

"Mister Douglass."

"Why, you think?"

Tub shrugged.   "I'm guessin, Mister Chestnutt. Woodrow yellin and Mister Douglass hurt, with a bloody face."

"Did you ask Woodrow if he hit Mister Douglass?"

"No, Sir. I thought . . . well, I thought . . ."

"Go on."

"I thought Porky had hit Mister Douglass with his flashlight.   Hit him in the face, and on his nose. I mean, it looked bad."

"Okay. Now, Mister Douglass is in the car. What happened next?"

"Woodrow said take Mister Douglass to the hospital, we'll meet you there."

"They didn't get in the car with you and Mister

151

Douglass?"

"No, Sir. There wadn enough room for everbody. By that time, everbody was awake and I think probably around the car with their lights. There was two other flashlights besides Porky's. Woodrow said git goin and I cranked up, turned the lights on, backed up, and drove to the road. In the headlights, I could see everbody was already runnin to the woods. I drove out to the farm-to-market road and turned to come to town. By the time I got down here, on the hospital street, they were runnin up, too."

"Who was runnin up?"

"Them. Woodrow and Grover and Porky and Babe."

"So they were there to bring Mister Douglass into the hospital?" Twig looked at Casey.

"Cross country, it's about a half-mile or so, maybe a little less, to Tanner's place," the Mayor explained.

"Through the woods at night? That quick?"

"There's a pretty good trail through the woods. And the way Tub had to come in the car is a mile-and-a-half, maybe. Less than two miles, anyway."

"I see." Twig looked at Tub. "So, they were there to help bring Mister Douglass into the hospital."

"Them and Doctor Gates. Somebody went inside, and Doctor Gates come out to help."

"Doctor Gates is in the hospital that early of a morning?"

The Mayor nodded. "I think Doctor Gates is there from midnight to mid-mornin. Doctor Burns is there too, late or early, sometimes. They come in and out all different times of the day and night. They're the only two we have. And Linda Salter and Agnes, Porky's momma. Geraldine is there too, but she's not a regular nurse like Agnes and Linda."

Twig took in a slow inhale and let it out slowly. "Is there anything else, Tub?   Anything else you remember? Anything else you want to tell me?"

Tub looked up at the Germans. "Are they Nazis, like in the *pitchursho*? On the newsreel?"

Twig looked at his prisoners. "I don't think so, Tub. Those boys have worked for me for several months out at the camp, and we've talked. I know them pretty good. I don't believe they're Nazis. They were in their Army just like your daddy and me are in our Army. Hitler is the Nazi."

"Do they talk like we do? In Palomino?"

Twig smiled.   "All three speak very good English, Tub.   Two of them, Duke and Will, lived in America before the war. Eddy lived in England for a while. They don't talk quite like we do here, in Texas, but they speak very good English. Anything else?"

"No, Sir."

Twig nodded at Casey.

"Okay, you can go on home," Casey said.

"Thank you, Tub, for talking with us," Twig said.

After Tub walked away, Twig spoke. "Tub seems like a fine young man, Mayor."

"He takes after his papa. Frank was a number one mechanic and he's a good family man. Tub's gonna be a good man, too. Who do you want to talk to next?"

Leroy's recollection matched Tub's. He admitted to being afraid and said he ran home rather than going to the hospital.

Emmett told about the boys coming into the house and opening the wrong door, the closet door, and Hale telling them where the bathroom door was. He said he stayed with Hale through the woods from Tanner's place because he had a flashlight, all the way to Hale's house. Then he ran home too.

Hale told much the same story as Emmett. Hale said he couldn't go as fast as the other boys so Emmett stayed behind with him, helped him down the trail with his flashlight.

After talking with Hale and Emmett, Twig told Casey he would pause for several minutes before calling the next boy.

When Twig looked up at the Germans, Duke nodded. Twig accepted it as a signal they were attentive and everything was okay.

"I'm gonna wait a couple of minutes and let the boys stew a bit, Mayor. They can see us but don't know what we're talking about. The order in which I want to talk to the last four are Grover, Porky, Babe, and Woodrow. Woodrow seems to be sort of a leader and the kingpin to this mess. I'm really interested in why he yelled. I have deep concerns why Babe was in the bathroom with Mister Douglass."

"When the boys were telling us where they were, I noted that too. There's something you need to know, Twig. It's about Mister Douglass, Clifford."

"You were going to say something about him this morning, when Nate walked up. You can tell me now, while I make the boys wait."

Casey looked up at the Germans, then over at the boys on the other side of the gym floor. "Well, okay, while the boys are waiting. I'll make it as brief as I can.

"A couple of years ago, um, maybe three now, Vernetta, Clifford's wife, had triplets. I had never seen anybody so happy about having babies than Clifford was. To look at him, and hear him talk about it, then, you'd say he'd be a perfect Dad.

"Well, there was measles goin round . . . "

Twig grimaced and frowned.

"Yeah, and chicken-pox, too." Casey nodded. "Yeah, it was a bad time here. Anyway, the babies got the measles, so did Vernetta. Doctor Gates, Pearly, was here by then, he'd been released from prison. Did six or seven years. The appeal court found him innocent – let's see, what do you call it, exonerated? I think the high court exonerated Pearly."

"Exonerated. He was innocent? The court said he was innocent?"

"Yes. He had been reinstated by the State, given his license back to be a doctor, and Doc Burns brought him to Palomino."

Twig smiled. "That's amazing. I've never heard of that happening before."

"Well, it was a rough go for him. People here didn't trust him, they were scared because of what he'd been convicted of doing, killing two elderly people with morphine."

"Morphine? The soldier's disease."

"Soldier's disease?"

"World War One. Medical people gave morphine to soldiers for their pain. It was called soldier's disease because thousand of wounded, maimed soldiers became addicted to morphine."

Casey looked across the gym, and pointed. Twig looked too. Two boys had their hands raised.

The Mayor and the Constable walked across Coach Byrd's polished floor.

"I need to go to the bathroom," Grover said.

"Me, too," Porky echoed.

"Okay," Twig said, "all of yall go on to the bathroom and come right back here, you hear?"

Twig and Casey stood alone. Casey continued.

155

"Pearly wanted Clifford to bring their babies and Vernetta to the hospital. He said he'd take care of them.

"But Clifford didn't trust Pearly, because of what had happened."

"I think you're going to tell me something very bad happened, Casey."

"Clifford's three little baby boys died."

"Jesus. Jesus Christ." Twig took a deep breath.

"And since that terrible tragedy, Clifford can't help himself."

"He feels guilty?"

"Yes, that, and the fact he's an affectionate, caring man. Always has been, as long as I've known him. So when his baby boys died, he turned his affection to boys, young boys. Somehow, in his heartbreak, we think he tries to make up for losing his babies by showing affection to boys."

Twig frowned and narrowed his eyes. "Is he . . . is he a . . ."

Casey shook his head. "No, not to anyone's knowledge. He's never pestered a boy in this town, and if he had, he'd be dead. I think you know that. No, he's affectionate, he's caring, he's . . . He means well, but some folks are wary. And of course, there's gossip. Clifford's aware of what some folks say, it hurts him, but he just can't help himself."

"Gossip can drive people crazy, I saw it in Vivian. Weldon Kreig couldn't stand the gossip about him. Broke his heart, put his shotgun in his mouth and ended it. A shame, too, cause Weldon was a good man."

The boys came toward them, and Twig pointed for the boys to return to the bleachers.

"Okay, Porky, Babe, Woodrow, you boys have a

seat. I want to talk with Grover."

Grover walked with the Mayor and Constable across the floor and they sat.

"Floyd would have a fit if he saw us walk across his floor as much as we have," Casey said.

"Grover, tell us what happened," Twig said.

Grover looked across the floor. Casey and Twig followed his gaze.

"Not much happened."

Twig shook his head. "You know that's not true, Grover. Somethin happened. Mister Douglass is in the hospital."

Grover looked at the Mayor, glanced up at the three Germans, and back at Twig. "Yes, Sir. I know. We went in the house to go to the bathroom. It was dark. We were tryin to find the door to the bathroom. Woodrow had opened a door and told Porky to turn his flashlight on. That's when we saw them."

"Saw who?"

"The gowns, the robes."

"Gowns?" Casey asked.

"Robes?" Twig asked.

"Whatever you call them."

"What are you talking about?"

"Woodrow opened a closet door instead of the bathroom. That's when Hale said the bathroom was on the other side."

Twig persisted. "There were gowns, robes in the closet?"

"Well, I guess you could call em white sheets. Like the pictures I seen in books, like the KKK wears. They had patches on em, too, like a badge, like a badge the sheriff wears."

Casey and Twig were speechless, their eyes fixed of

Grover.

"You saw white robes in Mister Tanner's closet?" the Mayor asked.

"Yes, Sir. And the pointy things, like a dunce cap or hood, like the hoods I seen in the pictures."

The winding up wail of the volunteer firehouse siren sang with an ear-piercing intensity. Everybody in the gymnasium looked at the ceiling, listening.

"Fire," Casey said. "We've got to go, Twig. That's a fire call."

Casey and Twig stood. The Germans stood too when their guard looked up at them.

"Go home, Grover," Twig said. He turned to the other boys. "Yall go on home, I'll talk to you later. We have to talk about Mister Douglass, but right now Mister Shipp and me need to help with the fire call."

Casey looked across the gym floor and waved his hand. "Go now. Go on home."

The boys jumped up and dashed for the exit, Grover right behind them.

Twig beckoned his Germans. "Come, there's another fire we need to take of."

Eddy whispered to Duke and Will. "This is a crazy place. It is a wild cowboy town."

"It is wild like a horse," Duke snickered.

"*That's* why it is called Palomino," Will muttered.

The men followed the boys.

As the boys ran down the hallway toward the doors, Porter Skaggs and Floyd Byrd came out of the coach's office and intercepted the Mayor and Constable.

"Fire call," Principal Skaggs said.

"We're going," Casey said.

"Where're you goin, Floyd?" Principal Skaggs asked.

"To look at my floor," Coach Byrd said.

"Never mind about your floor, Floyd, come on we need to go to the firehouse," Skaggs said.

Once outside, the screaming urgency of the nearby siren penetrated their brains. They could see the screen of black smoke drifting over the school and slipping north with the southerly breeze.

Porter and Casey jogged to the edge of the building.

Porter pointed. "It's coming from the other side of the Katy station, the south side of the tracks."

Floyd, Twig and his Germans joined them. They could see the funnel of bulging, gray and black billows rolling and twisting toward the sky. A dark covering overhead floated past them.

"I think it's Tanner's place. Winston Tanner's place is on fire, where these boys and Douglass were last night."

Twig pointed to the jeep. "Mount up." The Germans obeyed. "We'll follow the fire truck, Mayor, and lend a hand."

The men ran to the summons; the boys ran for home.

16

He heard his mother come through the front door, but he remained still, quiet, in his hiding place.

"Portland? Are you home, Sweetheart? Porky?"

She went to the kitchen. He heard paper sacks rattling and crackling. She put several items on the counter, cans, boxes, fruit, bottles. He heard the refrigerator door open and close. Finely tuned in, he could hear her moving from room to room.

Her voice came closer. "I know you're here, Portland. I want to talk with you."

He made no sound breathing, but he felt a shortness of breath. His heartbeat boomed in his ears and pushed on the side of his neck. He tried to swallow the dryness in his mouth.

He no longer could hear his mother moving about. Then he saw her white shoes, her nurse shoes. She was standing next to him, three feet away.

He kept his eyes on her shoes, expecting to see them move away. Instead, he watched his mother kneel next to the bed . . . her hands came down flat on the floor . . . then her face appeared. Her eyes – filled with surprise – met his.

"There you are," she said. "Come out from under there and come to the kitchen, I want to talk to you. I'll fix a glass of milk and some cookies."

Porky watched his mother's hands and knees disappear before her shoes walked away.

He waited a bit.

Milk and cookies.

Porky smiled; maybe he wasn't in as much trouble as he thought he was.

"Come out from under your bed, Porky. Don't make me wait on you."

Her tone of voice told him differently.

He stayed under his bed, watching for his mother's shoes to return. He knew he had no choice; he surely couldn't wait until tomorrow when his mother left for work. Anyway, sooner or later, he'd need to go to the bathroom, get a drink, or eat. He decided to surrender and face the music. Porky crawled out from under his bed. He straightened his shirt and rubbed his face with both hands.

Head down, he plodded into the kitchen without speaking.

His mother was standing at the sink, peering out the kitchen window. Her back was to him, but she did not speak. Red and blue polka dots alternated and shifted positions with the slight breeze on the white linen curtains.

He noisily plopped onto a chair, head still lowered.

She looked over her shoulder at him, turned, and opened the refrigerator door. She withdrew a quart bottle of Borden's and poured.

She brought the glass full of cold milk, a saucer with four chocolate chip cookies on it, and placed them on the table in front of him. She sat back in the chair, across from him, legs crossed with hands in her lap. She pinned him with her brown eyes.

He focused on the milk and cookies trying to avoid looking at his mother. He was unable to avert his eyes from her silent stare, sneaking glances around the glass.

She waited until he had eaten two of her cookies and slurped half of his milk. "I heard the fire call," she said. "At first, we didn't know where the fire was or what was on fire. I knew the Mayor and the Constable would go."

He nodded and took a small nibble, chewed, and swallowed a gulp of milk. He knew that keeping his mouth occupied was a way to avoid the interrogation at hand. He just needed time to plan . . . plan his response, his exit strategy, although at the time he hadn't thought of it in those technically tactical terms.

Agnes also had a plan, a strategy. She would not confront or cajole. Rather, she'd let it flow naturally, as she knew it would because she knew her son.

"I knew they'd let you come home when they went to the fire." She smiled, leaned forward, and laid her palms flat on the table. "You haven't hid under your bed in seven or eight years. Since that time when you . . ."

"I let the car fall into the ditch?"

"Well, yes, that time, too. But I was thinking of Miss Evans' living room window."

Porky nodded affirmation. "I knew I was in trouble."

"Yes, yes, you were. Even though you were nine years old, you had learned long before the difference between right and wrong. You knew you had done wrong."

He licked remnants of smeared chocolate from his fingertips and washed the sweetness down with the last two ounces of milk. When he set the empty glass aside, he looked at his mother.

"I waited on the steps to tell Daddy."

"That you did." Agnes nodded slightly; her eyes twinkled with heartfelt warmth. "And he was so proud of you. But you were still in trouble about it."

Porky nodded again and shrugged. "We sat out there on the steps. Daddy talked to me about it. Said I was havin fun without thinkin about others. I was thinkin about myself and my game, without thinkin bout Miss Evans' house, and their property."

Agnes kept quiet.

Porky stared at the empty saucer. "Daddy said that my knowin I had done wrong was my punishment."

"And what else did he tell you?"

"He told me to never again use Miss Evans' porch-facing as a backstop for drop kickin my football in to."

"We had to pay four dollars and eighty-three cents to replace Miss Evans' window. She told me it took an hour to finally get all the little pieces of glass out of her rug. She was not happy."

"I *apologized*," Porky said apologetically.

Agnes nodded. "I know you did. And Miss Evans' told me how she felt so sorry that she was mad at you." She paused. "And what did you do? Three days later?"

Porky raised his eyebrows. "I didn't kick it so hard."

"And your father came home when you were doing it. He saw you do it."

Porky shrugged. "I was surprised."

"I bet you were. Me and your daddy were, too. And we were disappointed. After he told you not to kick your football against Miss Evans' house, you were right back there doing it."

She waited, focused on her son.

"You broke a trust."

He met her eyes and managed a slight smile. "I know. I wanted to go under my bed then, the second time. I knew daddy was goin to get his belt."

His mother nodded.

"But it wasn't bad, I knew I had it coming. I knew better than to kick my football against Miss Evans' porch."

"Your daddy didn't want to use his belt. He sent you out in the backyard to select the instrument for your punishment from the row of hedges."

Porky grinned. "I brought back a limb from one of the bushes. I pulled off the leaves to make a switch."

Amused, she shook her head ever so slightly. "You brought your daddy a twig. It was about the size of a Fudgsicle stick."

Porky watched his mother's eyes sparkle, and he smiled.

"I wasn't hiding when you came home, Momma."

"Oh, really?"

"I was thinkin."

"I see."

"About what happened."

"Uh huh."

"About what happened at Mister Tanner's house. What happened to Mister Douglass. I was thinkin about what I should do. What I should say to the Constable. I know he's gonna want to talk with me. He just let us go because of the fire call."

"Do you know how he got hurt?"

"Yes, Mam."

"Did you hurt Mister Douglass? Did you hit him with

your flashlight?"

"No. No, Momma."

The surprise that flashed across Porky's face brought relief to his mother.

Porky was puzzled. With slight hesitancy, he shook his head. "No, Mam. I didn't hit Mister Douglass."

"Well, then, I don't understand? If you didn't hit him, how did he get his nose broken?"

Porky spoke slowly, remembering the sequence. "We were in the wagon and Grover, or Woodrow, said he had to use the bathroom, a number one. I did too. I drank too many Co-Colas. Somebody said just stand up in the wagon and go in Mister Tanner's yard." He paused for a response from his mother, an admonition. She waited. He continued. "When we went into the house to use the bathroom, Woodrow opened a door he thought was to the bathroom. He said turn on the light. I shined my light and it was a closet. There were white robes hangin in the closet. Grover said they was KKK."

Agnes' smile faded. She tried not to let the shock paint her face.

"I guess we woke up Emmett and Hale cause Hale said the bathroom was on the other side of the room. When I turned my light off, I couldn't see anything, it was so dark. I stayed next to Woodrow, touching his back as we went to the other side. He found the door and opened it. I turned my flashlight on, and Mister Douglass and Babe was in the bathroom. Mister Douglass was sittin on the commode. Babe was standin in front of him."

Porky stopped talking. He waited for his mother to speak. When she didn't, he continued.

"They both looked into the light like they was surprised, like we surprised them. That's when

Woodrow yelled and jumped into the bathroom."

Agnes found courage to move and dip her head as encouragement for Porky to continue.

"Babe turned around and put his hands up to stop Woodrow. I think he said no, maybe two nos, like no, no. Grover reached out and grabbed Woodrow's arm. But Woodrow is strong, so all three, Babe, Woodrow, and Grover slammed into Mister Douglass, and that's when he fell over."

"Fell over?   Mister Douglass fell over?   Mister Douglass fell on the floor?"

"No, Mam. He fell against Mister Tanner's bathtub. Mister Douglass hit his face on the side of the bathtub. Well, everbody fell in Mister Tanner's bathtub. They all fell on Mister Douglass, nobody hit him. I didn't hit him."

"It was just an accident?"

"Well, sort of. Yes, Mam. But Mister Shipp and Mister Twig thinks we tried to kill Mister Douglass. Woodrow said everbody is gonna believe we tried to kill Mister Douglass."

"Why did Woodrow yell and run into the bathroom."

Porky hesitated.   "Cause Mister Douglass was holding Babe."

"Holding him? Holding Babe?"

"Yes, Mam.   Mister Douglass had his hands on Babe's waist, on his side. His hands was on Babe's side like this, holdin him like this."

Agnes watched her son reach out and grasp an imaginary body.

"I see. I understand. Woodrow thought he was protecting Babe from Mister Douglass?"

"Yes, Mam, I guess so. Woodrow had told about Mister Douglass kissin Hale one time."

"Woodrow said that? About Mister Douglass?"

"Yes, Mam. Don't you remember?"

"Remember? Remember what?"

"We was sittin on the steps. Grover, Woodrow, and me. When you got the letter from the Army about daddy."

"Yes, I remember that. But I don't remember hearing Woodrow say that, about Mister Douglass."

"Well, we thought you did. So I guess Woodrow thought Mister Douglass was kissin Babe. When we went to the bathroom in the gym, Babe said Mister Douglass was askin him about why he was so sad."

"Babe was sad?"

"Yes, Mam. Babe tellin Mister Douglass he didn't know what to do about his brother."

"Which one?"

"Barber. Babe said he thought Barber cut Bobbette, with his big ole knife. He said he found Barber in their tree house. He said he told his brother that the Sheriff had come lookin for Barber and had asked their daddy about a knife. He said he told Barber to do the right thing and go to see the Sheriff. And Barber wouldn't do it. Babe didn't know what to do and was in the bathroom, in the dark, talkin to Mister Douglass about it when we came in."

Agnes's voice was barely a whisper. "Oh, my Lord. Oh, dear God."

"I saw Babe lookin in the campfire. He looked like he was lost or somethin. He said he started cryin when Mister Douglass asked him what was wrong. And after everbody had gone to bed was when Mister Douglass brought Babe in the bathroom, in the dark, to talk, so nobody would hear. They were talkin about what Babe wanted Barber to do. Babe said Mister Douglass was

167

just tryin to help, is all."

Agnes pressed her lips firmly together and put her right hand over her mouth while holding her left hand out to stop Porky.

"What's wrong, Momma?"

She brought her hands down and shook her head. "The fire. Mister Tanner's place was on fire. That was the fire call. Mister Tanner's house burned down. They found Wyatt and Barber out there."

"I guess they come out there to get Barber's car. It was parked beside Mister Tanner's house. Tub was gonna take Barber's car, but Babe yelled for him to take Mister Douglass' car, to take Mister Douglass to the hospital."

Agnes shook her head. "They didn't take the car. They brought them to the hospital this afternoon."

"Who?"

"Wyatt and Barber. When the Mayor and them went out to the fire they found Wyatt and Barber, there at Mister Tanner's place. Wyatt and Barber were dead, Porky. Both of those boys died. Wyatt burned to death in the house and Barber apparently shot himself. When they brought them in to the hospital, the Constable said Barber was holding a pistol in his hand."

Porky was unmoved by the deaths of two he knew. "Well, then, I guess bein a Boy Scout is over and done. There won't be no place to camp out. And I guess the case won't be solved neither."

Agnes was surprised that Porky showed no emotion. "I'm sure Mister Tanner can think of something for the Scouts. What do you mean the case won't be solved? What case are you talking about?"

"Remember when we were talkin about findin criminals, on the detective show?"

"Ellery Queen?"

"Yeah, that's one of them. They always found out who did it. And, there's the confession, they always say why they did it? We'll never know who cut Bobbette?"

"No, I guess not. Or why."

"We'll never know somethin else, too."

"What?"

"About the white robes."

"What about them?"

"We'll never know who they belong to and why they were hangin in Mister Tanner's closet."

"You've been listening to too many radio shows."

"I seen how the detectives work at the *pitchursho*, like Sam Spade did."

"Humphrey Bogart."

Porky's eyes widened and his mouth fell open. "The *pitchursho*."

"Yes, Humphrey Bogart was Sam Spade, a detective in the *Maltese Falcon*."

Porky jumped up from his chair. "*Casablanca*. At the *pitchursho*. I'm taking Sally to the *pitchursho*. I forgot. What time is it?"

Agnes put her hands together, gleefully, as if in prayer. "You're taking Sally to the *pitchursho*? How nice. I like Sally."

"I do too, Momma. I'm gonna ask her to be my girlfriend."

"How sweet."

"Can I have fifty cents, Momma?"

17

The Walking Liberty half-dollar his mother pulled out of her change pouch would pay for a night's entertainment for her son and Sally, his soon-to-be, hoped-to-be girlfriend.

She held the silver coin up at eye level. "I want you to walk Sally home after the *pitchursho*, you hear?"

He took it from her hand and stuffed it in his blue-jean pocket. "Yes, Mam. I always walk Sally home. Anyway, I wouldn't let her walk home in the dark. Girls are afraid of the dark."

Agnes smiled. "They are?"

"Uh huh."

"Who told you that?"

Porky shrugged. "Everbody knows that girls are afraid of everything. Spiders, a mouse, a snake, loud noises, they squeal and yell and scream like a . . . like . . . like a girl. Sally saw a bee one time and grabbed hold of me and held on tight . . . so tight I couldn't hardly breathe."

Agnes grinned. She reached out for her boy and hugged him. "One of these days you're gonna appreciate it when a girl grabs you and holds you tight. Mark my word." She pushed him back and straightened his hair. "Now, go have fun. Tell Sally I said hello. And hold Sally's hand. She'll like that."

He paused at the door. "I love you, Momma."

He hopped down the front steps and trotted most of the way. He passed the school, two churches, and the hospital. Using the small alley between Dulfeine's Grocery and Maybelle Winters' *Palomino Press*, he cut through the line of businesses and came out onto the Main Street sidewalk.

Across the way, in the bright lights of the marquee, he saw four adults and three children in line to buy tickets.

Sally was standing off to the side of the ticket booth; she was wearing her favorite dress. Porky felt a tinge of excitement and pride that a girl, his girl, was waiting for him. So were Rochelle, Bessie, Woodrow, and Grover.

Town was in its last stages of hectic activity for the day. Even though the slow passing traffic was sparse, Porky cautiously looked both ways before jogging across the wide thoroughfare. Dozens of cars and pick-ups were parked, angled-in, along both sides of the street. Their drivers and passengers were headed to, or inside, Jeeps Cafe, Kline's drugstore – the only store still open – or, the *Palomino Palace*.

Down the street at their station, near the water tower, Wolf Hunter and Caleb Joiner were accepting rationing coupons and pouring no more than five gallons of Gulf gasoline into vehicles' fuel tanks.

It was entertainment time now, time for leisure, time for a hamburger, corn chips or potato chips, and a glass of Royal Crown Cola, Coca-Cola, or Grapette in the cafe. A jukebox of relaxing cowboy music or songs sung by nationally renowned stars soothed the psyche.

After supper at home, folks would tune in to hear Edward R. Murrow's report from London. After the news, they would read a book, magazine, or passages from their Bible. Many of the men folk wanted to gather round the radio for a mystery program and become armchair detectives. Many of the women folk wanted to listen to their favorite vocalists sing the top ten songs on *Your Hit Parade*. Most often, with only one radio, the women folk got their wish. In the approach of the Labor Day weekend, a few could afford a cherished night out at the *pitchursho*.

A raging war was going on, on two sides of the world. Yet, in Palomino, there were no bombings, no threat of a sea invasion from Hideki Tojo or Adolph Hitler, no bunkers, no sandbagged anti-aircraft guns atop buildings, and no blackout. Citizens could enjoy the freedom from the fear that the conflict would reach their doorstep, as it were, in the last gasps of summer.

Admission prices to the theater had never changed, regardless whether it was an Academy Award Winner or a B-flick.

An adult ticket for *Casablanca* was ten cents.

A bag of popcorn was a nickel.

A cup of Coca-Cola was a nickel.

A box of Milk Duds was a nickel.

Porky developed a plan on the fly. For his plan to succeed, it depended on who was sitting in the ticket booth tonight. Porky thought he'd be able to buy tickets for a nickel apiece, the price for a child under eleven years of age. If he could do that, he'd be able to treat Sally to an ice cream soda at Jeeps afterwards.

On the other hand, if his plan failed, he'd end up

paying full price for a ticket. That meant buying only one box of the milk chocolates and sharing a bag of popcorn with Sally.

This was to be the last night for *Casablanca*. After its showing, Jake Little would rewind and secure the three reels of film in their tin containers. Like clockwork, he would tidy up his projection booth, centered in the balcony of the *Palace*, lock the door, bring the trio of cases down the outside stairs, and place them in the small lobby on the ticket-stub box.

After cleaning the theater, he would put the cans of film in a special lock-box out on the side of the building under the steps. Before securing the lock-box, Jake would unlock the chicken-wire cages on either facade of the theater, remove and roll the large paper posters for *Casablanca*, and stow them in the lock-box with the cans. In the wee hours, a driver would arrive from Paris, pick up *Casablanca* and the rolled posters, and leave the next film and posters in the lock-box. Mid-morning, Jake would bring the new film upstairs and load the first two reels on his projectors. Jake had been doing this for years. He had the process down to a tee. After loading the reels, he would go downstairs and retrieve the new posters.

Next morning, everyone at work or shoppers would occasionally glance out of store windows, anxious to see what posters Jake Little put up in the chicken-wire cages. Jake knew folks would be watching him, so he often played a game. He would come out to the cages, unlock the door, fiddle as if he were preparing to put up a poster, turn away, and go into the theater. It was his way to change the mundane monotonous chore and to create a bit of wicked entertainment.

"Hello, Sally."

"You're late, Porky. I've been waitin out here for you."

Humbled, Porky shrugged. "I know, I know. I ran most of the way cause I knew you were waitin on me. That sure is a pretty dress, I've always liked it." His smile shone with genuine infatuation. "Are you ready to see *Casablanca*?"

Appeased by his apology and compliment, she smiled. "We all are, Porky. Everbody already has their ticket."

The cue was obvious.

"Okay, let me get our tickets."

Porky slid the half dollar under the half-moon slit at the bottom of the ticket booth window.

"Two children, please."

Yvonne Leonard picked up the piece of silver and squinted. She lowered her fleshy chin and spoke, her tone friendly and amused.

"I don't see no children with you, Porky Baycann."

"It's for me and Sally."

Yvonne snorted and chuckled. "Yall ain't no children. A child's ticket is a nickel, and a child is eleven or under. Are you eleven or under, Porky Baycann?"

Busted, Porky tried a different tact. "No, but my cousin Sally, from Paris, is."

"I see. Is this your cousin Sally, from Paris, standin behind you? Sally Edmonds?"

Porky glanced over his shoulder and turned back to the ticket seller. "Two, please."

Yvonne grinned and nodded. "I thought so. Twenty cents." With fingers of her right hand each pressed on a coin, Yvonne pushed out three Mercury dimes. "You know what Miss Ruby'd do to me if I let you have a child's ticket?" She slipped the plump finger and thumb of her left hand holding the tickets under the glass. "Enjoy the show, all yall."

"Hey, friend."

Porky turned toward the voice. Sally and the others looked too.

"Are you done, Son?" a voice behind Porky asked.

"Yes, Sir." Porky moved away from the ticket booth. He walked to T J who stood at the corner of the theater. "What're you doin here, Butter Cup?"

"I'm goin to the *pitchursho*, just like you. Hi, Sally. Hi, yall."

"Hi, T J." Sally was the first to return T J's friendly greeting. The other four mumbled a weak 'Hi'.

"You didn't show up to pick cotton at Mister Church's field this mornin," T J stated.

"I know. We was bein held at the school gym. We was bein investigated by the Constable. He had his Germans watchin us all the time."

"The Constable? The Germans was watchin you? Wadchu do?"

"Mister Tanner's house burned down."

"Lordy Mercy. You set Mister Tanner's house on fire?"

"No. No, I didn't do nothin."

"Well, then, why you bein investigated?"

"Mister Douglass was hurt, he's in the hospital."

"Lordy Mercy, Porky, you done set fire to a house and hurt Mister Douglass?"

"No, T J. And, my momma told me that Barber Beck and Wyatt Posey died out there."

"They died out where?"

"At the house."

T J canted his head and narrowed his eyes. "You burned Mister Tanner's house down. You hurt Mister

175

Wyatt Posey. You . . . who died?"

"Not Wyatt Posey, it's Mister Douglass who's hurt."

"Who in the world is all these people you trashin up, Porky?"

"It's a long story. I'll tell you after the show is over."

Puzzled, T J shook his head. He pointed to his left. "The stairs to go up to the door is over there. I have to sit in the balcony."

Porky had forgotten why he was standing in front of the *Palomino Palace*. "We'll go sit with you in the balcony. We can talk."

Sally and T J said no, at the same time.

Porky glanced at Sally and turned back as T J continued.

"You caint go up in the balcony, Porky. And we aint supposed to talk while the *pitchursho* is goin on. You know that. Anyway, there aint no room up there for you. All them seats is reserved."

"For who?"

"For goodness sakes, Porky," Sally huffed. "For T J's people."

"That's right," T J submitted. "The balcony seats is the best in the house and they're reserved for us folks, the workin people of Palomino. We can see everything that goes on at the *pitchursho*."

Porky grinned. "You say *pitchursho* just like I do."

T J shook his head and matched Porky's beam. "Naw, I don't. I just say it like it's supposed to be said. *Pitchursho*."

"The show's gonna start any minute," Rochelle said.

"We better go on in," Bessie added. "We gotta get our Co-Cola and popcorn."

"We gonna go to Jeeps after the show," Porky said.

"Meet me here at the corner of the building after the show. I'll tell you all about it and something else."

"Okay, I'll meet you here. There's somethin I want to tell you too, Porky." T J turned away and scampered up the stairs. He stopped on the top step. "I'm gonna go to Paris." He waved, opened the door to the upstairs seating area, and disappeared.

Porky looked at Sally.

"Come on, Porky," Sally encouraged. "Let's go."

"Why is he gonna go to Paris? What is he gonna do in Paris?"

Sally answered as they approached the others. "He said he had somethin to tell you, so I guess it's gonna be about why he's gonna go to Paris."

Geraldine Skinner looked in the office first. The door was open, and the desk light was on. She expected to find him, but he wasn't there. She walked down the East corridor. Her white, soft-soled shoes, muffled against the black-and-white checkered linoleum, made no sound, not even squeaks or squishes. She stopped at each of the four rooms, peeking through the doorways. She made her way back, glanced at the empty chairs at the nurse station as she passed, and started down the opposite corridor. After looking into the other three rooms, she paused at the end of the West hallway, thinking. She focused on a door she had not opened and stepped to it. In a low voice, she called his name.

"Doctor Gates? Pearly? You in there?"

Behind the closed door, his reply was quiet. "Yes, Geraldine, I'm in here. I'll be out in a minute."

She heard the flushing, then running water. She stepped back and waited. She smiled when he opened the bathroom door.

He finished wiping his hands on the blue towel, draped it across the rack, and pulled the door closed.

"I was getting ready to go change Mister Douglass' bandages when I heard a voice. I thought it was you talking to someone. I went to every room. Miss Rogan, Mister Alexander, and the boy were asleep."

"I was about to make rounds, Geraldine. Bring your things."

"Were you talking to someone?"

"In the bathroom?"

"No, in one of the rooms."

"No, I came from the office to the bathroom. There's nobody here, except you and me and our four patients."

Geraldine shook her head. "I coulda swore I heard a voice."

Doctor Gates raised his eyebrows. "What did the voice say?"

"I dunno. I couldn't make out the words."

"Words?"

"Yes, maybe three, I think. Coulda been more. Strange soundin, too. Like cryin?"

"I didn't hear anyone talking or crying."

"Well, you were in the bathroom. With the door closed."

"Where do you think it came from?"

"I dunno. I was at my desk. That's why I went to everbody's room down there and to Mister Douglass."

"Well, let's go have a look."

Doctor and nurse made rounds. He checked their patient. She took vitals, wrote the information on the record attached to the clipboard, and tidied up.

Clifford Douglass was in the last room they entered.

The scent of raw alcohol permeated the small enclosure. A 15-watt bulb in a bedside table lamp gave off a dim light. Mister Douglass lay on his back, his arms and hands on top of the folded white sheet across his stomach.

Geraldine wrapped the blood pressure cuff around Douglass' left bicep.

Gates placed his stethoscope on an artery on the inside of the arm over the elbow. He squeezed the rubber bulb to pump air through the tube to the cuff and watched the pointer on the dial climb to 180 systolic. He listened to the heartbeat as pressure in the cuff tapered off to the diastolic, the lower number. Satisfied, Gates nodded, and Geraldine removed the cuff.

"Blood pressure is elevated, probably due to his intense pain."

"But he's in a coma, Doctor. How can he feel pain?"

"The body works in mysterious ways, Geraldine. Bring a vial of morphine and a syringe, please."

"Morphine?"

"Yes, I'll relieve his pain with morphine."

"But . . . but . . . I don't mean to question . . ."

Gates looked at his nurse. "You just did, Geraldine. Speak your mind."

"Morphine. It's what you . . ."

"It's what I've used on many patients. It's okay, Geraldine. Bring a vial and a syringe, please."

Geraldine left the room. Gates stood by Douglass' bed. While he waited for the medication, he searched his patient's closed face and wondered. He spoke softly, his words soothing for a soul in pain, in need.

It took longer than normal for her to return; when she did, she did not have the vial of morphine or a syringe.

"I called Doctor Burns. He told me to ask you to wait about the morphine until he gets here. Please don't be mad at me."

Greffen Gates took a deep breath. "That's okay, Geraldine. I'm not mad at you. I guess I'll have to live with distrust for the rest of my life."

"I just wanted to do the right thing, Doctor."

"I know, Geraldine. I know."

"It's better when Doctor Burns is here. Maybe he'll agree with you . . . about . . . about the morphine."

"Maybe he will. Why don't you go on back to the nurse station?"

She could not hide the concern in the tone of her voice. "What're you gonna do?"

"I'll wait for Doctor Burns."

"Here? Here, in Mister Douglass' room?"

"Yes."

"Maybe I should wait in here with you till Doctor Burns gets here?"

The doctor took Douglass' hand and pulled it up. He brushed the stethoscope aside and let the hand rest on his chest.

Clifford Douglass moaned but did not move.

"Oh, my," Geraldine whispered.

"Clifford, we are waiting. We're waiting here, in the room, for you."

Douglass' grunt sounded like a person clearing their throat before speaking.

"Clifford, can you see my light? Come to me, Clifford."

Geraldine stared at the side of Doctor Gates' face. In the diminished light, she focused on his closed eyelids. She could tell his eyes were darting behind the veil. Her mouth slacked into a gape. Her thoughts spun wildly, she imagined the doctor was in a trance – that she was witnessing a séance.

Geraldine spoke softly.

"Doctor Gates."

Her hesitancy was sincere. She was afraid, afraid of what she thought Doctor Gates was doing.

"Doctor Gates, can I help?"

Only their breathing filled the silence.

"It's okay, Clifford. They're safe now. They want you to know they're safe."

He laid his other palm across Douglass' forehead.

"There is no pain, Clifford. Come to us, Clifford."

Clifford Douglass' eye snapped open; he stared blankly at the two shadows on the ceiling. His voice was weak. "David? Daniel?" The Assistant Scoutmaster blinked twice. "Where's Donald?"

Geraldine's gasp bounced off the walls; its echo escaped through the doorway and careened down the hallway. "*Oh, my goodness.*"

Doctor Burns spoke from the doorway. "I'm here, Doctor Gates. Geraldine called about Clifford."

Douglass' eye clamped shut; a grimace gripped his face. He squeezed Doctor Gates' hand before going limp.

Burns stood beside Gates. His voice was quiet. "Did you bring him here, Pearly?"

"Yes. For a moment, Garland."

"I saw it, Doctor," Geraldine whispered.

"He had David and Daniel, but Donald wasn't here. I think I could have kept him with us if Donald had come along."

"His boys?" Geraldine asked. "His boys were with him?"

"Yes, almost, in his mind. That's part of his pain. A deep heartache."

Geraldine placed a hand on the iron frame at the foot of the hospital bed.

"I have to sit down. I think I'm gonna faint."

18

The kids entered the theater with Sally and Porky leading. All six dutifully fell in line behind several adults to present their tickets to Warrene Culp. As they shuffled forward, they could hear Warrene tell those in front about a drawing.

When it was their turn, Porky reached around Sally handing over their voucher of admission.

Warrene ripped the permits and handed back the ragged stubs.

"There's gonna be a drawin," Warrene announced. She raised her voice so all of them could hear. "Print your name on one of them little slips of paper and drop it in that there jar."

As one, the kids looked where Warrene pointed.

"Print, you hear me?" Warrene emphasized. "Print your name. And don't fold the slip of paper. Just drop it in the jar with your name printed."

"What's it for?" Bessie asked. "What's the drawin for?"

"A cook-out. Miss Ruby is gonna give a cook-out at the Porter House."

They grinned and moved as a squad to the table.

Grover was the only one who touched the lead of the Number 1 yellow pencil to his tongue before he printed his name. He kept dragging his tongue on his palette to swallow and rid the taste of the black carbon.

In only twenty seconds, they had printed their names and dropped the slips of paper into the jar.

Woodrow and Grover managed to submit five slips of paper for themselves.

"You can't do that," Rochelle chided.

"Who says?" Woodrow asked.

"It's against the rules," Rochelle retorted.

"I ain't heard about no rules sayin I can't put in as many as I want."

"Well, it isn't fair," Rochelle huffed. "I'm not gonna be a cheater."

"If I win I'll invite you to my party at Miss Ruby's Porter House. Then you'll think it was fair."

"She said it was a cook-out," Rochelle retorted.

"Whatever."

Bessie printed her name on two more slips of paper, and bent the edges of the strips. She reached into the jar and stirred the paper, dropping her two new slips on top.

"What're you doin?" Woodrow asked.

"I'm mixin up the names."

"Well, you ain't supposed to do that."

"Why not?"

"Cause."

Rochelle was exasperated. "So, now *you* makin up the rules?"

"It don't make no difference. Ain't none of us gonna win anyway."

"You never know. We might win. Luck of the

draw," Bessie said.

Grover pointed at the jar. "You see how many slips of paper is in the jar? Anyway, if I win, Miss Ruby ain't gonna bake no cake for me."

"Why you say that, Grover?" Porky asked.

"Cause."

Bessie pinned him with a stare. "You did somethin to Miss Ruby, didnchu? You always into somethin, always messin up or messin around. Tell whachu did."

"I was smokin in her barn."

"Good gracious, Grover."

"Well, I didn't think she'd ever come out there. Pinky and Patsy go in there all the time. They told me it was their smokin place."

"You'll set the old thing on fire and it'll burn down Miss Ruby's Porter House."

"Well, I was careful."

"Let's go get our stuff before the *pitchursho* starts," Porky said.

They all moved from the drawing table to the concession stand for their supplies.

With two of his three remaining dimes, Porky paid for a bag of popcorn, a box of milk chocolates, and two cups of Coca-Cola. With refreshments in hand, he led Sally down the right side aisle to the middle row of empty seats.

Sally followed her beau to the middle of the row and sat when he stopped.

Before he sat, Porky looked up at the balcony, searching for T J. He scanned all the faces peering down at him.

Woodrow led Rochelle, Bessie, and Grover down the row above Porky and Sally and chose a set of seats so Rochelle and Bessie would be directly behind the potential lovebirds.

Woodrow looked at Porky then turned and looked up at the balcony. He turned back to Porky. "Whachu lookin for?"

"I was lookin to see if I could see T J up there."

"Grown-ups sit up front, all the kids are on the back rows."

"How you know that, Woodrow?"

"I been up there one time."

The large screen brightened and Porky and Woodrow sat.

The bold white letters of *Coming Attractions* were superimposed across the scene.

"Heaven Can Wait." The narrator's trained voice was enthralling, exciting, demanding attention. *"He believed in love . . . honor . . . and . . . obey – that impulse. Spoiled playboy Henry van Cleve dies and arrives at the entrance to Hell,"* the barker proclaimed. *"A final destination he is sure he deserves after living a life of profligacy."*

With popcorn untouched and Coca-Cola unsipped, mouths agape, they watched in awe. The black and white scenes flashed by with the voice over continuing.

"The devil, however, isn't so sure Henry meets Hell's standards. Convinced he is where he belongs, Henry recounts his life's deeds, both good and bad, including acts of indiscretion during his twenty-five-year marriage to his wife, Martha, with the hope that 'His Excellency' will arrive at the proper judgment."

As the characters appeared in snippets of scenes, the children instantly recognized Don Ameche (*Henry*), Gene Tierney (*Martha*), Louis Calhern (Henry's daddy), and Spring Byington (Henry's momma).

They did not know Laird Cregar (*His Excellency*, the

186

Devil).

The screen faded to black.

"What is pro . . . prof-if . . . profiffaly-c?" Grover wondered.

"Profligacy," Rochelle corrected. "Prof-li-gacy. It means he's an immoral man."

Grover leaned forward and looked around Bessie. "Ain't you the smart one. Where in the world did you learn all that, smarty pants?"

Rochelle's exhaled annoyance was weighty. "Spellin bees. Webster's dictionary. Books, fool. I read books. Have you ever read a book?"

Bessie defended her boy, Grover. "I seen him read a funny book."

They did not even attempt to contain their convulsive giggling and snickering. Everybody was amused.

Everybody except Grover.

"I read books." Grover's voice was subdued. Defeat was evident; he spoke quietly. "I just finished *The Grapes of Wrath* about people goin to California."

They grew quiet in the three seconds before the bold white letters promoting *The Ox-Bow Incident* lit the whole room.

They filled their fingers with buttery and heavily salted popcorn and robotically lifted the snack to their lips. They chomped mouthfuls of the fluffy kernels and swigged ice cold Coca-Cola to wash the mush down. With eyes wide, they became immersed in the scenes as the storyteller guided them through the tale.

"*Gil Carter and Art Croft ride into a small Nevada town plagued by cattle thieves. Initially suspected of being the rustlers themselves, Carter and Croft eventually join a posse out to get the criminals, who also may be involved in a recent shooting*."

They all grinned as the featured actors appeared. They were familiar with Harry Morgan (*Art Croft*), Henry Fonda (*Gil Carter*), Dana Andrews (*Donald Martin*), and Anthony Quinn (*Juan Martinez*).

Their pupils had narrowed from the bright projection. When deep black swamped the room, they had no night vision, their eyes dilating to see in the darkness. The next dazzling installment nearly blinded them.

The *Universal Newsreel* logo appeared and for seven minutes, Lowell Thomas told the audience his latest observations about the war and spoke of President Roosevelt's nine trillion dollar victory loan, otherwise known as the war bond drive.

Finally, after devouring their bag of popcorn, dislodging sugary, sticky chocolate from teeth with sensitive tongues, and draining their cups of Coca-Cola, *Casablanca* started.

Sally reached out for Porky's hand. He intertwined his fingers with hers and, in the light of the huge screen, matched her sweet smile. She leaned forward; he met her lips in a soft kiss.

"Uh oh," a voice whispered. "It's gonna get messy."

"Good grief, Grover, why don't you be quiet and mind your own business."

"You are my business, Bessie Bee. Give me a kiss to hush me up."

And she did. Twice.

They followed the trials and tribulations of *Rick Blaine* (Humphrey Bogart), *Ilse Lund* (Ingrid Bergman), and her fugitive husband *Victor Laszlo* (Paul Henreid). They loved petty crook *Ugarte* (Peter Lorre).

Close to the denouement, the girls teared up as Rick

explained to Ilse that she would regret it if she stayed. *"Maybe not today, maybe not tomorrow, but soon and for the rest of your life."*

Their sniffles abated as Rick told the corrupt police *Captain Louis Renault* (Claude Raines), *"Louis, I think this is the beginning of a beautiful friendship."*

They all grinned with satisfaction.

Fade to black.

The overhead theater lights were blinding and the entertained covered their eyes with their hands. As eyes adjusted to brightness, all could see Yvonne Leonard and Warrene Culp standing on the stage.

Warrene was holding the jar filled with names on tiny slips of paper.

Yvonne's enthusiasm was exciting. "It's time for the drawing. Is everbody *ready*?"

The applause was encouraging.

"Drum roll, please," someone shouted, off to Porky's left.

"Pick my name," another hollered.

Warrene held out the jar.

Yvonne reached in and pulled out two slips of paper, one with a bent corner. She separated the two slips and dropped one back into the jar. She looked at the one remaining in her hand.

"I don't believe this," Yvonne said. She raised her hand and held out the slip of paper for Warrene to look at the name.

Warrene laughed and shook her head. "Whoda guessed that?"

A hopeful voice behind the children spoke up. "Tell us who the winner is, Yvonne."

Porky, Sally, and the others waited for T J.

"He's forgot," Woodrow said.

"T J's my friend. He don't forget a friend," Porky said.

"Why don't we go on to Jeeps," Grover said. "He'll probably come there lookin for you."

"Okay, I guess so."

They walked up the sidewalk together to the cafe.

Jeeps was crowded. Bobbie Jo Evans and Teresa Chestnutt were busy taking orders or serving pie and coffee to a dozen customers. Both looked up from their tasks when the screen door opened.

A dozen adult theatergoers quietly came into the cafe and moved to chairs at empty tables. Respectful of the present patrons, they talked in low tones about the great characters in the story they'd seen.

The six kids sat on stools at the counter – Porky, Sally, Rochelle, Woodrow, Bessie, and Grover. They did not organize the seating arrangement; it just seemed a natural set-up.

"Hi, yall," Bobbie Jo greeted. "We'll be with you in a hot minute."

Porky's voice was soft, congenial. "What kind of ice cream soda would you like?"

"Strawberry," Sally said.

Porky nodded. "I like strawberry, too."

Teresa appeared in front of them, order pad ready, pencil poised to record their request. Her smile was warm and friendly. "What can I get for you?"

She wrote each flavor of ice cream soda ordered and moved away.

They watched Teresa collect the glasses and set them in a row on the opposite lid of the ice cream chest.

Bobbie Jo appeared. She moved down the counter,

setting a small glass of water and a white folded napkin at each place. On her way back up, she laid a spoon and straw on top of the napkins.

"I hear yall tried to kill Clifford Douglass." The flat, accusatory voice was behind the children.

The chatter stopped, silence filled the room. The only noise in the cafe was the overworked motor on the red Coca-Cola ice chest.

As one, the kids turned on their stools.

Eliot Thurgood sat alone at one of the tables along the sidewall. He nodded; his face serious, showing no humor. "Which one a you boys beat on him? Or did all yall try to kill im?"

"That's enough, Eliot," Bobbie Jo said. Her voice was stern, authoritative.

Eliot persisted. "It'd been good riddance if yall'd succeeded."

Bobbie Jo reached under the counter. What she grasped stayed hidden. She moved out and stood at the end of the stools, her right hand along and behind her right leg. "I said that's enough. You leave these kids alone."

She paused.

The customers turned to look at Eliot Thurgood.

"Maybe it's best you go on home," Bobbie Jo said. "Your pie and coffee is on the house. Now, go on home, Eliot."

Thurgood stood and wiped his mouth with a napkin. He wadded the paper, ceremoniously opened his fingers, and dropped it on the pie saucer.

Porky slid off his stool and faced Thurgood. "Nobody tried to kill Mister Douglass."

"Porky. Porky, you sit down, you hear?" Bobbie Jo ordered.

"Porky?" Teresa whispered, "Porky . . . sit . . . down
. . . Porky." In a louder voice, she announced their
servings. "Here's yall's ice cream sodas." Quieter, but
commanding, "Porky . . . sit . . . down . . . now."

Thurgood stepped toward Porky. "We had a go in
the gin, Boy. You want some more?"

On her way to the other end on the counter, Teresa
picked up the butcher knife used to slice sandwiches
before she spoke. "Mister Thurgood, please, why don't
you go on home?"

Laird Weston and Pearson Keenan stood up. The
screeching, scraping noise of their chair leg bottoms
scooting on the floor was dramatic. Now, the cavalry
had arrived and was ready for battle. It wasn't only
Teresa and Bobbie Jo who breasted the bully of
Palomino.

Thurgood measured the opposition, scanned the
audience, and decided to capitulate. "I guess you're
right, Bobbie Jo. I'll be on my way. Thanks for the pie
and coffee."

All eyes followed Thurgood. He paused at the
screen door and pointed at Porky. "You and me and
that colored boy have some unfinished business."

Thurgood let the door slam behind him. The room
sighed; its loud exhale gave relief.

Weston and Keenan sat down. Their table partners
instantly engaged them in quiet accolades and
conversation.

Bobbie Jo walked behind the counter and released
whatever was in her hand. She placed both palms on
the counter and leaned out toward Porky.

"Sit down, Son," she directed. "Don't you ever do
that again to Eliot Thurgood."

Teresa shook her head. She propped forearms on

the countertop and thrust her face close to Porky's. "What in the world do you think you were doin, facin down that man? Eliot Thurgood is crazy mean."

Porky sat on his stool and grinned. "Mister Bennett said he's got bats in his belfry."

Bobbie Jo laughed. "Clive Bennett's got that right."

"I gotta go to the bathroom," Rochelle said.

All three girls stood.

Teresa chuckled.   "Don't be gone long, the ice cream sodas will turn to slush."

Bessie, Rochelle, and Sally headed for the restroom.

Teresa and Bobbie Jo leaned on the counter again; their faces close to Porky.

Bobbie Jo grinned. "Did you ask her yet?"

He shook his head.

Bobbie Jo's grin widened. Her blue eyes sparkled with curiosity. "Good heavens, why not?"

Porky shrugged.

"He's afraid," Woodrow said.

Bobbie Jo looked at Woodrow, then back to Porky.

"Of what? If you can stand up to the . . . to Eliot Thurgood, what in the world can you be afraid of, Portland Baycann?"

Grover snorted. "He's afraid that she'll say no."

Bobbie Jo straightened up and looked at Teresa. "They sure are takin a long time in there."

Teresa grinned, picking up on Bobbie Jo's clue. "I think I better go check to see if they're okay."

"Bobbie Jo," a customer called, "could we have some more coffee?"

"We'd like to order, too," one of the newer customers said.

Bobbie Jo's grin and effusiveness were contagious. "Well, we'll be right with yall. We gotta little love situation goin on at the minute."

Not a face in the cafe remained blank – smiles, grins, nods, head shakings prevailed.

Everyone was looking at Porky's face, which was redder than a ripe cherry.

"You stay right there, Porky. I'm gonna serve these folks and Teresa is gonna check on the girls in the bathroom. You've got some unfinished business to take care of." She picked up the coffee pot, check pad, and moved away.

Teresa tapped on the bathroom door. "Is everything okay in there?"

Bessie opened the door. "Yes, Mam."

Teresa went in.

Sally was sitting on the commode lid. Rochelle stood beside her with a hand on Sally's shoulder.

"What's wrong?" Teresa asked.

"She's scared," Bessie said.

"Of what, who?"

"Of what happened."

Teresa nodded and squatted at Sally's knees. She took Sally's hands in hers. "Eliot Thurgood is a bully, but I can't imagine that he'd have the gumption, the nerve, to hurt you, or any of you."

Sally shook her head. "That's not what I'm afraid of, Miss Teresa."

"What then?"

"That he'll hurt Porky."

"Porky shouldn't done what he done in there, Miss Teresa." The unease was clear in Bessie's soft voice.

"Mister Thurgood will be after Porky, Miss Teresa," Rochelle said.

Teresa stood and pulled Sally up into an embrace. She gently swayed, holding Sally tightly in her arms.

Her voice was soothing, reassuring.   "I will ask Constable Chestnutt to speak with Mister Thurgood. I know my husband will want to talk to Mister Thurgood, man to man. After that, I don't think Mister Thurgood'll bother Porky or any of you." She held Sally away and peered into the girl's eyes. "Would you like that?"

Sally smiled and nodded. "Yes, Mam. Thank you, Miss Teresa. You always are there to help us."

"All of my girls in Palomino are special to me. We got to stick together and stick up for each other."

Bessie, Rochelle, and Sally wrapped their arms around Teresa and held her in a loving hug for several seconds.

"Okay, let's go back. I'll make some fresh ice cream sodas. Okay?" She held Sally a moment longer. "And I think Porky wants to ask you something, Sweetheart."

Sally's grin was as wide as the Mississippi and her eyes shone as bright as a glowing harvest moon.

"I sure hope he does, Miss Teresa."

19

"What? Who?"

"T J Workman, Miss Ruby."

"Impossible."

"Warrene and I didn't know who it was, so we . . . so she . . . we . . ."

"Yvonne, you're telling me you announced this boy won the drawing for the cook-out . . . a colored boy . . . you made the announcement in front of the house full of people?"

"Yes, Mam. And he yelled from the balcony."

"I don't believe this."

The three stood in the Porter House foyer. Yvonne and Warrene twisted and balled their dresses in front of their stomach with nervous hands and fingers. They had difficulty holding their heads up to face Miss Ruby's wrath.

"How in the world could you both let this happen?"

Yvonne Leonard and Warrene Culp dared not look at each other for fear Miss Ruby would focus on blaming one or the other. Both of them felt verbally whipped, chastised, and raked over Miss Ruby Bostick's hot coals.

"We . . . we didn't . . . we . . ."

"If he was sitting in the balcony how could he write his name on a little slip of paper, drop that little bitty piece of paper in a jar, when the little bitty piece of paper, the pencil, and the jar was in the lobby of the *Palomino Palace*?"   She waited for three seconds. "Well?"

Yvonne shrugged. "I dunno, Miss Ruby."

"Neither one of you knows how a boy who was sitting upstairs in the balcony, could put his name in the jar that was downstairs in the theater?"

"Maybe . . ."

Miss Ruby cut Warrene off. "Ethel. Julius."

"*Yes, Mam*?" Julius answered.

"Yes, Mam, Miss Ruby? I'm a comin," Ethel called from the kitchen at the same time Julius responded from the back porch.

In six seconds Miss Ruby's housekeeper and her husband, Miss Ruby's chauffeur, stood in the dining room doorway.

"Come in here." Miss Ruby pointed to a spot near her, which would be at arm's length – within striking distance.

Ethel could see the fear and anxiety flooding Yvonne and Warrene's faces. She looked at her employer's black eyes and saw only wide-eyed boiling anger. Miss Ruby's face was fire engine red, ticks of white spittle stuck to each corner of her mouth.

"There was a drawing at the theater for the cook-out . . ."

"Yes, Mam."

"And a colored boy won . . ."

"Yes, Mam."

"His name is . . . his name is . . ." Miss Ruby glared

at Warrene.

"T J Workman."

"His name is T J Workman. Do you know this boy? T J Workman?"

Julius, standing a half step behind his wife, her left shoulder shielding him from an easy smack on his head, nodded.

Ethel stood erect. She had weathered many of Miss Ruby's storms. "Yes, Mam, I know the boy. Thomas James Workman. He goes by T J."

Miss Ruby waited. "Well?"

"He belongs to Miss Irene, Preacher Adams' sister."

"What do you mean *belongs*?"

"T J's daddy was killed. His momma jumped off a bridge in Tacoma, Washington. The government put T J on a train in Seattle and sent him here to Miss Irene. She's his only kin, his Granmomma. He calls Miss Irene momma. He's a good boy. It's been hard on him losin his momma and daddy and comin down here. He calls me his Auntie."

"You're his Aunt? Julius is his Uncle?"

"No, Mam, no, no," Ethel said. "He just calls us that. He ain't got no kin no more, cept Miss Irene and Preacher. You know the boy, Mam."

"Where did I meet the boy? When did I meet him? I don't remember."

Ethel usually was truthful. Sometimes her truth was her own making.

"I think it was last month, Miss Ruby. Maybe the month before. Wadn it out on the back porch, Julius? When we cut a watermelon?"

Attentive, Julius agreed. "Um hum." He knew how to catch on to his wife's diversions; he'd lived with Ethel more than twenty-five years.

198

"Maybe he was just comin by here to pick up somethin I had for his momma, his granmomma, Miss Ruby," Ethel continued. "I'm sure when you see his cute face you'd remember him. You do remember don't chu, Miss Ruby?"

Ethel had turned the table, so to speak.

Trying to recollect, Miss Ruby frowned. She shook her head in dismissal. "It doesn't matter. Never mind, it doesn't matter." She pinned Yvonne and Warrene with a murderous glare. "We just can't have this. One of you has to tell the boy he can't have a cook-out here at the Porter House."

Both women's instant expressions showed shocked surprise. "Miss Ruby, there was a drawin. A lot of people put their name in the jar hoping to come to the Porter House for a cook-out. We named the winner in front of a full house of folks, white and colored. If you don't have a cook-out for the winner of the drawin then everbody, upstairs and downstairs, will call it a renege."

"If I do have a cook-out for a colored boy it'll be a scandal."

"Yes, Mam, but if you don't, everbody'll say you went back on your word. It'll be the talk of town by everbody for a long, long time. It might even be printed in Miss Maybelle's newspaper, and even over there in Paris in *The Paris News.*"

There in the foyer of the Porter House, the three white women spoke about the "problem" as if Ethel and Julius were not standing in front of them.

"Why don't you invite some of his white friends to come, Miss Ruby? Then it'll look like a cook-out for them too. I think T J would like for his friends to come with him."

The four women were startled Julius spoke.

Tank Gunner   **Porky Baycann**

"He has white friends? Who's his white friends?"
Miss Ruby asked.

"That Baycann boy, Porky, Portland Baycann,"
Warrene said. Warrene's face brightened. "That's it.
That's it. That's who did it."

Puzzled by the outburst, Miss Ruby shook her head.
"That's who did what?"

"Wrote his name. Porky Baycann wrote his name on
the slip of paper instead of writin his own name,"
Warrene's glee at solving the mystery was infectious.
She nodded at Yvonne for support. "Porky Baycann
wrote down T J Workman instead of Porky."

"Yes, I can see that." Yvonne nodded with relief.
"That sure sounds like somethin Porky would do."

"And his friends coulda done it too," Warrene
continued. "They might of filled the jar with T J
Workman's name on slips of paper."

"Who're his friends?" Miss Ruby asked again.
"Who're his white friends?"

"Probably the ones who run with Porky," Warrene
said. "There's Sally Edmonds, his girl friend. And
Bessie Books and Rochelle Tucker. And Grover Lindsey
and Woodrow Collins," Warrene said. "They all came
into the *pitchursho* together."

"I've seen Tub and Babe and Hale and Pinky and
Patsy with him too, Miss Ruby," Yvonne added.

"I don't know about that Bessie. And Grover, I
know he's been smokin in my barn. And I know Pinky
and Patsy smoke in my barn. It's a wonder they
haven't burned it down."

"I think that'd be the right thing to do, Miss Ruby,"
Ethel submitted. "It'll be a small enough group and
everbody'd be happy you honored the winner of the
drawin. You kept your word."

200

Miss Ruby sighed. "Alright. Alright. But just those friends, nobody else, you hear?"

""Yes, Mam," Yvonne said.

"I don't know why I let you talk me into having a drawing in the first place, Warrene."

"Yes, Mam."

"And there'll be no more drawings at the *Palace*, Warrene. You hear?"

"Yes, Mam."

Ruby Bostick looked at the hugely grinning faces of her two employees. "Now, who is going to tell this boy, T J Workman, he can come to the Porter House for a cook-out . . . and can bring his white friends . . . how many?"

"About a dozen or so, Miss Ruby," Ethel said.

"Alright, then. You and Julius will go see about it."

Teresa led the three girls back into the dining area.

"Where's Tina, Miss Teresa?" Bessie asked.

"She's at home with her daddy, at the Porter House. Miss Ethel and Miss Ruby are there too. Miss Ethel said she'd keep an eye on Tina if I needed help."

Bessie, Rochelle, and Sally took their places on the stools next to the boys – their *dates*.

Bobbie Jo raised her eyebrows.

Teresa acknowledged the enquiry with a nod and smile. "Everything's just fine, Bobbie Jo. I'll make new ice cream sodas."

Bobbie Jo looked at Porky and winked. "Ask her," she mouthed.

Porky clamped shut his eyes and clasped his lips tightly together.

Bobbie Jo chuckled and nodded with understanding of Porky's shyness. She did not push his reluctance.

"How'd all yall like the *pitchusho*?" she asked.

"Nazis were in it," Grover said. "They wanted to arrest everbody and one of the . . . her husband . . . he wanted to get away cause he was tryin to hide and Rick had a letter from somebody and got mad at the piano player, Sam . . . Sam played the piano in the cafe cause . . . the police was looking for him . . . them . . ."

"Miss Teresa, are Mister Twig's Germans Nazis?"

The interruption stifled Grover who sputtered into silence.

Teresa's back was to her customers while she was digging into the ice cream tub and dropping scoops into the Coca-Cola glasses. "No, Rochelle, we don't think so. The General out there at Maxey said they're not. They worked for Twig at the camp. He was their guard and supervisor, like he is here. He knows them pretty well." She placed the desserts on the counter and the children went to them immediately. "They've said they're not Nazis, although when they were young they were in the Hitler youth programs."

"Do they have names?"

Teresa smiled. "Yes, Woodrow, they have names. They're just like us, they have the name their momma and daddy gave them."

"They're called Krauts," a voice behind the children said. "That's their name."

Bobbie Jo and Teresa looked toward the voice. The girls and boys turned on their stools.

"They're also called Heinies," a man said.

"Huns."

"Fritz."

"They probably worked in the concentration camps killin people."

Bobbie Jo used both hands, palms out, to wave off

the name-calling. "Okay, okay, we get the *pitchur*," she said, her voice friendly.

The girls and boys turned back to their ice cream sodas.

"Their names are Kraus, Edwin, and Wilhelm," Teresa said. "Like Portland's nickname of Porky, they have nicknames, too. Kraus goes by Duke, Edwin is Eddy, and Wilhelm is Will."

"Do they talk . . . do they speak English like we do?" Sally asked.

Teresa moved her head from side to side with a friendly grin. "Well, they don't exactly talk like everbody here in Palomino, but they all speak very good English.

"Will went to school near London, England for four years. That's where his father worked in a bank, in London. He said when he arrived at Camp Maxey, a toothbrush and toothpaste, a razor, shave cream, and soap were on his bed with a blanket, pillow, and clean sheets. He said at that moment, he knew he wanted to live in America for the rest of his life. Will is eighteen years old, the youngest of the three."

The cafe grew quiet. All of the customers were as intent as the children listening to Teresa tell about Twig's German prisoners.

Teresa detected the quietness and looked up from the children. Her eyes scanned the faces of the patrons who were staring at her with interested anticipation.

"Edwin, Eddy, is nineteen," Teresa continued, looking again at the children. "His hometown is near Frankfurt, Germany but he lived in Michigan for a while. His daddy worked at a Pabst brewery in Milwaukee but drowned in a boating accident on Lake Michigan. When Eddy and his momma went back to Germany, his momma got a job as a civil servant, working for the government. He wants to live in America too, after the war. He said his hobby is dancing, mainly the polka and the waltz."

Teresa looked again at the audience sitting at the cafe tables and included them in her telling about the German prisoners-of-war.

"Kraus, Duke, lived in Berlin. His father was a doctor and received a fellowship to study epilepsy at Northwestern University. For four years, Duke lived in Evanston, Illinois. He said he got speech lessons from a professor at the University. The professor was a family friend and was in charge of the school radio station so he let Duke read the sports news over the radio. Duke said he started at the radio station when he was fourteen and did that for three years. Duke is the oldest at twenty-one."

Teresa stopped. She waited for someone to speak. No one did, so she went on. "Duke and his family went back home in Nineteen-Forty. He said that the same day he finished communications school in Berlin the Gestapo killed his father. Duke said the Gestapo accused his father of spying for America."

Teresa looked at the children. "Duke said he listened to radio shows and news broadcasts and practiced saying what he heard. He wants to work in broadcasting in America after the war. He sounds just like an actor or a radio announcer when he talks."

Mouths remained opened, no one spoke for the longest time.

Grover's sucking on his straw and slurping up of the last remnants of ice cream and Coca-Cola broke the trance everyone seemed to be in.

"How about some more coffee, Miss Teresa?"

someone asked.

"Yes, more coffee, please, Mam," another said.

"You got a visitor at the door, Miss Bobbie Jo," a customer said.

Everyone looked.

"T J. That's my friend, T J," Porky said. "Come in, T J."

Sally's rebuke was sharp. "*Por-ky.*"

"Oh, yeah." Porky looked at Teresa, Bobbie Jo, and back to Teresa. "Can I bring my ice cream out to the sidewalk?"

"Yes. Yes, you may, Porky," Bobbie Jo answered. "And Miss Teresa will give you an ice cream to bring out to your friend."

Teresa cut out a scoop of strawberry, plopped it into a small Dixie cup, and stuck in a spoon. She handed it over to Porky.

Sally and the others followed Porky outside.

"Miss Bobbie Jo said you could have some ice cream." Porky handed over the paper cup.

"Thank you, Miss Bobbie Jo," T J said loudly.

"You're welcome, T J. Give Porky the spoon when you're finished."

"Yes, Mam."

T J sat on the edge of the sidewalk with his legs hanging over. His feet were a foot above the pavement. He began spooning the ice cream and guiding the sweetness and chips of strawberries with his tongue into his mouth.

Porky sat beside T J; Sally sat beside Porky. She hiked her dress above her knees and let her legs hang down too. The other children joined them.

"Um hum, this sure is good ice cream," T J said. "It's so cold it makes my head hurt if I eat it too fast.

But I like it."

"Why didn't you come to the side of the building when the *pitchusho* was over?"

"I had to go to the bathroom first."

"Did it take that long?"

"Have you ever been to the bathroom up on the balcony?"

Porky shook his head.

"Well, there's only one bathroom up there. Only one commode for everbody. So there was a line. All of us men had to wait until all of the ladies went in to pee."

The girls snickered.

"Then it was the men's turn, and it all just took a while. When I finally got my chance, everbody was gone cept me and momma. Momma helped clean up all the trash everbody left up there. Then the two ladies wanted to talk to me about the drawin."

"Where's your momma?"

T J pointed with the spoon. "Over there, in our truck. She's waitin till I tell you what I wanted to tell you."

"Watchu wanna tell me?"

"Well, the first thing I wanna tell you is I don't know if Miss Ruby gonna give me a party at the Porter House, but it sure was a lotta fun hearin my name called out from up there on the stage. I thought them two ladies was gonna faint when I yelled from the balcony that it was me, I was T J Workman."

Porky chuckled and shrugged. "I didn't think in a million years your name would be picked out of the jar."

"Well, none of us did," Sally said. "I didn't know that Porky wrote your name down instead of his, but I think it was nice of him to do it."

"Porky is my friend."

T J licked the remaining traces off the silverware and dropped the spoon into the cup. He handed the cup to Porky.

"Them two ladies said they'd have to talk to Miss Ruby bout it and they'd let me know what she said about givin a party."

"Well, that's gonna be the talk of the town for a while. If Miss Ruby gives you a party, can we come?" Bessie asked.

"You not supposed to ask somebody if you can come to their party," Rochelle said. "You supposed to be asked, not do the askin."

"You can come to my party at the Porter House, Bessie. And, you too, Rochelle. All of you are invited to my party at Miss Ruby's Porter House." T J paused. "When it happens. If it happens."

"Congratulations, T J Workman," a man's voice said behind them.

They turned and watched a man and woman walking away, down the sidewalk.

"Thank you, Mister. Thank you. Miss. Thank you."

"What else did you want to tell me?" Porky asked.

"I'm gonna go to Camp Maxey."

"Watchu gonna do there?" Woodrow asked.

"Sing."

They all leaned forward to look at T J's face, to see if he was grinning, playful.

"Really? Are you a singer?" Rochelle asked. "Are you a real singer or are you just foolin?"

"No foolin. I'm a real singer. I sung a lot over in Tacoma. I been singin since I was a child."

"Well, you are a child," Grover said. "We all are." He looked at Woodrow. "Ain't we?"

"You sound like one sometimes," Woodrow said.

207

"That sounds like fun," Sally said.

"What do you sing?" Bessie asked.

"Songs."

"Well, I know that, T J," Bessie huffed. "What kinda songs? Cowboy songs, Hit Parade songs . . ."

"Church songs. I was really pretty famous in the churches. I'd sing in one on Sunday mornin, sing in another on Sunday night. I'd sing at chicken dinners and fish fries. I'd sing in different churches on Wednesday Bible study nights, too."

"That's where you got all them sayins from the Bible," Porky said.

T J grinned.

The children fell silent, reverent at the mention of church.

"Sometimes, I got paid for singin."

"Why're you gonna go sing at Camp Maxey?" Sally asked.

"A Army Captain heard me sing many times up there at Fort Lewis, Washington. He was friends with my daddy and momma. His name is Captain Arthur Steinbeck. He's out there at the camp now. He asked me to come sing at the camp, they puttin on a show for all the soldiers."

"Will you sing a song for us?" Porky asked.

"Here? On the sidewalk?"

"Sure. Why not?" Sally asked. "I want to hear you sing."

T J looked down Main Street. In addition to the two small bulbs burning in the *Palomino Palace* chicken-wire frames holding the paper posters, he saw that lights were still on at Wolf Hunter's Gulf station. He leaned forward and could see lights through the front windows of Kline's Drugstore up the street. Farther down, the low-wattage yellow bulb over the front door of Henry Wilson's *Domeno Hall and Pies* was on.

"*Amazing Grace . . .*"

T J's clear notes sent chills through Porky and Sally. They stared at their friend whose voice was mesmerizing

"*How sweet the sound . . .*"

Talking and chatter in the cafe abruptly ceased.

"*That saved a wretch like me . . .*"

The rise in T J's enchanting tone echoed through the tough bones of Palomino.

Someone pushed open the cafe screen door. A half dozen people crept out onto the sidewalk and stood behind the children. Each onlooker, listener was careful to remain stealthy quiet.

"*I once was lost . . .*"

T J's momma got out of her truck and stood by it for a moment. She walked to the center of the street and stopped.

"*But now I'm found . . .*"

Bobbie Jo and Teresa came out. They wrapped their arms around the other's waist, moved by T J's gripping, powerful rendition.

"*Was blind, but now, I see . . .*"

Everyone on the sidewalk joined as T J sang the second stanza.

"*T'was Grace that taught . . .*"

Husbands put their arms around their wives, wives leaned their heads against their husbands' chests.

"*My heart to fear . . .*"

T J's momma walked closer and added her sweet voice.

"*And Grace, my fears relieved.*"

Kingston and Dora Kline came out of their

apothecary and looked up at the crowd in front of Jeeps Cafe.

"*How precious did that Grace appear* . . ."

"My goodness," Dora whispered.

Kingston put his arm around his wife. "I pray that our boy, Curtis, will be safe over there, Momma."

Henry Wilson and four domino players came out of Wilson's *Domeno Hall and Pies* and stood in a cluster, listening.

"*The hour I first believed* . . ."

Everyone stopped and let T J carry on solo. His expression on the last word of the sixth stanza hung in the night air as haunting as the call of a whippoorwill.

The applause was grand and lengthy.

T J, the performer, hopped off the sidewalk, turned to his adoring audience, and majestically took four polite bows. "Thank you."

In one voice, the adults showered T J with congratulatory praise. Coins and a couple of dollar silver certificates appeared on the sidewalk where he had sat.

"Thank you." T J could not stop grinning as he scooped up the money. "Thank you, one and all."

Many went back into the cafe; some lingered for a moment admiring the young boy with the golden voice.

"I didn't know T J could sing so good, Miss Irene," Porky said. "I didn't know my friend was really famous."

Irene laughed. "After he sings in Paris and Camp Maxey, he might be invited to Chicago or New York to make a record. He's got a beautiful voice."

T J collected two dollars and eighty-five cents. "This is a lot of money, Momma."

"We better be gettin on home," T J's mother said.

T J waved to his friends and walked with his Granmomma to her truck.

Porky watched the truck disappear into the night.

Peering into the darkness where the two red taillights faded away, Porky remembered what he wanted to tell T J. It was important, Porky thought, that T J and his momma know that he had seen three white robes in Mister Tanner's closet. Robes like he had seen in pictures in books at school, the white robes like the KKK had worn when they had marched down Pennsylvania Avenue in Washington.   Porky remembered those pictures and the white robes. He wanted to tell T J about them.

"I'd better get on home, Porky," Sally said.

"Okay, let me take this spoon back to Miss Bobbie Jo."

"Well, we gonna go on, too," Woodrow said. "We'll see you tomorrow, maybe."

The four children walked across Main Street and scooted through the small alley between Dulfeine's and the newspaper office.

Inside the cafe, Porky placed the cup with the spoon on the counter.

"Thank you for bringing the spoon back, Porky. T J sure has a wonderful voice. He's gonna be making records. Oh, I almost forgot to give you the check for the two ice cream sodas." Teresa presented the check. "That'll be twenty cents, please."

Sally looked at her beau with a pleased, satisfied smile.

She was anticipating their walk home and the question she hoped Porky would ask.

"Thank you for the *pitchursho*, popcorn, Co-cola, and a delicious ice cream soda, Porky."

Surprised by wartime price inflation for an ice cream soda, Porky pinched the lone, thin dime in his jean pocket.

Porky smacked his dry lips together.

He looked from Teresa to Sally and back to Teresa.

He tried to swallow the boulder lodged in his throat.

His mind found no words to explain his imminent default.

His heart found no refuge from the embarrassment he expected was sure to envelope him.

20

Porky pulled the lonely dime from his jean's pocket and laid it on the counter. As if it were a cautiously indecisive move in a championship checker game, he pushed the small, worn silver coin across with a single finger.

Teresa picked up the money. She understood the wide-eyed, flummoxed expression on Porky's face and smiled at the boy, empathizing with his predicament. "I'm sorry, Porky. You didn't know?"

He made the slightest head shake in response.

Sally leaned forward to peer into Porky's eyes. "What's wrong?"

Porky faced Sally. "Our ice cream sodas cost twenty cents. I only have a dime. I don't have enough money." He turned back to Teresa. "I don't have enough money, Miss Teresa."

"Last week, Miss Bobbie Jo had to raise the price from a nickel to a dime for a ice cream soda. Sugar rationing, I guess. And maybe the price of milk, too. So Blue Bell charged more for their five-gallon buckets. War-time inflation. The price for everything has gone up. Clothes, food, all that we buy costs more now."

Porky's face had drained of color. "All I have is that dime, Miss Teresa. I don't have another ten cents to pay for our ice cream sodas."

Teresa looked over Porky's head. Customers still in the cafe were watching, attentively listening. She winked at them.

They smiled, knowing a small Texas town game was about to begin.

She placed the Winged Liberty Head up on the black Formica and put her right hand on the countertop to prop her body. Teresa thrust her left hip out and placed her hand on it. She turned toward Bobbie Jo who was standing nearby.

Bobbie Jo saw the mischievousness in Teresa's sidewise, clamped lips.

"Miss Bobbie Jo?"

"Yes, Miss Teresa?"

Teresa dipped her head sideways at the ten-cent piece. "Mister Porky Baycann here doesn't have enough money to pay for two ice cream sodas. All he has is this dime, a wore out dime, enough to only pay for Miss Sally's."

"I see." Bobbie Jo raised her nose and eyed the boy, her glare ominous.

Bobbie Jo and Teresa watched Porky's Adam's apple bob as he swallowed with difficulty.

It was tough for them not to laugh and spill the beans.

Customers held their breaths; as children, they had experienced the same style of teasing going on here.

"What do you think we should do about it, Miss Bobbie Jo, if he can't pay?"

"I dunno, Miss Teresa? You think we should call

Constable Twig to come down here and arrest him?"

Porky's attempt at a formidable defense was weak. "I . . . I . . . I didn't mean to, Miss Bobbie Jo. If Ida been told a ice cream soda cost a dime now, Ida just ordered one for Sally. I wouldna had none, not even a strawberry one." Porky swallowed again.

"I don't think Mister Baycann can last a week in *The Calaboose*, Miss Bobbie Jo," a customer opined.

"A week?" Porky's squeak was faint.

"He'd go stir crazy," another customer chimed in. "Bad criminals can't stand bein locked up in *The Calaboose*."

Unaware it was friendly joshing going on, Sally turned on that customer, defiant. "Porky ain't no bad criminal." She asserted a defense. "I wouldna eat a ice cream soda neither if Porky hadda known it was a dime apiece."

Surprised by her aggressive tone and embarrassed they had provoked Sally's sharp anger, Teresa and Bobbie Jo backed off.

The teasing, good-humored mood in the cafe changed. A moment of fun at a child's expense became a sober realization; for the adults, the jolt was clear. Porky and Sally saw what was intended as play as a serious matter.

"We were just playin with Porky, Sally." Bobbie Jo spoke softly, soothing. "We were just foolin around. Havin a little fun is all."

"Well, it didn't sound like no fun to me," Sally snapped. "To me or to Porky."

Bobbie Jo moved around from the other end of the long bar and embraced Sally. "No, it wasn't, Miss Sally. It wasn't any fun for you or for Porky. We didn't mean no harm."

Teresa moved from behind the serving area and went to Porky. She took his shoulders, turned his back to her, and wrapped her arms around him. She whispered her apology in his ear.

The customer who had spoken about the small jail came up and laid a half dollar on the counter. "I'll make up for the shortage for Porky and Sally's sodas, and the rest is for the tip, please."

"Thank you, Jim," Teresa said. She swayed Porky gently and set the point of her chin on the top of his head. She met Sally's accepting, understanding smile. "Both of you are good kids. We were just playin."

Bobbie Jo offered appeasement. "Now, next time yall come in, I'll pay for a ice cream soda, okay?"

Teresa released Porky and turned him to face her. "Is that okay?"

Porky looked into Teresa's bright, friendly eyes and saw sincerity. He smiled. "Yes, Mam."

"Is it okay with you, Sally?" Bobbie Jo asked.

"Yes, Mam." Sally looked at the accuser. Her anger had not subsided. "Porky ain't no bad criminal."

Chastised, Jim nodded. "I know, Miss Sally. I know he's not. And I'm sorry."

"We're sorry, too," Bobbie Jo said. "We're all sorry. We shoulda known better."

"Well, we better be goin now," Porky submitted. He turned to Jim. "I'll pay you back, Mister Jim."

"No need, Porky. It's my small gift. Not for you to worry. It's alright."

"Everything is alright, Porky," Bobbie Jo said. "Yall go on home now. Be safe, you hear?"

When the screen door closed, Teresa busied herself cleaning up. She thought of Tina and felt remorseful to have teased Porky.

The adults stayed silent for a couple of minutes. Their eyes remained focused on the screen door.

Bobbie Jo went to the back bar and picked up the coffee pot. She poured the hot Joe for customers who wanted their cups topped off.

"They're good kids," someone said. "They're growing up fast."

"Sally wants Porky to ask her to be his girlfriend," Bobbie Jo said. "I thought he'd do it in here while they were eating their ice cream."

"Sally is fillin out," a woman said. "She's turnin into a fine young woman. I thought it was admirable the way she stood up for her man."

"Behind every good man is a woman," a male voice professed.

The women, *all* of the women in the cafe, huffed collectively.

"Well, behind that boy is a strong girl," one of them said. "She was onto Jim right away. She mighta takin him on, too."

"Sally is gonna be a leader in our community, in any community. She's always ready to help Malrie with the War Bond Drive. Many ladies said they'd never thought about buying a bond until Sally knocked on their door," a customer proclaimed.

"She helped Rita with the March of Dimes, too. I heard Sally collected over three dollars last month. They said she'd go door to door. When they opened their door, she'd hold her can out and shake it. The money inside made such a rattling racket people donated just to stop the clanging," another lady added.

Humorous chuckles recognized the visual.

"Three dollars?"

"That's what I heard."

"Eleanor said the ladies in her quilting party gave Sally two-dollars and thirty cents. She said Sally was so delightful and kind, it was hard to just say no."

"Well, I hope Porky asks her tonight," Bobbie Jo said. "She sure is sweet on that boy."

"I think they'd make quite a nice pair."

"Just like Patsy and her boy, Pinky. Now that's a pair of love-birds if I ever saw one."

"Two, Zandra. Love-birds are two."

"Well, you know what I mean."

"I don't know about Porky. Sometimes he seems so shy, the next moment he's the man about town."

"Well, Gene Autry sure took to the boy."

"I heard he had a tussle with Eliot over there in the gin."

"Yeah, I heard about that."

"Well, Porky's growing up. Remember all the antics his daddy told about – Miss Evans' window . . ."

"And the car in the ditch."

As one, they quietly laughed again.

Bobbie Jo had returned the coffee pot and was leaning on the counter. "It won't be long before he's ready to take on what comes at him."

"Yep, that boy is sure growing up. They all grow up too fast."

"How old are they now? Sally and Porky?"

"Fourteen? Fifteen? Fifteen, I think."

"Yeah, I think that's right. About the right age to start bein together."

"Yeah, well I asked Eve to be my girlfriend when we was ten."

Eve laughed. "You was ten, Darnell. I was eight."

Darnell snorted. "Eve and me been married goin on thirty year now."

Eve laughed again. "Good Lord. It's been thirty-four. You never could keep your numbers straight."

"We got six younguns of our own. Four boys and two girls. All growed up."

"Well, you got that number right, anyway," Eve said. She scanned the faces of their listeners. "Our boys are over there, like many of yall's are. One of our girls is in the Army, too. She's a nurse in the hospital down there in San Antonio. Where Agnes, Porky's momma, was."

"Their daddies are in the Army," someone said. "Sally and Porky's daddies."

"Porky's momma got a letter from the Army telling her his daddy is missing in action," Bobbie Jo said.

"What happened?"

"He was on a boat . . . a ship . . . or somethin, I guess, and it sank."

"Was it a torpedo? Bomb?"

"I don't think Agnes knows, she didn't say anyway."

"Where at?"

"Somewhere around Italy, or Sicily, or someplace like that."

"Did he drown?"

"We don't know. The Army said they couldn't find him . . . and a lot of others it seemed like. Maybe he did and maybe he didn't."

"Maybe Twig could find out?"

It became quiet.

The thought had never occurred to anyone in Palomino that their Constable, Military Police Sergeant Willow "Twig" Chestnutt, guardian and owner of three German Afrika Korps prisoners-of-war, might have connections.

To every person sitting there in the cafe, it now became important for them to know whether Twig could or would be able to find out what happened to Porky's daddy – or even locate Private Portland Alvin Baycann, Senior.

"I don't think Agnes ever thought of that, Jim. That Twig might be able to help. To find somethin out," Bobbie Jo said. She looked at Teresa. "Do you think he'd want to help?"

"Yes." Teresa nodded. "Yes. If I know Twig, I know he would. I think he'd go right to the top, to one of the bosses out at Camp Maxey. Twig would go straight to General Pace."

Sally led Porky across the street and through the small alley between Dulfeine's Grocery and Maybelle Winters' newspaper office.

They turned left and walked a block along the back street without saying anything.

Light from the full moon was bright enough they could watch their shadows precede them.

"Try to step on your shadow," Porky suggested. He raised his left foot and leaned forward.

Sally giggled. "You can't step on your shadow."

"I know. It won't stay still long enough for me to put my foot on it. Watch." He skipped-flopped-plopped, skipped-flopped-plopped, skipped-flopped-plopped but was unsuccessful at pinning his elongated shadow.

They strolled for many more paces.

"Why did you try to hurt Mister Douglass?"

"I didn't. It was Woodrow. Woodrow scared all of us when he yelled at Mister Douglass."

"Why did he yell at Mister Douglass?"

"I guess he thought Mister Douglass was kissin Babe."

Sally stopped. Porky stopped and faced her.

"Was he?"

"I don't think so. I mean, I didn't see him kissin Babe."

"What did Babe say?"

"He said Mister Douglass was tellin him everthing was gonna be alright."

"About what? Why would he say that?"

"Babe was sad and worried about Barber."

"Um. About Bobbette."

"Yeah."

"Bobbette was Tub's girlfriend."

"I thought Barber was her boyfriend."

"That was before."

They stood facing each other in the moonlight. On Pecan Creek, across Main Street, two blocks away, dozens of crickets chirped communicating their nightly mating calls. A dog wolfed at the man in the moon.

"Babe told us he thought Barber cut Bobbette."

"He mighta done because of Tub."

"Jealous, maybe?"

A whiff of tangy smoke found their noses. They could hear a man and woman talking in a low conversational tone.

"I smell Mister Crocker's Prince Albert pipe smoke," Porky said.

"I wish I had a cigarette," Sally said. "Do you have one?"

"Naw."

Betsy and Edgar Crocker sat in rocking chairs on their front porch, talking and watching the two children standing in the street.

"Who is that?" Betsy asked.

"Dunno, looks like kids to me," Edgar surmised.

Sally turned and stepped away. "They're dead, you know."

Porky fell in step and began walking beside her again. "I know."

"Wyatt died in the fire and Barber shot himself."

"Yeah. Momma told me they died out there at Mister Tanner's house. I don't guess I'm gonna be a Boy Scout."

"Why?"

"Cause of what happened. Mister Tanner's house is gone so there's no place to go, and cause of Mister Douglass. Everbody thinks we tried to kill him."

"You can still be a Boy Scout. There'll be another place to go besides Mister Tanner's house."

"Woodrow and Grover might know where we can go."

"They're your friends. They're Scouts. They'll want to continue."

"Yeah, I guess so. And the others. Hale, Tub, Pinky, all of em. And T J."

"Well, T J can't be a Scout."

"Yeah, I know. But that ain't fair."

"It's just the way it is in Palomino. You know that."

"Yeah."

"I like your friend, T J. Maybe he could be my friend, too." Sally took a deep breath. "He sure sings good."

They fell silent once more, walked around the corner, and headed up College Street.

"What're you gonna do after you finish school?"

"You mean after high school?"

"Yes."

"I dunno. I hadn't thought about it much. Maybe I could be a Constable like Twig. Or be in the Army like my daddy. Or maybe fly airplanes like my friend Gene Autry."

Porky stopped, looked up, and pointed at the moon. Sally looked up too.

"Maybe I could fly to the moon."

"There ain't nobody *ever* gonna fly to the moon, Porky Baycann. You know that. It's too far away."

He dropped his arm, looked at her face, and shrugged.

"Well, I guess I'll end up stayin in Palomino and pumpin gas for Mister Hunter like Mister Joiner."

Sally held his gaze. "Don't you have no dreams about whachu wanna do?"

Porky looked down then raised his head and avoided Sally's eyes. "The dreams I been havin is about my daddy."

"What kinda dream is that?"

"I'm in a boat and he's in the water. I have ahold of his arm . . . I'm tryin to pull him outta the water and into the boat. But I can't . . . I can't hold on." He looked into her eyes. "My daddy is gone."

He started walking again and Sally fell in beside him, her arm touching his.

In an off-handed way, Porky posed his question. "Wadda you wanna do?"

"Well, first, I wanna get married and have a bunch of kids. Four or five, maybe even six. Three boys and two or three girls. Then I wanna be a school teacher. I want to teach first, or maybe second grade."

"Like Miss Pruitt?"

"Uh huh. She's so pretty. Her beautiful dark eyes just give me goose bumps. And she smells so good all the time."

"I tried to bake some cookies for her when I was in

second grade."

"I remember that."

"They didn't turn out too good."

"That's cause you used salt instead of sugar."

They kept a slow pace, an unhurried stroll.

"Well, with five or six kids you gonna need a big house. And a husband who makes a lot of money to feed everbody."

They turned up Cherry Street. They stayed in the middle of the street instead of walking along the sidewalk. Porky kicked at a small limb lying in their path. He picked up the slim stalk and tossed it forward like a spear.

"And I wanna have a housekeeper like Miss Ethel is with Miss Ruby."

"Well, that's gonna cost a lot of money, then. All them kids and a big house. Where you wanna live? Here in Palomino? In the Porter House?"

"No. Not here. There's nothin here, it's a small town. I wanna go to Dallas. I wanna shop in Niemen Marcus. I wanna wear nice clothes. And buy perfume like Miss Pruitt wears."

"But this is where your momma and daddy live."

"I know. Palomino is their town. I'll come home to visit. They can come visit me."

Porky's fingers found Sally's and they intertwined without speaking. Together they lowered their heads and looked at their feet as they continued walking toward Sally's house.

"I'd like to go to Paris?"

"To the college?"

"Naw."

"To live?"

"Naw."

"Well, what for then?"

"To hear T J sing."

"He said he's gonna sing at Camp Maxey, too?"

"I sure would like to go there too, but that's a lot of drivin and gas. I don't know if momma would want to drive over there."

"Why don't you ask the Major for a favor?"

"What would I ask him?"

"Maybe the Major could talk to the Mayor and get a school bus so a bunch of us kids could go."

"You think so?"

"I do. I just thought of it, didn't I?"

"He said to come to him if I ever needed anything."

"The Major said that?"

"Yeah. When we was in the cotton field. Mister Church wadn gonna pay T J right and he'd picked more than me. I said it wadn right and the Major told me I was right and T J got paid the same. That's when the Major said if I needed anything to come see him."

They stopped in front of Sally's house. The porch light was on.

"So, you see. He could get a school bus for sure."

"Yeah, the Major's got a lot of money."

"He could even buy a school bus."

"Well, I better get on home."

Sally waited. She waited to hear Porky's words, his question. She held her breath in anticipation.

In the fleeting seconds, Sally realized that Porky was not going to ask. The words she had hoped for this evening were not to be. She sighed in resignation.

"Well, I'll see you tomorrow then."

"Bye, Sally."

She watched her beau walk away. She had not moved, standing in place, when he rounded the corner.

Sally went up the steps, opened the screen door, and turned off the porch light.

She sat on the porch, her feet on the top step.

Tears welled in her eyes, disappointment and hurt flooded her heart. She choked back a sob, her lips quivered with a sharp intake of August night air.

She shook her head and, in that motion, saw a figure running up the street toward her.

Sally stood, watching.

Anxious and puzzled, she swiped snot from her nose with the back of her hand.

She wiped away the tears with palms of both hands when Porky came into view.

He ran across the yard and stumbled. He threw his hands out to catch himself but fell onto the porch steps.

Porky lay prone on Sally's porch steps and moaned from the pain.

"Porky? My goodness."

"Sally," he gasped. "Will you be my girlfriend?"

She bent down and helped him to his feet.

Sally grinned, and the tears flowed again.

"Yes, Porky Baycann. I will be your girlfriend. Forever and ever."

Sally Edmonds bent down and leaned forward.

She passionately kissed Portland Alvin Baycann, Junior, her true admirer.

21

Love.

Love?

Porky felt differently.

He couldn't explain what just came over him.

After Sally said yes to be his girlfriend and kissed him – a kiss like one he had never experienced with her, his heart had fluttered.

Porky wasn't approaching the threshold of love; he had leaped over the line.

He felt . . . he searched for the word . . . he felt . . . he felt happy. Porky felt happy. He felt a happiness he'd never experienced until that night. Giddy happy.

He had never thought about love, as one might think about asking for mustard rather than mayonnaise and ketchup on a hamburger.

Eating a hamburger with Gene Autry didn't even come close to the dizzy, lightheaded excitement he felt after Sally's kiss.

Porky knew about love. He knew his momma loved his daddy and his daddy loved his momma. He had seen how deeply they loved each other by their affection and fondness. He had heard them say 'I love you' to each other, often, and knew they meant it.

He knew, too, that his momma and daddy loved him. They had told him so a kazillion times, and he felt their love in their warm embraces. In their love, he felt safe, protected.

He had seen how the actors at the *pitchursho* dealt with love, although at his age now, he knew they were pretending. But in a way, it was a role model for him . . . how the actors held hands, put their arms around each other, said soft, sweet things to each other, and kissed . . . a long kiss, sometimes. How they had sat together gazing into each other's sparkly eyes.

He wondered how they made actors' eyes so sparkly. And the women's skin so white and powdered looking. And the men's hair so black and shiny. He rubbed his fingers through his hair.

If Grover or Woodrow asked Porky if he loved Sally, the answer would be yes, even though he'd be embarrassed to admit it to them. Telling Grover in particular would be like the King sending out the town crier.

"Grover's got trouble keeping his mouth shut." Porky's soft-spoken words drifted out into the night breeze and floated who knew where.

If his mother asked if he loved Sally, the answer would be yes. Porky knew his momma would put her arms around him and congratulate him. He knew his momma liked Sally as much as he liked Sally. Maybe she loved Sally as much as he loved Sally. Well . . . probably not.

If Bobbie Jo or Teresa asked if he loved Sally, the answer would be yes. He knew how much they would tease him about it. But in the end, they would tell him they approved of the two of them being lovebirds.

I think I love Sally, Porky thought as he strolled down the moonlit street on his way home.

"No," he whispered, "I don't think I love Sally. I know it."

He walked a few more steps and said it aloud. "I love Sally."

"Really?"

Porky stopped in his tracks and looked up.

A man stood in the middle of the street, thirty feet in front, blocking Porky's path of travel.

The name flashed like a bolt of lightning through Porky's brain, along with a rising, frightening fear – *Eliot Thurgood*.

"So, you love Sally?"

Porky squinted. The voice didn't sound like Eliot's bullying whine. He tried to judge by size, but the figure didn't appear to be as large and as tall as Thurgood. In any case, he was not going to stand his ground and take any chances.

Mister Bennett had intervened in the fight in the cotton gin. Out here, alone, Porky was prepared to turn and run, to flee rather than fight. Porky knew Thurgood would kill him and leave ripped up and gnawed pieces of his shredded battered body in the street for somebody to find and everybody to know what happened.

His brain flashed the tsks tsks. *My, my poor Porky Baycann never had a chance. Just look at all the little chunks of skin and bone. Tsks, tsks, my, my.*

The figure moved toward him.

The smell of the strong whiskey was pungent even before Bastion Albert got close enough for Porky to see his face.

"So, you love Sally, do you?" Bastion asked. "Who are you and who is Sally?"

"It's Porky, Mister Albert."

Bastion stepped closer, now at arm's length.

"Ah, Porky, my boy." Bastion tottered, leaned in close to Porky's face.

Porky scrunched his nose at the biting aroma.

"How are you, Son?"

Mister Albert's speech surprised Porky. Bastion Albert's voice sounded like he always spoke, in a normal conversational tone, not the slurred, drunken way actors talked at the *pitchursho*.

"I'm fine, Mister Albert. Are you alright, Sir?"

Bastion straightened up, wobbled, leaned forward, and fell backward.

"Mister Bastion . . . Mister . . . Mister Bastion?"

Porky jumped forward and shoved out his hands to put them under Bastion's armpits. He decided against trying to help the man get up that way and went around to Bastion's head. He looked down at Bastion's face.

"Mister Bastion? . . . Mister Albert?"

"I'm down here, Porky. Help me sit up."

Porky reached down and with both hands grasped the man's shirt atop both shoulders and lifted, pushing Bastion up to a sitting position. Standing behind the man's back, Porky slid his hands under Bastion's armpits and tugged. The attempt was in vain. Bastion Albert's weight was too much for Porky to handle.

"I can't pick you up, Mister Bastion, I mean, Mister Albert."

Bastion laughed. "I know, Son. I know." He patted the pavement. "Sit here a minute with me." He patted the street several times. "Sit here with me and when I catch my breath then we'll be able to get my fat ass up."

Porky stifled a snickering snort at the amusing characterization – *fat ass*. The grin spread across his face. Fat ass. That's what Waldo was, a fat ass. Waldo was a fat ass bully, Porky decided.

He sat next to the intoxicated, very rich vegetable farmer.

"How have you been, Porky, my Boy?"

"I been okay, Mister Albert."

"I heard what happened. Cryin shame too."

"About what, Mister Albert?"

There was a pause.

Porky looked at the side of Bastion's face; the man's head was down, as if he was asleep or praying. Porky waited.

Bastion Albert's rumbling, rolling gut wrenching belch probably reached the outskirts of Paris. Bastion leaned to his left and grunted. His fart was a long whimpering whining whoosh of foul air.

"God, that felt good. Douglass. Clifford Douglass. Why'd you boys try to kill the Assistant Scoutmaster?"

Porky sighed. "We didn't try to kill Mister Douglass. It was a accident. Woodrow thought Mister Douglass was in the bathroom kissing Babe."

"Really? Woodrow thought that about Clifford? Woodrow thought Clifford was the kind who kissed boys? Really?"

"Well, Woodrow said he thought Mister Douglass kissed Hale, and if he kissed Hale then . . . well, he thought . . . he thought that wadn right. Woodrow thought he was protectin Babe."

"So it was Woodrow who beat up Clifford?"

"No, Sir. Nobody beat up Mister Douglass."

"That's what everbody was talkin bout tonight."

"It was a accident. Mister Douglass fell over and hit his face on the side of the bathtub."

"Everbody at the crap table said yall beat Clifford up. We didn't know why yall would do that."

Porky tried to imagine what a *krat* table was, what one looked like. He blinked three times, thinking.

"What's a krat table, Mister Albert? What's it look like?"

"Crap. *Crap*. Not Krat, Porky. Crap table. It's a table where men toss dice on it. They roll the dice on it. It has a wooden frame and a quilt or blanket covers the top. It's a table for a dice game. You ever heard of 'shootin dice'?"

"Oh, yeah, I know about that. Waldo has the dice. Shootin dice. Yeah, that's Waldo. But he don't have a krat table . . . crap table. He does it out in the street, dumps the dice against the curb. Sometimes he dumps the dice against Miss Winter's wall, there in the alley between her building and Mister Dulfeine's grocery store. I think he cheats. I think he uses different dice when it's his turn."

"You shoot dice, Porky?"

"I did a couple of times. With Waldo. We was in the restroom when school was goin-on. He took my lunch money evertime, so I quit."

"Well, I just won twenty-eight dollars and fifty-five cents, my Boy, at Blackie Beck's crap table. I was down over three hundred and won it all back, plus the twenty-eight-fifty . . . five."

"Mister Beck? Babe's daddy?"

"That's the one. That's where I got my refreshment as well. Blackie makes a mean strain, but it's good."

"From Babe's daddy?"

"That's the one."

Porky let the pause calm things down.

"Why do you drink, Mister Albert?"

"I used to have a drink now and then cause it was fun, relaxin after a hard day in the field. Now I do it to ease my mind, Son."

"To ease your mind about what, Mister Albert?"

"Life. Responsibility. Responsibility for others. This war. Some people can get through life without any waves. I don't seem to be able to. My situation is just the luck of the draw, I guess."

"I was in a drawin. Tonight."

"Really?"

"At the *pitchursho*. Everbody wrote . . . printed . . . everbody printed their name on a slip of paper and dropped it in a jar. Miss Warrene and Miss Yvonne did the drawin up there on the stage with all the lights turned on."

"Oh, yeah? What was the drawin for?"

"A cook-out. At Miss Ruby's Porter House."

"Really? That old bat is havin a cook-out?"

Porky turned away so Bastion could not see the huge grin. He leaned forward and looked up the street; he strained to hold in the out-and-out hollering laughter. Porky Baycann had never ever heard anyone address Miss Ruby Bostick as an *old bat*. Old bat. That was so good. He shook his head and covered his mouth to keep from yelling with mirthful hilarity.

Porky stayed focused on the long lane of emptiness. He wondered why a truck or car had not driven down on them, sitting there in the middle of the street in the moonlight.

Bastion Albert loudly yawned and exhaled.

"Did you win?"

"No, Sir."

"Well, tell me who won the drawin for the cook-out at Ruby's."

"T J won."

"Irene's boy?"

"Yes, Sir. Preacher Adams put us together when we was pickin cotton in Major Monroe's field. Miss Irene is his momma . . . his granmomma."

"I know the boy. Him and his momma . . . his granmomma . . . Irene . . . they come out to my vegetable fields and pick corn, beans, melons, squash, whatever sometimes. I really like the boy."

"T J is my friend. He said he's read a thousand books."

"He's smart as a whip."

"He knows a lot of Proverbs. He told me some of them."

"How could he win a drawin at the *pitchursho*?"

"His name was picked outta the jar Miss Warrene was holdin, the jar full of little pieces of paper. And Miss Yvonne reached in and pulled his out. She called his name out loud."

"Hum."

"When T J heard his name he yelled from the balcony. I thought Miss Warrene and Miss Yvonne was gonna faint. There was a lot of hoorays up in the balcony and a lot of hollerin and yellin down where I was. Some of the people wadn happy that T J won the drawin."

"How could he print his name on a piece of paper and put it in the jar?"

"He didn't, Mister Albert. I did it. I printed T J Workman on the slip of paper and put it in the jar. I never expected that Miss Yvonne or Miss Warrene would pick his slip of paper. Luck of the draw, I guess."

Bastion Albert roared with laughter. His glee turned into loud guffaws followed by a fit of violent coughing. He held his stomach before leaning back and laying on the street in boisterous merriment. He farted again, this time a rumbling locomotive blast.

Porky could not stop grinning.

Bastion's gasps for air followed his amusement. He lay quietly for a minute.

"You're always doin somethin for everbody, Porky Baycann. Will you help me get up?"

"Yessir." Porky stood, moved behind Bastion, and slipped his hands under the man's armpits. Bastion tightened up and this body movement clamped Porky's hands. Porky lifted as Bastion pressed the pavement with his Brogans, and in three seconds, the heavy man was up on his feet. Porky held on momentarily to ensure Bastion was steady then let go.

The vegetable farmer turned and put both hands on Porky's shoulders.

"You're always helpin young man . . . Porky. You helped me, I remember. At Nate's grocery store."

"Yessir, I did. I helped Mister Dulfeine help you, we was out there on the sidewalk."

"That you did. I remember."

"Your pants fell down."

Bastion snorted. "That was a sight to see, I reckon?"

"Yessir, it was."

Bastion Albert stepped back and smiled. In the pale cool light reflecting off the surface of the moon, he peered into Porky Baycann's shining eyes. He stuck his hand out for a handshake. "I'll be goin on home now."

Porky took the farmer's calloused hand and grasped

it firmly, man to man. "I'm gonna walk you home, Mister Albert. You don't seem to be steady on your feet, yet."

"I'd like for you to do that, Son. I'd feel right safer with you by my side."

Bastion put an arm across the boy's shoulders, and they turned together.

"You live the other way, Mister Bastion."

"That I do, Boy. You see, if you didn't walk me home Ida probably ended up in Hugo."

They laughed together and did an about face. Bastion put his other arm across Porky's shoulders and they stepped off, ambling down the street.

"You helped me at Nate Dulfeine's grocery store," Bastion repeated, "and now you've helped me again. Two times in one night. You helped me get my fat ass up off the street and helped me go in the right direction to get home."

"Yessir."

"You're a good boy, your momma and daddy raised you right. I've known you to be the one that always does the right thing."

Porky grinned, his chest swelled with pride. "Thank you, Mister Albert."

"Well, I want to repay the favor . . . the favors. Is there somethin I can help you with, Son?"

Porky didn't know what time it was when he bounded up the front steps. His stroll with Sally and the encounter with Mister Albert were happy spells, so the minutes didn't matter.

He knew his mother was home because the Chevrolet was in the driveway.

The huge fan he had built with his daddy was sitting

in the side door and running mid-speed.

He had helped his father assemble the three-foot-by-three-foot wooden frame and then painted it a very dark green.

His daddy had nailed a one-inch thick board across the mid-section and mounted the electric motor on it. He had spun the four blades to test clearance. Then he turned over the hammer along with small staples to Porky to pin the mesh screen on the front. There was no screen on the backside.

"Don't need one on the back, Son" Portland had responded to Porky's question. "Won't nobody think about reaching across the motor and sticking their fingers in the blades. But stuff happens, that's why you put the screen in front of the fan."

Porky could never figure out the fan business.

If the fan blew the air out through the screen door, he had wondered, how could the dispersed air travel out into the world and find its way back through the opened windows on all sides of his house, including the kitchen window at the back? Porky had yet to know about or study the laws of physics. He also had not realized that the fan was pulling the air back into the house through the windows and the breeze, the flow, had a cooling effect.

The light in the front window was on, so he suspected his mother was reading a magazine or listening to her radio program, or both.

When he noiselessly closed the screen door, she awoke from napping. A magazine lay in her lap. She had covered her nightgown with her favorite, button-less, raggedy, cotton housecoat.

"Hi, Momma."

"Where've you been?" She looked at the large,

round-faced alarm clock on the light table.   "My goodness, Porky, it's almost eleven. What've you been doing all this time after the *pitchursho*?"

Porky grinned at her friendly chastising tone, comfortable that he was not in trouble.

"Let me go to the bathroom and get a drink of water first. Then I'll tell all about what happened tonight."

"Well, go on to the bathroom, then come into the kitchen. I'll pour a glass of cold milk and put out a couple of cookies for you. Constable Chestnutt came by this evening. He wants to see you back at the school gym in the morning. He's bringing you, Woodrow, and Grover back to finish up about Mister Douglass."

Porky waited. He started to complain to his mother but decided against it. Instead, he only acknowledged her message.

"Okay, Momma.   But I have a lot to tell you, Momma. We can sit at the kitchen table while I tell you about Mister Albert's warts."

Agnes Baycann stopped mid-stride on her way to the kitchen. She turned around and faced her son. She canted her head with her question. "Excuse me?"

"When I got Mister Albert home, Miss Arlette . . . Miss Albert, said in spite of how much he drinks or what he does, she loves him warts and all. And I didn't even know Mister Albert had warts."

22

Agnes served the milk and cookies and sat across from her son. She found a mother's pleasure watching her boy munch the snack and wash the mush down. She smiled; her little boy was growing up. She resisted the urge to reach across the table to brush his hair up and off the eyebrow. She reflected on all of the precious time that had rushed past so quickly – her baby had pushed well into his teenage years.

"So, what's this about Mister Albert?"

Porky related the experience of sitting in the middle of the street. "When we started toward his house, Mister Albert said he wanted to show me the crap game."

"What?"

"Crap game. You know . . . they play . . . they throw dice on a crap table."

Agnes' mouth hung open. She stared at Porky. "You went to a dice game?"

He nodded. "It's behind Major Monroe's gin, over there on the other side of Main Street across Pecan Creek."

"I know where the gin is."

"Well, there's a spot where the table is . . . the dice table. The table is long and has high side boards all round. It looks like a big watering trough for horses or cattle. And there's a little edge on top of the boards where we leaned our arms on. It has a little platform all round too, to stand on so it's easy to look down into the bottom, they call it the pit. The table is on tall legs and there're two big lights hanging over it, really bright lights. A big cloth of some kind is laid over the boards on the bottom of the table. It looks like a . . ."

"Quilt? Spread?"

"No, more like a sack cloth. Oh, I bet it's cotton sacks sewed together."

Agnes nodded.

Porky continued. "When they shoot, they have to sling the dice hard to make them hit the end board and bounce back on the bottom."

"When they shoot?"

"Yeah, that's what they call it. Shootin the dice."

"Shootin the dice?"

"They get mad if somebody don't throw the dice hard enough, or far enough."

"Throwin the dice?"

Porky paused waiting for another interruption.

"Go on. This is fascinating that Mister Albert took you to a dice game . . . behind the gin."

Porky grinned. "When they shoot the dice they talk to em, they call the dice the bones, rollin dominoes, the ivories."

Agnes could not hide her amusement. She could not keep her mouth closed. "The bones. Ivories? Dominoes?"

"That's what they call the dice sometimes. They

blow on em too. And they talk to the bones."

"Um. What do they say?"

"Sometimes the bones are hot and sometimes they're cold . . . cold as a well-digger's ass in August."

Porky grinned at the shocked expression on his mother's face.

"Baby needs new shoes. Seven-come-eleven. Nina ross on a fartin hoss."

Agnes Baycann burst out in a choking guffaw. "Nina Ross on a . . ."

"Yeah. The point is nine when they call for Nina."

"You learned all those terms tonight."

Porky nodded, feeling safe his mother would not be upset. "And crap. Crapped out, too. That's when somebody throws snake-eyes, acey-deucey, or boxcars."

Agnes' head was in perpetual motion of denial.

Porky lifted the glass to his lips and let a thin line of white liquid slide into his mouth. He set the glass on the table, slid his tongue across his lips, and shrugged. "That's what I did."

She stopped moving. "What did you do?"

"Crapped out. My point was eight, a hard eight, and I threw snake-eyes."

"No, Porky. Oh, no. They let you play for money?"

"No, Mam. Well, yes, Mam. But it was Mister Albert's money. He bet a half-dollar and I threw a eight. Mister Beck said he had that bet covered . . . they called it even money. And the next throw I did was the snake-eyes. Mister Albert lost his half-dollar on me."

"Who is they?"

Porky thought for a minute. "Mister Albert. Mister Beck, it was his table. Henry Wilson, but he didn't play.

241

He sorta helped Mister Beck."

"His boy is dead and he's running a dice game?"

Porky understood the misgiving. He waited several seconds before speaking.

"Mister Stan was there."

"Stan Stern, Miss Maybelle's photographer?"

"Yes, Mam. And Miss Earlina and her twin sister, Miss Edwina."

Agnes nodded but held her tongue. "Um." She knew the reputation of the twin Cavanaugh girls and their family history. All had been in and out of the hospital clinic for one disease or another.

"And M D was there and Arty."

Agnes clamped her lips together and grimaced. "Those two. M D Draggert and Artemis Canton."

"Yes, Mam."

"Those two are a big mess. They're going to end up in big trouble someday. One day at the hospital, Geraldine said she thought those two boys were in cahoots with Ruby, Miss Ruby."

Porky could not recall when he last heard his mother speak ill of anyone. He knew M D and Arty had a bad reputation in town, knew they skipped school a lot.

Porky had heard that Arty had pulled a pistol on the school bus driver in Pattonville one time. One winter morning the bus was late picking Arty up. Porky had heard that Arty was cold, standin out in front of the house where he lived with his Aunt. When the bus driver opened the door, Arty pointed a pistol at him and told him he'd shoot him if he was ever late again. All the kids on the bus heard it, and that's how Porky learned about the pistol.

Porky had heard Arty bragging that Jimmy Madison, the Constable before Constable Twig arrived with his

Germans, had told him he'd put him in *The Calaboose* and throw away the key.

"Both have been in the hospital for patching up after fights or scrapes," Agnes said. "You just stay away from those two, you hear me?"

"Yes, Mam. Arty squeals funny when he loses his money and giggles like a girl when he wins. I think he's got bats in his belfry."

Porky's mother grinned again. "You like that saying, don't you?"

"Yes, Mam. Waldo was there too."

"What in the world are those grown men thinking, letting children hang around? I'm going to have to talk with Bastion about bringing you along."

Like a ship's horn blaring a collision course alarm, Porky's brain screamed *alert, alert, alert.* He picked up the miniscule crumbs with his finger and thumb while forming words in his mind. He swallowed the last drops of milk before he spoke. "No, Momma, please don't talk to Mister Albert about the crap game."

"Why not?"

"Cause, he didn't make me go. I was just walkin him home. He just wanted to show me where he'd been and what he was doin there, is all."

Agnes squinted. Her instinct or intuition or whatever it is mothers possess came into play. She knew, she just knew, there was something else. She pinned him with her half-closed eyes. "There's somethin else, Porky. What else?"

Porky took a deep breath. He knew he could not evade his mother's questions, there was no way she was going to let him brush them aside. He realized he had to *fess up*.

"Mister Albert is gonna do me a favor . . . some

favors . . . cause I helped him when he . . . when he was not feelin too good."

Suspicion clouded Agnes' peering eyes. Her voice was cautious, apprehensive, but stern. "What favors? What favors did Mister Albert say he would do for you?"

Well, now, imagine the Saturday matinee serial where Mister Portland Alvin Baycann, Junior is strapped down on that roaring conveyor belt rolling toward the gigantic whirling saw with a million angry, sharpened teeth about to gnaw his tootsies – or – being sealed in the soundproof room with no windows or no doors where a thriller novelist inadvertently had placed the protagonist. How in the world was the escape going to occur?

"It's about my friend, T J."

Agnes' facial expression changed. She frowned. "What about T J? What did he do? Are you two in some kind of trouble? What did you do, Portland?"

In the past five or six years, probably since the episode of his discipline for breaking Miss Evans' window, it was rare Agnes Baycann addressed her son as Portland. When she did, however, Porky paid attention. When his mother used Portland Alvin together, Porky knew he was in serious trouble.

He had blinked and blinked again in anticipation, not realizing he had not responded to his mother.

"Portland, I'm talking to you. Answer my question. Are you and T J in some kind of trouble? What did you do? What did the two of you do?"

Porky took a deep breath and let it out with his story. He told about printing T J's name, the drawing, and the winning. He told his mother about the ice cream for T J, his friend's singing on the sidewalk, and T J's invitation to Paris and Camp Maxey to perform.

Porky paused and swallowed. He gulped air. "We didn't do nothin, Momma. We not in any trouble." Porky swallowed again, this time with some difficulty. "I ask Mister Albert to help me get a school bus."

"What? A school bus?"

His voice was just above a whisper. "Yes, Mam."

"What on earth for? Why on earth did you ask Mister Albert to help . . ."

"To go to Camp Maxey."

Agnes closed her mouth. She sat back in her chair. She laid her hands in her lap and looked at them. She slowly shook her head.

"I've never heard of such a thing. A school bus. Why didn't you just ask me to drive you over there, or, if you're asking for favors, just ask Mister Albert to take you in his pickup?"

"I wanted a school bus so we all could go together."

"All? Who is all?"

"You and me and T J and his momma. And Sally and Miss Edmonds. Woodrow, Grover, Rochelle, Bessie, Hale, Babe, Tub, Pinky, Patsy, and their . . ."

"So you're the event organizer?"

Porky wasn't sure what an event organizer was. "If everbody had to go in their car then it'd be a lot of drivin. And there's a war on."

She smiled and spoke softly. "This is important to you, isn't it? To go see your friend . . . to see T J sing there? But, Honey, Mister Albert doesn't have school buses. They belong to the school. And besides all those you named may not even want to go."

"Mister Albert is rich. Maybe he could buy a school bus."

"Well, I know what you want to do but I don't think it's going to happen."

Porky closed his eyes and lowered his head.

Agnes felt sorry for her boy. She smiled. "You said favors. You asked Mister Albert for something else, something more than a school bus?"

"Yes, Mam."

His mother raised and canted her head to the right. She felt fearfully inquisitive. "What was the other favor you ask for? What did you ask Mister Albert to help you with besides a school bus?"

"To help you and me find out what happened to daddy."

After serving breakfast to the tenants in the Porter House, Julius drove Miss Ethel in Miss Ruby's 1942 black Crown Imperial Chrysler south down Main Street at a snail's pace.

"Why you goin so slow through town?" Miss Ethel demanded. "Everbody be lookin at us drivin Miss Ruby's car thout her in it."

"Um hum," Julius said. "That's the reason I'm doin it. I'm goin slow so folks can see we in her big car havin it all to ourselves."

"Well, you quit bein uppity. Miss Ruby'll hear about it soon enough."

"Well, she the one that we doin this for, anyway, Ethel."

"Now, you know bettern that. We work for Miss Ruby. We live in her house, we eat her food, and we take her money. When she wants us to do somethin, we do it. It's a job. And a good one. There's a war on, you know."

Julius was unmoved. "We don't live in her house."

From the back seat of the large sedan, Ethel looked out the window and nodded at gawkers standing on the sidewalk. "No, we don't live in the Porter House with her for sure, but we live in her house at the back. We don't pay no rent, neither."

"Miss Ruby oughta be doin her own bidness. Sendin *us* out to Miss Irene's and all. You know what Miss Irene's gonna say."

"Uh huh. And you know that's gonna be a big mess, too. Miss Warrene and Miss Yvonne got Miss Ruby in a fine fix alright don't you know it, callin out that boy's name in the *pitchursho* so everbody hear and see it. My, my, that woman is in a awful fix, any which way she go. If she does the cookout for him or if she don't. I swear to goodness."

At the junction of Highway 271 and Main Street, Julius stopped at the stop sign. Early morning traffic was thick. Heavy loaded trucks lumbered north along the highway going to Paris and Camp Maxey. Empty trucks from those locations roared south at high speeds headed to Mount Pleasant and the T and P railroad shops in Marshall to pick up another load of cargo.

He watched the huge trailer trucks, traveling salesmen in their shiny new cars, and military vehicles zip past. When he judged there was enough time and space, he pulled away and turned right on Highway 271. He accelerated and cruised north at the speed limit.

Two hundred yards before his turn off of 271, Julius stuck his left arm out as straight as he could. With his palm flat and fingers extended to signal a left turn onto Farm-to-Market Road 1503, he hoped high speed approaching traffic would not rear-end Miss Ruby's car.

Julius checked his rearview mirror and gritted his teeth as he watched a dark green East Texas Motor Freight tractor bearing down on him. The semi-truck driver pulled the cabin string for the air horn to blare his impatience at the black fancy car Julius was slowing for the turn.

They drove quietly along the two-lane road for several minutes. Julius slowed the sedan. He turned off the highway onto a dirt track Miss Irene used as a driveway.

He shut the engine and they got out. Miss Irene came out onto the porch, her smile inviting and genuine.

"My goodness. Hello. I didn't expect visitors otherwise Ida baked cookies to go with a ice cold glass of my homemade lemonade."

Julius followed Miss Ethel up the three steps. They cordially shook hands and exchanged pleasantries.

"Yall wanna sit in the swing and rockin chairs out here on the porch where there's a slight breeze or come inside the house where it's hot?"

"Why don't we sit out here," Miss Ethel said.

"Mighty fine," Miss Irene said. She gestured with her hand. "Pick your spot, swing or rockin chair."

Julius and Miss Ethel sat in the chairs.

Miss Irene sat on the swing but did not push it into motion.

"We come with a word from Miss Ruby, Miss Irene," Miss Ethel said.

Miss Irene nodded and smiled. "I see. Miss Ruby sent you out here. To give me some bad news I reckon. Why don't I go get us a glass of my freshly made lemonade first?"

Miss Ethel nodded. "Yes, please, Miss Irene. A glass of your lemonade first would be just right."

Julius grinned. "The more we talk about your sweet lemonade the thirstier I get, Miss Irene."

"I'll be right back with our refreshments."

The screen door had barely closed behind Irene when it opened and T J came out.

Julius leaned forward in the rocking chair and greeted the boy. "Hello, young man."

"Hello, Sir."

Ethel pointed at the swing. "T J, why don't you join us.. Sit here on the swing. We gonna talk with your momma about the drawin at the *pitchursho* and the cook-out at Miss Ruby's Porter House."

T J shrugged. "Okay." He moved toward the swing but stopped when Julius stuck out a hand. He looked at Julius, Ethel, and back to Julius.

"This is a big mess, you know," Julius said.

"Who for?"

"Miss Ruby. The town." Julius dropped his hand and leaned back and rocked slowly. "Your name and *pitchur* might even be in Miss Maybelle's newspaper, the *Palomino Press*."

T J walked past and plopped onto the bench; the swing wobbled with his weight. He pushed with his feet and the swing responded. He picked his feet and let the motion subside to idleness.

"Here comes some sweetness," Irene announced and pushed the screen door open with her butt. She brought forth the serving tray holding four glasses and held it so her guests and her son could take a glass and a napkin off the platter. She sat next to T J.

For several seconds, they sipped the cold drink in silence.

"Ummm. That is some good lemonade," Julius said. "You make it just right for my taste."

Irene probed. "Now, yall didn't drive Miss Ruby's car all the way out here to visit and drink my lemonade. I get the feelin somehow that Miss Ruby sent you about the drawin."

Ethel sighed.

Julius leaned over and sat his empty glass on a warped plank. He rocked back and folded his hands in his lap. He looked at T J first then at Irene. "The boy told you, did he?"

"Miss Ruby is in a awful fix about T J winnin this cook-out," Ethel said.

T J grinned. "My friend Porky wrote my name down and put it in the jar. I thought them two women was gonna have a fit when I yelled from the balcony."

"Um hum," Julius hummed. "Miss Ruby did have a fit when Miss Warrene and Miss Yvonne told her your name was called out . . . in front of everbody."

"Miss Ruby didn't want to do the cook-out but the ladies told her it'd be a mess if she *didn't* do it," Ethel said.

Irene nodded. She pushed with her toes and the swing swung. "When is the cook-out?"

"Well, that's why we here," Julius said. He looked at T J. "When would you like to have the party at Miss Ruby's Porter House?"

T J looked at his momma.

"After we come back from Camp Maxey, I guess," Irene said.

"Why yall goin to Camp Maxey? When yall goin?" Ethel asked.

Irene looked at her grandson. "T J's gonna sing for the soljer boys out there at the Camp. And maybe in one of the churches in Paris. That hadn't been fixed yet though."

Ethel's grin projected a pride that could cast the brightest shine on the republic star of the entire state

250

of Texas. "My, my."

"Captain Arthur Steinbeck invited T J to come out there to the camp to sing."

"The Captain went to the same church momma and daddy did in Tacoma. He heard me sing. I sung out there at Fort Lewis for him, too," T J said.

"When are yall gonna go? When are you gonna sing?" Julius asked.

Irene lifted a hand to gesture. "Saturday mornin."

"We could go over there Friday, but there ain't no place for us to stay the night," T J explained.

"It's just too dangerous for us to sleep in the car," Irene added. "So we'll leave early of the mornin."

"Um hum," Julius hummed.

"You got gas for that? Will the tires on your truck make it?" For Ethel, eighty miles round trip from Palomino to Camp Maxy might as well have been a thousand. In that time of rationing, everything seemed to be less in supply, harder to get, and more expensive.

"The Major gives me some of his coupons. The tires ain't bald yet."

A rattling drew their attention to the road. Julius rocked forward, searching for a clue who would be driving up the road.

Irene stood. T J put his feet down to stop the swing's wobble.

"That looks like Mister Albert's truck," Ethel said.

Irene moved to the front of the porch and waited.

"It is Mister Albert's truck," Irene said.

The truck turned onto the lane.

T J slipped off the swing and joined Irene. Side-by-side, they watched the pickup stop in their front yard.

"Somethin must be wrong," Julius said. "For Mister Albert to drive all the way out here of a morning, somethin bad has happened."

"Maybe it's about Preacher." Ethel's soft tone conveyed a mounting ominous feeling of bad news. "Oh, my goodness. Somethin's happened to Preacher. Oh, my. Oh, my."

23

"Sally?"

She woke at the call of her name. She stretched and curled her toes down. A big yawn accompanied the flip of the sheet off her chest. She pumped with her feet to push the cotton fabric off her legs. She lay motionless for several seconds.

"Sally?"   This time her mother's voice was demanding. "Get up, time for breakfast."

"Yes, Momma."

The child plodded to the bathroom. She sat, flushed, and moved to the sink. She washed her hands and face. She pressed the Colgate tube and lined her red toothbrush with a strip of white paste. She inspected and ran her tongue across her teeth then brushed them, and rinsed. She made her bed, dressed for the day, and went to the kitchen.

"I've made two slices of toast and two pieces of bacon for you," June Edmonds said. "Will that be enough, Sweetheart?"

"Yes, Momma."

"Butter and grape jelly are on the table."

Sally opened the icebox and pulled the quart bottle of milk out. She poured a half glass, replaced the top, and returned the bottle to its shelf. She brought the drink to her place at the table and sat.

In a coordinated routine, June placed the plate of breakfast in front of her daughter, lifted the pot off the stove, refilled her cup with black coffee, and replaced the pot.

Careful not to spill the coffee, June shuffled the four steps to the table and sat across from her daughter.

"Miss Belew called this morning. She said it was okay if you wanted to come so she could teach you how to operate her switchboard. Carsey said she would love to have you learn to connect the calls. Maybe you could have a part-time job working at the telephone company, helping Carsey."

"Maybe. I like Miss Belew, but she's a bit of a gossip."

June chuckled. "That she is. She listens in on people's phone calls. Sometimes she has told all the news before Maybelle can print it in the paper."

"Miss Malrie and Miss Rita wanted me to help them some more today. I thought I'd see what I can do. Miss Malrie says I do a good job with the War Bonds. And Miss Rita said I have a knack getting people to donate to the March of Dimes when they don't want to. I like to talk to people."

"I know, Darlin. And people like talkin to you. You're a good listener."

"Maybe I could do all three today?"

June blew on the hot coffee before taking a couple of sips. "So, how was the *pitchursho*?"

"It was good. I really liked the music, some of it made me cry, it was so romantic. There was a drawin after the show was over." Sally spread butter and jelly across both slices of toasted Wonder Bread.

"A drawin? For what?"

Sally told her mother about the events and aftermath at Jeeps Cafe.

June shook her head. "That Eliot Thurgood is crazy. You stay away from him, you hear. Porky had no business standin up to him, he's just a boy."

"Porky walked me home. We talked a lot."

June sipped coffee again and watched her daughter chew. "Um. About what?"

"What we want to be. What we want to do after school, when we graduate from high school."

June smiled. "What did you tell him you want to do?"

"I want to be a teacher, get married, and have six children."

June's mouth dropped open and her eyes grew wide. "What? Six kids?"

"Uh huh. Three and three."

"What did Porky say?"

Sally shrugged. "He said my husband needed to have a lot of money and a big house for six children."

June grinned. "So, he didn't say he was gonna be the husband with a lotta money to buy your big house and be the daddy of your younguns?"

"Well, I think he will."

"Oh?"

"He asked me to be his girlfriend."

June waited. She anticipated details but when none seemed forthcoming, she spoke. "And?"

"And, what?"

"And, what did you say?"

"Yes. I said yes. I've wanted to be his girlfriend

since second grade."

June nodded. Her grin remained in place. "Well, that's the first yes."

Sally crunched on a chomp of toast. "The first yes?"

"There's two more after the first one," June teased.

"What are they?" Sally washed the mouthful down with milk.

"The next is when you say yes to be engaged, to be a boy's fiancé."

"Porky's."

"Maybe."

"And the other one?"

"The other one is when you say yes when the boy asks for your hand in marriage."

"When Porky asks."

June raised her eyebrows. The grin had not faded. "Maybe. You both have a ways to go before that becomes an issue."

"I don't think so, Momma."

She paused to let her daughter finish the last bits of breakfast and drain milk from the glass. "Why?"

"I think Porky will ask me both times, and I'm gonna say yes both times. I want him to be my husband and I want to be his wife. And we're gonna have a bunch of kids."

June nodded and sighed.   There was sweet reminiscence in her smile. "I said yes all three times to your daddy. Your daddy and I married when we were seventeen. A Justice in Pattonville married us. You were born after we'd turned eighteen."

"I remember you telling me about that. You wore your purple dress with the white lace."

"I still have that dress in the closet."

They did not speak for several seconds.

"Is daddy alright?"

"As far as I know, Sweetheart."

"Will he go over there?"

"Probably."

"How old was daddy when he went into the Army?"

"Thirty-two. He was exempt because he is married with a child. But he wanted to go anyway. He wanted to do his part. And I didn't stop him cause I knew he'd be safe."

"How did you know that?"

"Your daddy is a clerk. He's an accountant out there at Fort Ord, near Monterey, California. He works in an office, like he did here at the bank."

"Porky said he had dreams about his daddy."

A cloud of somberness covered June's face. "Agnes didn't want Portland to go. He was exempt like your daddy. But men are men and he just had to join up, so she let him. Now, he's missing."

"Maybe they'll find Mister Baycann."

June shook her head. "When somebody is missing in action, the odds are not good, Sally. I don't think Porky and his momma should get their hopes up."

A few blocks from Sally's house, the urgent ringing of the telephone woke Porky. He heard his mother answer and lay still so he could hear the one-sided conversation.

"Hello? Oh, hello, Teresa. Yes, good morning. I'm fine . . . Really? . . . Yes, okay, that's good . . . I'll talk to him when I bring Porky to the gym . . . No, no, we've heard nothing from the Army . . . Yes, of course . . . Oh, I hope so too." There was silence. "I hope he will . . . That's very sweet of you to call and tell me . . . Thank you, Honey . . . Bye."

Porky didn't have to wait long for his mother's summons.

"Porky? Portland? Get up now. Get dressed, come to breakfast. Hurry up. We need to be on our way."

He obeyed and took care of his morning routine and chores before going to the kitchen. He sat in his place and watched his mother butter and spread peach jelly over two slices of toast. She placed the bread and a sausage patty on a plate and set it before him.

"Miss Teresa called this morning. She said Twig might be able to help find out about your daddy. Sergeant Chestnutt works for a General out there at the camp."

"Mister Albert is gonna help too."

"Well, the Sergeant knows the General. I'm not sure who Bastion knows out there, of any influence, anyway."

"I wish I didn't have to go to the gym."

"Well, it's the right thing to do. Our Constable needs to get to the bottom of what happened to Mister Douglass."

"Momma, everbody in town already thinks they know what happened. At the cafe they talked about puttin me in *The Calaboose*. Even Mister Albert wanted to know why we tried to kill Mister Douglass. Nobody is gonna believe whatever we say. Woodrow shouldna done what he did, he scared me when he yelled. We didn't mean for Mister Douglass to get hurt, it just happened."

Agnes sat across from her son. "I know, Porky. I know you didn't mean to hurt the man, but he's hurt. Bad hurt, so that's why the Constable wants to finish talking to you."

Porky finished his breakfast, Agnes cleaned the

dishes. "Go brush your teeth and go to the bathroom if you need to. We need to get moving. I'll drive you to the gym and talk with Twig before I go to the hospital."

Agnes steered the car on the streets to the school. The entire time along the route, they did not speak.

Porky could see the Mayor, the Constable, the three Germans, Grover, Woodrow, and Hale standing at the front doors of the gymnasium as his mother parked.

Twig pointed at the prisoners and pointed at the ground before he approached and greeted Agnes and Porky when they got out of the car.

"Porky," his mother said, "you go ahead while I talk with the Constable."

"The Mayor will bring everbody inside. I'll be there in a minute after I talk with your momma. Okay?"

"Okay." Porky joined the boys and followed the Mayor through the doors. The POWs remained in place.

"Teresa called this morning, Twig. She said somebody mentioned it might be possible for you to help find out where Portland is. To talk to somebody out there at the Camp. Maybe my husband is just hurt and still alive."

"We know the invasion of Sicily just ended. Patton and Montgomery swept up both coasts. The Italians surrendered. The German forces, a hundred thousand or more, fled. At Messina, they got across to the mainland and got away."

Agnes put her hand up. "I know all of this, why are you telling me old news?"

Twig shrugged. "I'm saying it so you'll understand how busy everbody must be over there."

Agnes nodded. "Too busy to look for Portland."

"I'm sorry, Agnes. It's a trite phrase but . . . there's a war goin on."

In spite of her worry about her missing husband, Agnes managed to smile. "I've heard that said in this little bitty town so many times I want to scream. Of course there is. We don't need a reminder every minute of every day."

"I'm glad you can be reasonable about it.

"Do I have a choice, Twig?"

"I know you're concerned. I can appreciate the anguish you must feel."

"Thank you."

"I promise I will raise it with my superiors." Twig paused. He glanced at Duke, Eddy, and Will. All three nodded their attentiveness. He reached out and touched Agnes' arm. "But you must be prepared for the worst news you did not ever expect to hear."

"That Portland is dead?" Tears shimmered in her eyes.

"Worse, I'm afraid, Agnes."

She wiped away moisture from her cheeks and dried her palms on her white nurse's skirt. She shook her head, puzzled. "I don't understand, Twig. What could be worse than learning that Portland . . . that my husband is dead?"

"Not being able to find him and bring him home."

"Yes, of course. I had not thought about it in that way." She nodded. "Of course, that's a possibility, but I never thought that would be the case. I don't believe, I can't believe, Portland is dead. In my heart of hearts, I believe he is alive. The Army just doesn't know it."

Twig took in a deep breath and exhaled slowly. "I know, Agnes, I know that's what you believe and wish for. In your work you have to deal with the families, the hardships, so you'll be better prepared than most if the news – whatever the news is – is that bad."

"Yes, of course. I suppose so."

A honking horn interrupted their seriousness.

Major Monroe stopped his pickup along the curb. He rested his arm and elbow on the open driver's window and his stump on the top of the steering wheel. "Good morning, Agnes. Mornin, Constable."

They stepped to the truck's running board.

"Can I help you, Major?" Twig asked.

"Actually, I came to see Principal Skaggs. Is Porter in his office?"

"Probably, the doors were open when Casey and I got here. We're gonna finish up talkin to the boys about Mister Douglass. Porter and Coach Byrd are probably inside."

"Well, I better be off to the hospital or I'll be late for work," Agnes said.

"I'm here because of what your boy asked Bastion about, Agnes."

The nurse frowned. "What do you mean, Major?"

"Your son had the idea that Bastion could get a school bus to bring him and his friends to Camp Maxey to hear T J sing. There must be twenty, twenty-five people your boy wants to go on the bus."

"Porky told me about Bastion offering favors. I was surprised when he told me about asking for a school bus. But he never said anything about twenty-five people."

"If I know Bastion he's gonna make it happen, Agnes. He's out there now, at Miss Irene's, to find out when her boy is supposed to be at Maxey. Bastion asked me to talk to Porter to arrange the school bus." He grinned and shook a finger at Agnes. "Your boy, Porky, has sure stirred the pot, Agnes. He's got everbody runnin round doin his biddin."

Agnes grinned. "He has, hasn't he. Should I call Doctor Burns and tell him I'm gonna be late?"

The Major shook his head. "No, I don't think that's necessary. You go on ahead to work, Agnes. We'll let you know the details when it's all worked out."

Twig and Agnes stepped back when Major Monroe eased the truck door open.

"Yes, of course," Agnes said. "I'll be on my way then." She turned away and went to her car.

Sergeant Chestnutt and Major Monroe waved as she drove past.

"Agnes asked me to try to find out about Portland."

"Do you think you can?"

"I'm gonna do whatever I can. I'll talk to General Pace."

Twig walked alongside Major Monroe as they moved toward the doors. Twig pointed and the German prisoners formed up in a column and silently preceded the Major into the building. "I'll speak to General Evans on her behalf, Twig. With you talking to the Deputy Commander and me having the ear of the Commanding General of Camp Maxey, we ought to be able to get them interested in finding out about Portland, for sure."

The Major stopped at the Principal's office door and peeked in.

The Germans stopped in the hallway.

The Major greeted the school Principal. "Hello, Porter." He turned back to Twig. "I'll let you know what kind of response I get from General Evans."

"I'll do the same, Major, after I talk with General Pace." Twig waved at the school Principal. "Hello, Principal Skaggs."

"Casey's in the gym with the boys, Twig. Hello, Clay. Come in."

The Major went into Porter Skaggs office.

Twig pointed and the POWs led the Constable through the double doors. They mounted the bleachers and sat on the same bench as before.

The trio looked at each other first, then they looked across the gym floor at the young boys perched on the bottom row of the bleachers, and finally peered down at Twig and the Mayor before speaking quietly, almost in a whisper, their lips hardly moving.

"I think I would rather be picking cotton than watching all the goings-on in this small town," Eddy said. "Sometimes I have trouble keeping up with the who and the what."

Will agreed. "Um. If we were in the field, I could talk to Dallas. I think she likes me a lot."

Duke cleared his throat. "You and Dallas and me and Odessa. I hope I can remember all of this. It would make a great book or film for the cinema."

"I have heard everyone pronounce it as *pitchursho.*" Will exaggerated the word. "*Pitchursho.*"

When Twig looked up, the three of them slightly raised their fingers in recognition. He nodded and spoke to the Mayor.

"Mayor, the order I'm thinking about talking with these boys will be Hale, Grover, Woodrow, and Porky. What do you think?"

"I agree, Twig. We'll know soon enough if they've made up any story."

Twig called for Hale.

The boy rose and had a silent audience as he oddly bounded across Coach Floyd Byrd's polished floor. Cerebral palsy affected Hale's ability to walk in a normal pattern, one foot in front of the other while maintaining balance and an erect posture. Both of Hale's feet pointed inwardly; his forward movement was accomplished by bouncing on his toes – his heels did not touch the floor. He carried his left arm over his chest and the hand seemed to dangle. His right arm and hand swung with the rhythm of his pace.

"Hale is a bright boy, Twig, in spite of the brain damage he suffered at birth," Casey Shipp whispered. "He is a voracious reader of the classics and a history buff. He never accepts pity or sympathy from anyone. Even at Scout camps, Hale hustled firewood without assistance. That boy is as intelligent as any man I know, smarter than most of us."

"Hello, Hale," the Mayor greeted. "Have a seat here with Constable Twig and me."

"Hale, I appreciate you coming to talk with me," the Constable said. "I'd like you to tell me what you know about what happened to Mister Douglass."

"We were in the house when Babe began to cry. We all heard it. Mister Douglass got up and turned on his flashlight. There's no electricity out there at Mister Tanner's house . . . what was his house. Mister Douglass asked Babe what was wrong. When Babe kept crying Mister Douglass asked him to come into the bathroom. I think he did that so Babe wouldn't be embarrassed for crying in front of Emmett and me. A few minutes later Woodrow, Grover, and Porky came in. I asked what they wanted and somebody said the bathroom. Somebody opened the closet door and somebody turned on a flashlight. Blinded everbody. Emmett said to stop shinnin the light. In the dark, they found the bathroom and turned the light on again. That's when Woodrow yelled. There was scufflin or fallin sounds, then Mister Douglass was hurt. Babe said all Mister Douglass was doin was talkin about how it was okay to cry when you're sad."

"Do you know why Babe was sad?" Twig asked.

"What Barber did. Babe thought his brother cut Bobbett Moon." Hale looked at the Mayor, at the Germans, and at Twig. "The scufflin was Grover and Porky holdin Woodrow and they all fell on Babe who fell on Mister Douglass who fell in the bathtub and hurt his face. Nobody hit Mister Douglass. It was just a accident."

"Do you know why Woodrow yelled?"

"He thought Mister Douglass was bein a bad man with Babe, that's all. But he wasn't, he was just tryin to be a friend with Babe."

They waited to see if Hale had more to say.

"Okay, Hale. Is somebody gonna come pick you up?"

"No, Sir, I'm gonna walk home. I just live two blocks from the school."

Twig nodded at the Mayor who spoke. "Okay, you can go on home. Thank you, Hale."

All of them watched with pity and sympathy, believing Hale struggled to walk out of the gymnasium and through the doors. But for Hale, he felt normal.

"Tremendous baseball player," Casey said.

"Really?"

"Twig, that boy can throw a baseball from deep center field to home plate in three seconds. Coach Byrd timed it."

"But . . . how can he do it with his arm . . . ?"

"He wears the glove on his right hand, catches the ball, and in a fluid movement squeezes the glove under his left arm while pulling the ball out. And . . . I've seen him do it. It's a fireball, a real zinger."

"Can he bat?"

"With his right hand."

"How can he run the bases?"

"Well, he can't, that's the problem. So, Floyd has Hale catch fly balls in batting practice and see if runners from third can beat the throw. It helps instill a sense of urgency with the players and keeps Hale involved in sports. Hale loves the challenge."

"Mayor, I think talking with these boys is just a matter of formality. It seems to me that everbody in Red River and Lamar counties knows what happened to Mister Douglass was an accident. There may have been an intent to stop him, Woodrow may have thought Mister Douglass was – how did Hale say it – *bein a bad man* to Babe. But I don't think anybody would think he intended to hurt Mister Douglass."

"You're right, Twig. It is a formality."

They talked with the remaining three.

"I thought Mister Douglass was kissing Babe when Porky turned the light on," Woodrow said. "Babe has told us Mister Douglass was just talkin. I'm really sorry Mister Douglass got hurt. I think it's all my fault, Sir. I'm ready to go to jail."

Grover and Porky supported Woodrow's explanation and expressed regret for what happened. Both said they grabbed hold of Woodrow and all fell forward on Babe. Just as Hale had described it.

Mayor Shipp and Constable Chestnutt concluded the investigation, and deemed the affair an unfortunate accident. No further interviews were scheduled.

But Mister Douglass was still in the hospital, hurt, and Miss Vernetta, his wife, and Miss Bertha, his sick momma, were distraught.

24

The Sergeant eased out the clutch on the downshift and the jeep slowed on the uphill dirt trail. His passenger stopped talking on a signal to halt by two armed sentries. The Sergeant braked. The vehicle stood at an idle twenty meters in front of two massive, closed, wrought-iron gates.

No one spoke. The two occupants in the military quarter-ton truck kept wary eyes moving, searching for threats from the approaching guards who each hefted a sawed-off shotgun.

One sentry took up a safe position off to the side and forward of the Sergeant.

The other found a spot away from the front bumper on the passenger side. His shotgun hung limp over a forearm but his eyes remained fixed on the Captain.

The Sergeant's lips barely moved; his words were almost a whisper. "I think we're okay, but don't make any kind of a sudden move. Sir."

The Sergeant dipped his head in salutation. He kept his hands high, his fingers wrapped around the steering wheel. He did not want to cause a calamity. He tried to swallow the cotton ball stuck in his craw.

The guard crooked his right index finger and touched the front of the stained, weatherworn, and rumpled woolen black Beret covering shaggy hair. He returned the Sergeant's greeting. "*Salve, Signore. Ciao.*"

The Sergeant plastered an appeasing, friendly smile on his face. "*Siamo qui per vedere Don Vito Scarpinello, Signore.*"

The guard stepped forward. He stuck his hand out, unsmiling. "*Documenti.*"

The Sergeant turned to look at his front seat passenger. "He wants to see our papers, Captain."

"What papers?"

"I'm afraid to ask, Captain. Show him something. Show him your I.D. card, Sir."

The Captain flashed his hands, palms out, at the guard before leaning forward and reaching into a rear pocket of his khaki trousers. He withdrew and opened his wallet, holding it high toward the requester. His military identification card and military driver license appeared side-by-side in the billfold.

The guard stepped close and peered at the two cards. "Okay." The pronounciation had a thick Sicilian twang. He raised an arm and two men with shotguns grappled with the heavy gate. "You go there. *Aspettare.* Wait."

The Sergeant shifted to first gear and eased forward. Ten meters through the entrance he stopped on a signal from a young boy with a pistol strapped to his hip.

"Jesus," the Captain whispered. "All we need is James Cagney and Edward G. Robinson."

The Sergeant snorted. "They might be up there in

the big house, Captain."

They heard the gates clang shut. The Sergeant and Captain looked at the jeep's side mirrors to see what activity was going on at the rear of the vehicle.

"These guys are scary, sure enough," the Captain opined.

"These boys are the real deal, Captain. Mafioso."

"Why do they have so many weapons?"

"Protection."

"From us?"

"No, Sir."

"The Germans were here and now we are. Maybe they're scared of us?"

"No, Sir. They ain't scared of anybody. These guys are threatened by Mussolini," the Sergeant said. "*Il Duce* promised to wipe out all of the Sicilian gangsters. He got close but no brass ring. These boys mean business whether it's Mussolini, Germans, or Americans. We're on their turf."

"You come." The voice came from behind the Captain before the figure walked past. The man swept his hand along his leg, beckoning. The shotgun was now slung across his back, attached to a rope over his chest. Its muzzle pointed toward the ground.

"Go ahead, Sorvino, follow our leader," the Captain said.

Sergeant Sorvino revved the engine and rode the clutch just enough for the jeep to creep along behind the guide. On signal from the escort, Sorvino stopped the vehicle and shut it down.

They sat without speaking, waiting for an invitation from their host to dismount.

The old woman clamped her remaining dark,

tobacco-stained teeth together and grimaced. She knew it was useless to try to open the heavy bedroom door quietly. When it squeaked and creaked and moaned, she shook her head in resigned surrender.

She gathered her apron in both hands and moved toward the bed. A small candle stood in its brass holder atop the bedside table. It was the only light in the darkened space. She turned and beckoned with a finger, the gesture known by people of all continents.

The Captain and Sergeant responded to her invitation and entered the room. Their shadows along the wall were eerily tall, broad, and erect.

She pointed at the man lying on the bed. Only a heavy cotton sheet covered his legs and waist. His chest was bare and showed signs of deep, restful sleep.

"This is creepy," Sergeant Sorvino said. "I don't know why the room is so dark in the middle of the afternoon."

"Ask her his name," the Captain said.

"*Il suo nome?*" the Sergeant asked.

"*Mi dispiace, Signore, non lo sappiamo.*"

"They do not know his name, Sir."

"They? Who is *they*, Sergeant Sorvino?"

"The villagers, I imagine, Captain."

"When did he come here?"

"*Quando è venuto qui, Signorina?*"

"*C'erano quattro soldati. Suo zio li ha trovati sulla spiaggia e li ha portati qui con il suo mulo e il suo carrello. Non avevano vestiti. Don Scarpinello disse a suo zio di tenere qui gli uomini. Due sono morti.*"

Sergeant Sorvino nodded. He looked at the Captain. "She says there were six soldiers. Her uncle found them on the beach and brought them here with his mule and cart. They had no clothes."

"No clothes? They were naked?"

"Don Scarpinello told her uncle to keep the men here. Two are dead."

"Don Scarpinello? *The* Don Scarpinello?"

"Yes, Sir. This is his province, Captain. Along with the two adjacent ones. Known killer, everbody's scared of The Don. They say he is a mean, ruthless character."

The Captain frowned and looked at the signora. "Where are the other men? The live ones?"

"*Dove sono gli altri uomini? Quelli vivi?*"

"*I morti sono sepolti nel cimitero della chiesa. Mia figlia ha le altre tre a casa sua, due case in fondo alla strada.*"

"She says the other three are in her sister's house, two houses down the street. Two are buried in the church cemetery."

"No names? No clothes? No identification. So we don't know if this man is an American, British, Canadian, or whatever. Or the other three." The Captain looked at Sergeant Sorvino. "Every hour we seem to be chasin down leads about found men."

"This operation has been a mess from the get-go, Sir. We've got dozens of these guys who've washed up on the island, some dead, some unconscious, like him, Captain. We don't know . . . we don't know who they are or who they belong to."

"This man could even be a German, Sorvino."

The three of them looked toward the creaking bedroom door. A squat man filled the doorway, his whiskered features grim in the diminished light – but his flaming red hair was unmistakable.

The signora brought her handsful of apron up under her chin and shrank back. She brushed against the nightstand and the candle wavered.

The Captain and Sorvino looked at the tottering candle holder then up at her face. They saw terrified fright and an expression of dangerous confrontation. They looked back at the man.

"*Signore Scarpinello?*" Sergeant Sorvino asked. "*Don Scarpinello?*"

"*Si.*" The voice was gruff, unfriendly, threatening. "*Tu chi sei? Cosa vuoi?*"

"*Sono il Sergente Sorvino e questo è il Capitano Hayworth. Veniamo per gli uomini, Don Scarpinello.*"

"*Devi lasciare gli uomini qui fino a quando non avrò preso accordi. Sto aspettando una lettera dall'America.*"

Sergeant Sorvino nodded. "*Comprendi, Signore.*" Sorvino looked at the Captain and back at the Don. "He's not going to let us take these men away, Captain."

"We're the Army. These men belong to us, or to somebody. He can't *keep* him, them, Sorvino."

"I think he can, Sir. You don't understand, Captain. Don Scarpinello has four bargaining chips. To him and his people these soldiers, American or whatever, can mean a lot of food, a lot of clothes, a lot of stuff . . . just a lot of everything. He says he''s waiting for a letter from America."

Captain Hayworth glared at The Don. "A letter from America? He's waiting for a letter? That's crazy. Who does he know in America? Who's writing this letter he's waiting on?"

"*Da chi arriva la lettera, Don Scarpinello?*"

"*Salvatore Lucania.*" Then The Don spoke English. "*Luciano in America.*"

"Luciano?" Sergeant Sorvino repeated the recognizable name.

"*Si,*" Don Scarpinello answered.

Captain Hayworth recognized the name too but wanted confirmation. "Salvatore Lucania? Is Salvatore Lucania, Luciano? The gangster?"

Sergeant Sorvino stroked his chin. "Luciano, in New York?"

"*Si.*"

"Yessir, Charles Luciano, Captain. Lucky Luciano, the gangster." Sorvino smiled at the Don. "*Charles 'Lucky' Luciano*?"

Don Scarpinello grinned and nodded. "*Si.*" In English he said, "Lu-ky Lu-chi-a-no, yes. He is no gangster, he is a business man."

Both of the American soldiers raised their eyebrows in surprised disbelief. "You speak good English, Don Scarpinello," Sorvino said.

"*Un po,* Sergeant. A little bit of English, *Si.* Your tongue is native."

"My mom and pop come from Catania. My father is a fisherman, Vito Sorvino. I am Vick Sorvino."

"You are one of us, My Son."

"I'm Captain Harry Hayworth, Mister Scarpinello . . ." the officer interjected.

"I know, Captain. The Sergeant said your name."

"It's *Don* Scarpinello, Sir," Sergeant Sorvino corrected.

"I'm sorry. Yes. *Don Scarpinello.* Sergeant Sorvino and I work for General Patton. For the last month, General Patton receives messages that many soldiers were found in the water and on the beach after we came ashore. One of the messages was about men here in Nicolizia. My Colonel sent us to investigate. I must arrange to bring these men back to my headquarters. Sir."

"I am sorry, Captain Hayworth. I cannot release these men. The two who are dead must stay buried as well."

"Do you know who they are? Their identification? American, British, Canadian?"

"Yes, we know who the three are." Don Scarpinello pointed at the man on the bed. "I am sorry, Captain, but we do not know who this man is. He had no clothes. Fishermen found him on a small crate with the others and brought them to my friend who brought them here. The other three are at a house, down the street. One is from New York, one is from California, and one is from Texas. They are many kilometers from where they were supposed to be, in Gela."

The Captain frowned. He wondered how the Don knew these soldiers were supposed to be in Gela.

The Don paused when he saw Hayworth's expression. "We know about all of the locations, Captain."

Hayworth nodded without speaking.

The Don continued. "They are hurt, broken bones. My associates found them and hid them from the German soldiers. I had those three brought to another pkace. I have had Doctor Nicodemo Gallotti look after them. His message to your Army of their presence with us was premature. I am waiting for instructions."

"From . . . from Luciano?"

"Yes, Sergeant Sorvino."

"He is in prison, Don Scarpinello. He is in an American prison. He will be there for thirty or forty years," Captain Hayword said.

"Yes, I know. Salvatore sent word to us to help the Americans, so we want the Americans to help us . . . to help him."

"To help with what?"

Don Scarpinello smiled. "The war, Captain. You do know there is a war."

Hayworth smiled, agreeable. "Yes, of course."

"So, you must rid this country of Mussolini. That will help us."

"We have made the Germans leave Sicily. Your King, Victor Emmanuel, has removed *Il Duce* from the head of government and placed him in custody. Badoglio is the new Prime Minister. That's what we have done here. But how can we help Luciano?"

"Release him from prison. Let him come back to his home in Lercara Friddi."

Vick Sorvino chuckled. "The government ain't gonna let that happen, Don Scarpinello. Even if they wanted to help, Governor Dewey won't do it."

Don Scarpinello shrugged. "Then I will keep them."

"I must see the other three. I must report who they are and what unit they belong to, Don Scarpinello. Will you allow that?"

"*Si*. We can go in your *camionetta*, your jeep."

Captain Hayworth pointed at the man on the bed. "Has he spoken at all?"

"No, but he awakens when we shake him. He eats, he goes to the toilet, he does normal things but does not speak. He never stays awake more than an hour. Doctor Galloti believes brain damage, maybe a loss of oxygen while in the water. I believe he is a lost soul. The doctor thinks this man may never recover, may never be normal again."

"May I wake him?"

"Of course. English may be his native tongue. He might speak with you."

25

"See if you can wake him, Sorvino," Captain Hayworth directed. "See what you can do."

Sorvino moved to the side of the bed.

The man opened his eyes on the third shake of an arm.

"My name is Sergeant Vick Sorvino, Seventh Army Adjutant General's office."

The man's mouth opened but he did not blink.

"What's your name, Soldier? What's your unit?"

The man's mouth remained ajar. He stared at Sorvino.

The Sergeant looked at the old woman, the Don, and Captain Hayworth. "No, response, Sir."

"Maybe he's German," Hayworth offered.

"*Sprichst du Deutsch*?"

The man's eyes turned soft, a faint movement of his lips tried a smile.

Sorvino paused. "*Sie sind Deutsch*?"

The man blinked, twice.

"This is a German soldier, Captain." Sorvino touched the man's arm. "*Konnen sie sprechen*?"

The man kept his mouth wide and held it open for several seconds before pressing his lips together and swallowing.

"I think he hears me, Sir, but apprently he can't talk. Or won't talk."

"Don Scarpinello, you have a German soldier here," Hayworth said. "We must take him into custody as a prisoner of war. He needs medical attention and we are required by the Geneva Convention to give that."

"You are welcome to take him away, Captain. I have no use of a German."

"When I return to my headquarters I will arrange for medical personnel and an ambulance to come for him and the other three."

"I agree you can take the German, Captain, but the other three will remain here. We can go see them but I will not release them to you. You are a soldier, you understand orders. Like you, I follow orders. My orders are to keep them until I receive a letter from America. From Salvatore . . . from Luciano. He will tell me what to do."

Hayworth took a deep breath and exhaled slowly. He looked at Sorvino for help.

"That is not reasonable, Don Scarpinello," Sorvino said. "You must release these men to us."

The Don shrugged. "I am sorry, Vick, my Son. It is not within my power to disregard instructions."

"Then we must see these three soldiers now, Don Scarpinello," Hayworth said. "They may need medical attention as this soldier does."

"That I will grant, Captain." The Don spoke to the old woman. "*Sofia, prenditi cura di questo tedesco fino a quando gli americani non verranno per lui.*"

"*Sì, mio Don.*"

"I will take you to the other three, Captain."

Sorvino touched the man's arm again. "*Wir sind amerikanische Soldaten. Sie sind jetzt ein Kriegsgefangener. Versuche nicht zu fliehen. Diese Leute werden dich töten. Wir werden einen Krankenwagen für Sie organisieren. Sie werden dort eingesperrt, wo Ärzte für Sie sorgen. Verstehst du?*"

"I told this man he is a prisoner of war, Captain."

The POW blinked. He smacked his lips together twice and swallowed again.

"Very well."

"I said we will send an ambulance for him and doctors will care for him while he is imprisoned."

"Very well, Sergeant Sorvino."

Vick looked at the Don. "I said you would kill him, Don Scarpinello, if he tried to escape."

"He did not try before you came, my Son. I do not think he will try after you leave. He is happy he is safe and the war is over for him."

"Let's go see the other three," Hayworth urged.

Come with me," Don Scarpinello instructed.

Two men with shotguns sat in chairs out on the walk. Both stood and silently greeted their Don as Sergeant Sorvino parked.

The three visitors entered the tall, narrow building. They climbed the stairs to the top level. It was hot inside the house, but the lower floors seemed cooler than the third floor. Another man with a shotgun rose from a wooden chair a few feet from a door. He bowed at his Don, but neither spoke.

They watched as Don Scarpinello fiddled with a large key and unlocked the door.

Blistering heat consumed the slight breeze that

found its way through open windows on two sides of the small room.

The three soldiers in their skivvies lay on flat, grubby mats on the floor. They struggled to their feet when Captain Hayworth appeared from behind Scarpinello.

"At ease, Men. As you were," the Captain ordered. "Relax."

Two took a seat on a soiled, tattered divan, the other sat in a straight back, heavy wooden chair. There was no other furniture.

"I'm Captain Hayworth and this is Sergeant Sorvino. We are from General Patton's Seventh Army Adjutant General's office." Hayworth pointed at their host. "I think you might know Don Scarpinello, or know of him. The Don speaks English."

One of the soldiers on the couch ventured a question. "Have you come for us, Sir?"

"Yes. Yes, I have. But there is a problem that has to be resolved. I see your bandages. I see all three of you are hurt."

"We've been pretty well taken care of by Doctor Gallotti, Captain," the soldier in the chair said.

"Okay, good. Now, tell me who you are. Tell me about your injury, your unit, and how you ended up here. Let's start with you, Son." Hayworth pointed at the other soldier on the sofa, a youngster.

The soldier in the chair spoke. "I'm the senior Non-Com, Captain. I'm Corporal Dennis Raymond." The Corporal pointed at the youngster. "That's Private Ross Connors and this is Private Grant Sweeney. All of us are in the First Infantry Division."

"I see. The Big Red One. General Allen's Division. Okay, Corporal, let's start with you."

"Acting Squad Leader, C Company, First Battalion,

Twenty-Sixth Infantry Regiment, Sir. Our landing craft was hit by a shell. An eighty-eight, I guess. Maybe a mine. Blew the back end of the boat off. Shrapnel in my left thigh and hip." Dennis Raymond reached up and touched the bandage on his neck. "We were in pretty deep water, chest-high. It was a rough sea, the wind musta been blowin forty miles an hour. We was supposed to land at Gela, but the Doctor said we were found somewhere around Licata."

"You ended up in the Third Infantry Division sector, General Truscott's area," the Captain said.

"We were on a crate paddling through the high waves for a couple of hundred yards or so. When I went ashore and got up onto the beach, a bullet cut a trough on the side of my neck."

The Corporal paused. He looked at Don Scarpinello and then back at Hayworth. "His men found us on the beach. Nobody was around, from any unit. They had left us to die or thought we were already dead.

"That was the order, Corporal. Get ashore and fight, no stopping."

"We were exhausted and hurt, in a lot of pain. We were captured, Sir, by his men. Well, not captured, I guess, maybe rescued. What pieces of uniform we had on was taken away. The doctor came to the house and patched us up."

Connors swung the arm lying in a bandanna sling. "When the landing craft was hit, I jumped out. Jumped over the side. Pulled my shoulder out of joint. I thought I was gonna drown. Some guys did. We had so much gear on, it weighted us down, Sir. I'm a rifleman in the Corporal's squad, Sir."

Sweeney answered when Hayworth nodded. "Rifleman, Sir. I either ripped a hole in my leg when I jumped out of the boat or I snagged it on a steel pylon under water. Tore my pants off. My leg was infected, but the doctor drained the puss and it's healin now, Sir. I also hurt my ankle, thought I broke it but the swellin has gone down a lot since we been here. Probably just sprained it. I lost my rifle in the water. I had to shuck all my combat gear off and my boots and uniform to keep from drowning. It was pitch dark, we couldn't see anything and guys all around me were yellin and screamin and bein killed. I was scared, Sir. Scared of drownin and scared of gettin shot. I guess I passed out on the beach. I woke up in a cart with everbody else."

"There were five of you, and the German," the Captain said.

Corporal Raymond frowned. "The German, Sir?"

"Yes. The man in the other house, at Don Scarpinello's house," Sergeant Sorvino confirmed.

"Don Scarpinello will only let us take the prisoner, the German. Sergeant Sorvino is a linguist. Speaks several languages. He talked to the German but got no response, so I guess he won't or can't talk. Maybe brain damage."

"Could be a hearing loss, Sir. All the shelling and explosions."

Hayworth narrowed his eyes, sensitive, noting the unusual softness in Raymond's voice.

"The German was found on the beach, like the rest of you," Don Scarpinello said.

Corporal Raymond looked at the Don. "You'll let the German go with Captain Hayworth?"

"*Si.* I have no use of a German soldier."

"Don Scarpinello is waiting for a letter from America before he will release you three men, Corporal. I will report this to my Colonel when I get back to headquarters. I will return with an ambulance to pick up the German prisoner, and maybe all of you."

"A letter?"

"It's complicated, Corporal. It'll have to be handled by General Patton. General Eisenhower will have to go to the President about it, I suspect."

"Because of a letter?"

Hayworth shrugged. "Afraid so. Now, who are the two buried in the church cemetery?"

Connors held up a handful of dog tags hanging from neck-chains. "The two men in the cemetery are Sergeant Randolph Dell, our squad leader, and PFC Merle Barnes. Don Scarpinello's men buried them and gave me their dog tags, Sir. I have *all* the dog tags, Captain. *All* of the dog tags."

Hayworth's suspicions were aroused with the emphasis Connors placed on the word. He became more attentive, listened for nuances. "Don Scarpinello told me you're from California, New York, and Texas."

"I'm from San Diego, Sir," Sweeney said.

"Buffalo, New York, Captain," Connors answered.

Raymond smiled and slowly closed one eye as he squeezed his nose. He slid an index finger down the bridge, over the tip, and across his lips. "Me and Pig, Texas, you know?"

Hayworth caught the drift. He squeezed his nose. "Yes, I know Texas, Corporal. Lots of cowboys and horses."

"Pretty horses, Captain. Really pretty horses in Texas, Sir. Connors, hand over the dog tags. You better take *all* of the dog tags with you, Captain. *All* of the names are there. You'll see."

Sergeant Sorvino took the chained nameplates from Connors' hand and held them up as an angler would when showing off with a large-mouth Bass.

Hayworth hesitated, staring at Corporal Raymond. "Yes, I see. I know there are pretty horses in Texas. I think I know what you mean." He looked at the Don to see if the slyness, signal, and coded communication had registered – realizing it had not he nodded at the Corporal. "I understand. Of course. Pig. Texas."

"It's like falling in a pigsty, Miss Ruby. Once you get the stink on you it's terribly hard to get the stink off."

"I know, I know, Maybelle. If I let it happen, half the town will not let me live it down. Having a cookout for a colored boy."

"I think it would be a feather in your cap, a ribbon in your bonnet, for sure, if you did it."

Ruby's mind was racing. She acted as if she had not heard the publisher of the town newspaper. "If I don't do it, then the other half will hold it against me. This is an absolute mess."

"Well, either way, I think this will be the talk of town for a very long time, Miss Ruby. You can't deny that."

"Well, that's why I sent for you. I know you want to write about this and put it in your paper."

"I do so want to, Miss Ruby. I will write about it. It's my obligation to report the news."

"What if I asked you not to do it, Maybelle? What if I asked you to just let it die its own death?"

Maybelle Winters grinned. She loved twisting the saber in the wounded beast. "You know I have to put it in print. If I didn't put it in the *Palomino Press*, the *Paris News* would have two front page stories. One about the drawing and you not doing the cookout and the other story would be about the *Palomino Press* not reporting the news, not telling a hometown story, a cover-up.   Once it's in the *Paris News*, then the *Texarkana Gazette* will pick up the story.   Then, all of the Dallas and Fort Worth papers are going to print their stories about the event.   And once that happens, it could even go national."

Rudy Bostick sighed.   "We have to decide how you're going to write about it in the paper."

"I started thinking about how I was going to write the story that night, right after the drawing.   I think six or seven people called me after the show was over to tell me what happened.   Carsey Belew had all of the details."

"Maybelle, you and I know this wasn't supposed to be.   That Baycann boy, that Porky . . . who in the world gives their child a name of Porky, for goodness sakes?"

"His daddy did it, Miss Ruby, so Porky wouldn't have to fight bullies in school.   With a last name of Baycann, it woulda happened sooner or later anyway.   His daddy knew it all too well.   I can't remember anybody in town ever calling Porky's daddy Portland."

"Well, anyway . . . what was I gonna say?"

"I think you were about to blame Porky."

"Yes.   Yes, of course.   If he hadn't put that boy's name . . .   Warrene said she thought that's what happened, that Porky wrote that boy's name and put it in the jar."

"T J.   Thomas James Workman.   Miss Irene's boy . . . her granson.   Preacher's nephew.   T J calls Irene his momma since his real momma and daddy is gone."

Miss Ruby waved her hands, dismissing Maybelle's carrying on.   "Warrene and Yvonne.   I couldn't believe they made the announcement."

Maybelle Winters grinned.   She shoved and twisted the blade deeper.   "I heard they did it in front of all the people in the theater. According to Carsey, it was a packed house, including the balcony. And there was a lot of yelling and hollering and whooping, too."

"I wasn't going to do it but . . . Warrene and Yvonne both said it'd be bad if I didn't do it . . . the cookout . . . for him."

Maybelle nodded. "Remember the pigsty, Miss Ruby."

"What?"

"The pigsty. The stink."

"Yes. Yes. Warrene suggested I invite the boy's white friends to the cookout."

"So, I guess if you invite T J's white friends you're going to do the cookout?" Maybelle sawed with the razor. "I'll have to write about it either way, Miss Ruby. You know that."

"Yes, I guess I will, Maybelle. I'll have to invite white friends if I want to make it seem normal. I've sent Julius and Ethel out there to Irene's to tell the boy we'll do it this Saturday, Labor Day weekend. I want you to say I am pleased to put on this cookout for the winner of the drawing, as promised."

"For Thomas James Workman, T J."

"Do you have to put his name in the paper? Can't it just be a cookout for the winner of the drawing?"

Maybelle slowly, slyly shook her head. "No, I think it'd be proper for the *Palomino Press* to identify the winner. And I"m going to bring Stan here to take pictures for the paper."

"Oh, my goodness. Pictures? Please, Maybelle."

"No, no. There has to be a picture with the story. And I think it would be great if we made a picture of you with T J and put it on the front page. Maybe T J could sit on your lap, Miss Ruby? With Porky standing next to you?"

They heard a car pull into the driveway.

"That's Julius and Ethel coming back from the boy's house."

Maybelle followed Ruby through the dining room to the front door.

When Julius and Ethel started walking toward the back of the house, Ruby pushed open the screen door, went onto the porch, and stopped at the edge of the steps. Maybelle stood just behind Ruby.

"Here," Ruby commanded.

The servants changed course, came back to the steps but did not come up them.

"Well?"

Julius removed his hat and placed it over his chest. "Scuse me, Miss Ruby. I gots to go to the bathroom, right now. I will come back as soon as I can and tell you what we know."

"I need to go too, Miss Ruby," Ethel said. "We'll be just a minute, I promise."

"Okay, okay. Go ahead. Come to the back when you're done. I'll meet you on the back porch, don't make me wait forever."

Julius bowed. "Yessum."

"I'd like to stay too," Maybelle requested. "If you don't mind? This story is really building into a suspenseful drama."

"Oh, alright, Maybelle. Let's go sit on the back porch and wait. I'm as anxious as you are, I guess."

Maybelle followed Ruby through the foyer, back through the dining room and out onto the long, screened-in room. There were four rocking chairs and beside one was a small table. On top of the table were an opened pack of Old Gold cigarettes and a small, red box of Diamond matches.

Purposefully, Maybelle made her way to the chair beside the table and poised her backside to sit.

"Maybelle. Don't sit there, Maybelle." Ruby pointed to another chair. "There. Sit there."

"Oh, is this your favorite chair, Miss Ruby?"

"It's where I sit when I want to smoke a cigarette. And I want to smoke one now. So sit there."

Maybelle moved to the designated chair and settled in. She pushed with the tip of her toes, rocked back, then let the large chair roll forward. She pushed again, ever so slightly. It was a casual, smooth movement of nervous anticipation. She kept a side-eye glance on her hostess, waiting.

Ruby sat majestically for a moment, staring straight ahead. She turned and picked up the pack of smokes and the matches. She shook the cigarettes and a loose one popped up in the opening. She pulled it out and stuck it between bright red lips.

Ruby slipped a match out of the box, dragged it along the striking surface, and flared the tip of the butt. She inhaled the satisfying nicotine. She puckered her lips and blew out the flame. She dropped the stem into an amber glass ashtray on the table beside her chair.

She drew another long inhale from her cigarette and exhaled smoke through her nose. She positioned an annoying bit of tobacco onto the tip of her tongue and placed her tongue between her lips. Instead of using a finger to remove the fragment, she stuck her tongue out between her lips, quickly pulled her tongue back in while at the same time blowing a puff of air to expel the grain of tobacco.

Maybelle watched this routine in awe. She had never realized Ruby Bostick smoked cigarettes.

Maybelle pulled on the sides of her nose to dispel the annoying scent of the smoke.

"I didn't know you smoked, Miss Ruby?"

"I started a long time ago, Maybelle. I just don't smoke in public. It's unladylike, you know."

"Uh huh."

"I also drink whiskey now and then."

Maybelle chuckled. "I've been known to take a sip or two, myself. But *never* in public."

"Unladylike."

"Um hum."

"Okay. Here they come." Miss Ruby snubbed out her cigarette. She laid the matchbox on top of the gold pack and rubbed her fingers together. She remained still, unmoving, in the rocking chair and watched Ethel and Julius mount the steps and stop at the screen door.

"Well, come on in."

Julius opened the screen door and stepped aside for his wife to enter. They stood aside of Miss Ruby, waiting for instructions.

Ruby pointed at the two empty rocking chairs. "Sit there."

Julius followed Ethel as they crossed between the two white women.

Maybelle watched the stage play unfold, mesmerized by the commanding voice of the servants' employer. She had never seen Ethel and Julius Watson move so meekly. She thought on it as they sat without speaking and reached the conclusion that they were embarrassed to be treated so abruptly in front of a visitor. It was then Maybelle became embarrassed for them and uncomfortable there on the screened-in back porch of the Porter House.

Julius and Ethel sat quietly. Ethel clasped her hands

together and rested them in her lap. She smiled at Maybelle.

"Well?"

"Yessum," Julius answered.

"Well, tell me what Irene and the boy said about the cookout."

26

After leaving Porky at the gym, the lingering moments of hope Twig had given to Agnes turned into minutes of crushing anguish when she came into the hospital.

Doctor Burns had his arms wrapped around Geraldine. They stood in front of the nurse station. His voice was soft. "It's not your fault, there's nothing you could do. It's not your fault, Geraldine." He looked at Agnes and pressed his lips together.

Agnes put her hands on the back of Geraldine's shoulders. She did not speak but raised her eyebrows, inquisitive.

"Geraldine . . . Pearly. It's Clifford . . . he's . . ."

Agnes rushed down the corridor to Mister Douglass' room. All the while, she imagined, and feared, what she might find. She stopped at the doorway, one hand on the doorframe for support the other on her stomach.

Douglass' sheets and blanket were rumpled; they were hanging over the side of the mattress. The bed was empty. Crumbs, serving tray, and shards of a coffee cup were scattered on the floor; in the amber liquid that covered the white linoleum was an unbroken jar of marmalade.

Agnes hurried back to Burns and Geraldine. "What happened?"

Doctor Burns caressed his lips with his tongue and shook his head before he spoke. "Clifford woke and left the hospital."

Geraldine eased back out of Burns' grasp and looked at Agnes. "He said his life was over."

"Why?"

It was Geraldine's way. Her unbreakable habit was to tell someone how a clock worked when the person only asked for the time. So, instead of just answering Agnes' question of 'why', Geraldine began telling the what, when, where, and how.

"I was doing his vitals, blood pressure, temperature, oxygen, when he woke. Scared me half to death. He asked for breakfast, said he was hungry. I went to get coffee and a couple of biscuits for him. I told Doctor Gates that Mister Douglass was awake and asked for something to eat. I went to the kitchen and put two biscuits in the oven to warm them. I poured a cup, put the biscuits on a plate and put all of it on a tray with the jar of peach marmalade, and was bringing them to Mister Douglass. When I came back to his room, he was coming out of the bathroom, almost running and Doctor Gates was behind him saying that everything was gonna be alright."

Agnes tried again. "Why? Why did he say his life was over?"

"The talk?" Geraldine wiped her cheeks and rubbed her palms together. "The talk, I guess."

Agnes was near exasperation but controlled her impatience. "Geraldine, please."

"Well, I'm telling you what happened." She looked at Doctor Burns. "I'm telling you."

"Yes, Geraldine, we know you are." Doctor Burns smiled. "It's just that we'd like you to be more precise, to tell us why Clifford said his life was over."

"The talk. What people believe he was doing with Babe in the bathroom at the Scout camping. The talk in town."

Doctor Burns shook his head. "This is not good. The state of mind Clifford is in is not good. He could hurt himself."

"I know. Maybe Pearly will bring him back."

Doctor Gates came through the front door and walked to them. "I lost him. He ran faster than I could to keep up. I thought he might have gone home but Vernetta said he hadn't. Of course, when Vernetta saw me and I told her I was looking for Clifford, she went into a panic. I got her calmed down and came here. Clifford is somewhere out there in town in his underwear."

"This is not good," Doc Burns repeated.

Gates rubbed his face. "I'm sorry. This might be my doing. When Geraldine told me Clifford was awake, I went to him. He was in the bathroom. The door was closed, so I waited a moment. I knocked on the door and called his name.

"He was sitting on the commode when I opened the door . . . just sitting there . . . the lid was down. I asked how he felt and he just looked at me. I could see fear in his eyes, his face was drawn.

"He said the boys meant no harm, they didn't know what was going on with Babe in the bathroom. He said it was the talk . . . the talk of the town. The talk had ruined his reputation and the boys thought he was hurting Babe. Everbody thought of him as a mean man with boys.

"'My reputation was bad enough, now it's completely shot', he said. I asked him to come back to bed. He just sat there a moment. Then he looked at me and asked how I dealt with adversity . . . with what happened to me. 'The talk, it never stops', he said.

"I told him that I take one day at a time. I know how he must feel because my reputation suffered, too. People will talk, I said, and what we must do is live our life and pay no attention to gossip.

"Clifford jumped up and looked in the mirror. 'I might as well dive head first off the water tower', he said and then pushed past me. I stumbled against the sink and called after him, told him to come back. I said everything is going to be alright. He ran into Geraldine bringing the tray with his breakfast. He paused a moment, I thought he was going to help pick up the tray and things, instead he shouted 'My life is over' and ran out of the room. I helped Geraldine first, then ran after him."

"I'm afraid he'll hurt himself if he believes his life is over."

"Yes, Garland, I'm afraid of that too. It's the state of mind he's in."

"That's what I said he said," Geraldine added, pouting.

"Agnes, call the Mayor," Doctor Burns instructed. "We have an emergency on our hands. We need volunteers to help find Clifford and bring him back to the hospital. He's in bad shape, both physically and mentally."

"For sure, mentally," Doctor Gates added. "I'm going over to the water tower, Garland, just in case."

"Yes. Of course, Pearly. That's a good idea."

Agnes went around the counter of the nurse station. Before she could take the receiver off its hook and crank the handle, the two brass bells on the wooden faceplate started ringing. She adjusted the arm, turned the mouthpiece down, and placed the receiver to her ear.

"Hospital, this is Nurse Baycann . . . Yes, Carsey, we know . . . He woke a bit ago . . . Yes, Carsey . . . Where was he? . . . I'll tell you about it in a minute . . . Okay, Carsey . . . Yes, I know . . . I know, Carsey . . . Please ring Principal Skaggs office . . . No, I need to reach the Mayor, he's with Constable Twig at the school gym . . . We have an emergency, Carsey . . . Please ring Porter's office or Coach Byrd's office . . . Thank you . . . Okay, Carsey, I will . . . I promise . . . you'll be the first to know . . . Okay, please ring it now . . . I'll wait . . .

"Principal Skaggs . . . Yes, it's Agnes, I need to speak with the Mayor. Please ask him to come to the phone . . . it's an emergency. What? When? Oh, my goodness. Okay, thank you. Yes, thank you, Porter. Carsey . . . Yes, Carsey who's on call for the fire department? Yes, okay, ring Winston . . . His house, I guess, Carsey . . . first, anyway . . . Hello, Mister Tanner . . . Yes, Nurse Baycann . . . Please sound the alarm for volunteers . . . No, no. No fire. Mister Douglass left the hospital and we need to find him . . . No, Doctor Burns and Doctor Gates are here . . . at the hospital . . . We're all here at the hospital . . . Yes. He woke and ran away . . . Well, we're afraid he's not well . . . We need volunteers to look for him . . . In town, here in town . . . somewhere in town . . . And we need a couple of volunteers to standby at the water tower with Doctor Gates . . . Yes, the water tower . . . because . . . you

294

know. Yes, we believe he might . . . Okay, thank you . . . Thank you, Mister Tanner . . . Yes, bring him to the hospital . . . Bye."

Agnes replaced the receiver and pressed on her forehead forcefully with thumb and fingers to relieve the throbbing stress beginning to sting her temples.

Before she could turn back to report the developments, the siren atop the roof of the firehouse came alive and began a yawning wind up. Its call to action filled the streets and alleys of Palomino with an insistent, crying howl.

When Twig dismissed the boys, they left the gym together. They walked slowly so Hale could keep up. The four of them stopped at the corner of Church and Powell Street.

"We don't deserve goin free," Grover opined.

"Why not?" Woodrow questioned. "We didn't do nothin wrong."

Porky disagreed. "Yes, yes we did do somethin wrong, Woodrow. And it's your fault. If you hadn't yelled and jumped at Mister Douglass . . ."

Woodrow shrugged. "Well, it's over. There ain't nothin I can do about it now."

"Yes there is."

"Well, smarty pants, what is it?"

"You can do the right thing. First, you can tell everbody in town it's your fault that Mister Douglass got hurt and next you can tell Mister Douglass hisself that you're sorry."

Grover snorted. "I wanna see that."

"I ain't gonna do neither one of them," Woodrow said. "If I go up to him, he might choke me or beat me up. Anyway, he's in the hospital and won't wake up."

"Well, that's where I'm goin. To the hospital. All of you should come with me. And if he wakes up, we can tell him we're sorry."

"I'll go with you, Porky," Hale said.

"Okay, Hale." Porky looked at Grover. "Well?"

Grover looked at Woodrow.

Woodrow sighed. "Okay, okay. I'll go to the hospital. That way, if he beats me up, Doctor Burns can save my life."

"I'll go too," Grover said.

"Okay, Hale, you and Grover lead the way."

They turned from their small circle and began the trek down Church Street toward town. Hale set the slow pace with his handicap, and Grover stayed alongside him. Porky and Woodrow followed. They had gone a hundred yards along the sidewalk at a methodical march when Grover broke the silence and pointed.

"Look over yonder," Grover whispered.

The foursome stopped and stared at a figure in white underwear sitting on the back steps of the Presbyterian Church. The front of the church faced Church Street, but from their position, forty or fifty yards away, they could see the full length of the west side of the building and the back steps.

"That looks like Mister Douglass," Hale said.

"He's in his underwear," Porky whispered.

"What's he doin sittin on the *Prespertiurn* Church steps in his drawers?" Grover asked.

Woodrow snorted. "He's waitin on a bus, Grover."

Hale started out on tiptoes, bouncing onto and across the street. The other boys quickly caught up and followed him.

"Whachu gonna do, Hale?" Grover asked.

296

"Mister Douglass is supposed to be in the hospital."

"Well, he ain't there, Hale," Woodrow said.

"I'm gonna find out why and if he's okay."

"I'm with you, Hale," Porky said. "Maybe he needs our help?"

"I wonder what Mister Douglass is doin sittin out on the church steps in his underwear?" Grover wondered again.

"Maybe he's waitin on the preacher instead of a bus," Woodrow countered.

They walked across Pastor Fred Bishop's manicured lawn, skirted the tiny rock wall encircling a bed of Posies, and stopped at the corner of the church.

They stood mute.

Hale spoke first, quietly. "Hello, Mister Douglass. Are you alright?"

They watched the math teacher rise up and massage his cheeks. He turned his head toward them, leaned forward, and placed his elbows on his knees.

"Hello, Hale. Hello, Boys."

Hale moved to the side of the steps; the lagging trio closed in behind him.

"You feeling better?" Hale asked.

Douglass smiled. "I am now since you came up to say hello, Hale."

"Weren't you in the hospital, Mister Douglass?" Grover asked.

"I was, Grover. I ran away."

They were frozen in place and speechless for several seconds because Douglass' admission surprised the boys.

Hale shuffled to the front of the steps, facing Mister Douglass. The others moved around too, standing on Hale's right.

They faced Douglass; encroaching his space. Caught off guard, the youngsters lowered their heads, embarrassed by his red face. In spite of the bandage over his swollen eye, they could tell Douglass had been crying.

"Have you been crying, Mister Douglass?"

Douglass wiped his uncovered eye. "No, no, not at all, Porky."

"Mister Douglass?" Porky began and paused. "Mister Douglass, I'm sorry we made you get hurt." He looked at Woodrow.

Douglass bobbed his head.

"I'm sorry, too, Mister Douglass," Grover said. "I tried to stop . . . I tried to stop it." *He* looked at Woodrow.

"I'm . . . I'm awfully sorry, Mister Douglass I yelled at you," Woodrow said softly. "If I could take it all back, I would. I am sorry, Sir."

"While you were in the hospital, Mister Tanner's house burned down," Hale said.

Douglass straightened up. "My goodness. What happened?"

"Wyatt Posey and Barber Beck was out there. They died and the house burned up," Porky reported.

"Why did you run away, Mister Douglass?" Hale asked.

"I've lost my faith, Hale. I've lost confidence. I was sitting here thinking about what I should do. I think I'll have to leave Palomino."

Stunned by this revelation, Porky pled his case. "We don't want you to leave, Mister Douglass. You are the best math teacher we've ever had."

"You're the best Assistant Scoutmaster we've ever had," Hale added.

"Did you kiss Hale, Mister Douglass?" Grover blurted.

"Jeez, Grover," Porky groaned.

Douglass smiled. "Did I, Hale?"

"Yessir." Hale raised his strong arm and stuck a finger on his forehead. "Right here, on my head."

"Why did I do that, Hale?"

"Cause I did a good deed, Mister Douglass."

"And what deed was that, Hale?"

"I helped Miss Douglass plant roses for your . . . for David, Daniel, and Donald."

"For our baby boys." Douglass tried to smile.

Porky saw tears shimmer in Clifford Douglass' eye. Embarrassed, he looked down.

"And what did Miss Douglass do, Hale?"

"Miss Douglass hugged me and kissed me." Hale raised his strong arm again and stuck a finger on his forehead. "Right here, on my head."

"And after Miss Douglass gave you a kiss, what did your momma say, Hale?"

"Momma said I deserved a peck from you, too, Mister Douglass."

"You're a good boy, Hale." Clifford Douglass went from one face to another, looking into their eyes. "All of you are good boys. You're good Scouts."

"I want to be a Boy Scout, Mister Douglass," Porky said.

"You're the best Assistant Scoutmaster we've ever had, Mister Douglass," Hale repeated.

"I want to be a Boy Scout, Mister Douglass," Porky repeated.

"We can sure swear you in, Porky. You'll make a good Boy Scout."

"We don't have a place for our Scout troop to camp anymore," Hale said.

"Well, Mister Tanner and me will find a place. We need to have Boy Scouts in Palomino."

"Does that mean you ain't gonna leave, Mister Douglass?" Grover asked.

Douglass took in a deep breath and let it out with a shake of his head. "I just realized I have work to do here, with you and the others, with my boys, my Boy Scouts."

"We better take you back to the hospital, Mister Douglass," Porky suggested.

Douglass stood and lost his balance. Hale wobbled, unable to reach out. The three jumped forward and reached out for the math teacher's arms.

"I guess you better help me. I may not be able to make it to the hospital by myself."

Just as the four teenagers moved in close and grasped his arms to help Mister Douglass off the church steps, the Palomino firehouse siren started up.

"Well, Miss Ruby, we talked to Miss Irene about it," Julius reported.

"And the boy," Ethel added. "He was there and had a say."

"We told her you'd do the cookout for Thomas, for T J, on Saturday," Julius continued.

Ruby checked her impatience. She knew how long it took sometimes for Julius and Ethel to tell a story. Julius and Ethel Watson had been with her for almost twenty years, through the Great Depression. Even though she was short with them at times, they were her family, they were special to her, and Ruby loved them in her own way.

"Mister Albert drove up in his truck while we was there," Ethel said.

The diversion piqued Ruby's interest. "What did he want?"

"He wanted to know when the boy was gonna sing out there at the Camp."

"Sing? The boy is going to sing? Camp Maxey?"

Julius nodded and absentmindedly rocked in the chair. "Yessum."

"Will you stop rockin and tell me what Irene and the boy said?"

Julius tensed his legs and grasped both arms of the chair in his hands to stop the movement. "Miss Irene said the boy had been invited by a Army Captain to sing for the soldier boys Saturday night."

"What about my cookout?"

"T J said you could . . ."

Ethel cut him short. "*Julius.*"

"Uh huh. The boy said he would not be able to come to your cookout for him."

"He can't do that," Ruby sputtered. "There was a drawin and he won the cookout."

Maybelle grinned. She had seen displays of Ruby's false indignation before. This time it was cover for the relief of not having a cookout at the Porter House for a colored boy.

"Well, well." Maybelle snickered. "Looks like I got three or four good stories out of this drawin you put on at the *pitchursho*, Miss Ruby. Who is this Army Captain?"

Ruby kept quiet. She was as interested as Maybelle.

"He's Captain Steinbeck," Ethel said. "He was friends with T J's momma and daddy in Washington and knows how good T J sings. They havin a show out there at the camp for the soldier boys and the Captain asked T J to come sing for them."

The investigative reporter wanted to know more. "What does Mister Albert have to do with it? Why was he out at Irene's?"

Ethel took over. "He needed to know when T J was gonna go so he could arrange school buses?"

Ruby could not control the volume of her voice. "School buses?"

"Yessum," Julius answered. He did not rock the chair.

"T J's friend, Porky . . ." Ethel started to clarify.

"Porky? Is that boy into *everything*?"

Maybelle couldn't resist. "Seems so, Miss Ruby. What does Porky Baycann have to do with Mister Albert and school buses?"

"Uh huh." Ethel appreciated Maybelle's leading question. "Mister Albert and the Major are . . ."

"THE MAJOR?"

"Yessum," Julius said again.

Ethel waited, but the next outburst she expected did not come. After a few seconds of pause, she continued. "Mister Albert asked the Major to help. The Major was goin to the schoolhouse to ask Mister Skaggs for a couple of school buses to take the boy and his momma and Preacher and their friends . . . and Porky and T J's friends to Camp Maxey to hear T J sing."

Ruby's exasperation was evident to the three she faced sitting there in rocking chairs on the Porter House back porch. "For goodness sakes."

They kept still and quiet, watching Ruby pick up the pack of Old Gold and shake it. When no cigarettes popped out, Ruby dug a finger into the opening and peered inside. She crumpled the paper and dropped it on the table. She went to the porch closet where Ethel stored sundries, can goods, and preserves. She pulled an opened carton off a shelf and removed a fresh pack. In a smoker's routine, Ruby grasped the red strip of the wrapper and pulled. She removed the top of the packaging, lifted the corner of the silver paper, and tore the top half off. She pressed the bottom of the pack, pulled a butt out, and stuck it between her lips. As a femme fatale in a film noir would display her tough side, Ruby let the cigarette hang from the side of her mouth. She released the scrap onto the table, pulled a match from the box, and lit the tip of the tobacco. She sucked in the nicotine and expelled smoke through her mouth and nose. She poked her tongue out and touched the tip with a finger to remove a grain of tobacco. She wiped the finger on the side of her dress.

"The boy made the decision, not me. If he wants to go to Camp Maxey and sing for our soldier boys, doesn't seem like I can do anything about it, Maybelle. I support our boys in uniform. And you need to be sure and write about it that way in your newspaper."

When she shook out the flame, the siren atop the firehouse came alive with a whirling windup groan. Its call for volunteers filled Palomino with an urgent wail.

"That's a fire-call," Julius announced.

Ethel stood and went to the screen. "I don't smell no smoke cept what's on this here porch, so I guess it's a piece away."

"Well, Maybelle?"

"What, Miss Ruby?"

"Aren't you gonna go to the fire?"

Maybelle drove in a final thrust for the fatal cut with her imaginary knife of vengeance. "I might as well since it looks like you're not going to honor a cookout for T J, the winner of the drawin at the *pitchursho*."

27

Eliot Thurgood and Ruby Bostick had not been on speaking terms for only God knew how long. But Eliot had agreed to take his fifteen-year-old nephew, M D Draggert, and M D's fourteen-year-old cohort, Artemis Canton, to Paris because they had a job to do for her.

He had parked outside Estelle Kerns' boarding house while M D and Artemis had gone inside to speak with a man they called Herr Higgins.

Artemis had often served as driver for Higgins, but there had been a falling out between Ruby and Higgins so she had instructed Artemis to go to Paris and take care of business. Artemis had asked M D to go along, and M D had asked his uncle to take them.

Thurgood had found an empty, angled space almost at the front door and waited in his truck while the two teenagers had gone into Estelle's place. When he had a spare two dollars, or needed an adjustment, he had been in the establishment a time or two or three or four. While sitting there, possibilities had floated across his mind. He had thought about his two favorite ladies who worked for Estelle. Delilah . . . what was her last name – usually these ladies didn't like giving out their last names – Delilah . . . Wheeler, that's what it was, Delilah Wheeler, and Ginnie, Ginnie Tyler. Thurgood had smiled, remembering how well both of them were frisky, enjoyable entertainers. He had wondered if he had time for a quick visit, so to speak.

A honking car horn, and a 'Hallo Purvis', behind Thurgood's Ford pickup had brought him out of his reverie. He had checked his rearview mirror and looked out both windows. No threats or intrusions had been apparent.

Artemis and M D had returned in fifteen minutes.

"Well?" Eliot had asked.

"He ain't there," Artemis had said.

"What was yall gonna talk to him about?" Thurgood had asked.

"Miss Ruby wanted him put out of action," Artemis had replied. "I was prepared to do it, too." Arty had flashed his small caliber pistol.

"Put out of action?" Thurgood had asked. "You mean like permanent?"

"Yep, with extreme *preciousdous*," Artemis had answered.

"With that little pea shooter? That little thing is like a bee sting. You need a bigger persuader, Boy."

Thurgood had dropped off Artemis in Pattonville where he stayed with his Aunt Maude, and had driven in silence back to Palomino.

When he had pulled up in front of M D's house, he had cautioned the boy.

"You be careful with Ruby, she can turn mean quick."

M D had opened the truck door but paused. "I know. I've just about had my fill with her, Uncle Eliot.

She don't pay Arty and me like she promised."

"Well, you got to decide whether to fish or cut bait, Boy. You mind my word, you hear? Ruby Bostick is not somebody to fool with. You're either with her or you ain't, there is no in between. And when you're out, that could be permanent, like this Herr Higgins job."

"Extreme *preciousdous*?" M D had mocked.

"You know what I mean, Boy."

"I know, Uncle Eliot. I know. Maybe I could end the arrangement myself in a permanent way."

"Don't be stupid, Boy. You listen to me."

"Okay, Uncle Eliot. Thank you for takin us to Paris."

"You better think about givin up Artemis, too. That boy is gonna screw up bad one of these days." Thurgood nodded at his nephew. "Okay, go on."

Thurgood drove away and looked in the rearview mirror. He was satisfied that M D was going in the house.

Now driving south down Church Street, headed to the gin, Thurgood heard the firehouse siren and saw the boys with Clifford Douglass coming from the back of the church. Porky was in his sights. He stopped his truck and waited, to see their direction.

Twig with his Germans in the Army jeep sped past Thurgood's pickup, followed by Mayor Shipp in his car.

The boys waved at the Constable and the Mayor before turning toward town.

Thurgood checked his mirror. A car was three blocks behind him. He eased out his clutch, and rolled down the street, passing the contingent.

He stopped and got out of the truck, facing the boys and Douglass.

"I been lookin for you, Baycann," Thurgood snarled. "I ain't forgot how you acted up at me in the cafe. You a snot-nosed kid that needs a good whippin and I'm the one to do it, right here in the middle of the street, Boy."

"You leave us alone. You leave Porky alone," Hale said.

"You keep your mouth shut, Perkins. I don't care if you are a cripple, I'll whip you, too."

"You won't whip any of these boys, Thurgood," Clifford Douglass asserted. "You go on now, leave us alone. We not botherin you."

"Well, look at you, Douglass, all bandaged up. You already got a whippin, you can't stand another one."

Douglass straightened up. "I can hold my own, Thurgood."

"You might think you can with this gang of babies you probably foolin around with, Douglass." Thurgood snorted. "I guess all the stories goin on around town about you is true."

Porky moved in front of Mister Douglass. He took up a stance, feet apart and his fists balled. He was ready.

Thurgood reached out, and Porky parried with his left forearm.

The car that had been coming down the street stopped.

Distracted men and boys looked.

June and Sally got out and walked to them.

Sally stood by Porky and June put a hand on Douglass' arm.

"My goodness, Clifford, what are you doin out here on the street all banged up?" June asked. She looked at Thurgood. "What's goin on?"

"You mind your own business, woman," Thurgood snapped. "We was just talkin about past times."

"He was gonna jump on Porky," Grover said. "He

tried to grab him."

June Edmonds' anger flashed. "What? What for?"

Woodrow nodded at Thurgood. "He said he was gonna whip Hale, too," Woodrow said. "Called him a cripple. But we ain't gonna let that happen."

"We sure are not," June said. She took Sally and Porky's arms, pulled them back, and moved in his place. She faced Thurgood, two arm lengths away. "You go on about your business, Eliot. Leave everbody alone. If I hear that you are after any of these boys, or any of the children in town, I'll come lookin for you and it won't be about talkin, you hear me? Shame on you." June swept her fingers at the tall, big man. "Now git, go on about your business."

Grover and Hale grinned. They were witnessing a phenomenal event, a six-two giant being cut down by a five-four sassy, brassy lady.

Without saying a word, Thurgood turned away.

No one spoke; they waited and watched the pickup drive away.

June Edmonds turned on Porky. "What in the world do you think you're doin, Porky Baycann?"

"He did that in the cafe, Momma," Sally revealed. "He was gonna fight Mister Thurgood."

"You stay away from Eliot Thurgood, Porky. He's mean crazy."

Porky grinned. "Bats in his belfry."

"That's for sure. And what in the world are you doin out here in your drawers, Clifford Douglass?"

"He run away from the hospital, Miss Edmonds," Hale said. "We was takin him back."

"I thought my life was over, June" Douglass answered. "The talk. I didn't think I could handle the talk any longer. I was prepared to . . . well, you know."

The boys and Sally stared at Mister Douglass.

"Well, what about Vernetta?" June prodded.

"Yes, of course. She's suffered through the talk, too. And the loss of our babies."

"And your momma, Miss Bertha. They need you more than ever after . . ."

"I know, June. Of course, you're right. I had lost my faith, until these boys came to me and restored it."

"We apologized to Mister Douglass for him gettin hurt," Grover said. "We didn't mean for that to happen, Miss Edmonds."

"We was helpin Mister Douglass back to the hospital, Miss Edmonds," Woodrow said.

"Well, I'll take him in my car. Come, Clifford, come to the car."

As a group, they escorted Douglass to the car. Grover opened the passenger door and they helped the Assistant Scoutmaster in.

Woodrow closed the car door and turned to Miss Edmonds. "It's all my fault, Mam. If I hadn't yelled at Mister Douglass out there at the Scout camp he wouldn't be hurt."

"Why did you yell at him, Woodrow?"

"I thought he was kissin Babe, Mam."

"Oh, my goodness. Babe? Blackie's boy?"

Woodrow rushed his words, apologetic. "But he wadn doin nothin wrong, Mam. I made a big mistake. I'm really sorry, Mam."

"Well, Woodrow, there's enough mistake for everbody to have a piece of. All this talk about Mister Douglass, for goodness sakes."

"I apologized, Mam. And I want to tell everbody in town that Mister Douglass got hurt because of me, because of what I done. He didn't do nothin to Babe,

Mam. He was just tryin to help, is all."

Grover, Hale, and Porky were impressed listening to Woodrow man-up, admitting he was at fault, and taking responsibility. Their chests swelled with pride for their friend.

"You're a good boy, Woodrow," Douglass said from the window.

"Okay," June said, "Sally and me are gonna take Mister Douglass to the hospital."

"Yes, Mam," the boys answered.

June started the car and began to pull away.

Sally waved at Porky.

"I won't forget, Porky," the Assistant Scoutmaster said. "You will become a Boy Scout. I'll make it happen. I have a uniform for you."

The four of them stood there a moment watching the car move down the street.

Sally was still looking at her beau through the rear window, and Porky watched his girlfriend's face fade in the distance.

Grover broke the silence. "Let's go to Jeeps and get a ice cream cone. I got two dimes in my pocket."

"Yeah," Hale said. "That's a great idea. I got twenty cents, too. I'll buy us a Co-Cola with the ice cream cone."

"I dunno if twenty cents is enough for ice cream, Grover," Porky cautioned. "Miss Bobbie Jo doubled the price for a ice cream soda, so a ice cream cone might be a dime now. She said it was the war, prices went up because of the war."

"The war," Hale said quietly.

"Well, I got a quarter." Woodrow was cheerful. "So we got enough to buy ice cream and Co-Colas if they cost more."

"Okay," Grover said. "I think we deserve a treat. We got cleared of a crime, helped Mister Douglass, said we was sorry, and backed down Eliot Thurgood."

"You didn't back down nobody," Woodrow countered. "Porky did it."

Hale's musing provoked Porky's thoughts.

The war. Sicily. His daddy. Porky thought about his daddy, wishing he knew where his daddy was — knew that he was alright, alive. Porky swallowed the gnawing fear that his daddy might never come home, that he might never see his daddy again. Ever. He quickly wiped both eyes with the palm of his hands.

"What's wrong, Porky?" Grover asked.

"Nothin. Nothin is wrong."

"I thought I saw you . . . I thought . . ."

"You didn't see nothin, Grover." Porky swallowed and wiped his cheeks.

"Okay."

Porky felt a smile creep out of his despair. "Okay. It's okay, Grover," he said. "Come on, let's go to Jeeps. I'm gonna get a strawberry ice cream and a Grapette."

"Eeewwww." Grover's groan was emphatic. He shook his head. "I can't believe a Strawberry and a Grapette? That's nasty."

With raised, waving hands and shaking heads, the Scoutmaster, Palomino Mayor, and the Constable finally controlled the chaos at the firehouse.

"Now, quiet down everbody," Winston Tanner ordered. "Please. There's no fire. Nurse Baycann asked me to sound the alarm because Clifford Douglass left the hospital and she's afraid of what he might do."

"Like what, Winston?"

"Like he might hurt hisself, Bryan. I sent Bill and

Tobin over to the water tower to be with Pearly, just in case."

"He's gonna jump from the water tower?" a voice asked.

"Well, he won't be able to with Pearly and Bill and Tobin there to prevent it."

"Last time somebody jumped off the tower was Thirty-Six," another voice said. "The Dustbowl."

"Yeah. Jessup Worthy. Lost his money and his farm. Shame, too, he was a fine man."

"His wife and younguns had to leave town, *humilatated*," someone said.

"Well, Clifford is a fine man, too. We need to find him and bring him back to the hospital."

"Where do we start, Winston?"

"Wait a minute," the Mayor said. "I know where Clifford is."

Silence.

"Where, Mayor?" Tanner asked.

"He was at the church, the Presbyterian Church, with the boys."

"Oh, my God," a voice whined. "Clifford, with boys again?"

The Mayor turned toward the voice and his own was sharp. "*That's enough*. There's been too much mean talk in this town about a man who lost his babies and suffers more heartbreak and heartache than any of us can imagine. That is enough talk about Clifford and boys, for Chrissakes. It is not true, and you know it."

Silence prevailed for several seconds.

"You're right, Mayor. You're right," another said.

"We finished with the boys at the school, Twig and me. After we talked a bit with Porter and the Major, we heard the fire call and were coming here to the firehouse. I saw them with Clifford, who was sittin on the back steps at the church. He was in his underwear. I'll go back to the church." The Mayor turned to Twig. "Why don't you go to the hospital in case the boys brought him back there already?"

"I will, Mayor." Twig signaled the Germans and they walked to the jeep.

"Okay, then," Winston Tanner said. "Let's all go back about our business. Tim, please walk over to the water tower and tell them we know where Clifford is and have everthing in hand. Okay, let's move along."

Duke sat on the passenger seat, Eddy and Will in the back of the jeep. Under the steering wheel, Twig leaned over and eased his Army caliber .45 pistol and holster out from under his right leg. He cranked the engine and pulled away. They had gone several blocks when Duke spoke.

"This little town is sometimes crazy," Duke said.

"Small Texas town," Twig said. He looked at Duke and smiled. "Aren't there small towns in Germany?"

"Yes. Many."

"Some are like this town, Palomino," Eddy said. "Small. A few people live in town and farmers live out of the town, just like Palomino. But none of the towns in Germany have so much that happens like here."

"Palomino is interesting," Will added. "Very interesting. And different."

"Vivian was about the same," Twig said. "Lots of intrigue, lots of small town goings-on."

Twig parked in front of the hospital. The Germans piled out of the jeep and formed up in ranks. Twig pointed, and the prisoners faced right and in single file formation marched ahead of their guard through the doors of the hospital.

Agnes was sitting at the desk behind the counter of the nurse station. She looked up when they approached. She nodded but did not speak to the POWs.

"Hello, Agnes. We're all looking for Mister Douglass. Is he here, maybe?"

"Yes, Twig. June Edmonds brought him in a couple of minutes ago."

"Well, I'm glad he's safe."

"Doctor Burns and Geraldine are down in the room with him, cleaning him up. I just called Carsey. She's going to find the Mayor and Winston and tell them we have Clifford."

"Well, the Mayor saw the boys we dismissed from the gym with Mister Douglass at the Presbyterian Church. Casey is going over to the church to have a look, and he asked me to come here just in case. Winston released everbody from the fire call."

Blackie Beck came through the front doors of the hospital and, with walking cane support, shuffled his way toward the nurse station.

"Hello, Mister Beck," Nurse Baycann greeted.

"Miss Baycann." Beck nodded at Twig. "Constable."

"How do, Mister Beck." Twig pointed at the prisoners and at the floor.

Duke, Eddy, and Will sat on the hallway floor, their backs against the wall.

"Can I help you, Mister Beck?"

"I'd like to see Clifford, Agnes," Blackie said. "My boy, Babe, told me he was with Clifford out at the Scout camp."

Twig became concerned. He spoke before Nurse Baycann could. "I've looked into the affair, Mister Beck. Your boy didn't have anything to do with Mister

Douglass gettin hurt."

"I know that, Twig. Babe told me Clifford was bein kind, tryin to be helpful. I just want to ask what he was tryin to be helpful about?"

Twig took a breath. "It was about Barber, Sir. Babe was worried that Barber had done somethin bad. Babe had tried to get his brother, your son, to do the right thing."

"Bobbette Moon."

"Yessir."

"I been over to see Frank and Francine. To do the right thing."

"The right thing?"

"I gave my condolences and a good amount of money to Bobbette's ma and pa, mind you, cause I believed Barber – and that Posey boy – had done more than . . . Posey was a bad apple." A faint smile tried to grow on Blackie Beck's whiskered face. "Barber wadn no saint, neither, you know."

"Yessir," Twig acknowledged, noncommittal.

The German prisoners watched and listened, intrigued.

"I wadn much of a Pa, myself. My business affairs got in the way while my boys growed up." Tears shimmered in Beck's eyes. "I've lost three of my boys, Constable. Two to this war and one to meanness. I only got Babe and my youngest, Billy, left. I want Clifford to know I appreciated that he was tryin to help Babe."

"I will tell him for you, Mister Beck," Nurse Baycann said. "Right now, though, he's bein looked after by Doctor Burns. Mister Douglass is not ready for visitors."

"Very well. I'll be on my way. Constable." Beck stopped after a couple of steps and stuck his cane out toward the prisoners. He looked back over his shoulder and spoke as he jabbed the stick at the Germans. "They didn't hurt my boys, but their Hitler and them Japs is the reason Buster and Butch are gone."

No more than a minute passed after Blackie Beck left, than a commotion erupted at the doors, and a gaggle of men poured into the foyer.

The Germans quickly stood and plastered their backs tight against the wall, apprehensive and exposed to potential attack by men of Palomino.

Bastion Albert, the Major, Mayor Shipp, and Principal Skaggs led the group of eight to the nurse station.

"These men need to talk to you about this Camp Maxey trip, Twig," the Mayor said. "About the time I was leavin the church, they came outta the gym. Said they were lookin for you. I brought em here."

"What was Blackie doin here?" the Major asked.

"Twig, we need your help on two things," Bastion said, preempting the Major's question. "We need you to call your people at Maxey to tell em we're comin and we need to know from you who all's gonna go."

Twig blinked. "For what, Bastion?"

"For the show?"

"What show? What are you talkin about?"

"They're talking about Porky's friend, T J, Twig," Agnes said. "T J is invited to sing at Camp Maxey tomorrow night and Porky asked Mister Albert to arrange for a school bus to take some friends."

Twig blinked again.

The Germans slid down the wall and sat on the floor. They were amused at the goings-on here in the Palomino hospital.

"I don't know anything about this, Bastion." Twig looked at the Mayor and the Major.

"Will you call your boss at Maxey and arrange passage for a school bus full of people comin to watch the show?" Mayor Shipp asked.

"Yessir, I can do that. How many people? Who are they?"

"About forty, Twig," Agnes answered.

All the men looked at the nurse, their eyes wide and mouths ajar.

Duke, Eddy, and Will were grinning and shaking their heads.

"Forty?" Bastion whispered.

Agnes grinned, too. "About that, I think. I've made two lists of names. One list is for the people close to T J who will be going, Miss Irene, Preacher, probably Miss Ethel and Julius, too, maybe even Henry Wilson and his wife. The other list of the names is who Porky will want to go, like me, Sally Edmonds, Woodrow, Grover, probably Bessie and Rochelle. There'll be others, I believe. Twig, Teresa, and Tina . . . and them. Palomino will be well represented to support T J when he sings for the soldiers out there at Camp Maxey."

"Forty people?" the Major mused. He looked at the school principal. "How many people can sit on a school bus, Porter?"

"Twenty. Two rows, ten seats each row. Twenty people on a bus. Nobody can stand while a school bus is moving. State law."

"We'll need two buses, Porter, for forty people."

"I don't know Major. Who's gonna pay for em? Who's gonna pay for the gas?"

"I said we'll need *two buses*, Porter," the Major repeated. "Twenty people on one bus plus twenty people on another bus is two buses for forty people. I'll pay for the gas."

"What in the world is going on here?" Doctor Burns asked.   He and Geraldine came up the hallway, approaching the convention. "Agnes, what is all these men doing hanging around your station?"

"They're here to talk to the Constable and arrange buses to go to Maxey," the nurse reported to her boss.

"Well, this is a medical environment, not a meeting hall. There are sick people here who need peace and quiet. Yall, all yall, will have to find another place to have a confab." Doctor Burns used both hands to shoo the group away. "Now, git. Git outta my hospital."

"Jeeps," the Mayor said. "Let's go over to Jeeps. We can have a cup of coffee while we work out the details."

"Good idea, Mayor," Bastion agreed.

Twig pointed at the Germans. They rose, formed up in military single file, and awaited instructions.

Agnes reached across the counter, two sheets of paper in hand. "Here, Twig, take these. It's the names I thought of who will want to go to Maxey to hear Porky's friend sing, there may be more."

"Porky is responsible for all this?"

"I'm afraid so."

"Well, we can't go," Twig said. He shoved out the papers to Bastion.

Mister Albert did not reach for the lists. "Why not?"

"My charges. The prisoners. Public place. People might not feel safe with them in the cafe." Twig eyed the trio. "*They* may not feel safe."

Bastion, the Major, Mayor, and all the other men looked at the three standing in at military attention, their left shoulders against the wall, looking straight ahead.

"They'll be alright, Twig," Casey Shipp said. "You'll

318

be with them, so it'll be alright. We need you to be the leader of this situation so you'll be able to talk to your people at Maxey. Anyway, the town is gettin use to havin German POWs."

"Come on. Let's go to Jeeps," the Major encouraged. "I'm gonna have a strawberry ice cream cone."

28

Warrene and Yvonne were the only customers in Jeeps. They sat at a table enjoying a mug of rationed, black coffee with a spike of whiskey from their flasks.

Warrene raised her tiny silver container and invitingly jiggled it. "You want a taste of this, Teresa?"

Teresa added water to the second pot of the eight-cup percolator. "Um, no. No thank you. If I was off duty I might take you up on it."

"Adding a little mixture makes up for the weakened coffee," Yvonne said.

"I know," Teresa answered. "Usually, I dump eight spoonfuls of Hills Bros into the basket but rationing has hit us hard. We're drinking a lot more coffee in Palomino, these days. Bobbie Jo said to cut back, to use four level spoonfuls instead of eight heaping spoonfuls for each pot, now."

"I don't know why?" Warrene questioned.

"Why what?"

"I don't know why we have to ration coffee. The countries where the coffee comes from are not in the war and they're still growing the beans."

"Well, it is the war."

Warrene chuckled. "Seems like we all are in the habit of using *the war* as a excuse. It's the war this, it's the war that. Pretty soon we won't be gettin any because of *the war*."

The three women looked at each other straight-faced before roaring with mirth. They fell silent after the last bit of snickering.

"Well, this time it's true, it's the war," Teresa answered. "It's the ships and the military. All the ships are taking stuff over there instead of bringing coffee here, and the coffee that is brought to America mostly goes to the men and women in uniform."

"Well, that makes sense. Did you ever listen to Eleanor's radio show *Over Our Coffee Cups*?"

Teresa prepared the second pot of coffee and plugged in the cord. She wiped remnants of granules and dabs of water away from the bar with a cloth. "Never did. Why?"

"I dunno." Warrene sighed. "We was talkin about coffee and that jumped into my head."

"That was last year," Yvonne said. "That show went off the air in the spring of last year."

"Do you think she loves Franklin?"

Teresa laughed. She brought her half cup of coffee and sat at their table. "Goodness, Warrene, you got all kinds of things going through your mind. What's wrong?"

"It's Jake. He wears me out."

"With Jake, everthing's got to be done just right, at the right time," Yvonne said. "He was on a tear this morning, so me and Warrene just walked out and came over here."

The screen door opened, and the four boys came into the cafe.

The women turned and looked.

Yvonne chuckled. "Well, the gang's all here."

"Hello, boys," Teresa greeted.

"Hello, Miss Teresa," they replied in unison. "Hello, Miss Warrene. Hello, Miss Yvonne."

The boys went to the counter and sat on stools.

Teresa got up, cup in hand. "Let me take care of these young men." She placed her cup on the back bar, turned, and leaned on the counter. She looked into each of the boy's eyes and smiled.

"What can I get for you?"

"How much is a ice cream cone, Miss Teresa?"

"Ten cents, Grover. Used to be a nickel, but now they're a dime."

"Told you," Porky said.

"How much is a Co-Cola, Miss Teresa?"

"A nickel, Hale." Teresa's smile grew larger. "Are yall counting pennies?"

"Yes, Mam," Woodrow said. "We got sixty-five cents."

Now, this calculation puzzled Grover. He mentally went through the addition of amounts declared at the church. He had twenty cents, Hale had twenty cents, and Woodrow had a quarter. Twenty plus twenty plus twenty-five was . . .

"We ain't got enough," Grover deduced.

"Enough for what?" Teresa asked.

"For a ice cream cone and a Co-Cola," Grover answered.

Teresa grinned. "What grade are you in Grover?"

"I'll be in the ninth grade when school starts."

"Well, school is gonna start next Tuesday, after Labor Day. Are you going to be in Mister Douglass' math class?"

"Yessum."

"Then you'll be able to catch up on your adding and subtracting."

"Yessum."

Porky grinned. He had quickly solved the math problem. "We do got enough, Grover. A dime apiece for ice cream is forty cents and a nickel apiece for the Co-Colas is twenty cents. That's sixty cents. We'll have a nickel left over."

"Well done, Porky," Warrene called out. "You're a math genius."

Porky's grin spread with the accolade.

After serving the flavor of ice cream each boy ordered, and setting the choice of drink by a glass of ice, Teresa picked up her cup and went back to the table.

The noise of men's chatter and laughter reached them before the screen door opened. The boys only glanced, but the women took notice of the new gang coming through the door and taking seats at tables. They could not tear their eyes away from the Germans who sat with Twig at a table along the wall.

"How do, Ladies," the men individually saluted.

"Looks like there is going to be a meetin of the great minds of Palomino," Yvonne remarked.

"Where's Tina?" Twig asked.

"She's in the kitchen with Bobbie Jo. They're makin a batch of Hush Puppies, Cajun style," Teresa said. She stood. "Yall want coffee?"

"Yes, Mam," in unison.

"I can smell the Hush Puppies," Porter Skaggs said. "Makes my mouth water."

The boys kept attacking their cones and swallowing the last gulps of their sodas, before swirling their stools around to face the men and women.

It took several minutes for Teresa to put out cups and spoons and pour out all of the caffeine in both pots. She busied herself making fresh brews and plugged in the pots again.

"Porky Baycann," Bastion Albert said. "We're gonna need your help."

"Yessir."

"What do you need Porky's help with, Bastion?" Teresa asked, cautiously, protectively.

"Porky's friend, T J, Thomas James Workman, is going to sing for the soldiers at Camp Maxey, tomorrow evening. Mister Baycann, here, asked a favor. He wanted a school bus to take some folks to Maxey to see his friend perform . . . and to support him. Turns out Porky's momma prepared two lists of some people who she believed might want to go."

"I wanna go," Warrene said.

"Me, too," Yvonne sang.

"Okay, I'll add your names at the bottom of the list." Bastion Albert laid the two sheets on the table. He began reading the names Agnes had written.

"T J. Irene and Preacher. Ethel and Julius. Porky and Agnes. Teresa and Tina, and Twig and his three Germans."

"Sally," Porky said.

Bastion nodded. "Your momma put down Sally and her momma, June."

"If their momma and daddy's will let them, Hale, Woodrow, Grover, Babe, Tub, Bessie, and Rochelle," Porky said.

"Yeah, the boy said he'd leave it up to you about friends. 'White friends', he said. Lookin at the names, I think your momma wrote all those down. Say the names again, slow, so I can check em off."

Porky said a name and paused, waiting until Bastion was ready for the next one.

"Okay, we've got the Mayor and Sue Shipp, the Major and Sunny Monroe, Principal Skaggs and Dana, Winston and your wife, Clara, me and Arlette, and our girl Lana. Let's see, that's thirty-three."

"And us," Yvonne urged.

"I just thought about it, Yvonne. We can't go," Warrene said.

"Why not?"

"Who'd run the *pitchursho* Saturday night if we was out there at the camp? Miss Ruby wouldn't let us go anyway."

Yvonne sighed. "You're right. We can't go, Bastion."

"I've scratched your names off."

"Better add Maybelle and Stan Stern. She'll want to write about it and Stan'll want pictures," the Mayor said.

"Okay, I've put em down," Bastion said. "That's thirty-five."

Bobbie Jo and Tina came out of the kitchen, each holding a platter of Hush Puppies.

Bobbie Jo grinned. "What in the world? What are all yall doin?"

"Countin noses," Bastion said. "We makin up a list of folks to go to Camp Maxey tomorrow night. We got two school buses going and there are three seats left. Wanna go with us, Bobbie Jo?"

"I got a place to run. Can't do it Saturday night. Are you gonna go, Teresa?"

"I am, if you don't mind."

"Fine with me."

"I wanna go, too," Tina said. "Can I? Can I,

Momma?"

"Yes, Tina. We're going with your daddy and Duke, and Eddy and Will."

"Oh, goody."

"Who wants some fresh Hush Puppies? Me and Miss Tina worked all mornin makin these spicy balls. I think there's enough so everbody can have at least one." She and Tina passed their plates around.

Teresa got both pots and refreshed everyone's cup, including the prisoners. She posed an issue. "You know, Bastion, once the word gets out those three seats won't be enough. There'll be other people who'll want to go. Who are you going to turn away?"

Bastion looked at Twig, then the Mayor.

"Teresa's right," Casey said. "There's gotta be some kind of control."

Bastion laughed and pointed at the Constable. "Twig wears his gun all the time, that's gotta be pretty good control."

Duke, Eddy, and Will peered at their armed guard. Twig winked at them.

No one else found Bastion's remark humorous.

Bobbie Jo took Tina's plate and moved to the counter.

Tina hopped onto her daddy's lap. She licked the taste of batter off each finger, one at a time.

"You and Bobbie Jo sure made some good Hush Puppies, Sweetheart."

"Thank you, Daddy."

"You need tickets," Bobbie Jo said. "Give the people a ticket to ride, just like the Greyhound. If they got a ticket, they can get on a bus. If not, then they stay in Palomino. Pretty simple, huh?"

Bastion frowned. "Tickets?"

"Where we gonna get tickets?" the Major wondered.

"Tickets," Warrene said.   "I got tickets.   Wait a minute." She got up and walked out the door.

"Who's gonna drive the buses?" the Mayor asked.

"Coach Byrd'll drive one," Principal Skaggs said. "Clive Bennett is a regular bus driver, so I think he'll probably be glad to drive the other one."

Teresa was walking back to make more coffee when she posed another matter. "Who's going on which bus, Bastion? Bus number one and bus number two?"

Bastion looked at Porky.   He smiled, his eyes friendly. "See what you've done, Porky Baycann?"

Porky shrugged. "I didn't mean to cause this much work, Mister Albert."

Bastion shook his head. "Not to worry, Son. I'm doing this . . . we're doing this because we want to, not because we have to. This little trip out to Camp Maxey will be a lot of fun for everbody."

"Write down who's gonna be on which bus," the Mayor prodded.

"Why does it matter who's on which bus, Casey?"

"Cause we need to have it organized."

"Okay, okay." Bastion studied the list.

"Let me help with an idea, Bastion," Twig offered.

"Go ahead."

"Bus One will lead. It'll be the first one at the gate at Camp Maxey. It'll be my duty to get us through the guards, they all know me.   Plus, I'll call Colonel Sanchez, my boss, and tell him we're coming in two buses. I wrote down the names when you and Porky was going through the lists. So, in Bus One'll be me, Duke, Eddy, Will, Teresa, Tina, T J, Miss Irene, Preacher, Miss Ethel, and Julius. Porky, Agnes, Sally, and June. Mayor Shipp and Sue, the Major and Sonny, and Lana. That's twenty. And Coach Byrd will drive Bus One.

"Bus Two . . ."

"Hold on, hold on a minute. I can't write that fast."

Twig waited. All watched the vegetable farmer scribble on the sheets of paper. "Okay, go ahead."

"Bus Two. You, Bastion, and Arlette, Principal Skaggs and Dana and Winston and Clara."

The children on the stools listened intently, waiting for their name to be called.

"Okay, got them. Go ahead."

"Maybelle and Stan. Grover, Bessie, Rochelle, and Woodrow. Hale, Tub, and Babe. That's fifteen. Clive will drive Bus Two. There's five seats open."

"Pinky and Patsy," Tina cried.

"Yeah, Pinky and Patsy, too," Porky said.

"Pinky and Patsy and me, we're the three mustard tears," Tina asserted.

Bastion nodded. "Got it. That's thirty-seven. Three seats open. That's well organized, Twig."

"I'm a soldier."

Chuckles and nods affirmed Twig's remark.

The screen door opened and Warrene hurried in. She stuck out both hands to Bastion, holding theater tickets. She shook her right hand. "These purple tickets are adults." She shook her left hand. "These orange ones are kid tickets. Twenty apiece."

Bastion took the tickets. "That's good, Warrene. Okay, the purple is for Bus One and the orange is Bus Two." Bastion began handing out the vouchers.

He gave all the children tickets to Porky. "Tomorrow morning, make your rounds and give out these. If somebody can't go, bring the ticket to me, just in case. Okay?"

"Okay, Sir. What about T J, Mister Albert?"

Porky's voice froze the cafe. Children and adults looked at him as if he had cussed.

"I'm going to bring his ticket in the morning. For him and his momma and uncle."

"I mean, what about T J? Don't he have any friends to come?"

The quietness was pronounced.

"I see," Bastion said. "I asked about that when I was out there. No, Porky, I'm afraid not. You have to understand that T J hadn't had time to make any friends here, colored friends, because he just came down from Tacoma a little while ago. You and them," Bastion pointed, "are the only friends he has in Palomino."

Some looked away and lowered their heads.

"We're his friends, too, Porky," Teresa said.

"All of us are," Bobbie Jo submitted.

"What time does T J need to be at Camp Maxey, Bastion?" Mayor Shipp asked.

"Six o'clock. He said the show starts at seven."

"What time do we need to leave?"

"I think we ought to meet at the school at three-thirty, to be safe, and leave at four."

"Two hours to drive to Maxey? It's only forty, forty-five miles."

"These school buses are not cars, Major. They can't move fast like cars and trucks. There's a lot of traffic these days. It's the war."

Yvonne and Warrene snickered. Teresa smiled.

"What?" Twig asked. "What's funny, you three?"

"Nothin," Teresa said to her husband.

"Well, it is," Winston Tanner said. "There's a lot of big trucks going to and coming from the camp along

Two-Seventy-One, from and to the T and P shops in Marshall. All kinds of cars and pickups going fast. I think the extra time will give us some breathing room. We all know from experience that if something bad can happen, it will happen."

After Irene parked her truck, she, Preacher, and T J got out.

T J retrieved the small suitcase out of the truck bed.

Together, they walked toward the two buses parked in front of the gym.

T J asked about her keys. "You left the keys in your truck, Momma. Aren't you gonna lock your truck?"

"We don't lock our cars and trucks here in Palomino, T J," Preacher said.

"We don't even lock our house," Irene added. "Goodness, I don't even know where my house key is."

"Won't somebody take it? Take your truck?"

She laughed. "Sometimes I wish they would so I could get a different one. I leave the keys in the truck so anybody can move it if it needs to be moved."

"They might even need it for a chore, to haul stuff, while it's parked at the schoolhouse," Preacher offered. "Folks here don't mind, we all one community."

Bastion greeted them. "How do. My, my you sure look ready for church, T J."

T J smiled. "It's a new suit, Mister Albert. Mister Wilbert gave it to me."

Bastion raised his eyebrows.

Irene nodded and admired her boy. She matched Bastion's expression. "Mister Wilburt gave T J this new black suit, two white shirts, a pair of suspenders, and new shoes."

"Mister Wilburt said I needed to be a well-dressed

performer, so he dressed me up. Gave me two pairs of underwear and two undershirts, too." T J caressed his tie. "Even gave me this red bow tie."

"You sure look nice," Bastion said. "Are you excited, T J?"

"Bout what, Mister Albert?"

Bastion, Irene, and Preacher laughed. "Bout singing for the soldier boys, Son."

"No, Sir. They just like everbody else, I reckon."

Bastion pointed. "Yall are on this bus, Bus One. Everbody is here except the Mayor and his wife. We bout ready to go, ahead of schedule."

Ethel and Tina sat in the left seat, second row. Julius sat alone in the right seat, first row.

Irene paused. "Whachall doin sittin way up here?"

"Mister Twig said," Julius answered. "You and T J supposed to sit there, behind Mister Byrd – the driver – and Preacher, you supposed to sit with me."

"In the front of the bus?" Preacher questioned.

"Cause of the Germans. Security and safety, Mister Twig said."

Irene laughed. "Lordy mercy. Sittin in the front of the bus, on the front seat. Wonder of all wonders."

T J placed his suitcase under the seat and sat beside Irene.

"Why you bringin a suitcase, T J?" Porky asked.

"It's my clothes and toothbrush. I ain't comin back to Palomino."

They no longer had settled down in the seats when a ruckus outside the bus jolted the serenity.

Bastion raised his voice. "I said I know there are three empty seats on the second bus. All I need is your ticket to let you get on."

Twig swept past and went down the bus steps.

All on the bus could hear the exchange; some rose from their seat and peered out the windows to see who was stirring the pot.

"I see Ethel and Julius, Bastion. You let colored on the bus but you won't let us?"

Bastion turned to Twig. "Thurgood, M D, and M D's friend, Artemis, want to go to Camp Maxey with us. They tried to get on that bus but the Scoutmaster told em they needed to see me."

Thurgood pointed. "And them Nazis."

Twig turned. Eddy stood on the top step; Duke was one step below, just behind their guard.

Twig could see Will standing behind Eddy. He used a slight movement of his head to signal a return to their seats. "Go back."

Thurgood looked at his nephew and Artemis. "Colored and Nazis, they think they're better than white people." He looked at Bastion. "Get them off and let us on."

"We all have tickets to ride this bus, Eliot," Bastion said. He held his purple ticket up for the trio to see.

Twig pulled his purple stub out of a shirt pocket and wiggled it. "Show me your ticket, Thurgood, and you can get on that bus."

"Ticket?"

"Yes. Everbody on the bus – everbody – has a ticket. Show me yours," Bastion demanded.

Casey and Sue Shipp walked up.

Thurgood smacked his lips. Defeat flooded his face. He looked at the Mayor. "Where do we get a ticket, Mayor?"

Bastion spoke before Casey could open his mouth. "You might try Miss Ruby. I hear she has the three tickets. I guess she's not gonna use them. We're ready to leave."

"Ruby. I'll die and go to heaven fore I ask that woman for spit."

"Well, then. Step aside. We'll be on our way."

The three turned, walked to Thurgood's truck.

Bastion and Twig waited until the pickup turned a corner up the street.

"That Teresa of yours and Warrene sure had a great idea about tickets," the Mayor said.

"Well, Sue, Mister Mayor. Yall go ahead and get on the bus. We're ready to go," Bastion said.

Twig drew in a deep breath. "Eliot Thurgood is a piece of work. This coulda been a nasty situation, Bastion."

Sue Shipp boarded the bus. The Mayor paused with one foot on the lower step. "I think your Germans scared him off."

"No, Mister Mayor, if anything, for them to come to the front of the bus for him to see them is inciting for a man like Thurgood. He's dangerous."

"And so are the two with him," the Mayor added.

Bastion held out his hand toward the bus door. "Okay, Twig, let's go to Maxey."

Floyd Byrd closed the door and cranked the engine.

The buses pulled out of town and headed west toward Paris on Highway 271. Chatter was loud because all of the windows were up, letting the hot air circulate inside the cabin.

They had been on the road for twenty-one minutes when everyone noticed the slowing of the bus. They tried to get a position to look through the windshield. Up ahead they could see a flashing red light atop two cars. One car was near them, on the east side of Pattonville, and the other on the west.

A train was stopped and a mass of people were moving about.

Coach Byrd's loud voice could be heard by all the passengers.   "Somethin's going on up there in Pattonville. Train musta run over a car at the crossing." He downshifted and let the bus creep forward.

A Deputy Sheriff stood in the middle of the highway, fifty feet in front of his car.   He raised both hands, signaling a halt.

"I just need you to go slow, Driver," the Deputy instructed.   "There's a lot of pedestrians crossing the highway, so proceed with caution, about ten miles an hour until you get alongside the other car."

"Yessir. What's going on? Train run over a car at the crossing?"

"Prisoners, more German prisoners of war comin out of Sicily."

"I got three German POWs on my bus.   We're headed to Camp Maxey."

"Well, go along, but keep it slow."

"Yessir." Bastion pressed lightly on the accelerator, the bus moved at a snail's pace.

Porky never looked at the train, never looked at the commotion. He kept staring at the back of his friend's head. Porky heard nothing else except T J's words – they kept echoing in his ears.

The occupants of both buses could see citizens of Pattonville, with thermoses, coffee pots, cups, trays of small sandwiches, fruit, and odds and ends serving the POWs hanging out the train's windows.

"My goodness," a woman standing near the train said. "They all look so young. Welcome to America."

Duke and Eddy sat on the right seat on the back row, Will and Twig sat on the left.

"That was us, two months ago, Twig," Will said.

"We stopped here, too," Duke said.   "I got a sandwich and an apple."

"The same greeting, too," Eddy said. "I want to live in America after the war."

"Welcome to America," Will said quietly.

29

As the bus moved along, Porky got up from his seat and walked forward.

Porky's approach to the front of the bus caught Coach Byrd's attention. He watched the boy in his rearview mirror.

Porky stood next to T J.

"Why did you say you're not comin back to Palomino?"

T J looked up at his friend and grinned. "I'm going to Dallas after I sing at the camp."

"You're gonna sing there?"

"Uh huh. Then I'll get on a airplane and go to Chicago."

"On a airplane? I've never been on a airplane."

"I haven't either. I'm kinda scared about it, too."

"Whachu gonna do in Chicago?"

"Sing and make a record. That's why I'm not comin back to Palomino."

"Does it take a long time to make a record?"

"I dunno, I never did one."

"Where you gonna stay, in Chicago? You got people there?"

"No, Capn Steinbeck is arrangin things for me."

Porky looked at Irene. "T J is gonna live in Chicago?"

Irene nodded. "It's a great opportunity for T J. He wants to be successful and that's not possible for him in a small town in Texas. There's nothin for the boy in Palomino."

"Nothin?"

"There's no future for him, Porky. In Chicago, we are better off – our people."

"Are you gonna go to Chicago, Miss Irene?"

"I might just do, Porky."

Porky looked at both T J and Irene as he asked the questions. "Are you gonna live there, in Chicago? All ways?"

Irene nodded and answered for both of them. "I think we will, if things work out with T J's singin and the record."

"I'm gonna be singin in different places, too. Churches, restaurants, cafes, nightclubs, theaters. There'll be a lot of places, Capn Steinbeck said. He said there might be a band that would want me to sing with them, and travel to different places. Even Baltimore, Philadelphia, Saint Louis, and New York."

Speechless, with his mouth open, Porky peered at his friend.

"Porky?" Coach Byrd called. "Porky, you better take your seat. We're gonna be goin faster up the highway now. It's not safe for you to be standin up."

Porky looked at the back of Floyd's head, then looked in the mirror, and met the Coach's eyes.

"Go on now, take your seat, Son."

Porky looked at his friend again and shook his head. "I might never see you again, if you live in Chicago."

337

T J's smile hid sad eyes. "We'll see each other again. We'll always be friends. You're my pal, Porky."

"Porky?" Coach Byrd's voice was more firm.

"Yessir, I'm goin. Bye, Miss Irene. Bye, T J."

Irene shook her head and smiled. "It's not bye yet, Porky."

As Porky made his way up the aisle, he discovered Tub had moved from the seat he had shared with Lana and was now sitting next to Sally.

Porky looked at them. "That's my seat, Tub. You're sitting by my girlfriend."

Sally's voice was flat, cold. "Lana says she wants you to sit with her."

"Lana asked me to move, so you could sit with her," Tub said. "Sally doesn't mind if I sit with her. Do you?"

Porky could not hide the hurt. "No. I guess not. Whatever Sally wants."

Sally pinned Porky with her icy stare. "It seems, *whatever Lana wants*," she huffed. She looked away, toward the front of the bus and Coach Byrd.

Porky, defeated, shrugged. "Okay, whatever Lana wants Lana gets."

He looked at the Chestnutt family.

They, and Twig's Germans, were taking this fuss all in. Their soft eyes and faint smiles hinted at the empathy they felt for the teenager's angst.

Porky plopped on the seat next to Lana Albert.

Will leaned over and whispered his question to Twig. "He has lost his girlfriend?"

Twig leaned in. "I think Lana likes Porky. Or, maybe Lana doesn't like Tub."

"Um," Will mused. "Maybe Lana does not like Sally. She uses Porky as the talon?"

Twig looked at Will. "A talon, you mean like a

claw?"

"Yes. In a way."

"Like Lana is being catty and uses Porky as a claw?"

"That is a simile, Twig."

"A simile?"

Will's grin was large. "I read books. I use a dictionary when I need to look up words, English words. I am learning American words."

Twig blinked. "I thought they were the same."

"I wanted you to sit with me so I could thank you," Lana said, her voice sweet and gentle.

"For what?"

"For what you did for my daddy."

"Well, he was . . . it was nothin."

"I heard you helped him two times."

"I did."

"And that's why he's doin this favor for you."

"Yes, he said it was. I only asked for one bus, though. I didn't know all these people was gonna wanna go."

"Will you do me a favor, Porky?"

"Sure, Lana. Whachu want me to . . ."

Before Porky could finish, Lana had intertwined her fingers through his and squeezed.

Porky found that he didn't mind – Lana's hand was delicate and tender, thrilling, exciting, arousing.

"Your hand is very warm, Porky, and your fingers are long and slim. That feels good."

Porky swallowed. "Yes. It does feel good."

"Do you like it?"

Porky swallowed again and looked into Lana's inviting, hazel eyes. "I do. It's nice."

"Would you like to kiss me?"

Porky couldn't understand why his mouth was dry.

He slid his tongue across his lips to wet them, hoping the moisture would help him swallow the brick lodged in his throat.

"Here?"

"Uh huh. If you want to."

"I . . . I . . . I, ah, I . . ."

"That's okay. We can wait until we get to the camp, and when it's dark. That way it'll be better."

Sally turned. She peered at her boyfriend and discovered he was holding hands with Lana. She turned back, her flushed ears and cheeks felt fiery. She looked at Tub, who was dozing. Sally took Tub's hand and slipped her fingers through his.

Tub woke instantly. "What are you doing?"

She held his hand in her lap.

"I'm holding your hand."

"I know that, but you're Porky's girlfriend."

"Not anymore, I'm not."

"Well, I'm Porky's friend and I don't want to get between you two."

"You're not between us, Tub. You're next to me. Porky's obviously found a new girlfriend with sweet *Daisy Mae* Lana. And he's already holding her hand."

Tub leaned forward and reached for the cuff of his jeans with his free hand. He turned to spy and saw Sally's words were true. He sat up, paused, and spoke. "Okay. I see what's going on." He patted her hand. "We'll be friends, okay?"

Sally could not hide the weighty sadness as tears formed in her eyes. "He's gonna be sorry."

"I'm sorry, Driver," the Military Policeman said. "No pass, no entry. You've got to turn around and get both these school buses out of the way."

"I'm tryin to explain," Coach Byrd pleaded. "We're comin to the camp by invitation."

"I don't see no invitation, Driver. Now turn around."

"Twig?" Coach Byrd looked in his rearview mirror. "Twig, I need your help here. The soldier won't let us through the gate."

Twig stood. "I'm coming, Coach." He pointed at the prisoners. "Stay put, not a sound, you hear?"

Duke, the senior Wehrmacht soldier, answered. "Yes, Sergeant Chestnutt. We'll stay seated, and quiet."

Coach Byrd turned back to the MP. "We're late because of the trains."

"Uh huh." There was no interest evident in the response. "I don't know about any trains, Driver. And I don't know about any invite you got. I am not asking you, Sir, I'm telling you, for the last time. Turn this bus around and get out of the way. There's cars lined up behind you that need to come through. Now follow my order. Sir."

"Open the door, Coach, let me out," Twig said. On the bottom step, Twig turned back. "When I'm out of the bus, close the door. There are prisoners of war on your bus and it needs to be secure to confine them."

"Yes, Twig. I understand."

Floyd Byrd gripped the metal handle and pushed. Once Twig was out, he pulled the doors closed but kept his hand on the lever.

Twig walked around the front of the bus. He hefted his holster and heavy pistol to ease the weight on his hip.

"I'm Sergeant Chestnutt, with . . ."

"My officer, Lieutenant Schultz, is coming up behind you," the MP said.

Twig spun around.

"Twig. How have you been?"

"Ollie? *Lieutenant* Schultz?"

They shook hands and patted each other on the back. "Three weeks ago I was a Corporal, Twig. Two weeks ago, I was a Sergeant. Yesterday, I was anointed an officer and a gentleman. A brand, spankin new Second Lieutenant. A Butter Bar. Ain't war hell?"

The MP smiled at their real laughter and apparent camaraderie.

"I ordered the bus driver to turn around and get out of the way, Sir."

"Okay, Kiley. It's okay. Sergeant Chestnutt is an old friend. He has a trio of German POWs. They're comin in from Palomino."

"Oh. Yessir."

"We're a little behind schedule, Ollie, there was a holdup in Pattonville because of trains and . . ."

"I know. More POWs coming in. From Sicily, this time. Colonel Sanchez told us you were bringin a boy, a teenager, who is part of the show tonight. A singer."

Twig jerked a thumb over his shoulder. "He's on board, here. T J, Thomas James Workman. Captain Steinbeck is expecting us, him. Waiting for him, actually."

"Captain Steinbeck? Captain Art Steinbeck is a staff officer for General Pace."

"That's the one, I guess. I don't know the man, the Captain. He was friends of T J's momma and daddy at Fort Lewis, Washington."

"We didn't know there'd be two buses, two school buses, full of people, Twig. I'm sorry, but my men'll have to board and inspect. Security, you understand. It's the war."

Twig grinned. "The war. Of course, Ollie. It's the

war."

"And Sergeant Chestnutt, in front of my men, *Lieutenant*, okay?"

"Yessir. Sorry, Sir. Thank you, Lieutenant."

Ollie smiled. "Kiley, you go check that bus, I'll check this one. And be quick about, there's a lot of cars lined up waitin to get through the gate."

In less than one-hundred-thirty-eight seconds, Lieutenant Schultz was back. Kiley walked up, too.

"Folks on my bus is okay, Sir," Kiley reported.

"Was there colored on that bus, Kiley?"

"No, Sir. Some adults with just a bunch of kids."

"There's colored on this bus, Twig," the Lieutenant stated. "I can't allow a bus load of colored people on the camp without proper authorization."

"They have authorization, Oll . . . Lieutenant. They're his family, the family of the invited performer." Exasperation crept into Twig's voice. "Call Colonel Sanchez and Captain Steinbeck and tell them we're out here. Waitin to get in, Ollie."

"At ease, Sergeant," Lieutenant Schultz commanded. "Kiley, get on the horn and call the OD."

"Yessir." Kiley went to the gate shack.

"The Officer of the Day will find the Captain, Sergeant Chestnutt. In the meantime, I want you to get these buses off the road so all of the backed-up traffic can come onto the installation. All these people behind you are comin to see the big show tonight that's bein put on for the soldiers and prisoners here at Maxey."

"If you don't hurry up, Lieutenant, they'll miss the main attraction. He's sittin on this bus."

The Provost Marshal, Colonel Sardanna-Sanchez,

ordered Lieutenant Schultz to permit the buses from Palomino to enter Camp Maxey and personally lead them to The Hut – the building used by visitors and dignitaries.

There, boys and girls used restrooms and refreshed themselves before Lieutenant Schultz escorted them to the outdoor seating of the theater.

Captain Steinbeck took charge of T J and brought him backstage to meet the Army bandleader. They discussed the songs T J wanted to perform, and the music. As artists, they were one. There was no indication of superiority – adult to child. T J was the star of the evening and treated that way, with great, endearing fanfare. There was no thought or mention of segregation.

The Colonel also instructed Ollie to have Twig place the three Germans in the confinement area. Penned, they could see the show with other prisoners behind the wire enclosure.

The security guard, armed with a Thompson sub-machine, closed the gate behind Sergeant Chestnutt's prisoners. The loud clicks of the two locks on the hasps were distinct.

Eddy, Will, and Duke stood impassively. They waited, hoping that Twig would tell the guard to open the gate and bring them along with him.

Duke put his fingers through the chicken wire, his nose through a hole. It was a pitiful sight. "I have the feeling that they will want to keep us here, confined at the camp."

"Why you say that, Duke?" Twig asked.

"Attitude. This is a concentration camp and the guards are grim."

Twig looked around. "It's a serious place, Duke.

These guards mean bidness. You boys are prisoners of war, not citizens of Palomino."

"We got used to living in America, Twig," Will said.

Twig nodded. "I know, Will. I know."

"I am scared, Twig," Will whispered. "This is all strange to us now. We got use to being with you and your family."

Eddy joined Duke hanging on the wire. "Will you come get us, Twig? When the show is over?"

"Yes, Eddy, I will." Twig met their somber stares. He could see the pain and despair in Will's eyes, the youngest of the three Wehrmacht soldiers. "I promise you, Will, I will come get you and take you back to live in Miss Ruby's Porter House and work in Palomino."

"I trust you, Twig," Duke said softly. "We have trusted you with our lives. You have always been truthful with us. When you say you will take us back with you, I believe you. But . . ."

"What? But, what, Duke?"

"Ollie has changed," Duke said. "He was always a soldier, a Corporal, with us. But I heard what he said to you, as a Lieutenant. He is different now. The camp is different now. I feel it. If your Colonel says we must stay here, there is nothing you can do. Is there?"

Twig sighed. "No, Duke. You know I must obey my orders, whether I like it or not. You obeyed Hitler's order to fight in North Africa. You obeyed your General's order to surrender. All three of you are soldiers. You know . . ."

"We know, Twig," Eddy said.

Will nodded. "To know that you will take us back with you, if you can, is promise enough for me, Twig."

Twig placed the palms of his hands on the wire. Eddy, Will, and Duke placed the palms of their hands against their military guards.

"I will do my best. I promise you that."

The tuning of horns, beat of drums, and bows across strings of violins reached them. "I have to go, now." He pointed at them and grinned. "Stay put."

Sergeant Chestnutt saw where Teresa and Tina sat and inched his way in front of those already seated, excusing himself as he passed.

He sat between his wife and daughter and took their hand in his.

They sat enthralled for two full hours. Dozens of talented people entertained them.

Once the show was over, all the performers came back on stage. They lined up, held hands, and faced the audience for a curtain call. One by one, the Master of Ceremonies announced names and that person stepped out of the line for a bow. When it was T J's turn, at the end of the line, he stepped forward. He stood at military attention. The audience went wild, jumping to their feet, hollering, whooping, and applauding non-stop for eight full minutes. He gave a magnificent salute and took a deep bow. When T J stepped back into the line, he took the hand of the girl next to him, turned, and led the performers off stage.

"That was great," Teresa said. "T J is going to be famous one of these days."

The spectators began to file out of the seating area, moving toward The Hut where after-show refreshments waited. There, they would be able to meet and talk with all of the talent.

"I've got to go to the bathroom, Momma," Tina whispered.

"That's where we're going, Sweetheart."

"Okay. I can hold it. Maybe."

Teresa chuckled. "I hope so." She took Tina's hand. "Let's hurry so we can get at the front of the bathroom line, okay?"

Twig and the Palomino contingent followed and eventually reached The Hut. Lights were now illuminating porch, steps, and yard.

Irene, Preacher, Ethel, and Julius stood off to the side.

Twig approached them. "What's going on? Why are you standing here?"

Irene smiled and canted her head. "Really, Twig?"

"Oh. Yes." Twig held out his forearm. "Miss Irene Adams, may I escort you and your party inside?"

Irene's smile turned into a wide grin, her hand found his arm. "Please, Sergeant Chestnutt. We thank you." Ethel, Julius, and Preacher followed them up the steps, through the double doors, and into a massive room.

A long banquet table draped with white cloth was in the center of the floor. On the table were jugs of coffee, iced tea, and water. Platters piled with small triangular pimento cheese sandwiches and dishes of chocolate cake lay invitingly exposed. Silverware, plates, and napkins held strategic spots on the table, as well as large ashtrays. The good people from Palomino intermingled, they became one with all in the room, including the show crowd.

Porky had taken up a tactical position near the cake and helped himself. He was about to slip another slice onto his plate when his mother signaled for him. He set his dish aside and joined her.

"Porky, this is Colonel Sanchez. He is Sergeant Chestnutt's superior officer, his boss."

"How are you, Son?" Colonel Sanchez greeted. "I like your nickname. Your momma told me your daddy gave it to you when you were two years old."

"Yessir."

Another man came up beside Porky and spoke to the Colonel.

"General Pace is ready, Sir."

"Thank you, Tommy." Colonel Sanchez pointed. "That's Major Monroe, Mayor Shipp, and Sergeant Chestnutt. Please bring them to the conference room."

"Yes, Sir."

"I'll bring Miss Baycann and this young man with me. We'll meet you there."

"Yes, Sir." Tommy turned to walk away and Colonel Sanchez reached for his arm.

"Oh, and Captain Thorson, please be discreet."

"Of course, Colonel."

Porky watched and listened. Inwardly, he felt a swell of pride. He and his mother's diligence had paid off. They were about to meet the man, a General no-less, who knew where his father was. Excitement filled Porky's heart.

The Camp Maxey Deputy Commander, fifty-year-old Brigadier General Charles Pace, Junior, was a grossly overweight chain-smoker. He sat at the head of the gray-metal military conference table sucking on a Lucky Strike. Blue-gray smoke floated to the ceiling. The General stood and walked to Agnes with an extended hand when she entered the room.

"I'm General Pace, Miss Baycann. And this must be young Baycann?"

She shook the General's plump hand.

"Agnes, and Porky, General Pace."

He pointed at chairs at the table. "Please have a seat." He greeted the others and invited them to take a chair at the table, too.

Once everyone sat, General Pace returned to his position of authority. "Miss Baycann, Agnes, Sergeant Chestnutt made a request to Colonel Sanchez, and Major Monroe talked to our Commanding General, General Evans, about helping you. We understand you seek information about your husband, Private First Class Portland Baycann, listed as missing-in-action in Sicily. It is unusual, indeed rare, that we hold a meeting with family members about military affairs. However, the circumstances in this case are different because of personal connections. You see, Major Monroe and General Evans served together in the First War."

Agnes looked at Major Monroe. "He lost a hand in that war," she said.

"Indeed, he did," the General replied, and then he went on with his little speech. "Accordingly, General Evans asked me to sit with you and tell you what we know."

Agnes kept still, anticipating, wondering.

Porky was busy scoping out all of the business about Army matters that filled the walls: maps, bulletin boards with tacks holding sheets of paper, photos, and flags. Two large fans stood in the far corners of the room, their blades whirling at low speeds.

"As you well know, the Allied Forces finally drove the Germans out and captured Sicily two weeks ago. I have a Major who was in Sicily, here in my operations and planning office. I will bring him in. I've asked him to give you a detailed overview of the situation that occurred there so you have a picture of what we're dealing with. I caution everyone, Miss Baycann, gentlemen, that this briefing is classified. Once you leave this room, what you've heard must not be discussed.   Even   among   yourselves.   Please acknowledge this."

They did.

"Okay, Tommy, bring in Major Binna, please."

After introductions, Barry Binna sat across from Agnes and Porky.

"Major, you are free to reveal classified information to this group about Operation Husky."

"Miss Baycann, gentlemen, Son, General Patton's Seventh Army and General Montgomery's Eighth Army were the assault force. We were on ships from North Africa. The seas were rough. Most soldiers were seasick. The wind was forty-miles an hour. Heavy fire from defenders scattered the approaching armada. The LCVPs were targeted by German eighty-eights and blown out of the water. Men, burdened with their weapon and all of their equipment, drowned."

General Pace interrupted the Major. "Wait, Barry. Miss Baycann is not familiar with military equipment and guns."

Agnes did not look at General Pace. "I know what an eighty-eight is. The newsreels have shown us the German gun and what it can do. I do not know what the LCVP is, Major."

"I'm sorry, Mam. LCVP is Landing Craft Vehicle Personnel. It is a small boat that brings men and equipment from the ships to shore."

"These boats carry the attacking force to the beach landing," General Pace added.

"Anyway . . ."

Agnes held up her hand. "I don't need to know all of this about military stuff, Major Binna. What can you tell me about my husband?"

Major Binna closed his mouth and looked at the

General.

Pace cleared his throat. "Miss Baycann, Agnes, the operation had a lot of difficulty from the beginning. High winds and anti-aircraft fire broke the formation of aircraft carrying paratroopers. Many planes were shot down. Some paratroopers were dropped fifty-five miles off course. Heavy guns on the beach dispersed landing craft out of their zones of attack. Many of the boats were destroyed . . ."

Agnes had had enough of the briefing. "Where is Portland?" She looked at Major Binna, then fixed General Pace with her stare. "Where is my husband?"

General Pace sighed. "Miss Baycann, one-hundred-forty American airplanes carrying reinforcements, an infantry regiment of the Eighty-Second Airborne Division, came in low, at six-hundred feet, in the night. American sailors mistook these planes for German bombers and shot down twenty-three. Our own men – our own men shot these planes down, Miss Baycann. Over three hundred soldiers and airmen died from this friendly fire. For weeks, we have had teams on the water and in the countryside. They search for the dead and wounded, they follow up leads. Most who are recovered can't be identified. We have a major tragedy on our hands."

Agnes Baycann's concern involved only one of those soldiers. "And?"

"I'm afraid the news we have for you is not good, Miss Baycann. Your husband may have drowned and we'll never find him. I'm sorry."

All the men jumped to their feet when Agnes stood.

She looked at her son. "Let's go home, Porky. Thank you, Major. Thank you, General. We're sorry we bothered you and interfered in your war."

Agnes led the group out of the building to the bus. T J was by the door. "I waited for you, Porky. What did you find out about your daddy?"

Porky shrugged. "Nothing. He's probably dead."

T J touched Porky's arm. "I'm sorry. I wanted to tell you something before I go to Dallas and you go back to Palomino."

"What?"

"Remember when we were on your bicycle after the Germans came to town? We were singing Gene Autry's songs. You stopped and we watched the Germans go into Miss Ruby's house? Remember that?"

"Yeah."

"And I pointed over your shoulder and said look at that? Remember?"

"Yeah. The water tower."

"And what were the letters on the side?"

"P-A-L. That's part of the letters all the way round, for Palomino."

"You're my friend, Porky Baycann, my white friend. You will always be my P-A-L. My pal."

30

It was Tuesday, September 14, the second week of classes in Palomino. The day after Labor Day, Tuesday, September 7, had been the start of the new school year, and the official ending of the summer of '43 for Porky Baycann.

The absence of people in his life was striking for Porky.   There had been no further word about his father; the finality of the meeting with the General was heavy on his shoulders.

His mother had cried herself to sleep that night, after they got home from Camp Maxey.

He had lost an important friend when T J had walked away into the darkness.

He felt alone, loneliness was only a thought away.

Sally had forgiven him for sitting with Lana and holding her hand on the bus. But Sally now seemed cautious, insecure about their relationship. He had done all he knew to do to make her comfortable.

In a way, he was happy to be back in school. Yet, he found classrooms, teachers, even friends, had changed over the summer. Porky looked at them, thought of them, differently. It was the war.

The war. He was watching a battle develop in the schoolyard. He was detached, but felt a part of it – rooting, encouraging, egging-on.

He stood at an open window in Miss Madeleine Menden's history classroom on the second floor. History was his last class for the day. Looking out, he listened to the argument between Waldo and *the three mustard tears* – Pinky, Patsy, and Tina.

He knew the feud. Waldo was stealing Pinky's paper route customers.   When Pinky complained to Miss Maybelle, Waldo tried extortion – a quarter a week to leave Pinky alone.

Porky snorted when Tina kicked at Waldo, and caught his breath when Patsy drew back and, with full force, planted her fist square on the chubby bully's nose. Waldo's yelping whine drew attention.

He looked beyond the playground and watched traffic speeding along in both directions on Highway 271. Trucks, cars, even motorcycles moved east toward Bogata and west toward Paris.

Only one car stopped at the stop sign at the Main Street junction with 271, the others only slowed before turning and merging.

It was rare when a car would turn off the highway to come into town. But now, as Porky watched, two slowed to do just that. The car in front was a sheriff's car, its rooftop red light flashing. Porky could faintly hear the siren. Behind the patrol car was a huge black sedan pulling a fancy horse trailer.

Miss Menden clapped her hands. "Everbody take your seat, please."

Porky turned away from the window, made his way up the aisle to the center of her classroom. He sat in his assigned place, three chairs back from the top of the center row. Sally sat even with him in the row on his right. He touched her arm.

Miss Menden began their lesson. "New Italian prisoners of war are arriving every day at Camp Maxey, along with hundreds of Germans. Yesterday, we talked about the island of Sicily. What else did we cover? Sally?"

"The war there, Miss Menden."

"And? Tub?"

"The surrender of all the Italians. All the Germans escaped."

"Very good, Tub. But the *Movietone News* tells us not all of them escaped, but enough did to fight another day.

"What other important event of history took place over there? Lana?"

"The removal of the dictator, Benito Mussolini, Miss Menden. A lot of people were very happy."

"Yes, they were, Lana. Weary people. They were weary of Mussolini and weary of the war. Very good.

"Years from now all of you will be able to recognize that you lived during a period of great history. Now, today, we'll talk about what you think will happen next. Who wants to go first? Any volunteers? How about you, Porky? What's on your mind?"

Silence.

His twelve classmates looked, waited, anticipated. Sally lowered her head and glanced at her beau's blank face. Porky didn't hear her whisper his name.

Miss Menden prodded her student. "Porky?"

The sheriff's car pulled into an angled parking space in front of Jeeps.

Shoppers and merchants poured out of stores, disturbed by the hullabaloo.

Deputy Gully shut off the siren and police light.

The black sedan eased up behind the cruiser and stopped.

Maybelle Winters called from the sidewalk. "Stan? *Stan*? Bring your camera. Hurry, bring your camera."

The phone rang at the nurse station.

"Yes, Carsey?"

"Geraldine, let me talk to Agnes."

"She's not here."

"Where's she at?"

"On an errand."

"Where? I need to talk to her right away. It's about Porky."

"Oh, my. What happened to Porky?"

"I'll tell you later. Tell Agnes to call me when you see her. Bye."

Agnes sat at Wolf Hunter's Gulf station, waiting until Caleb Joiner put two gallons of gasoline in her car. She held the coins and ration coupon in her hand.

She and Caleb heard the siren and watched the two cars come down Main.

"Looks like somebody is under arrest. Must be horse thieves."

Agnes laughed. "Horse thieves don't pull a fancy trailer, Caleb. They have big trucks and huge trailers."

"Well, maybe they just wanted one horse, Agnes, and got caught stealin it?"

Agnes agreed. "Maybe."

"Carsey, ring the hospital. I need to talk to Agnes.

356

She needs to bring Porky down here right away."

"I just did, Bobbie Jo. She's not there."

"Where is she at?"

"We don't know. I've called Dora and Margie, they haven't seen Agnes."

"Well, call the Mayor, we need to sound the alarm."

"I just talked to him, Bobbie Jo. He's the one who wanted me to find Agnes."

"Call him back. We need the alarm."

The siren atop the firehouse wound up. Its aching wail stung Agnes and Caleb's eardrums.

"Good Lord," Agnes shouted. She got out of her car and looked at the siren. "It's right next to us. How in the world can you stand that noise, Caleb?"

"We get use to it." He pointed. "There's something going on up there at Jeeps."

"Why are all those people standing in the street and on the sidewalk?" Agnes asked. "What in the world are they looking at?"

Caleb replaced the nozzle on the pump and wiped his hands on a red rag. "Let's walk up there and see what's the matter."

Miss Menden called his name again. "Porky? What do you have on your mind?"

The urgent screaming of the siren reached them before he answered his teacher.

Porky jumped to his feet. "GENE. CHAMPION. The car. The trailer."

"Who is that?" Miss Mendon asked. "What car?"

"They've come to Palomino. My friend, Gene Autry. He's brought his horse, Champion. He said he would. I bet they're at Jeeps."

"PORKY," Miss Menden called at the boy's back as he dashed from the classroom, followed by his girlfriend. "SALLY."

Sandy opened the door for Gene and their passenger.

Palominoans gasped and stared as the trio mounted the sidewalk and stood majestically in front of Jeeps.

Bobbie Jo and Teresa came out.

Stan ran across the street, camera in hand. He put the tip of the flash bulb in his mouth to wet it.

Porky came through the alley between Dulfeine's Grocery and the *Palomino Press* building. Sally was on his heels, reaching for his belt.

They saw the flash from Stan Stern's camera. It flashed again. And again.

Sally pulled and Porky lingered. He glanced at her but focused on the three standing on the sidewalk – all three familiar faces.

He stepped forward and paused in the middle of Main Street, mesmerized. Sally stood at his elbow.

Caleb and Agnes got closer and stopped when Stan's camera flashed and flashed and flashed.

Caleb put a hand on Agnes' arm. "Porky," she whispered.

Caleb held on as Agnes quickened her pace. She hurried into a trot before breaking into a dead run. The gas coupon, the two dimes, and two pennies slipped from her fingers.

"DADDY," Porky cried.

"PIG," Agnes screamed.

Portland Baycann, Senior, mouthed their names and jumped down from the sidewalk as his wife and son rushed into his arms.

Tears and applause erupted in an outpouring of love from the onlookers.

Gene Autry turned to Jim Dudley. "I think I've earned my Army pay today, Sheriff." Then, to his driver. "Okay, Sandy, it's time for us to get on back to San Antonio. There are other soldiers at Brooke Hospital who may need a ride home."

Tank Gunner is the pen name of a retired combat cavalry trooper, Senior Parachutist, and Jumpmaster awarded a Combat Infantry Badge and decorated with a Silver Star, three Bronze Stars, one for Valor, and a Purple Heart. He served his nation with pride and honor for more than a quarter century as an enlisted soldier and officer. An award-winning author, Tank wrote and published *Prompts a collection of stories* at age 76, *Prompts Too another collection of stories* at 77, *Cookie Johnson*, his Vietnam historical fiction novel at 78, *Palomino*, his immensely popular WWII historical fiction novel at 79, and *Porky Baycann* at age 80. He and his wife live with Toby, 100 miles southwest of Palomino.

PROMPTS
a collection of stories

Tank Gunner

Available at TankGunnerSix.blogspot.com

PROMPTS TOO
another collection of stories
Tank Gunner

Available at TankGunnerSix.blogspot.com

TANK GUNNER'S BLOG & BOOK SHELF
tankgunnersix.blogspot.com
all 5 books available here

COOKIE JOHNSON
Vietnam Historical Fiction Novel

COOKIE JOHNSON

His journey along paths never imagined

TANK GUNNER

Author of *PROMPTS* and *PROMPTS TOO*

Available at TankGunnerSix.blogspot.com

TANK GUNNER'S BLOG & BOOK SHELF
tankgunnersix.blogspot.com
all 5 books available here

PALOMINO
WWII Historical Fiction Novel

PALOMINO
Afrika Korps POWs Come to Town

Available at TankGunnerSix.blogspot.com

TANK GUNNER'S BLOG & BOOK SHELF
tankgunnersix.blogspot.com
all 5 books available here